By Rod and Staff

Danny Aglugub

publishing

All praise be to God.

By Rod and Staff, let us walk in comfort.

To Dad and Mom. You have shown me everything. I can write, because first I observe. If parents have one job, that would be to teach their children how to look and how to listen. With these eyes and ears, I gaze at the world of five hundred years ago so that you may visit. Enjoy the trip.

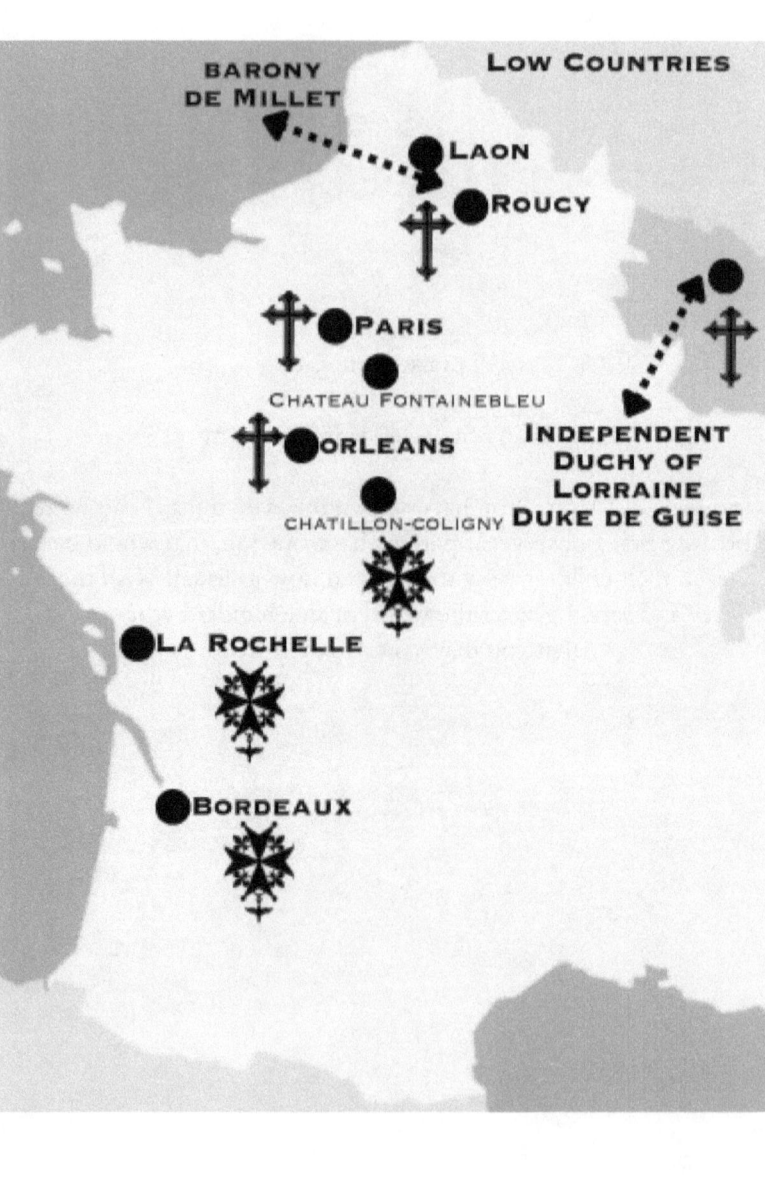

Characters:

Millet Family
Maurice Millet
Tonya Millet(Wife)
Jean Millet(Father)
Christopher Millet(Brother)
Marie Millet(Sister)
Thomas Sunstone(Brother in Law)

Sophists of Mausien Brook
Danilo
Janeau
Heather
Torry
Robiere

Various Authority Figures
Seigneur of Laon
Phillipe
Reeve of Laon
Gascon
Sir Thomas(Cavalier)
Pastor Rohn
Priest Borges

La Paussion Family
Robert la Paussion
Claude la Paussion
Lisbeth la Paussion

Chauvre de Sois
Herndon Calais
Christopher Millet

Conspirators of Amboise
Charles Avon
Seigneur de la Renaudie
Prince of Conde
Admiral de Coligny
Arthur Pontillon
Barry Benique

Politiques
Michel de L'Hopital
Chancellor
Lady Dowager Emily
Smolliet
Lehman
Daniel Laurent
Marcel Ruben

Ultra Catholics
De Guise brothers
Robert La Paussion
Priest Borges
Gaultien
Pope Paul III
King Philip II of Spain

Nobility:

House de Guise
Duke of Lorraine
Francois de Guise
Cardinal of Lorraine
Charles de Guise
Chevalier du Lay
Queen of Scots
Mary Stuart
Antoinette de Bourbon
Duke of Lorraine
Henri de Guise

House Valois
King Henri II
Queen Mother
Catherine de Medici
King Francis II
Queen of Scots
Mary Stuart
King Charles IX
Margot
King Henri III

Francois-Hercules Duke of Alencon

House Montmorency
Anne de Montmorency – Constable of France
Francois de Montmorency
Henri I de Montmorency

House Bourbon
Antoine de Bourbon King of Navarre
Jeanne d'Albret Queen of Navarre
Louis de Bourbon Prince of Conde
Henry III de Navarre
Margot de Valois
Antoinette de Bourbon

House Coligny
Gaspard de Coligny Admiral of France
Odet de Coligny
Francois de Coligny

Chapter One

August 1, 1559

Laon, France

Maurice watched his sleeping wife through new eyes. A father looks upon his family differently. Perhaps even ferociously. *The Lord is my shepherd, I shall not want.* Maurice and Tonya Millet were blessed with their first child. The midwife just that day confirmed Tonya's feeling.

Tonya had insisted he send for the midwife, as she was feeling nauseous and for a fortnight suspected she was with child. The midwife came on horseback, alone. She was an elder of their town of Laon, and dedicated to ride until her dying day. Maurice had to force the reins from her old sturdy hands so that he could tie off the colt himself. She went inside to attend to Tonya while he remained in open air and busied himself securing the stable posts with more nails. When that did not sufficiently run out the time, he set about sharpening an axe on the wheel grind. The sound pleased him. *Best to leave them alone, this is woman's domain.* The buzz of stone and iron dueling and the mesmerizing flurry of popping sparks almost caused Maurice not to hear the midwife come out.

But hers was a booming type of voice. Terrifyingly so Maurice decided, as he listened in on her proclamation. "Yes, your wife is with child. In five or six months she should expect to birth."

"Is it a boy?"

"For that you would speak to a stargazer."

Maurice was impressed that such an old lady would not subscribe to the old superstitions. "In half a year then I should be a father."

"I said to expect a birth. That could very well mean the extrication of a dead fetus or a babe so weak that it would not survive its first chill."

Woman's domain. "Of course, excuse me, and what is owed?"

"Should you like to send me away then, or employ me for the duration?"

Maurice wondered what was wrong with himself. He was offending the good woman at each turn and he usually understood people's nature quite well. The woman's face hardened, her leathery lines curved and wizened, and made no less handsome for it. Half the day working outside and strong enough to face labor a dozen times in fifteen years. "I should very much like to employ you and for five ecus would you feed her personally, I am not altogether satisfied with her present girth."

"Accepted, and you are quite right Mr. Millet. I shall fatten her up and should be glad to know that shan't affect your fire for her. Bedding at this stage is—"

He had to offend her a final time as he could not stomach being lectured to on the matters of the bedroom by the midwife. "When shall we receive you again?"

"Expect me in a fortnight."

Maurice walked her to the stable post and tried to unmoor the beast but the leathery woman took that upon herself. She rode off and they both understood that she would be back somewhere between ten to twenty days. Enslaved to time they were not. Churches in various towns knelled out tolls for specific hours of prayer, but none more. These tolls, sunrises and sunsets were the mechanisms by which the people of Laon found the Lord's rhythm.

In the late hours they lay safe and sound. And Maurice wondered if he would ever rest again. Perhaps a child would cause them to fall in love with each other. His was a modern family. The Millets of Laon. Considered literati, humanist, and of the reformed religion. All these appellations being true, yet here he lay within the confines of an arranged marriage. Quite the old-fashioned tradition that his own father thought would be for the best.

Maurice had no complaints. Their respective families matched them well. Tonya had taste and was sharp minded. Her recent escapades around town involved teaching the other bourgeoisie women to have their pigs killed humanely. She also advertised guide books of similar content to help drum up business for the Millet family book shop. He knew she would be a good mother, for it was his duties that now kept him up.

The village herald had made the unofficial announcement that day, the king was dead. Succession is always an uneasy affair. *This one will be especially trying for the reformed protestants of France.* The babe now in her womb makes me doubt; he told himself.

He counted his shortcomings and virtues alike and presently relied on the latter to navigate the way. Maurice winced at a sharp pain induced by a head scratch. The Queen mother, Catherine de Médici, would lead the moderates through a peaceful regency, he was sure of it. Yes, all will be fine. The boycotts should end and the family bookstore would thrive again. Maurice prayed one last time before resting his eyes. Fatherhood is disquieting business is all.

Woeful thoughts were not the only culprit invoking Maurice's insomnia. Tonya's style for the right furniture made her an authority with the women on how to elevate their homes beyond station as a form of manifestation. "It all starts with the bed before it can start in the bed," she would say. "A quality feather and linen bed should be among the first family heirlooms to pass on to your children. The next generation, without having to make that investment for themselves, could make some other, for their own children, and that is how family wealth is built." Maurice was forced to put his foot down on the matter of quality, they purchased what they could afford which excluded her desire for Renne linen.

Give me back my sack of straw, he pleaded. It was well beaten and molded with a firmness that a classical stoic would admire him for. Murmurs of voices from the other rooms could be heard. Perhaps he could even make out his sister Marie singing. Through heavy-lidded gaze, the *fleur-de-lis* wallpaper blurred into mighty visages. Thusly he entered his dream world. Imagining himself more like the men he most admired. Maurice thought of himself a typical soft man-child of the nouveau bourgeoisie, an old critique made raw by the new luxurious bed thrusted upon him. Neither strong and hearty like his friend Janeau, nor great like the mythical men in Plutarch's 'Lives'. Maurice found his sleep inside a world where the simple farmer Janeau fought alongside Alexander, and such a beauty as Cleopatra could capture hearts at will.

He was jolted back awake, still staring at the walls. The *fleur-de-lis,* a symbol of fertility. Maurice introduced himself to his child. *It is me, your earthly father. You can hear me can't you? Oh heavenly father permit.* A spear impaled the child in the womb. *I will do anything to protect you.* The spearman menaced again but this time Maurice had a sword of his own. A sword too heavy and he was quickly put out of his misery. His child, born now, wailed in hunger. *I will do anything to provide for you.* Maurice begged from his knees in a strange land. The people of this land walked past the beggar. He could not speak their warbled tongue so pinched his child again to induce another cry for food. Surely the passing folk understood he was only asking for food, then the dream state sent him yet again to another test. The fleur-de-lis also a symbol of the Virgin Mary and church authority. Wearing a blackened cloak he prayed on bloody knees to the corrupted ones. His child burned. Royal authority was also represented by the symbol. *Your earthly king is Francis II. Mine was Henri II.* The womb impaled again. *Your king is a boy yet and is surrounded by slaves to power.* Maurice screamed with all of his might. The child matched his father. It seemed nobody was listening.

    Seigneur Phillipe drew in a deep breath looking out at a bad sky. An unusual summer rain was amidst. Some hours prior tolled the final church bell. Marking an end to the hour of vespers, candles snuffed out leaving only those with troubles awake.

    On this night the good people of Laon rested, Catholics and Protestants alike. Laon, like much of northern France, was majority Catholic. Seigneur Phillipe's late father converted to the reformed religion nearly twenty years prior. When Phillipe inherited the estate, la Paussion family pressured him to convert back to Catholicism but he would not yield. As lord over his family estate with their own peasantry, private and rented farms, and a decent town, truly Phillipe should have been a baron. His father's decision to reform doomed his son to be only a seigneur, the lowest rank of nobility in France. Seigneur Phillipe worried somewhat about the rash of boycotts on protestant businesses in town but protocol demanded that the Reeve Gascon, have time to handle it himself before the lord could intervene. Reeves, or Sheriffs, in France were known as the former. Seigneur Phillipe had to allow the Reeve to enact local authority of the law. It was another decision he made that day that he now wondered about. Traditionally, when a herald made a sanctioned announcement, that message was to be considered as true fact. Today when the Herald of Laon announced the tragic news: that King Henry II had indeed died, Phillipe decreed that it not be considered a true fact until the news periodicals publish confirmation. The old tradition was now in flux. Phillipe's cousin, who was a catholic baron, argued that rumors only become news when the printers type it. With a predilection for compromise the seigneur allowed the herald to make the announcement per pending confirmation by the press masters. After all, it is treasonous to speak about your king being dead when he is not so. He did hope that a news periodical would arrive on the next day.

As far as Lord Phillipe was concerned, on this night, King Henry II was still his king. He still was fighting to survive the wound he incurred from jousting. He still was issuing anti-protestant edicts from his deathbed, and Phillipe still had no reason to expect any better from the dauphine Francis II.

Phillipe pitied his fellow reformed citizens of Laon. The peasants, commoners, and even bourgeoise families who converted to Protestantism across France over the last few generations; would not have provoked the coming persecution. No, this only began when noble houses such as his began to convert. Upon bent backs would lashes strike the sharpest.

Seigneur Phillipe's herald had no reason to fret about being set aside since his works as personal historian were invaluable. The seigneur read over some of the latest entries, complete with advice, trying to glean the enemy's strategy:

15 January 1552 - Treaty of Chambord

King Henry becomes Defender of German Liberties and Imperial Vicar of the three bishoprics, war declared against emperor in February.

Do not mistake this as a sympathetic act towards protestants!

This was French speaking territory and popular victory!

Friend and ally, the Constable of France Lord Montmorency earned renown

Greater prestige won by our enemy Duke Francois de Guise, hero of Metz

July 1552 - Italian Wars

King Henry becomes Liberator of Florence spurred on by Catherine de Medici to reclaim her family demesne.

Our moderate party led by Montmorency lost

De Guise and de Medici factions pressed Italian Ambitions

Franco-Papal alliance signed on 15 December 1555

10 August 1557 - Battle of St. Quentin

Seigneur Phillipe put the book down. He need not read about a battle that he himself had fought in. A two-year anniversary of that humiliating defeat fast approaching. Lord Montmorency himself was captured that day. While de Guise floundered in Italy, we fought to defend France in a war we never asked for. Now they dare question our loyalty simply because our faith differs from theirs? It plagued him that the Duke of Guise was still remembered as the defender of Metz and himself as part of the infamous losers at Saint Quentin. People still spoke of how the Guise brothers needed to be recalled from Italy to clean up the mess. Charles Guise, the Cardinal of Lorraine, even took over many of Anne Montmorency's duties which should have been given to the lord's nephew, Admiral Gaspard de Coligny.

He closed the book and let days agone remain yesterdays. With a snuff of the lone reading candle, Phillipe took to bed and endured a restless night

Chapter Two

August 2, 1559

Laon, France

Danilo had strapped on an extra tarp over the wagon cover for additional protection from the rain. It was all that he could think to do, owing to the precious cargo entrusted to him. My life will now certainly change, he thought as the courier listened to the excess of the flimsy tarp taking slaps from reaching tree branches.. He would have driven the carriage asunder as by then his anxiety toward anticipated completion overtook fickle caution. Alas the boughs of that pasture lane proved as fluffy as they looked and despite the superfluous girth of wagon, he and the horses passed through unscathed. The narrowness of that lane was the lone source of any misgiving he had while outfitting the wagon. So when emerged into the verdure of the dell, he at once decided to keep the tarp as a permanent feature. Oh the look on Maurice's face, he remembered that day when he presented a stack of dampened copies of 'Utopia' to the bookseller of Laon. Nothing would stop Danilo from making the current delivery though, with its contents dry.

The courier could hear the torrent of a nearby stream as he gazed upon an approaching stone edifice that had the look of not once tolerating an assault for which it was designed. Up an anthill through the unguarded postern, he proceeded into the leafy gardens of fruit and berry whose bounty surpassed their rude placement. Encircling and amongst, abandoned

spires whose only belligerents now were lizards, who preyed upon the destructive herbasects. These lizards fell prey themselves to the field cats and the world marched on. Who could foresee how long those towers would stand with their self-reinforced circular stair structures.

As soft and welcoming as the dell was for these peasants were only a pitiful book or two. Though the poor villagers could ill afford new prints, the good owner of the printing press, for whom he was delivering, decided to donate a periodical to the village since the news was of the utmost importance to these states. King Henri II died from complications following a jousting accident. In short order, the men and women and children alike would be called to encircle the village wordsmith who would impart the news. It would have been a surprise to Danilo, if one in twenty of the villagers could read. They would have the news read to them. He had no need to remain and would leave the briar patch as he had found it. He would depart before their simple folk cried in lament over a dead cankerous king. The fools.

The death of King Henri II left his wife and eldest prince in a precarious state. Though succession to the throne was not in question, King Francis II and Mary Stuart, were indeed nominally the crowned rulers of France. The age of majority was fourteen and Francis was indeed fifteen years of age. However, due to his sickliness and low energy, a Regent was to rule officially. Henri's grieving wife, and now Queen Mother Catherine de Medici sought the regency.

France had been under mounting religious division for over twenty years. The national religion was Catholicism, though a growing number of reformed followers broke away from the church. From this divide arose several political factions, each wanting the authority of the regency for their purpose.

The most dominant group were the ultra-Catholics. They were zealous radicals who sought elimination of the reformed protestants through policies of intolerance, forced conversion, Papal decree, execution, or civil war. The ultra-Catholics wanted France to be once again a unified country under one faith. Their leader, ironically, was a foreign prince. Duke Francois de Guise and his brother Cardinal Charles were princes of Lorraine, a sovereign state. Though the Guise brothers were not even French, they were in position to rule France temporarily as regents. Ethnic questions aside, Francois de Guise was a favored general and friend to the late King Henri II. Furthermore, Duke Francois and Cardinal Charles were uncles to Queen Mary Stuart. They had her ear, and she had Francis'.

The protestants had been growing in number, but what became alarming to the Guise faction was when many from the noble, bourgeoisie, and administrative classes began to reform. Though they were growing in power, they had no political leader to appoint for regency and thus threw their lot in with Catherine de Medici.

As Queen of France, she tended to keep King Henri appeased with the fact that the protestants were loyal to the crown. As now the Queen mother, she was looked upon to continue the same influence as Regent. While a devout Catholic herself and unquestioned royalist with always the Valois house sanctity in mind, she cooperated with the moderate politiques.

The moderates also wished for a unified France but they hoped the reformed would abjure and come back into the folds of the church on their own terms. This group wanted to prevent a religious civil war and promote tolerance. They also feared a return of the inquisitions and crusades such as those inflicted upon the Cathars of Languedoc of the 14th century. Such a sign of regression was counter to the day's climate of renaissance humanism. Danilo gave his wagon horses a rallying whistle. Best to get his friends the news as soon as he could. His visions haunted him. The courier could more than imagine the protestants of France being in mortal danger from the upcoming regency.

The lane gave way to the high road of the country connecting Paris to Reims. If green and grey were a color, that would be France. The mongrel race of Celts and Normans unlike us Italians who are all good Romans. The courier was travelling north, the natural route of intelligentsia. It was easy travelling from this point forward. Joie de vivre, he could then roam through the stability of northern France, where his protestant friends were the minority and the rebellious south returned to the dust of eternity. Danilo suffered the oppression of his friends and students, but nonetheless was happy to cross the line of demarcation which all but now assured a safe crossing into Germany towards a new life. He whistled the horses into an excited gallop, the load and his soul, mostly unladen.

Maurice was not used to being alone at the bookshop, usually his father was there with him, humming as he unwittingly tended to do. "Dad, you are humming a tout le monde." "I don't know that tune," he would say to which the son would respond, "well you are humming it." It was common for his younger sister Marie to come in and lend a hand. She loved to arrange the books in order of size and color paying no mind to subject material. They would chat and sing and hum and do the dance of labor, while filling out ledgers, dusting the nooks, and tending to customers.

Lunches would be spent out on the flat rocks along the Mausien Brook. Maurice would be welcomed by Janeau, Torry, and Robiere. The bookman would be teased for being stuck inside the shop all morning and made jealous of their outdoor frolics of the day. Maurice did indeed grow tired of the stuffy shop, but would not give his friends the satisfaction. Well, you all need a head start on the day's reading for there is no other way to keep up with the likes of me! At that moment though, he would have basked in the company of his friends and family. These being dangerous days of boycott and harassment. A young sickly boy king, succeeding his father, while his mother and uncles vied for regency over the throne. A more chaotic situation Maurice could not have dreaded. It would not have been prudent, and it was at his insistence that he alone tend the store during these troubled times.

In conspiracy with his thoughts, he looked up and out through the window and gazed upon the source of a row: the courier, or more accurately a trio of boycotters harassing the courier. I should wait and see what transpires, I don't want to make it worse.

"Halt right there sir, what is your business?"

Three men stepped in front of the courier's wagon. One wearing third-hand finery unbefitting his lot, another pox marked, and the third with a hooked nose and bulbous forehead. Danilo assumed these were boycotters. It was not an uncommon tactic of the Catholics to disrupt protestant businesses. After all it was not until the reformed religion crept into the merchant communities and noble houses of France, that it became a problem. He mustered a response to the cohort though it seemed "monsieur finery" fancied himself the leader:

"I pride myself in knowing the reeve of every shire I deliver to, or they pride themselves in knowing me? Well whatever the score on that; the point gentlemen is that my business is none of your business."

"Fair enough, your business is your own. But this establishment and all other stores or markets or merchants of reformed propriety is our business. You see we have no quarrel with you, and you said you make deliveries, well it just so happens that Laon now also has a bookstore run by a proper catholic family, I could direct—"

"You have the right of it..." Danilo now nearly yelling. "I make deliveries and pickups and I am but a simple courier. A highway man of the decent sort. Such a simple task for such a great man. Yes this job is far inferior to my skills and abilities and resolve sirs so I will make this delivery!"

The men were taken aback by such bravado. The man with pox about the neck shuffled, his boots grating for purchase as he thumbed at a sheathed dagger. Since they began upon this self-anointed quest to boycott the many protestant merchants of Laon they had relatively easy work of it. This southerner was of a different stock yet their leader, monsieur finery, continued on:

"Would you then consider visiting the catholic stores and making other arrangements with them? We would love to have such fierce responsibility taking highways for us and not for this reformed bookman."

This part was always the point of the highest degree of inner anxiety for Danilo. The courier would often bluff with bloated breast but in truth, he was not much of a fighter and violence sickened him. He was not a coward, just not good at fighting and if violence never solved anything, then for him it was trebly so. Such was his motto.

"Yes, that sounds quite reasonable but I can make no promises. Yet if the prices are met, my employer may be persuaded to change affiliations at a later time and in the meantime my grave honor may remain intact."

That concluded the matter and the boycotting ruffians allowed the man to pass and conduct his business with Maurice the bookman.

"You fool Danilo what was all of that?"

Danilo nodded. "Well, it worked and how long has this boycott been going on Maurice?"

"Too long. So long that in fact I have no orders to place and would not hazard to accept any new stock. Not even the 'Book of Hours' leaves our shelves. I fear ruin is imminent for our little book shop."

"Would you purchase the latest editions from any of the periodicals? You know the king is dead?"

"Yes we are aware, of course I do believe these boycotts ramped up since that damned jousting accident."

"What of your edicts..." Danilo quipped, "your protestant rights?"

"Increasingly ignored. If the royal train nears Laon then we are reprieved, but once the lords move on, the edicts become once again worthless pieces of paper..." Maurice continued with gathering aplomb, "the king had been ill-counseled, but that will change now that the Queen Mother will gain regency."

The courier scoffed. "The Queen Mother? The Black Witch? The Tradesman's Daughter? No matter the connotation you Frenchman can't get the correct appraisal of Catherine de Medici. Her father was Lorenzo the Duke of Urbino, no mere tradesman. The Medici clan has been a scourge on us Florentines for centuries, I would not put your faith in her sir."

"Enough Danilo, I will hear no more of the Queen Mother. Friend to us or not, I believe she fosters for peace and she alone can keep de Guise's whispers from the young King Francis' ears, and for that matter the Dauphine Charles as well."

Danilo had grown fond of Maurice over the years and considered himself a bringer of news for the young literati. "Maurice, how exactly is it that positions are being drawn up in your head when I am just now delivering the news of the King's death?"

"Oh dear Danilo the world does not start and end with your delivering "the news" as you call it. Indeed not, here in Laon a succession is well anticipated and who comes out the victor for the seat of regency, hinges all our poor hopes to Catherine. Besides it is not so much that the King was hurt jousting, but that he was jousting at the lists of a royal wedding and even more to the point, a wedding symbolizing the end of the Italian wars. Now the radical Catholics can shift their gaze internally, namely on us protestants. Deportation of Calvinists to Geneva shall increase, forced conversions and as you can see - unlawful boycotts."

The courier imagined the scene of the joust wistfully, sticks into ribbons under thunderous applause. "Oh what a tournament that must have been. In all seriousness though I am pleased by the end of the Italian wars, I fear you are right of the true effect of one peace leading to civil war eternal in France."

"I said nothing of a civil war. The young King Francis II is bankrupt—"

"Oh Maurice, a king always finds a way to pay for wars. Financed by the Church no doubt, your lady de Medici shall see to that. The Medici old family business—"

"Yes, yes bankers to popes and all that," the bookman whined in jest.

"Maurice listen, your people cannot win. Listen to your father, you are not yet as wise as he. Flee! Though I am not so sure the low countries are any safer, it is just a matter of time until Spain puts down iconoclasm in the Netherlands." Danilo could see his friend was too far engulfed in pride, too smart for his own good.

"No matter, our family will not be moving there and there shall be no civil war in France. The Queen Mother shall moderate for us. And if there were a war, why do you discount the possibility of us winning? If the English could do it, why not the French?"

"Indeed, why not." Danilo thought now would be time to shift topics. "I do have some more sad news of the more personal type. Had you any new orders to place, I would not be able to take them from you. I am away to Germany and shan't be delivering for the press any longer."

Maurice became shocked but listened on.

"For me though this is a fantastic improvement. I carry with me something of value which will surely improve my own lot, and the press master assures me that you will have a new courier soon. You should however prepare yourself to begin your own purchases in bulk at market. I am afraid the delivery method to each shop is just not working anymore. Sooner or later, the presses will be only distributing to major markets who will then supply the proprietors directly. Perhaps you can arrange deliveries from these new wholesalers."

It started to dawn on the courier what a slow-witted ass he was sounding like.

"Of course when all this blows over I am certain to return again someday as you and your flock of the Mausien Brook are some of the more promising socratics in all of the land."

"Oh can we not go to the brook now? The men all surely await," Maurice begged.

"My cargo is very precious, and really those ruffians gave me a scare." Maurice appeared injured at that. What an ass I truly am, the courier thought to himself. "Of course Maurice what am I saying. Let us have one more discourse at the brook. I know exactly the lecture."

They hurried about finalizing all past bill of sales. The Millet Bookshop was a dark den with little natural light. During normal business operations many candles were lit for customers to browse titles comfortably. Under an effective boycott, he kept only the one personal candle lit, a cocoon of light surrounded by grey. Maurice had knocked over the small glass bottle of ink as he dashed out his signature with his quill pen. His friend helped by moving a pile of papers away from the gushing black goo, when a particular draft caught his eye.

"Yes my friend, if this boycott does not end soon we shall be forced to shutter."

"My friend is it really that dire?"

"I dread it so. My great grandfather started our collection, he was a manuscript hunter,"

"A man of the world he was?"

"Not like you, but yes," A slip of pride beamed. "My grandfather continued our family collection of original texts, but he also began buying reprints and original runs. He and father ran it together for a couple of years, then it was just my father, then my father and me. I dread that our family legacy will be lost. Under my watch, it shall all be lost."

Danilo could not meet his friend's eyes.

"Yet, I am determined to save it!"

Business was hence concluded and the pair left off the bookshop of Laon towards the Mausien Brook.

The heat of the day had taken a toll on the courier's wagon horses so he granted them a most leisurely pace. The pair chuckled about rushing to leave the book shop only to dawdle about.

"Maurice could you sell some pieces from your family collection?"

Maurice kicked a rock, an answer in itself., "No, grandfather made my father promise to never mix the retail business with our collection. He was convinced they will only gain value with time…"

Town folk came up to the slow-moving wagon to ask if King Henri II truly had died. Maurice told a few to gather a collection and on the strength of the yield, to buy as many editions as they could, directly from the courier.

"I can sell you none, they are running me out of business!" Maurice announced to his folk.

"Repent Maurice and we should gladly buy your books again," replied a Catholic woodsman.

Maurice knew that oaf well, "You've not picked up a book in your life and the bible is read to you!"

Horses be damned, Danilo gave a whistle and a click commanding the horses to quicken the pace. Maurice was sorry for the outburst and wanted to enjoy time with his friend. So Maurice hopped out and began gathering pebbles to pelt the wagon with, a bit of fun is what they needed. "Be gone you scoundrel," the courier shrieked. Boys of the bourgeois class took notice and arose from their neat porches to join in. Rocks then rained upon the courier, "I cannot escape for my horse is lame."

"The Italians are invading," proclaimed the little gendarme. The rough-housing of the Laon kids proved too much for the men. Maurice hopped back in proclaiming himself a mercenary with a new pay master. Other boys went rogue too and now there were two armies facing each other down as the pair continued down the road, happy that they could still play the games of children. And it was the same game Danilo and Maurice would have acted out as kids, where two sides established often morphed within the midst of battle, mercenary soldiers abandoning their kin for the higher paying lord.

"All joyous again?"

"Are you Danilo?"

"Indeed. Not only for my treasure," gesturing to the cargo bin beneath remaining books. "I am joyous for all of us. There is an easy solution to this puzzle Maurice, and you are too wise for it to elude you long."

The Sophists of the Mausien Brook, as they called themselves, sat upon rocks and hurled quips at each other. Robiere was tall and meek. Janeau was strong and jovial. Torry was stubby and mischievous. There ended any differences and what remained was a homogenous brotherhood of hard-working farmers. Faithful protestants and the only true academics according to Maurice. He would say that "nobody worked harder for knowledge." The few hours of daylight not working the fields they spent at the brook learning. They allotted more of their budget than other commoners to candle wax so that they could read into the nights.

"Do you think Maurice will be here today?"

Torry replied to Robiere, "As sure as you are a son of the Vaudois."

"Lay off Robiere now," Janeau commanded of Torry before answering Robiere. "If not Robiere, it would be for good reason."

"Should we not help him with those sons of Vaudois boycotters?"

Torry carried on with his latest quip but this time Robiere parried.

"It doesn't even make sense Torry, the boycotters are cath-o-lics." Robiere grinned at his response. "I swear when you learn a new term you use it for everything." Torry only shrugged.

Janeau concluded, "No Torry we should not help him, he expressly stated for us to stay away from shops. He will handle the matter with the reeve." At that both Robiere and Torry looked at each other skeptically. "Have you ever known Maurice to be wrong about such matters?" Jan continued. "Maurice has a way of understanding people and events and well everything." At that they nodded together in the affirmative. "Anyway here he comes now, and look Danilo is with him."

"So it's not just rumor, the king is really dead?" said Robiere.

"Yes." Maurice confirmed bluntly.

"From his injuries, from jousting at Princess Elizabeth's wedding?" Robiere always a fountain of questions.

"Yes."

"Well what are we doing here? We should make for the church at once," said Robiere.

"The bells have not yet rung."

"Waiting for the bells toll is a statement within itself Torry."

Maurice and the courier looked at each other proudly. Their students were learning at a great pace. Like moths to a flame, they read as voraciously as they reaped the fields and with the same dogged determination and rhythm. Knowledge was hard fought for simple farmers, they were the real scholars. They worked the land all day and read and participated in discourse whenever they could steal the time.

"What do you say Janeau?" said Danilo.

"Perhaps the most solid of defenses for us protestants, is that we are no less Frenchmen than the Catholics. We are loyal subjects to king and country and we absolutely need to protect that reputation even for image sake."

Robiere protested at the implication, "but I do love King Henri."

Maurice interceded, "Well spoken Jan and indeed you are correct, but there is one other piece of news concerning our dear Greek here, or Italian is it?"

The young sophists laughed at the inside joke of the courier's ever-changing claim of origin. When the cackling ceased so that the pigeons could return home, Danilo took his cue.

"It shall be time to update my lore again gentlemen farmers, brave Frenchmen, and dear fellow humanists. It may be some time before I can return and may well never sit aside this brook again to enrich my knowledge with you."

"Where do you go?" "What of the book trade?"

"Maurice will fill you in. But be assured friends my station is more secure today than yesterday. May I propose one final quick lesson as your visiting tutor before returning you to the capable hands of our bookman."

Jan replied, "Yes a final lesson we can not only afford but are ever grateful for every drop of truth from our wise teacher.

"Even though you are not a real Greek," Robiere jokingly added.

They laughed and took their places around the courier sitting on the Speaker's Rock. "Dante's Inferno," announced the teacher:

Upon which the circle of sophists closed their eyes. They were each in their own way scanning the halls of their mind's storehouse. Places mapped out as familiar haunts and houses and other buildings with furniture arranged just so. For Maurice it was the second shelf of his childhood nook. A dusty copy lay there. For Jan it was under a pillow in a wooden shed where infrequently less than healthy farmers took extra breaks. In classical times this was a common enough tactic for academics. Even the greatest schools had but one copy of any given text, and as such the students only had brief turns to commit the whole to memory. This was but one of the classical traditions being raised from the dead.

"Now class recall the third Canto. NINE," Teacher commanding the students to recite the ninth line.

"Abandon all hope ye who enter." Replied heartily. That was an easy one and one of the teacher's favorite lines.

"But of course Dante would later clarify what we all here know so well, through Christ one can hold hope, as easily as a small girl." Danilo lectured with the purpose of stoking the French protestants. "You see we renaissance thinkers do not idolize the pagans, but only admire their accomplishments, given their limitations as pagans. What lay beyond this frightening gate, was the vestibule of hell. Dante reserved such a place for the likes of Celestine V. FIFTY-SEVEN!":

Near silent murmurs to which Danilo gave pause. Maurice answered for the group due to their accelerated pace of the day as he did not want unanswered questions to linger. He also wanted to demonstrate to the students that partial answers were better than none.

"Something about cowardice and denial."

"Well enough. It was Celestine V who allowed Benedetto the Papacy and unleashed the Boniface on Dante's people. He denied his obligation to oppose evil and such gave up his right to rationalism. That he would not use his intelligence when it was needed most, he was doomed to the vestibule of hell." Time to wake them up. "You reformed are the opportunists of the day!"

Janeau parried, "But we have reformed our churches and carved the words of Christ not by rune but by plain speak."

"Uh hu, Jan, today will be a short lesson. I did not agree to allowance of retort." No more time for debate, they must have the truth, ready or not.

Torry piped, "Surely Maurice and Danilo are great teachers who allow for hours of discourse of the back and forth kind, today is only an exception. Though I query if he dons the cloak of dictate with ease."

The good-hearted group laughed together.

"Admittedly it does feel good to simply tell a fool the right of it and be done with the whole matter. In this case I tell you protestants, you endanger yourselves to the vestibule along with all the other opportunists who refused to take sides excepting only for worldly gain. My travels through France always leads to the same conclusion. The protestants should either abjure!"

Yelps in the negatory.

"Exodus"

A quieter moan.

"Or fight."

Which garnered only small croaks from the toads of the brook.

"By doing none of these three you are not taking sides. You must not side against all the Catholics as they are not all evil. You could rejoin them or leave, but by remaining you dangle yourselves as fodder and allow evil doers to take you down, village by village, town by town and province by province. You must not continue to withhold aid to your fellow protestants simply because they are facing an evil while you currently are not." Back to the lesson at hand Danilo thought. All in its own time.

"Next is the fourth canto where Virgil and Dante come upon the first circle of hell. They passed through the gate which sucked hope from their soul, and since the pagans knew not of Christ they could not regain it. Otherwise the pagans were not tormented any further but by being stuck in limbo. In limbo was also the citadel of human reason where only those who reached the very limits of knowledge could enter. The members were Virgil, Homer, Horace, Ovid, and Lucan, but of course Dante had the audacity to make himself the sixth member—"

To which the group chuckled like school boys, earning them their next test.

"One Hundred Six," queried Danilo. Recalling lines this deep into the text was a natural filter leaving only the more gifted students.

The students grumbled. Torry gaped then quickly withdrew. Robiere ventured some non-sense but it was Janeau who proclaimed:

"Come on men, its why we gather at this place!"

Maurice smiled proudly while the courier privately wondered if Jan, the hearty farmer, was the wisest of them all.

"The brook surrounds the citadel and represents a moat which keeps the ignorant at bay. We study here in effort to cross the brook. Once crossing the brook, we would then have to topple each of the seven battlements of philosophy. Or I could just anoint myself the seventh."

The sophists laughed heartily at that, then the courier boomed.

"Was it arrogance or righteous self-awareness for Dante to recognize himself as a virtuous pagan in addition to carrying Christ's light?" The group tensed at his change in tone. "Maybe Dante could have humbled himself but humility is simply recognizing reality without shame or pride. Who could argue that Dante did not climb each tower and deserved his place there. Perhaps you Jan are the seventh, after all a brighter student I have never known." Janeau blushed with embarrassment which the courier immediately regretted. "One final thought before I bid you all adieu." Coincidentally Danilo would strike again at another parallel of Dante and Janeau. Unbeknownst to the courier, Jan was the only one of the group to have true love. Danilo concluded the lecture:

"Our friends now eternally preside at the citadel and have gained all possible knowledge that can be gained without Christ. With the love of the lord one can progress further. This divine light is symbolized by Beatrice...Dante's true love. It was through her guiding spirit that inspired Dante to pass forward even when Virgil's influence was not sufficient. Whence Virgil explained that Beatrice, and the Virgin Mary, and others indeed came to him; so Virgil could temporarily hold the divine light and aid Dante to gather the heart to continue the descent. To summarize good men of Laon and followers along the brook - Choose a side. Blaze your own path to the citadel. When angels come, do not hesitate to follow."

Dinner at the Millet home consisted of the patriarch Jean, his eldest son Maurice, his wife Tonya, daughter Marie, and fifteen-year-old Christopher. Jean took in the news about the courier and the approaching changes to the delivery methods. He sighed. Final nail in the coffin.

"So Maurice, the boycotts continue. Did you get any sense that this was related?"

"How do you mean father?"

"That the printer is merely brushing us aside too?"

"Quite the opposite. Danilo chased the mongrels away and was more than prepared to sell us stock that he had in tow." Maurice continued with his summary report on the sad state of the family business. "However, since we have no orders to place, nor a courier to place them with, we instead drew up a final settlement for past bills of sale—"

"I see, and with such letters being called in; we are nearly broke," Jean Millet stated with finality.

The Millets had been preparing themselves for this moment. It was shocking how quickly a family on the rise could experience a turn in such drastic fashion. None at the table knew of life without bourgeoisie means.

"I shall see the banker Quentin tomorrow for payment and about the other business."

Jean glared at Maurice in disbelief. "Even in the face of all this you would still drag Torry down with us."

"In what world is helping a small farmer to open his own drapery business, anything but an elevation."

"In this world, France, right now! Look Maurice I know you believe in Torry, and perhaps you are right about his capabilities but Christ can only show us the signs, and it is up to us to read them."

"I will see the Reeve again."

"We've been to the Reeve!" piped in Christopher. "He has done nothing. It is time to plead with Lord Phillipe."

Maurice droned his typical response, "We have rights, edicts that guarantee our rights to worship and do business—"

"There is also an edict that dictates pigs are not to be penned with goats, have you walked across Laon lately."

The whippersnapper makes good points, the father thought. Tonya aimed to change the flow of discussion.

"What does Danilo think?"

"He agrees with father, we should move away."

"Ah hem."

"But not to the low countries."

"Hrmph."

"He also thinks we are heading to a civil war that we can't possibly win."

"I fear the same," Jean replied.

"I welcome it, and we will win," Christoper said.

"Is no one on my side?" Maurice asked.

"I am." Put in Marie but that only drew a skeptical consensus.

Maurice made his point for optimism or at least patience. "Yes it must seem strange but I see potential here. Our friends, relations, countrymen are all here. I believe the Queen Mother can put things to right, and that the reeve shall have to put down the boycott. Our business can recover and thrive again. Torry will open up a draper's shop, yes we can all thrive."

Tonya looked at him prodding another subject.

"There is something else. Tonya is with child. We must think of the financial security of this family."

Christoper rose up gallantly, ever the picture of a long lost chivalry. "So it begins, we shall begin making our own children which makes us men Maurice, we must fight for them."

"Enough," the father proclaimed. "I have made my decision long ago. And all the news of today has not swayed me, not even the happy news of my emergence to grand-fatherhood." Jean stood shakily and seemed ready to burst in delirium. while he managed to open the floodgates. "What I have decided is something radical. Perhaps even unheard of, but there is another way. I need not be the dinner table dictator nor hold court over a dinner table democracy. We could all simply choose what is best for each of us. Except for you Marie, even I am not that progressive."

"What do you speak of father?"

"When I was younger than you Christopher, I remember too being the young pup at the table, but it was a much larger table and what was decided at those tables had to be for the entire family. Uncles, cousins, sisters, and nephews all had to be considered. Then my Great Uncle Tobias stopped attending and said he would make decisions for his own kin. He was the radical humanist back then, but in time many of the protestants embraced humanism. Some of the Catholics too in their own way. Now while we are here tonight having this discussion the Millets of the northern quarter are surely doing the same as are the Millets in Reims and our cousin house here in Laon. Tonight I am Tobias, the new radical humanist. Marie and I are indeed moving to the Netherlands, the arrangements are in motion—" Marie ran off in a great state.

"Maurice I leave to you the shop which is nearly bankrupt as you know. Christopher you are right, we are all here men now—" but he too ran off in tears tripping and stumbling over a wayward stool. Jean calmly picked it up and fiddled with a snapped stretcher piece. "Maurice we shall meet with my broker friend he will purchase our family library and we shall divide it into thirds. One for me, one for you, and one for Christopher. There is one other proposal I have for you, but it shall wait until we meet with the broker as it is something he and I have conspired about, if only in brief detail."

"Father, your logical deduction is sound and perhaps this is rational choice. But does it not seem, wrong?"

"It does, quite wrong."

Chapter Three

August 4, 1559

Laon, France

Maurice wondered when the last time he had been so near the Manor Estates of Laon (personal home of Seigneur Phillipe). Certainly the bookman usually traveled west then south on the high road toward the briar patch aside the lake. From the high road one could barely make out the luxuriant palace as it was tucked neatly into Phillipe's woods. The mansion was accessible only by a lane which took such a wide angle, one's approach from the high road to the manor itself, would be semicircular, rather than a perpendicular route. It was here that Maurice received a torrent of old cob webbed memory of his youth.

"Father I remember this place." They happened upon a roughshod orphanage conjoined with a stony church. In the plain field a cohort of little ruffians ran about playing no-rules ball creating a real dust up. He was immediately dropped into the heady days of his youth. He had played ball on this very field with orphans of his age. A few times even. Though the modern version of no-rules ball seemed rougher and the field certainly less grassy; he had played here just as they did now. It was all coming back.

"It was from the time of the plague, when we lost mother." Laon had been hit particularly hard by plague when he was one and ten. For their family, only the soul of Grace Millet was claimed, which was atypical in two ways. Firstly, losing anything less than a third of your loved ones was seen as a mercy and secondly in that final bout of the plague it was

the children who suffered the highest mortality rates. As the surviving kids got on, they no longer had the numbers to play a proper match, so they took to joining up with the orphans for such games. The games however devolved into further mischief as the orphans took to daring village boys to haunt the seigneury woods. Not to poach so much as to generally dare violation and perhaps muck about the groundskeeper's shed. He had seen this place before and began to regale his father with more of the story, but Jean said, "No son, some memories are best kept to oneself." They soon arrived at the home of the book broker who lived upon a proper rue. As if another degree of intrigue was lacking Jean said, "Son understand this, I fear we must run and I wish nothing else for you come—"

"Perhaps as a colonial, but a vagabond. Father, anything but banishment."

Jean Millet eyed his son with bewilderment, wondering when he would learn that starting again in a new country is no longer taboo. "Maurice, If you must stay and trust in reconciliation, perhaps here is a way that you may affect it and not just wait upon it."

Maurice quite enjoyed the company of Charles Avon who evidently his father secreted away as both friend and business associate. For the plot which they were hatching was of the pre-arranged variety. This monsieur Avon was a speculative broker who specialized in a longer viewed approach to appraising period literature. His was a comfortable house on the Rue Magnon with not only the necessities of life but many decorations and luxuries as well. There was the fattest cupboard the bookman had ever seen. Lamps of polished brass, silver spoons clanked upon porcelain cups. He decided however that it lacked taste, yet he realized too that it was a fashionable abode for the bourgeois of the day. Within the cozy confines of Avon's parlour they were delighted with viands, oaky wine, and sheriee. Maurice now properly buttered up, their reason for the rendezvous was put forward.

"Your father tells me that you are the most well-read person he knows and that you tutor your own band of sophists along a rocky brook." Monsieur Avon continued quite forwardly on the assumptions he was led to believe about Maurice. "He also tells me that you have excellent intuition and a gift for delivering a synopsis on just about any important text. But I think a father surely boasts."

"I tell you Charles I love to be tested because pass or fail someone will learn something." Maurice guessed the man a rascal, perhaps up for a game. "You can pick any book and I shall attempt to summarize it for you. Then you can correct me on any missed point or misinterpretation. At the end we shall decide if I learned more from you, or, you from me."

"He also said you were a sport. I will make you a deal, you answer this one." He grabbed Erasmus' Adages from a nearby shelf. "And you get to keep this copy, begin a new personal collection today. If you falter though, you must hear out my proposition. Are these agreeable terms?

"Indeed monsieur Avon, as I understand Erasmus of Rotterdam quite well."

"Allow me to set the scene. You are at a soiree and a lady far out of our league inquires to you about these adages. A subject that has become so fashionable in Paris society. She complains of socialites repeating these phrases of Erasmus, but she takes his works as purely unoriginal and quite literally a collection of other authors' works, long now dead. So, she asks you, what is the significance of his publications?" Charles Avon laying down the gauntlet, indicating to Maurice that a battle of wits had begun.

"Hmm, I don't quite understand the scenario," Maurice rubbed his chin, a sure sign of wisdom. "But I would explain to this grand lady that Erasmus understands that these proverbs do not belong to any author but to everyone, especially the living. These expressions exist out of time and that is self-evident to the hearer when Erasmus shoots the adage like an arrow which instantly leaves a sting upon your ear; whose mark does not easily fade, so that for some days or even weeks an itch causes the hearer to recall the trauma with greater and greater clarity. The fact that they are universally recognized as not non-sense, gives Erasmus rights to compile them for posterity."

Jean leaned back into his lounge triumphantly, but his prodigy was not quite done. Avon listened on though already quite impressed.

"In a way we can view Erasmus as a collector of these metaphors with tremendous festivitas, to be modernized specifically into a more familiar tone, which the entire operation itself is a microcosm of the Renaissance."

"Brilliant." Charles Avon clapped.

"Una hirundo non facit ver," said Maurice with a playful bow.

"Enlighten me," Jean said, not well versed in Latin.

Clapping with more gusto, Charles translated for Jean. "One swallow does not make a summer. It is one of Erasmus' simplifications Maurice just talked about, and in the context that I should not have praised him by only one swallow. Maurice you are talented—" he began to hand over his copy but pulled back mockingly, "yet maybe too condescending."

Maurice swiped his prize. "Well it was a stupid question."

Charles now leaned back in the chaise and replied. "It was a soiree...all the questions are stupid."

Maurice now mocked writing a new passage to the collection of adages. "You just added a new proverb Charles."

The three rolled in their chaises in glorious laughter and Jean tied the bow. "You better credit him Erasmus."

Maurice enjoyed the company of his father's friend indeed and so they dined and drank on. "You know Charles my dad was right about one thing, I am a good sport and although I did not falter, I shall like to hear your proposal after all."

"I know of your family history and I too have shared with Jean my similar background."

"His family are Lutherans but we shan't hold that against him." Jean pointed at their host. "Like us Maurice they have been

31

in the book business for a few generations now, but Charles Avon here has discovered quite a different method."

Now Charles explained. "You see Maurice, royalists are coming around to the humanities. It has been fashionable for some time now for any respectable lord and lady to have a well curated library and to be able to speak half intelligently on the books they pretend to read. Within this realm book dealers are becoming quite influential and welcomed members of court life. Now here is the crucial aspect of my novel approach, I do not deal in money, I have adapted to their practice of trading influence, association, and favors."

"Am I to understand that the nobility still looks upon the bourgeois avarice with disdain?"

"No, that has largely passed for the lower nobility. But many see the advantages to the royalist currency of favor—"

"Are you suggesting that I enter this business?"

"No, well yes, but not for personal gain. I wish to enlist you into the protestant cause and to join the court of Lord Admiral de Coligny."

Maurice scoffed and his father took a hearty drink of brandy.

"You are connected with Lord Admiral de Coligny?"

"Yes Maurice, this is where my influence has taken me. But we believe you can take us further. You see, more than anything else, you would be interpreting these humanist texts for the Catholics, to grow the politique which is the moderate base. Your father has told me of your ability to bring out the best in others, to guide them and perceive their true motivations. All these innate skills along with your expertise as a literati; I have passed on to the admiral, I shall now send him word of my confirmation of your capabilities and I have no doubt that he will invite you forthwith to an apartment of your own at his chateau."

"This seems, surreal and I fear father and Charles, that you are dreaming."

"Oh son, you have not heard the most fantastic part yet. Admiral de Coligny believes that you can work your way up to Catherine de Medici directly with our Machiavelli letter—"

"Our Machiavelli letter?" Maurice was now utterly confused as Charles continued the double attack.

"Yes, the provenance of that piece is fantastic. The way your great grandfather won it from Niccolo himself in a card game! Fantastic, and how the story goes he all but gave up on the Medici ever returning him to favor or accepting the advice of 'The Prince'. That was a man who understood the currency of favor."

"Let me see if I can fathom this. Admiral de Coligny wants to furnish me an apartment at his chateau, as a member of his court, fulfilling the role of book broker and sophist to the Catholics, with aim of currying sympathy and influence to the point where the Queen Mother may at some point attend to me and my offer of a gift to her as somewhat a family heirloom?"

Charles formed a mischievous look. "Why stop there? Teach her of the Machiavellian methods her ancestors ignored and she can begin to contend with House Lorraine on equal footing."

"How so monsieur Avon?"

"The de Guise faction of radicals are persecuting us village by village. The reformed of Laon won't stand with the reformed of Lyon because why?

"In Lyon they are heretical and their crimes of iconoclasm are being punished—"

"No Maurice, that is the game the radicals are playing. Machiavellian to the core, divide and conquer. We need to employ similar methods. Knossos Maurice, you understand it at the rational, but what of the relevant, the useful. You taught me something tonight but I have knowledge you cannot learn from books. Did you know Maurice that an edict of re-education is being issued?"

"I have heard no such thing."

"You will. Your Danilo kept you informed well enough but even a traveler only scratches the surface, and I fear you will know even less without him. Knossos, it is how we will win our rights—"

"Tell me of this edict."

"It was one of King Henri's final dictums and one that King Francis II will not overturn. The edict is not being issued everywhere."

"The Machiavellian way," noted Jean.

"Strategically divisive and as you said yourself Maurice of the Lyon. The counties where it is not read will convince others that the counties affected, brought it upon themselves and now need re-education. They too will call the protestants of Laon, heretics."

"It will be issued in Laon?"

"Yes."

"What does it read man?"

"That all maidens receive catechism some hours a day for some months and upon completion need to confirm their faith once again."

"Is that all?" Maurice grinned at the failing of the climax. "Nay father, nay Charles. I will not flee nor conspire. This could not be the way. I could only imagine a life abroad. A refugee, a stranger...a leper. Begging for ply, being of strange tongue, a Frenchman no more. I dare reserve some optimism to be found embedded in this edict. I notice a hint of reconciliatory spirit of harmony in this re-education program. Father, you and grandfather knew well the Catholic prerogative and those parts which needed reform, yet think on my fellows who have known nothing but the protestant faith. Shouldn't they be reacquainted with superstitions if only to reject them anew? The Queen Mother shall affect further such moderations."

"Ah Maurice your true knowledge could surpass mine. You could be one of the most influential protestants at court." Charles Avon's disappointment now was replaced by some paranoia. "I put myself at great risk exposing myself and the conspiracy yet I will reveal to you a final fact. Lady de Medici has already lost. Duke Francois de Guise is the ruling regent to a sickly boy king."

"I shall never utter a word of this to anyone" Maurice assured Charles.

"I have heard such things before. God gave you an extraordinary gift Maurice, do you not feel any responsibility?"

"I am responsible for my dying business, my wife, and an unborn child. I am trying to keep my family together so my father and sister don't leave their ancestral home of the Millets. I am teaching a band of wise farmers, mes amis, to aid them in their own elevation."

How could Charles argue further with a young man so determined, so utterly sure that a return to normalcy was just over the horizon? "Now let us conclude our business. Firstly, how shall we guard the delivery of your magnificent library Jean?"

Jean asked his host for pencil and paper and began drafting a crude map. France was generally a lawful country but the significant value of the haul could not be ignored. The brush of the lead sweeping parchment gently and the rhythm of the elder Millet's strokes caught Maurice's attention. He always adored his father's style. Father was deeply disappointed; a son could tell. Snapping back to the present Maurice uttered, "There, remember, didn't bandits rob a train of priests last year?" A general recollection of the event was confirmed, and in the end they decided to just hire out a few aged veterans with nothing better to do.

Marie was puzzling over how she could get an excuse to go down to the market square. Her father, and her brother Maurice, gave strict instructions to stay away from the bookshop. Why were they being so obtuse? The proper thing to do would be to abjure.

We would still be children of Christ and our souls would be in better hands. A priest is closer to God than father is, a bishop under a cardinal and so on. That is the order of things. Men know best of worldly things, but only certain men know of heaven. She found herself at an impasse. With every fiber she wanted to obey her father, but one day soon she would obey her husband and he would be Robert, she was sure of it.

He was a Catholic of a leading family of Laon, la Paussion. Just convert you donkeys. Marie thought that the next time she would have to hear about the honor of her dead mother she would scream. She became a reformed Calvinist for father. Oh how I wish she was here. That would just muddy things. She could never admit what she did with Robert. It wasn't exactly sex, she was pretty sure of that, but she was also pretty sure it was something that only married couples did. No, she would not have told her, but again would she have done it if her dear mother was still alive?

If she had been raised by her mother, and not a couple of nannies, she would have been raised a proper woman. The nannies would come and go, in accordance with her father's ability to pay . Since they had grown up, father could barely afford part time maid arrangements. The proper thing was for father to remarry but no, he was much too progressive for that. Not progressive enough to allow her to make her own decisions at sixteen. What a cruel joke. Of course that would be unheard of, however, she noted to herself, it is also unheard of for a man to run off to the Netherlands leaving his two sons behind, one being just fifteen.

It is all so muddy. It is done now and without being at market who knows when she would see Robert again. Her tears swelled up and she sniffled to a near sneeze. Oh Robert, take me in your arms, lead the way. She stiffened her upper lip and steeled herself. He did tell her what to do in an event like this. He promised to see about ending the boycott and she was to work on convincing her family to repent. She was to inform them of their pending courtship and with his relations and connections with the House of Lorraine, whose star was surely rising.

Tonya and Marie paced around the already nervous maid who was glad to hear miss Marie suggest that they take a turn around their modest grounds.

"This appears to be the end. Father and Maurice are finalizing the deal with monsieur Avon and that will be the end of our family dynasty. You know I never felt quite comfortable with literary relations but now that I can no longer make such claims, I fear I am going to miss it. I should have made more of it, cracked open more of the books myself. I had free reign at the shop for years and let it all waste away."

Tonya tried to raise Marie's spirits but they were a gloomy pair indeed. "Nothing is over dear Marie but I admit I am deathly afraid."

"And in your state. I will miss you so sister."

Tonya was startled by the affection. "Sister, you have never called me that before."

"I don't want to waste anything ever again."

"Marie, I don't know if I should tell you this but Maurice suspects you are having an untoward romance."

"Tonya, sister, I am indeed having a romance but nothing so untoward. He is a Catholic."

"Maurice suspects that as well. Do you love him?"

"I do, ever so. Well, I don't know I am just a silly girl, but I think it is love. How did you know you were in love with Maurice?"

"Oh Marie, I have not seen my own sister in years and she was the last person I told this to. I do not love Maurice."

Marie was not prepared to hear such a confession as the two had a rapport of dancing around the taboo. "This day is surreal is it not?" Marie noted.

"Here we are alone with the men out making the final decisions on our futures. The Millets and my own Troyes family, known in Laon as such humanists, yet my marriage to Maurice was no less arranged than perhaps our great grandmothers."

"I fain to know all about it."

"No Marie I will not bore you, this day is too dazzling for all that. Suffice it to say that Maurice loves me not. I fain to hear of your beau and what can be done."

"His courtship has been incognito and that wounds him, but he could not allow the present circumstances to be an obstacle from winning my hand. He finds it best to remove such obstacles first."

Tonya crunch-facedly touched Marie's wrist, as if to draw in some of her charms. "Some girls have all the luck."

"He plans to make his intentions known to father but wanted to give me time to convince father to allow me to abjure first."

"Abjure, you would do that?"

"Is that not love Tonya?"

"Dear sister I do believe it is."

They giggled away morning dew and returned inside with sun high above and hearts beating. Plots in mind as well. They had decided that together they could concoct the means of rendezvous and that Marie should never plant a foot in the Netherlands. Here was a beau that was showing his love, what her worth was. Tonya would sip some of its honey too and let it flavor the matrimony of the mundane. Marie regretted not taking fuller advantage of her life as a bookseller and not becoming closer with Tonya. In a day she gained herself a sister. What would a fortnight bring, a husband.

Chapter Four

August 4, 1559

Joinville, Lorraine

Duke Francois enjoyed a wonderful breakfast. Though it was his typical juicy pear brought down with hot coffee, on that day it was received with greater satisfaction. He had seen his brother Charles off to do his bidding. The Cardinal of Lorraine, Charles de Guise fancied himself a co-regent of France. Francois shattered such fancy. To rule France from outside, as a sovereign of Lorraine, would require more tact than Charles could muster. Perhaps in being a Cardinal of Rome, or perhaps owing to something else, Charles' inclination towards provoking the new protestant nobility was obstructing Francois' way. He had finally convinced his younger brother to shift his attention to papal backing of their new licensure program. Francois, as both regent and treasurer of France, began to call in all debts from the military-clique. So many noble families ran delinquent to the point where he had the authority to revoke landed titles. Such crisis events were not altogether unheard of in France. Granting those vacated titles to commoners was both risky and novel. Francois most needed church backing on that point. That he wished to grant landed titles to such families, was audacious enough. That the Duke wished to make these families into nobility, retroactively and without question, bordered on the absurd.

The families he had in mind were staunchly Catholic though, and rich. "Why challenge the newly reformed lords when we can just replace them," pointed out Francois to his brother.

To Charles' credit, he balked enough for the accord he truly craved. Cardinal Charles wished to champion the Gallican cause. An independent Gaulic-Franco church with certain autonomy from the Papal States. Francois assured him such ambitions were in reach, and thusly the brothers were of single mind.

Their mother, Dowager Antoinette de Bourbon, came upon breakfast late and with the disposition to altogether ruin his morning.

"You shall forgive my lateness son as I am altogether distressed."

"I beg of you, what distresses the great dowager of Lorraine?"

"On my very passing through Vassy last evening, it was on the hour of Vespers we passed and so most appropriately stopped."

"Most appropriately."

"Yes, well son I shan't have to tell you that many of those home worshippers disturbed this holy liturgy."

"Mother I implore you, on the very morning I set Charles straight can I not do the same with you."

Antoinette de Bourbon boomed. "I care not for their souls, I care only for your princely authority. You go chasing a kingdom while our dukedom may be the cost. You issued decree for they to worship afar did you not?"

"I did."

"Your father would have brooked no disobedience—"

"Father would not have grasped at France herself either—"

"Fool yourself son but you shan't fool him. They offer nothing but a temporal regency. In the end you shall only have the Lorraine he procured for you, and it will be run afoul."

"We shall see mother."

Francois excused himself and set directly upon guests his mother knew nothing about. The western wing of Chateau de Joinville was made a ready part-time residence of King Francis II and his beloved Mary Queen of Scots. In ousting all other protectors including Catherine, Duke Francois made it a point of charging himself with the royal couple's security. This included spiriting them away at his pleasure.

Duke Francois checked in with his niece, seventeen-year-old Mary. She reported to him much the same as before. The fifteen-year-old King was a sickly boy, and could not keep up with her vigor. King Francis was gratified by Mary and completely under her spell. Mary's own lack of satisfaction was of little importance. Uncle Francois walloped her with praise. "Mary, you shall not only rule the Scots but will also rule the French. Listen to your uncle who knows best and loves you most. If ever his mother makes herself near him again, gently remind him who keeps the coffers full.

Chapter Five

August 5, 1559

Roucy, France

Three cavaliers paced upon the village of Roucy at a brisk pace. Though they were not in proper imperial uniform they were adorned quite equally. They had spent well the stipend pay from the Chevalier Dulay. Their commander ordered, "to adorn yourselves such as kingsmen, yet without formality." Looking at one another they thought the chevalier would have been proud of them.

They strode upon horseback in crimson and gold. Their shirts dyed of crimson, and rustic colored vests to better match with the bronzed baggy pantaloons and browned jack boots. Scarves and gloves of white, inspiring chivalrous memory; contrasted with the leathern cross body straps which sheathed their subtly angled swords.

Frequently assigned as advance scouts, they were to hasten upon the village postmaster. At Roucy, they were to prepare chargers, to relay the following ecclesial troup. The Abbe de St. Clair, a congenial man for somebody that high in the Catholic Church order, was travelling by post. From Reims to the Ardennes, swapping for fresh horses at any number of stops.

If the approaching Abbe de St. Clair so commanded, they would make frequent or infrequent stops.

The postmaster at Roucy was also to freshen up the cavalier's horses while the scouts took stock of the mood of the peasants and villains, whose protestant number was growing. Sir Thomas recalled the caution given to him by the

Chevalier du Lay before departing. The Abbe was on a mission of delivering an edict of the anti-heretic kind. Du Lay ordered his loyal cavaliers to pay special attention to any protestant nobility, a center of stir.

Sir Thomas was the captain of these cavalier scouts. He was recently dubbed a captain by the Chevalier du Lay and would do anything to earn the promotion. Thomas' wife and children struggled to survive in his absence, but if he could return it would be worth the sacrifice three-fold. All Thomas needed to do was identify the protestant leaders and condition them for the legal edicts that followed. Thomas found a tactic to effectively irritate certain protestants into converting back to the true faith.

Sir Thomas elevated himself to speak with protestant nobles, as if he were equal to them. On the basis that he was Catholic and they were not. This single fact induced permission to violate official decorum. In this way he was daring them to render him back to his original position. The tactic was simple: annoy his superiors enough that they would do anything to restore their superiority. It had worked many times before.

Firstly, Sir Thomas had to deal with Pastor Rohn. By the quality of the pastor's dress and his manners, he judged him to be lower nobility. Thomas then deployed his rude arrogance which was meekly ignored. "The Baron of Roucy was still a Catholic", Pastor Rohn told Thomas, as if warning him to drop the superiority act. Rohn argued quite effectively that a post scout was not the same as a post messenger. Rohn submitted that either a post messenger or the ecclesial party itself could warrant an audience with his lord.

Thomas and his chevaliers submitted and opted to observe the town for names that the Abbe could persecute at later dates; Pastor Rohn was now first on that list. There was one thing that Thomas realized quickly. Though the town was still mostly Catholic, a majority of attractive maidens were reformed, suggesting that within a generation, yet another Catholic principality would fall, unless intervened upon.

Thomas and the other two cavaliers ate and drank openly in disbelief. Was Catholicism going to defeat this reformed religion?

Pastor Rohn seated himself with his own mug of ale without being asked. Rohn noticed the group of girls who captivated their gaze.

"The Baron does not allow bigotry here. We protestants worship in our own homes as the law requires but other than that we are left to do with our freedoms what we will."

A heavy-lidded cavalier replied with a slight slur, "Do I seem bigoted towards her priest, I should have her just as she is."

"I am not a priest," said the pastor.

"You're all priests to me."

Ignoring the man, Rohn nodded to Thomas instead. "Sure, they are pretty, but Thomas you must understand the entire wave of young protestants outshine the Catholics in nearly every way men find attractive in a partner. You want a woman who will find a clever device that adds two more whole reels to her daily output, you marry a protestant girl. You want a woman who will support a man in taking a business risk—"

"I marry a protestant girl. Now that you are done giving me mating advice please be on your way."

"No Thomas, I give you spiritual advice, I think I see a protestant in you." Eye to eye, followers would look upon their gods. Eye to eye, gods would see their followers.

The church bells tolled the final hour - the completion of vespers. Maurice led his wife to their bed. He tried desperately to get the thought of the midwife out of his head. *What gossip did Tonya pass?* He knew the midwife would have inquired about their bedding habits of late. Tonya would have told her the truth of it, that there had been none. Maurice despised her at that moment. *Did you tell her why?* He accused. Tell them all that you never loved me and can't respect me, even worse you often fail to pretend.

But he was desperate for companionship and he wanted it to ring true. Maurice had judged what Tonya desired and was building this false ego. *Don't scratch your head, you are not a thinker, you just do* (like Christopher).

"Maurice tell me truly, what do you feel about your father leaving?"

It was a trap and he knew it. His feelings, his dread, would turn her off. "It is for the best dear. He may not have raised a fool, but that does not mean he is not a fool himself."

"Maurice," she feigned to chide. "What should you mean by that?"

"I get my inheritance early! I know just what to do with it. The boycotts will shutter businesses and I will buy them up. One by one."

Tonya grasped at him with abandon. He knew it was not him. She knew it was not him. The roleplay was the best they could muster. A substitute for a union that naught have been.

The market streets were noticeably quieter in Laon. This pleased Robert who was clanking and creaking about the empty store searching for anything of value left behind in haste. He recalled the last time he was in this butcher shop. Men, women, and children crowded the place. Protestant deplorables huddling around the counter shouting out for a pound of swine flank or pheasant wings. Banter infected the aura and wild children ran about. Laon was still a majority catholic city, but the ascending bourgeois class was nearly all reformed. They ordered for a week's worth what a peasant catholic family would consume in a month. This he did not take personally as his was the richest family in Laon. But when the Millet family rose to be nearly as prestigious as his, that he did take personally.

Robert and Maurice were once even friends; however, he never gave Maurice the satisfaction of knowing why he retreated from him. Maurice assumed that it was the natural age where teens began herding along co-religious lines, letting go of the halcyon days of youth. Of course that was mostly true, Robert la Paussion thought, but for him there was something more personal. He could recall vividly what happened on that long ago day. The boy of four and ten finally marshalled the courage to approach Coralin de Suzier. He had asked her if she wished to study with him and received a most vile of rejections.

"Why should I want to read with you?"
A tightness overtook him.
"Only protestant boys understand books."
He could picture Maurice smugly reading to Coralin.
"My father won't allow me to become a protestant,"
A flash of sweat, seeing them smile at one another.
"But one day I shall marry one and then I will be converted."
Robert grabbed Coralin by the throat and squeezed while seething, "How dare you, I am la Paussion, you go home and tell you father that, and see if he runs off to the Reeve or if he gives you a spanking instead!"

He shook off the daydream and muttered to himself about the tardiness of fools. Nobility was in reach. What was once an impossible dream was now actually just upon the horizon. The closer that he got, the further away it began to feel. *Where are these fools?* Through the Guise faction's control of the treasury, many houses would fall. However through licensure new titles would also be established. The scrolls opened and new names inked into the halls of nobility. Ah here are the fools at last. Robert gawked at the doublet Leon bought for himself but decided he could spend the money however he liked as long as he earned it.

"You have been doing a fine job really, but why was a delivery of books permitted?"

Leon did most of the talking for the boycotters. "Monseigneur Paussion, it was only a small stack of periodicals, no books were delivered, and we assumed that the bookman could not pay."

The poxy boycotter added, "Maurice can barely pay for the news."

"Fair enough, and like I said you have done an adequate job, so here is your pay and I will no longer require your services." Robert slid them a pouch of ecu crowns.

"We thank you my lord, but as you recall we organized this boycott of protestant businesses, and we shall only end it as we see fit."

"Of course Leon, you are good catholic, of course, but I can only continue funding if you are willing to do more."

"What do you have in mind Monseigneur?"

"Two things. For one it surprises me that the upcoming art faire is still scheduled."

"Well, we have made assurances to suspend the boycotts temporarily for the faire, after all the Flemish and Italian masterpieces provide works that appeal to the culture of Laon. Pretend reformers or not, we are all keen to gaze upon the latest examples of the ugliness, and frailty of humanity, and to shudder at how far we have fallen."

"Yes Leon, let it not be said that only the protestants are learned humanists. We Catholics too feel our worth, the pearly gates of heaven may be everything, but that does not make our lives, nothing."

The boycotters looked uneasily as Leon queried slowly. "Then are we still in disagreement my lord?"

"Mark my words, this is no time for a sectarian feast of our shared love of art. Now I have my own plans in motion to stop the faire from coming here. But it would help if you kept the boycotts in full force and withdraw any promises to stop."

"I see, and the second request?"

"If I want to see any particular business shuttered for good, it would be the bookstore."

The men were dismissed from the shop. Robert now owned two storefronts which were abandoned by their previous protestant owners. This particular one smelled every bit a butcher shop that it was. Is this where I should make her my whore? Sweet Marie. He delighted in the thoughts of the way he used her mouth. She was not fully a whore yet but would be. He had long hated families like the Millets. The ever-rising protestant class thought to be the enlightened and industrious people to lead France into prosperity. One by one their numbers grew converting catholic merchants and bourgeois and even the nobility. They were vile heretics who needed to be demoralized, converted, and demoted. Or hunted down and killed. He preferred the former. That uppity Maurice who thought himself his peer, but no. Robert would become a lord and Maurice and his whore sister would be back in the fields where they belonged. He pulled out a letter from his pocket and allowed himself one more read before he would burn it as he should have done much earlier. Too savory were its contents:

de Guise is the regent.

Edict of reeducation to be issued in Laon.

Continue boycotts and prevent the faire from happening.

Your reeve is our friend.

You are our friend.

Scrolls being opened.

Treasury is ours.

Licenses being issued to friends such as yourself.

He lit the note afire and dropped it in a bucket. Watching its flames, the stink of the place now wafted. Yes, this is where he shall stick the pig. Just another injury for the Millets to endure.

Once the ecclesial post arrived in Roucy, Sir Thomas again demanded an audience.

The local baron and his brother were harried from a duck shoot. Both had been long away from their respective bows and as such were forced to quit without a single bird bagged. Pastor

Rohn had advised his lords about the trio of cavaliers who were comforting themselves with gnarled formality. The pastor of the reformed of Roucy was praised for his denial to their initial request of audience.

"The cavalier by the name of Thomas beckons you at haste my lord."

The Baron, his brother, and the Pastor came upon the lead cavalier near the village square.

"So I have been beckoned by one Sir Thomas acting the lord of my own demesne."

"With no ducks," his brother added.

"With no ducks Thomas."

Thomas nodded a bow with only as much deference as such proceedings dictated.

"You are surely lord here which is precisely why I am required to serve you this notice of edict."

"An edict of whose issue?" said the baron. "The late King Henri? God rest his soul." The cavalier Thomas stared blankly giving away nothing. "Ah so not our King Francis then."

Thomas ignored the implication that any just order from King Henri upon his death bed could thus now be called into question posthumously.

"You are to gather your town leaders to the square within the hour as by then the Abbe de St. Claire shall surely be ready to shine light upon all to which you inquire, and to which I am fully ignorant."

The cavalier issued some motion for him to set about, yet the baron remained still. For certain the town leaders, if not the entire town, were already coming upon the square with strained souls. Neither the Catholics nor the protestants desired any intervention upon the harmony that the Baron had so carefully nourished in Roucy.

"Now do you acknowledge my duty of delivering you this notice of edict has been fulfilled?"

"Yes."

"Upon your return to the square please have the letter bear your own seal—"

The baron's brother could no longer remain silent, "We should not put our House seal upon an edict of unknown contents from a late King."

"Brother you do Sir Thomas a disservice. Surely these weary cavaliers have been ahead of post which departed a living king." The trio nodded in the affirmative. "And the cavalier does not know the nature of the edict and thusly we are putting our seal to a notice only, giving no consent to the heretofore unknown edict."

"The edict needs no consent," stated the cavalier.

"As Thomas says." The baron concluded as he turned his back on the cavaliers and the noble brothers strode briskly toward their faithful subjects trying to remain distinguished in this most decidedly undistinguished afternoon. With no ducks.

The Abbe de St. Claire was affable enough, but the priest Borges was venomous and ill-tempered. Regardless of any charm exuding from the Abbe the situation was that of a trampled people bracing for another buck.

The Abbe cleared his throat which was his way of calling attention without the overtone of authority:

"Ahem…per royal Edict of the late King Henri II; deus misereatur anime suae":

The baron scanned over his flock hoping that all repeated the Latin tongue without disgust.

"DEUS MISEREATUR ANIME SUAE"

Afterall the King was a Catholic and the baron knew it only meant 'have mercy on his soul'. Priest Borges seemed displeased with the showing, but the Abbe carried on.

"And to our young King Francis…LONG LIVE THE KING!" Here the priest whispered into the ear of the Abbe. "May it also be known that this edict has been confirmed—"

Then a crack in the sky.

"What does it mean, to confirm the edict?" pleaded one Pastor Rohn.

The Abbe turned agape, the priest livid, and the baron feigning shock, yet he knew this pastor too well.

"How dare you interrupt!" shouted down the priest.

Abbe de St. Claire hushed the priest with a simple hand gesture. "It's a fair enough query, these are certainly complicated times, and I remember you fondly from last summers' council."

"And I you, your holiness."

The baron was pleased to see his own pastor make such impressions at what he presumed would be fruitless councils of Catholic and protestant ecclesial convened for purchase of common ground.

"Pastor Rohn, to confirm means King Francis II does not necessarily support said edict, but does not wish to void his father's command. The edict commands the following:"

"All maiden daughters brought up in the reformed faith of any sect be it Lutheran, Protestant or Calvinist or any such similar sect…shall be re-educated in the one true Catholic faith."

The crowd frozen by seconds unto a frenzy by moments. The cavaliers menaced on horseback towering over the livid Roucy men.

"I really must call for order my lord."

The baron bellowed, "This is a royal edict. We shall hear it in its entirety and rest in the bosom of our wise king."

Priest Borges would have been shocked by the devotion of the sympathetic lord had he believed it sincere. He knew as soon as the Abbe continued on the post, that these nobles would appeal to the Queen Mother, but he would remain here in Roucy and see after this edict. For he feared rebellion in this town almost as much as he did for Laon.

"The maiden daughters are to be schooled according to the Priest Borges' conditions and will receive their opportunity to abjure from this misguided reformation and rebaptized with full sacrament. That is all."

"The women may choose not to abjure," said Pastor Rohn.

"Only after a proper catholic education, since they have been denied this by their reformed fathers."

"Once they know of Catholicism, they may choose to remain reformed?"

Abbe de St. Clair bristled at thick headiness. "Yes Pastor Rohn. But I beg you to see that they will abjure a thousand times over upon basking in the light of the Lord's true words as they have never heard before."

"It is off to the convent for them?"

"Oh no fear of that, the edict does not stipulate anything but a reeducation which can be accomplished in the wee hours before their duties of the day begins."

The next morning Thomas gave instructions to his men to ride with the Abbe until a halfway point where one should ride ahead to Laon as a scout. The pair of cavaliers departed leaving Thomas and Borges in Roucy to set about establishing the re-education of those beautiful protestant women.

Nearly an hour into the travel, the troup was approaching the high road when a cavalier felt a sharp bite into his thigh. He nodded his head downward hearing a whoosh of air pass by and seeing a dark stain blossoming around an arrow embedded in flesh. A fiery ball pitched from behind a rock landed atop the wagon cover. The unharmed cavalier charged the boulder where three bowmen revoked their cover to take direct aim. Each of their arrows missed and the cavalier swiped his sword into a neck. His momentum caused the blade to stick in cartilage. With lost grip he circled wide and grabbed for a dagger. A bowman nocked another arrow, but a thunderous crack knocked him to the ground, with a shredded hole in his back. The injured cavalier lowered the smoking gun, in as much awe as the remaining bowman who but dropped his bow and quivers. Abbe de St. Clair and the driver put out the cover fire by standing upon the window ledges of each side and swatting with blankets. The Abbe dropped down and walked toward the attacker. It was a farmer from Roucy. He wondered if Borges had the right of it, that harsher measures were called for.

Chapter Six

August 7, 1559

Laon, France

The herald-historian of Laon just left his seigneur to ponder on the latest information. The herald did well to keep Phillipe informed but it was vexing. Two pieces of news, both bad. The more concrete of the two was the fact that an edict of re-education had just been issued in Roucy, with the ecclesial troup now apparently on its way to Laon. Protestant maidens to learn the catholic catechisms, would not go over well. Especially with the boycott of protestant businesses which had already led to a few shudders.

In the second, the herald stressed that it was not yet confirmed, but it appeared that Robert la Paussion was behind the boycotts and that Reeve Gascon was in league with them. The thought of Gascon betraying him grieved him most of all. Additionally, it was suspected that Robert was attempting to get the travelling art faire to avoid Laon.

Phillipe wondered what issue he should address first. Gascon would be the final problem and there was nothing that could be done about a royal edict, so that left the boycotts or the faire.

The boycotts, he had been advised, would be broken soon on the strength of the catholic consumers who grew tired of being without their goods and services. A catholic literati complained to him personally that the new catholic bookshop was shit. This would be good news for the Millets who he knew were nearly bankrupt.

Finally, Seigneur Phillipe looking to help the greatest amount of all his people in the name of unity, prepared to deal with the travelling art faire. He would travel to the faire himself and assure them of the excitement and ecus Laon wished to welcome them with. Phillipe brought more coinage with him than he had ever travelled with on a mission. He sought to procure pieces himself if the art faire administrators still refused to visit Laon. Latest examples of the Flemish technical masters and the naturalist Italians would be carried back to Laon by his own train and auctioned off at a faire of his own. Perhaps he should even donate a piece to the first catholic family willing to openly break the boycott.

Chapter Seven

August 13, 1559

Laon, France

Janeau and Heather frolicked through the dell beside the Mausien brook. They embraced each other in all manner. They locked eyes, interlaced fingers, and swam through the oceans of their minds. He spoke of losing his teacher sullenly to which she buoyed him back up. "This means you no longer need him." He was unconvinced but accepted her faith anyway. He always believed Heather over himself. Better by her, better than him.

Suddenly they took to running, nearly at full sprint, where he bested her by three sticks. Whence she caught up, she threw herself upon him and they skidded through the damp grass. He laughed with glee, but she growled in primal delight.

"You may out run me with your legs, but I shall never be far behind."

"With more succor to spare I see." Jan knew that her spirit would always out run his own. He surrendered to her. She kissed him frantically and then nervously. Sobs. Tears of sorrow from her cheek to her lips and to his.

He begged to know what could turn her from their love. She was always the giver. Januea panged to know what had wounded her. He suffered her pains three times over. *I have always taken from her. Now I must give.* She always knew what to say to him, but Januea never once was needed to come to her rescue.

"I have been working on a rhyme for you." Her eyes lit up. There by the babbling brook he recited:

> She shook her tree
> Leaves fell to the ground
> A wind shuffled aroused
> From all around

To a star on the horizon
A chain is formed
The final link found a man
Whose heart was warmed
From out in the open
He followed along
Leaf by leaf to a forest
Where the roots run strong
The canopy to envelop
His chest made bare
Heart made to develop
Layer by layer she peeled
Layer by layer she peeled

It worked, she was beaming. "It is not quite done."

"Yes Jan, it is." He was not sure if he expressed his true feelings but she would have no interpretation. He would read it over and over to her for all the days of their life and she would wonder. Each day they would make love to each other without carnal knowledge. On this day she faced temptation, for her lessons of re-education were upon them. The priests would rob them of the few precious hours she had in a day. She disrobed and Jan turned away. Noble, faithful Januea. Heather clothed herself quickly and sighed a deep breath.

"I shall not see you for some time Jan."

"Of course you will see me."

She grinned and playfully shoved his shoulder. "You know what I mean. The love we have for each other, the love of a mother to her daughter that is but a glimpse of how so Jesus loves us. What else is there to know? I need no re-education."

"God loves even me?"

"Oh yes, he favors you."

"That is what he said you would say. At our last lesson, Danilo told me that like Dante I would ascend each tower of knowledge and that I also would have a Beatrice. An angel from God who would show me the way. I know how I should fill my time while you are learning catechisms from the Catholics."

"How so?"

"With your father, speaking with him, working with him."

"You will!" she cried, tackling him to the ground again. "He will warm up to you."

"I shall try my best Heather. You will be a re-confirmed protestant and made a wife."

They heard then jolly strumming from what sounded like a stringed instrument of some implement. It was their friends who they received with both excitement and heartache. Heather told the group of Jan's poem. It was settled, they would harp and recite poetry on the strength of the sunrise; all this before trudging off to the fields to meet the demands of the day.

Robert loomed on the portico of his familial manor, thinking about God's plan for him. His two younger brothers dying in the plague so many years ago. He recalled the time mother slapped him for his 'coming of the Cain' quip, that he loved to throw around after the deaths of his younger brothers. The look of disdain in her eyes. It was only a joke, a bad and childish joke coming out of the mouth of a child. Robert's outward rationale was that his jagged demeanor resulted from the terrible loss he had to cope with. Though he never voiced that phrase again he always kept the concept near to his heart. Cain represented the Catholics, the ancient landlords. Abel represented the protestants, the classical shepherds. Cain would once again need to kill Abel.

Now these heady days have arrived to complete his prophecy. God calls upon me and I shall answer, Robert pledged. The bell rung, indicating the arrival of their esteemed guests. Make way father, here comes Cain.

Father took his proper place at the anteroom, greeting and ushering in Chevelier du Lay and Priest Borges. With proper decorum his father led the way to their small conference room. All which was expected of a bourgeois gentlemen was demonstrated. Robert though, had been brushing up on customs of the blue bloods.

"May I?" Robert gestured his intent to kiss the priest's ring. This was a noble custom when hosting an ecclesial that outranked the house.

Robert's father, Claude la Paussion, pulled his son by the shoulder subtly. "Forgive me, the lad is getting ahead of himself."

"Not at all," The priest said as he raised his hand slightly to receive the bow and kiss. "In truth, this is the kind of initiative warranted in a situation like this."

Monsigneur la Paussion, Robert, Priest Borges, and Chevalier du Lay seated themselves as Borges continued.

"You see there is no such thing as new nobility, only a lost status of a family; that is recalled and reconfirmed. This is why noble houses continue to behave noble even when their fortunes are lost but names remain in the scrolls." Serving maids in their cream work gowns entered to serve lunch. Their presence was barely perceived. They set porcelain bowls of broth and heavy beer into mugs before briskly exiting. "If I do my job well, I will press your claim for House la Paussion to be reinstated as the Lord Seigneury of Laon. A common basis for objective would be your family's etiquette, that they—"

"Don't seem noble," the chevalier interjected.

"Don't seem noble?" Claude repeated.

"Quite right for the chevalier to intercede here."

Chevalier du Lay continued, "None of us here at this table are of the nobility but I alone spent a great deal of time with them. Your son's gesture with the priest seemed noble. You will need to embrace more habits like that."

Robert was basking in the adoration but took care not to yield momentum just yet.

"Father, I have brushed up on some books from our library which highlight such manners. We should continue to practice from this material."

"Indeed son. Now Chevalier du Lay, what of our current standing with your lord, and how is this opportunity even possible?"

"Although our young King Francis is fifteen and old enough to rule, our lords the brothers of Guise, thought it wise to establish a controlling regency. Francois the Duke and Charles the Cardinal of Lorraine are effectively ruling France as brothers as we speak—"

"I must put in that of course the Guise brothers are raising their niece Mary Queen of Scots and young King Francis II in holy tutelage to assume the throne fully as blessed husband and wife as soon as possible," stated priest Borges with a noticeable squirm.

"Yes, indeed father. More specifically and to your question Claude, my lords have been delegated to fund an empty treasury. In that task they have deftly disbanded legions and considerably decreased the payroll of the army. Given that we are at peace finally and cannot afford anything other than peace, our natural enemies will be those of the militant factions. The old houses of the standing army, yes. Hence Duke Francois delegated to his brother Charles acting as cardinal to revoke licenses from these houses and offer them for purchase to families such as yours. Claude please do understand in your situation you could not muster the funds near what other bourgeois have been paying. So for you to continue to be in the favor of Francois de Guise, depends very much on your son Robert's abilities to stamp out Protestantism in Laon. On that score the Priest and a cavalier of mine named Thomas will remain in Laon awhile and report back to Joinville their findings of your progress young Robert."

"I am confident that your lord shall be pleased. I have organized effective boycotts of their merchant shops and have even taken steps to prevent the art faire from making a stop here in Laon."

"What steps?" demanded Claude, "I gave no such authorization and fail to see how this helps our cause."

"It is only a simple gossip campaign, father. Cheap and with no risk, I thought it of minor importance and beneath your greater purview."

Priest Borges was increasingly more impressed with the son over the father as the meeting bore on. "What to you exactly, is a simple gossip campaign?"

"Pay the prostitutes of the artistry train a bit to whisper rumors of rebellion in Laon. I spent a few more crowns and hired a rogue printer to counterfeit a known periodical with such a headline."

Claude was sensing all too well that he was being sabotaged by his ambitious son. Monsigneur la Paussion wondered if an exit from this plot was warranted; he felt an instinct to go directly to the old military families and warn them. "How secure of a hold do the Guise brothers have on the regency?"

Chevalier looked at him blankly. "l'Hopital. Conde. Montmorency. Coligny. Lady Medici. Are all but sidelined."

The moderates are in shambles, now for the coupe de grace, thought Robert. "Excuse me Priest Borges but in my research of our family history I could not help but notice that my mother's line may be easier to resurrect and even perhaps it would make the most sense to put myself forward as pressing her claim on Laon directly."

The church bells of Laon struck miraculously for Claude. He had been saved. "I am afraid we must conclude at this time. For whether we want the art faire to come or not, we must appear as if we do. Our Lord Phillipe expects my son and I at his manor by the next toll, to discuss this very matter—"

"Fear not Claude," said Priest Borges, with such a look that Claude could only grow in fear from. "Our matters here are quite concluded. De Guise puts his faith in you. The claim shall be pressed by the la Paussion paternal line, though your son brings up an interesting point. On the matter of the art faire, that is completely within your purview. Your tactics matter not. I am only concerned with one thing, reporting back to Joinville that protestantism is not an issue here in Laon."

At the conclusion of the meeting, father and son retired to their own chambers to prepare themselves for their next important meeting of the day. Claude took a slight detour to the chamber of his daughter, Lisbeth la Paussion.

"Father!" She ran to him and gave him a kiss. "Shall you be off to the lord's manor?"

"It is so."

"Please father make a large bid, you promised me a fine piece of art to be included in my dowry holding—"

"On that very matter I have come to speak with you. Your brother vexes me. Are you ready to carry the torch for our family name?"

Chapter Eight

August 13, 1559

Laon, France

Lisbeth kneeled and kissed her father's hand. "I am."

"Very well. You may not get a fine Flemish piece this year, but the husband we have in mind shan't require a dowry."

Claude dressed himself appropriately for his audience with the Seigneur and met Robert in the anteroom.

"Tell me son, was that all boast with the priest or have you truly set in motion a plot to stop the art faire?"

"It was no boast father."

"Will it work?"

"I believe so."

Father and son arrived at the seigneur's manor of Laon. Phillipe was hosting a fine dinner with the aim of raising enough bids that the art faire would be sure not to skip making a stop in Laon. Not once, under Phillipe's reign, had they skipped.

Maurice eyed Robert until catching his attention, then beckoned him over for a chat. Maurice wished to converse with Robert on two items of importance: his aid in ending the boycotts and the rumors he had been hearing about Robert and Marie. The latter of course could not be discussed openly, but he hoped Marie's absence from the meeting would warrant some visual cues.

"Maurice my old friend, how are you?"

"I have seen better days."

"Will your father make a bid this year?"

"Our family rarely bids on anything else but literature and given the boycott—"

"Ah yes. Maurice I have spoken with Reeve Garcon at length about the damned boycotts. They benefit no one, yet it seems these are legal matters between the Reeve and our Lord."

"It seems so Robert. Thank you for the attempt on my behalf."

Robert made no inquiry about Marie then took his leave, yet Maurice was not convinced there was not an affair. They had once been friends. As boys, more than once did Robert's fists get Maurice out of trouble that his own mouth got him into. They grew into manhood and each accepted their religious differences would be a wedge socially. But Maurice still thought of him as a friend, and hoped he was not capable of besmirching his family name by consorting with his sister.

The evening ended as Maurice expected. The Millet family entered no bid for the art faire. Claude la Paussion entered a rather large bid though. This puzzled Maurice. He concluded though that la Paussion was desperate to gain a rich Flemish piece for Lisbeth's dowry. A beauty such as she was in danger of becoming an old maid. Catholic suitors dwindled over the past few years with many rich families of Laon becoming reformed.

A week later, Maurice awoke abruptly, which was his typical routine. He long had the sense of being afraid of waking up too late. As a bookman he often wondered if he was cheated out of his manhood, and waking at the same hours of other men was his way for making up for it. Pathetic as it may be to rise early only to rearrange books, it was all Maurice could think to do. At times he wished he was born into the agrarian class, and allowed to reap the fields with strong back. He respected Jan, Torry, and Robiere too much to allow himself to sleep in just because he could. Besides today was to be an auspicious day, he thought while allowing himself a smirk of irony.

The bookman nearly tripped leaving the bedroom. Maurice did not like to wake Tonya by lighting the candle near her. The hallway flickered alight for only a moment before darkness returned. Something must have dampened the wick. He gave himself a moment for his eyes to adjust before traversing the hall.

Here I lament my false manhood all the while aiming to help Torry rise from a hearty farmer to a petty bourgeoisie. Despite his misgivings, Maurice's intentions were pure. He saw the potential in each of his friends. Torry worked well with his fingers, especially with finer tasks, and he had the acumen required to transfer domains. Although Maurice had his own insecurities, he also knew he had the skills that his friends presently did not and would be needed for the future. Skills such as negotiation, ordering in proper quantities and knowing when to enter a 'bill of sale' or require hard currency. Furthermore, sometimes foreign currency might be offered, in which case one must know the prevalent rates and the state of credibility of the coinage. Pooh, Torry you will hate me for making you a draper. Drapery, of course, was a solid business neither in its infancy nor infirmness. Maurice had spent much time nurturing a relationship between a protestant investor and Torry, which had finally led to an agreement of funding to open a new shop.

Drapery, like other trades of the burgeoning petty merchant class, was of the self-perpetuating type. The bourgeoisie consumers demanded more and more novel luxury items. Thus proceeded new suppliers to satisfy new demands therein, creating new members of the class. Like dominoes they would fall, and such like dominoes, they would be erected one at a time.

Maurice's knowledge of the game of dominoes was indicative of the heady times for humanist Europe. As a learned man, one of the most well-read men in France, he had come upon a text from the Far East. This peculiar little book alluded to the game of dominoes yet he never encountered anyone who had ever heard of it. Strictly speaking, Maurice too did not know the game of dominoes because in the text (he had read as a child) he mostly took in illustrations which shown Chinese people using the domino blocks to create intricate patterns. The pieces used would number in the hundreds. Each block would be carefully erected just near enough to the other, so as they did not have enough independent space to be safe from preceding or successive pieces. The final illustrations displayed onlookers above the structure, which stood ever so precariously. When all the blocks had been arranged, the final one was tipped over carefully, and then this set off an entire effect which happened so quickly that it could be imagined that a giant snake meandered through the valley. The fall of one domino would crash onto the next, and so on, until they were all left toppled. Maurice was never able to remember which text it was or who they sold it to. But this domino effect resonated with him through his life. So much that in recent times he conflated the extraordinary economy of his era with this image.

From his father's generation and until present, the dominoes were being set up. The opening of a bookstore leads to the opening of a draper which leads to the opening of a tanner. When the tanner shutters then so soon will the draper, until finally even the book store is gone. Maurice had tried ceaselessly to convince the Reeve Gascon of his duty to stop the boycotts, not just for the tax revenues in annum, but in safeguarding the entire domino structure.

Thus far the boycotters had only managed to shutter businesses in such a disparate fashion that thankfully the entire chain reaction had not been triggered, and after all, dominoes can be set up once again. So, he was in the business of putting up dominoes while others were tipping them over. Torry will stand with his domino as a draper and one day, when we are picking up our fashioned jack boots from the tanner, he will forgive me for drowning the yeoman in drapery. He and his would be more secure and in good standing, and perhaps Catholics and Protestants could once again stand side by side as countrymen and not topple each other over.

Maurice saw Torry waiting outside the banker's office and ran to him. They embraced and said a prayer together. It was all smiles and joy, for they were there to finalize and receive the loan. They entered the building and began the meeting. The beginning of a new day was over before it began.

Maurice sat crestfallen across from the banker and at the side of Torry who almost seemed amused.

"You see this man here, I am ashamed he counts me as a friend—"

The spooked investor tried to interject, but Maurice was in no mood for listening.

"All this time we have spent analyzing and speculating Torry's fitness and all the while he should have been speculating our own honor, we bourgeois whose word apparently is just a drop of nectar."

Torry shifted, a slick of mud on his breeches caused him to slip off the smooth chair. Putting back on his wool cap as if to say: *back to the fields for me then.*

Quentin defended his decision to deny the loan request. "I should not have to sit here and listen to—"

"Your word was given man!"

"We have not put to print any signatures—"

"Quentin, you and I both know how we protestants do business in Laon. The signing is a formality, today was to be just a formality."

The banker sat back and called upon a measure of courage, "Strictly speaking I am no longer a protestant."

Torry was no longer amused. "You...abjured?"

"I had to. They took my Lydia to the convent and Perisol was to be next—"

"You speak nonsense, the girls are to learn catechisms, a few hours here and there for a few fortnights which at the end they will simply confirm their protestant belief and the obligation fulfilled."

"No." Quentin boomed fists down upon his desk. The tiny drawers rattling as the banker continued his tirade. "It is you who speak nonsense Maurice. Lydia was scheduled to report to the convent in the morning for her first lesson and was never again allowed to leave. For two days and two nights we were not even permitted a visit. By the third day we abjured and I was given a special condition to call in all loans to protestants and to issue none further."

"It is purgatory for you and yours," Maurice said sullenly.

Quentin in his snug doublet leaned in as if to reveal a secret, "You don't actually have to believe it. You just pretend."

Torry rose and spoke directly, "God does not play pretend." The farmer concluded the meeting as such but not before the banker could offer one more ponderance.

"Your first child Maurice, is it to be a girl?" Other such utterances could be heard as they stamped down the staircase from the third floor. Knees wrenched from their hasty exit upon the robust medieval stone steps.

Maurice begged forgiveness. "Torry, I apologize about this."

Maurice's friend only nodded but asked, "Why did you say that about our friendship?"

"You are right, God does not play pretend, but the bourgeois do. We pretend we are better than the peasantry… that we have honor, yet I have never known you or Robiere or Jan to say a false thing. I told you I would make you a draper and I have not."

"Pooh Maurice, I took your word as an oath to try and that you did. You left nothing undone and I am not ashamed to count you as a friend." The pair began their walk back home. "For the record, Jan once promised to help me stack some hay bales…but he didn't." They chuckled.

"Maurice."

"Yes."

"I don't blame you. But if you want to make it up to me, I just thought of a way."

"What is it?"

"Well, many times at the brook I have questions that I am too embarrassed to raise."

"I suspected that were the case."

"I know I am the least of your students."

"Listen Torry, last, first…it doesn't matter. The only thing that matters to me is that you keep learning. So you must ask."

"I ask you to keep it a secret."

"Of course."

"When the edict was read out, I did not truly share completely in the anger. You see my brothers and I come from one of the strictest protestant families and quite frankly we know nothing of Catholicism and for me the Abbe spoke true, I never had a choice. So I ask you this: Tell me of the Catholics and of the split and by the end of the walk I shall never think about it again."

"Perhaps what I tell you will tempt to you to abjure."

"Can the Catholics breathe fire?"

"Ha no."

"Then I promise I won't want to abjure."

"Where shall I begin? I shall start with Martin Luther. Forty years ago, a monastic theologian named Martin Luther began to criticize the church, specifically the corruption which was rampant. He wrote individual theses, a hundred or so of them, all spelling out the indulgences and sins of the clergy. He even wrote about the pope himself with one of the theses asking why such a rich man would not pay for St. Basilica himself. His pamphlets circulated around Germany in a frenzy as the printing press distribution system was being established. Some even took to nailing theses on church doors. Whether he intended to or not, the reformation began."

"What else would Martin Luther have intended?"

"Not to trouble ourselves with semantics but some say that he only wanted to fix the church from the inside. Root out some corruption here, cut a branch off there. Repair as opposed to reform. It has been said that while Luther brought the idea of reformation to our heads, it was John Calvin who brought it to our hands. Calvin's followers organized the reformation by building some new modest churches or makeshift temples in followers' homes. Layman pastors and elders read from bibles that were translated to their own languages. Of course this led to Calvinists splitting from the Lutherans and many other new denominations. Whatever the specific style of reformation, we are all protestants and simply Christians. Simplification is the essence of our religion. We think of Catholicism stripped of its rituals, pomp, and the papa—"

"The papa?"

"Let me try to list the significant differences we have with them:"

"One, we don't believe the mother Mary is the ark of the new covenant."

"She was a wonderful woman," Torry insisted.

"Of course, we point out no flaw with the woman herself, only that *we* are all flawed. If we are tempted to sanctify the virgin Mary then, we would struggle with our next disbelief. Two, we protestants don't believe Jesus dictated a framework for a delegation of authority before easter. No hierarchy of bishops, saints, and cardinals each with varying degrees of authority to represent God's kingdom on earth. The papa is the Pope and sits atop just like a King. No, we reject this wholly. God's kingdom is the earth and here he has no deified representatives. We are all fallible. There was Jesus and there will never be another. Every man, woman, and child is a sinner and there are no exceptions."

"Why then should we listen to pastor Etienne if he has no holy authority?"

"We revere Etienne because of the example he sets, not because he holds the title of pastor, which we can strip from him whenever he stops leading by example. We are nearing the last leg of our trek so let me arrive at a conclusion. Understand Torry this is not a complete discourse on the nature of our religious divide."

"No, I shouldn't think so but this is sufficient, exactly the things I wanted to know."

"Three, they pray to particular saints for particular issues. Imagine our dear friend the courier, if he were a Catholic, he would pray specifically to St. Christopher to bless his travels."

"So not to Jesus?"

"It is complicated, but it smacks of paganism all the same. Let me conclude with one of the most critical of Luther's arguments, which underpins the entire problem with Catholicism, and why I believe it could never have been reformed internally. Higher level clergymen such as Cardinals or archbishops can sell letters of indulgences to the nobility, which wipes a set of sins away. The more serious the set of sins, the more such a letter will cost you."

"What types of sins were they getting forgiveness for?"

"Good question student, I am at a bit of a loss. One of the prevalent activities is something that helped produce the bourgeoisie class here in France and was something we were about to take part in on this very day. One of the mortal sins, if not the mortal sin, Jesus preached about was charging interest on loans. Families such as the de Medici in Florence became prominent money changers and convinced the church to update their understanding of modern money lending. They explained that the charging of interest was not for personal gain, but rather a remedy for the money lender to receive back their original sum. The borrower may appear to pay back more money, but because of fluctuating rates, it really was not more money."

"Dubious."

"Quite so, though I would posit that we may not have our Da Vincis and Botticelli's today if the church did not allow this. They did in fact accept this argument and the money changers became large scale bankers who grew extraordinarily rich from the money that really isn't money. I believe that these good standing Catholics did not quite believe their salvation was truly secure, so they often purchased letters of indulgences to set them at ease. Payment was most often that they funded commissions of high art, sculpture, and architecture for the church."

"How could the priests do that?"

"Not how Torry, but by what means? Of course, they could do it because of the authority delegated to them, but how exactly do they accomplish? How did they communicate to God that: Lorenzo the Great had settled a massive and systematic manner of sinning without true repentance. Does the Pope speak in Latin to westerly winds at just the right hour? Does he have to wait for confirmation from God before issuing the indulgence?"

Torry replied with wonder, "What wizardry they must employ."

"Alchemy they call transubstantiation, turns their wafers into actual eucharists. Yes Torry they believe they can still partake in the body and blood of Christ."

"Blasphemy indeed," he exclaimed. Torry's mind was racing. If only he could have these personal lessons more often. "If as you state the bankers of Italy have brought about your present class in France and then followed great commissions to our renaissance thinkers, then is it not good?"

A merchant's train passed by the pair. An axle beam bowing under the pressure of the overloaded wagon, which Torry could see contained mostly sacks of sugar branded as an Egyptian export.

"Remember Torry we are all sinners, and had today turned out differently, you indeed would be a greater sinner than you were yesterday. A protestant humanist such as myself cannot fault de Medici for sinning, but rather for trying to circumvent his own judgement—"

"I would have been paying the interest so how would I have sinned?"

"You would have sinned because you had an ambition for a station not truly available to you. You asked Quentin to sin for you. I sin because I did not abdicate my station once I learned how we all benefitted from the bankers of Italy, from the original sin as it were. The domino effect." Torry knew not the term. "Never mind."

"Tell me one better thing about the Catholics."

"Excellent Torry, you make me truly proud. One must also look for the positive within that which we reject. I have been to a mass or two in my life. They put on a good show. Their devotion to catechisms really does create a wonderful harmony—"

"Maurice," whispered his friend turned ashen.

"Yes Torry."

"Catechisms."

"Jan's Beatrice."

The horizon quaked for the pair running as hard as they could. Upon a short grassy matted path they nearly slipped on wet blades but they ran on and panted with terror.

Chapter Nine

August 20, 1559

Laon, France

Torry and Maurice belatedly realized that if the banker's daughter was held hostage, then would not the same fate await Heather?

They needed to get across the town center to the south fields where Jan was to be preparing the cabbage plots for an early harvest. They came upon a row in town and it was the Reeve, a pair of boycotters, and Maurice's brother Christopher.

From the look of it. There appeared to have been a brawl. The young scrap emerged the victor even against the two to one odds. Or was it three to one? Yes, three on one. The reeve was not breaking up the ruckus but participating. Torry leapt into action by first blocking the oncoming blow of the pox-marked boycotter, then pulling him away from Christopher. The reeve seemed shocked to see Maurice and immediately shifted in visage. Though the reeve was not fearful, Maurice did hold some sway in those parts. The reeve commanded everyone to break up, and recognizing the new dynamic, Christopher was released by hook nose.

"What has happened here?" Maurice demanded.

"Your brother assaulted these two men," answered the reeve.

"For what reason?"

"It was unprovoked," said hook nose.

"Unprovoked," the bookman haggled with the reeve. "Two of the boycotters that I have formally laid complaints about—"

"Get out of here you two." The boycotters ran off. "I have told you Maurice, they are well within their rights to protest merchants."

"Not to physically prevent my opening the shop," Christopher wheezed, just getting his air back.

Maurice was not aware that Christopher would be opening shop.

"You were what?"

"There you have it, a misunderstanding." The reeve took the opportunity to frame the fight in more neutral terms. "They did not recognize the boy. They thought, perhaps he was attempting to break in."

"I will hear no more sir. I have trusted you to this point, but I see now that my faith has been misplaced."

Christopher looked to Maurice tellingly. "There is more brother. Tell him reeve."

The reeve Gascon obliged. "The art faire has cancelled on grounds that there are reports of fresh rebellion in Laon."

"Tell them otherwise," Maurice commanded.

A crooked grin formed. "I don't know Maurice. Seeing as how three protestants before me just attacked a couple of Catholics."

"You bastard," Christopher cried.

"Don't worry little brother, I shan't be formalizing any charges. Yet I will note such disturbances as reason not to appeal the artist train's decision. They think it unsafe to pass through Laon. Who am I to tell them otherwise?"

"There is another matter for your attention Gascon, for I shall call you reeve no longer. You were supposed to uphold our laws! Monsieur Quentin has told me that his daughter Lydia was detained at the convent for three days when the edict called for hours per day."

Gascon, the Reeve of Laon, shot back too knowingly, "I believe the edict also read that Priest Borges was given explicit authority over the matter, and it just so happens that he is presently gracing our town with his oversight."

"This it then. You won't do anything in the name of justice."

"All that I do is for justice Maurice," he snapped back.

They arrived at the southern field and cried out for Jan. There were at least three separate clusters of farmers in different directions, so they split up and each headed towards one group. Finally, one of the farmers yelped back, then another. Maurice turned around and saw that Torry found their quarry. He and Christopher joined up and ran towards Torry, and Jan who ran towards them.

Jan told all he knew. "She left for the convent this morning. It was to be her first lesson. She should be back home."

They continued their run with Jan at the lead to the stead of Heather's family. Jan was inside for only a few minutes when out he came with four more men. Both Heather and another farm girl named Jenelle failed to return from convent.

The now group of ten were in disarray and mindlessly headed to their church. It was a rude temple on the edge of the southern fields, which Seigneur Phillipe stated was far enough from town, for worship to be held. Another group of concerned villagers already found Pastor Etienne and had surrounded him near the windmill. The two groups merged. Frantic voices contended with the whirling mill.

"Maurice can you confirm any of this?" said Pastor Etienne dreadfully.

"Monsieur Quentin, the banker, has converted to Catholicism. He and his family were forced to abjure. Their daughter was held captive in the convent for three days and that is how they secured her release." Fists clenched and boots kicked rocks. The humidity of late summer gave rise to the flushing of jowls and boiling of blood. A lone mangy wolf caught the attention of several ranchers who rushed toward it to scare her away. The wolf was near their church. A poor field temple with only three quarters of a roof as the congregation saved to purchase the rest of the slate.

"My daughter was there for two nights and returned a Catholic," cried a mother. "She says she chose to stay and only came back to beg for our confessions."

"This is no program of re-education," yelped another.

"Our women are held as hostages," concluded the pastor.

"It appears so Etienne; however, Gascon will not lift a finger."

"The reeve, the reeve Gascon?"

"I won't call him that, but yes, that is of who I speak. He claims that the edict stipulated authority to a priest named Borges for the specific conditions of the program. And this Borges is at the convent now, issuing these orders lawfully."

Janeau impatiently demanded, "So now we should go directly to the Seigneur."

Etienne raised his hands in effort to calm his flock, "No the seigneur left last evening on urgent business. What business, I do not know."

"I may venture a guess on that score," young Christopher volunteered. "He may be riding toward the train of the art faire on our behalf. You see the guild has decided to no longer make a stop here in our town, as they got it in their heads that we are rebelling."

The mob was now in full disorder. The irony occurred to Maurice. The Machiavellians orchestrating it all. "Aren't we though? Look at us."

"What are we still doing here? Off to the convents to get our daughters," shouted Heather's father.

Pastor Etienne shouted back with equal volume. "No, we mustn't! For that is the rebellion they full now expect. A mob quitting the fields and storming their convent, with no reeve nor lord at our mast. Let Maurice and I go and speak with this priest. Look to the lord! He is our shepherd."

The crowd dispersed and Maurice scanned for Christopher, as he wanted to give him his own instructions to stay away from the bookshop. He could not see him. How long had he been gone?

Christoper looked around not a little nervous. He had never been this deep in the seigneury woods alone before, where all were forbidden. If nothing else, he would be alone, so he picked the feather from his pocket and inserted it snuggly into his cap. From here he was to stay along this side of the brook. He forgot the tune he was to whistle, so he whistled the only one he knew. And just like that.

"Wrong tune Millett."

Seven members of the *Chauvre de Sois* were upon him from everywhere.

"You'll have to teach me the right one again, I simply forgot."

They bantered, Herndon Calais, their leader knew full well that his band of chauvre de sois had taken an immediate liking to their newest member. "What brings you here at this unappointed hour?"

"Even you are not going to believe what has happened," Christopher panted.

"Astonish me."

"Herndon, the edict of re-education is a farce. There are at least two of our women being held hostage at the convent. The price of freedom is to abjure immediately."

"Is a priest named Borges involved?" said the captain of the forest bandits.

"Indeed."

Herndon considered for a moment, "That means he has cavaliers with him. No more than three, maybe just one. What is it you want to do?"

"Free our maidens."

This drew a stunned enthusiasm from the band.

"Your spirit Christopher," Herndon declared before turning to his chauvre de sois. "How many are known in Laon?" Four raised their hands. "That leaves us with eight."

"No, I am going," said the young Millet.

Herndon chided the youngster. "Firstly, I have decided nothing yet. Let me explain how the chauvre de sois get away. Nobody likely to be identified comes along. Also, we do nothing without a plan. A plan that entails nobody getting killed. You are a firebrand, unlike your brother, but if you don't have half of his brains then you are useless to me. Now here is how you could be useful. It is likely that Borges has imprisoned girls back in Roucy as well. These maidens of Laon, their men, could you recruit them?"

"Some possibly, yes."

"Good. Go now, and bring them back here. We could send a band from Laon into Roucy, where their faces are not known."

"I see." *I could learn a thing or two from him.* "This is how we grow a rebellion," proclaimed Christopher. He understood why these jolly bandits admired their captain Herndon so.

"Go, I have planning to do."

Borges was a drafting a quick report for his associates at Joinville, which served as the capital for House de Guise. The priest highlighted the successes of his mission. He paused to privately recall, some of the finer details. *Oh the maiden-heads I had taken so far.* After regaining his concentration, he went over the number of converts he gained; and then flubbed the quantity just so as Cardinal de Guise would not care for a list of names. The list of names went to the Abbe, who in his infinite ignorance, was displeased with the results. As soon as Abbe de St. Clair learns of the incarcerations, the priest would be reined in. Oh, the irony.

The fool really believes there would be willing converts, but of course there were none, and if it were not for his craftiness, the Abbe would have a lot more to lament.

The priest in his crisp black robe stood up to look out the window at the strange potato field. Beneath dying foliage, tubers of an unnatural off-white color burst forth. Apparently the first harvest of this new world staple was only a fortnight away.

Borges also made note of the fine job Robert had done. Monsieur Paussion managed the art faire cancellation by orchestrating a scheme where the news of protestant rebellion in Laon was heralded by an established press. Of course, these versions of the periodicals were counterfeits, and would not be discovered for some time. Robert was a man who understood the importance of propaganda in this war. Furthermore, Borges learned of an added benefit of Robert's campaign. The Seigneur of Laon had personally taken leave to attempt to convince the artists they had been duped. Now, the priest had time enough to bring in one final group of protestant girls, and there was one particular maiden-head he craved next.

There was a tiny rap at the door. Oh sister Marie was a timid one.

"Yes, enter."

The sister came in, accompanied by Sir Thomas.

She spoke, "There are two gentlemen wishing to speak with you."

"That would be Pastor Etienne," Borges guessed.

"Yes father."

"The other, sister?"

"Maurice Millett he is a book shop owner."

"Reformed I presume?"

"Yes, but the town gossip say he is more humanist than heretic."

"Hmm, a literati, they are an uppity lot, with all those fancy words." The priest considered a moment before addressing his cavalier guard. "Thomas, show these two gentlemen in." The cavalier turned smartly, putting tanned leather gloves on as he did so and strapping down the attached forearm guard.

Sir Thomas, having escorted the pastor and bookman in, eased behind the seated guests.

Etienne prayed before speaking. Lord forgive me for wishing to strangle this man to death here and now, he thought before clearing his throat. "Thank you for allowing us to see you without the proper decorum."

"Decorum, oh is this an official visit pastor?"

Patience be damned Etienne now thought, "Yes this is an official visit before God, for you to release our women at once!"

The cavalier menaced behind them, Maurice could sense it. "If I may, Priest Borges, I am Maurice Millet, my family owns the bookstore in town and I was present when the Abbe de St. Clair read the provisions of the edict of re-education. I myself found the edict quite reasonable."

"Did you?"

"Yes, you see I have been digesting pamphlets reporting on the matters being discussed at the Council of Trent and their discourse drums up conciliatory attitudes on both sides."

"You shall forgive me Maurice, I am a simple priest who tends to limit his reading to just the *one* book."

"What I mean to say is that it seems to be a time of Catholics and Protestants finding our common ground again, of which there is ample."

"Well said young man," the priest growing weary of the protestant. "It is not every day I meet someone so astute and that is the sentiment I receive from the council as well. For example, here at this convent the sisters are dedicating themselves to God, which is the holiest union a woman can make. A reformer such as yourself would argue that the holiest union is that of man and wife—"

"Living for god," Etienne added. "We believe in the union of husband and wife, for god."

Borges continued, "A counter reformer at the Council of Trent may now say, perhaps the protestants are not so wrong. We too can change ways. In the old ways, once these maidens renounce their false gospels, they would be made to remain at the convent for the rest of their days, in atonement. In our newer ways; however, we see it fit for them to be released as Catholics to find good catholic husbands. As you say our common ground is…ample?"

"Ample, yes." Maurice could not believe it, he was being outwitted by a simple priest. "Let us turn then to where we disagree, which is holding these women in confinement in this convent while they are not presently Catholic."

"I am holding no one sir," the priest gasped in feigned besmirchment. "As the Abbe suspected, most of the maidens quickly found the error in their ways and wished to convert immediately. However, what was not expected was the level of fear they have of their fathers, brothers, and suitors. You see, they fear being released."

Pastor Etienne's awe was not feigned. "Let us talk with them to hear that for ourselves."

"Oh their great fear extends to the pastors, too."

"And bookworms?"

"Your reeve or even your lord may have an audience with them, in fact I want the matter settled quickly, too. You see the extra mouths to feed was not expected and my allotment grows thin."

The pastor and bookman exited the convent defeated. What else could they take from us, Maurice wondered. They staggered along a country mile or so before Etienne insisted they stop to pray, right then and there on the side of road. A mossy branch served as a kneeling pew, as did a robin serve to witness.

"Just us and Jesus," the pastor proclaimed.

"Pastor, I don't understand what is happening to me. My judgement of character has... suddenly been lost. I have been so keen in the past to see people's true potential and intent. I fear I have grown to depend on my own conclusions."

"Yes Maurice, God has endowed you with certain skills as he sees fit, as he does with each of his children. Now the time has come for you to be humbled before the lord."

"Gascon, I truly believed him a man of honor. My readings on the papers disseminated from the council of Trent, erroneous conclusions. Quentin the banker. Lady Catherine lost the regency already to de Guise."

"Jesus works through you if you allow him the autonomy to do so. If instead you demand full control at all times, then his works of brilliance are caged, while yours of fallibility are loosed. Come now, let us pray."

Maurice shot up from his praying knees furiously.

"No pastor I cannot pray to God now! He shall not do everything for us. There is turning the other cheek...then there is this," He gestured back towards the convent. "We gather our men and storm the convent to free our innocent women!"

"Yes Maurice we could do that. With enough men they would merely give themselves up to us, and then what?"

"We could just let them go. It should all be settled by the Seigneur and the Abbe at a later date, yet for now I cannot look the other way."

"At that later date of yours would be Civil War!"

"No, you don't understand everything. Etienne, the moderate party is stronger than anyone knows. La politique has more influence than—"

"Shut up now you fool. You are caught in your own vanity Maurice. You make an idol of yourself! Humble yourself before Jesus and ask for forgiveness."

"If anything happens to them I will wreak vengeance."

Pastor Etienne roared at that and pointed at Maurice mockingly, "Now I know who you remind me of, Jonah. Was it not Jonah who wished destruction on Nineveh?

Maurice understood his pastor wanted an answer. "Yes, Jonah fled from God's command."

"And what of Jonah's own will?"

"He was swallowed by a great fish and dropped precisely where God wished him to be."

Once again a tiny rap on the door. "Yes sister do come in."

"Monsigneur there is a small fire near the road just west of us."

"Thomas, do investigate."

Momentarily the cavalier reported back without real alarm. "A fire that seems to have started on a passing wagon leapt into the potato crop adjacent us, but it does not seem to be spreading and they have formed a bucket brigade. Come down to the entry room father for the best vantage point or let me go outside and check on them directly."

"Yes, out with you, and I will remain close to our entryway." Marie timidly, "Father, this is Laon's very first potato crop. Destruction of this novel vegetable from the new world could vex the Abbe."

At that Borges got up and rushed outside to see for himself. The fire seemed bigger than what the cavalier and the sister made out, but any preliminary evacuation was out of the question. Priest Borges watched the cavalier exchange words with one of the field hands and was running back.

"Your grace, the fire is getting worse as they are almost out of ditch water."

"Sister Marie, what is the nearest water source?" demanded Borges. She fumbled for further meaning. "Come look over here." Borges pointed to Marie, "See the fire there?"

"Yes," she stammered.

"Now judge the length those men could extend their bucket brigade, where upon the convent could they draw the water from?"

"Right through here sir where we stand back to the pantry."

That was not truly close to where the girls were quartered, but not ideal. The priest puzzled over his options. He wanted the fire out, without anyone hearing the cries of the maidens. Paramount was to get the fire out before the Reeve arrived, for the Reeve would be forced to issue an evacuation of the convent. Borges asked more specifically, "What about from the exterior sister Marie?"

"Oh no, those have not worked in years."

"Very well. Get the water started." Sister Marie obeyed, then to the cavalier. "Thomas you must get that fire extinguished and fast, I suspect it was started on purpose, the Reeve would have to call for the convent to be evacuated if he gets here." The cavalier obeyed to set about the redirection of the bucket brigade to draw water from within the convent.

One of the field hands came. He bowed respectfully to the priest and was shown the way by the cavalier. Once the buckets began their circuit, Borges inquired with the field hand.

"Did anyone see anything?"

"Oh yes I certainly did father. Two men stopped their wagon and came to the edge of our field. I could not see what they were doing, but suddenly I saw flames lick around them. It seems the fire spread to their wagon and they were forced to flee on foot. Quite intentional did the chauvre de sois begin this fire."

Priest and cavalier instantly froze, "chauvre de sois, how do you know?"

"I saw their feathered caps. And who else would start a fire near a holy convent," the field hand answered casually, paying more attention to passing the next bucket along.

The priest continued with the frightful interrogation of him. "You are sure you only saw two?"

"Yes, two."

"Where did they run?"

"Towards town."

At that the cavalier remarked, "Rogue bandits started a fire and ran towards town and not the forest."

The field hand continued passing buckets of water to and fro, taking an extra step closer with each iteration. "Hmm, that is strange, perhaps I am mistaken. All I know is the field is afire and we must get it under control before we lose our entire crop of tubers."

"Quite right, come Thomas you and I must help, with us added to the chain each man can move closer to the other."

Herndon Calais could come up with a plan, no doubt about that. Everything was happening just as he predicted, even down to the cavalier being commanded to help. *Now the Priest jumping in was an added bonus.* This supported what Herndon suspected, which was there be just the lone cavalier to deal with.

One, two, three, Herndon gathered much momentum in the full bucket of water he held, and spun a full revolution, knocking the cavalier flush on his nose, and the man went down instantly.

It happened so quickly the priest could hardly comprehend what occurred. The cavalier was out cold. Herndon savored the awe in the priest's unbelieving eyes gazing upon his guard's limp body. The captain issued orders to the rest of the field men, his *chauvre de sois!* Herndon lashed the priest across his dazed face. "Easy way, or hard way?"

"There are three girls. Sister Marie has all the keys needed."

"Stay with them both." Herndon directed a bandit to guard duty.

The priest, bandit and cavalier remained in the entryway. The bandit eyed the priest warily while rummaging through Thomas' possessions. Finding it difficult with just the one hand, the bandit put down his own weapon with a smirk, the priest would be no trouble. Screams and shouts echoed the halls. Thomas stirred weakly, but not before his short arquebus gun and dagger were confiscated. The cavalier was still again, the bandit went in for a second rifling, this time acquiring matches for the pistol and a pouch of ecus. Borges could do nothing but hope his man still lived.

Then it occurred to the priest that the bandits had not simply executed Thomas. He surmised they were attempting to rescue the maidens without committing murder. This made Borges chuckle to himself, knowing he would still win. Robert's tale has now come true. Heretic rebellion in Laon. The king would be made to act swiftly. The convent was all screams and shouts and thuds when Heather emerged first. From the priest's loins emerged an image of him taking her.

The priest could not resist a slur, "I still win."

Out of complete humiliation she wailed, "You bastard!"

Heather attacked the priest like a crazed animal. Flailing and clawing, a banshee set upon her own tormentor. "You bastard!"

The bandit had pulled her away and his grip was shaken by her inconsolable vibration. She sobbed and shuddered, but then pulled away and his dagger was in her grip not long before landing in the priest's shoulder. There was another onslaught of slaps before she went suddenly limp.

The priest had pulled the dagger from his shoulder in one motion and slit Heather's throat with a counter slice. She seemed to stand frozen before she piled to the ground. Herndon, who had just arrived, punched the priest square in the jaw and he, along with his guard, was knocked out.

"You fool," captain admonishing the guard. He knelt and pleaded with her to look him in the eye. The captain of the forest bandits, not shuddered from violence, made his prognosis. "It is not as bad as it could be, the artery has been nicked for certain but it is not wide open. Hold this to the wound firmly, help is on the way." At that Herndon continued with the daring escape into the woods.

Just before the end of that unfortunate hour, the mob, now perhaps a hundred men or so, converged on the entrance of the convent. They shouted and hurled cabbages at the reeve and a couple of soldiers.

Reeve Gascon had secured the convent ahead of the mob. Heather had been dragged out and tended to by her kin, until Janeau arrived and he was left alone with her. The cavalier and priest had come to, and stood behind the entry door which they held ajar. The church bell of Laon rung sharply, reverberating through bone and soul.

Heather gurgled in Janeau's arms. Her eyes fixed upon his for the eternal gaze. Jan rubbed her arms to warm them back up and began to shush her. She gurgled and struggled to speak so he found the strength to cease his sobbing and hear her wishes. He bent lower to hear Heather's final utterance. "From, fro. Heaven. I peeeeeeel. Peel."

Chapter Ten

February 25, 1560

Germany

Outside the alehouse a bright day was passing by. These Germans were hard drinkers. Pints were the standard quantity of choice. The utility of oaken barrels reinforced with iron straps were shrunken down into mugs for their swarthy hands. The German drinkers roared with deep bellows as the southern stranger was celebrating with libations for all. A sunny day lost on them as the den had few windows, fewer still unmolested. Patrons would use old newspapers, dabbed with grog and hastily stuck to glass until the barmaid got around to tearing them down.

Danilo was trying to read one of the old papers, but it was lined upside down. Indeed, his life had changed after that final delivery. The item was placed in the proper hands and Danilo was promoted within the organization. Not so high to brag, but high enough to ensure that he would no longer be a mere courier. Curious item it was, a shield with a lion emblazoned centrally upon it. The shield seemed most ceremonial and likely was not retrieved from any battlefield.

He was born for this raise and more to come. Still he could not pretend to miss the road. He did miss his many friends and associates across distant kingdoms. Danilo certainly was less informed those days, but had taken to maintaining letters of correspondence with many. Some of the more sensitive information they had taken to using a simple encryption. In

that manner, he took information from Maurice and others which he compiled into a full account of the aftermath of the Laon incident of late August 1559. The following had been conveyed to Maurice using the encryption Danilo taught the lad so many years ago:

Dear Maurice, here is a summation of all that I have learned about August 20, 1559. Your brother Christopher was associating with the chauvre de sois band led by Herndon Calais. He was not yet a member, but he was trusted with ways to find them. On that day he did just that. While you and the pastor were approaching the convent to confront Borges, he was in the forest telling the tale of the kidnapped girls. He was sent back to the temple in your southern fields and recruited a few men for Herndon. I expect you know more about who those men are. Back at the forest the bandits split up into two groups. One group to infiltrate the convent of Laon and the other for Roucy. Your brother went along with the group bound for Roucy.

Herndon is a competent tactician and devised a plan that included starting a fire near the convent in the potato field. He figured that such a fire would pressure the wayward priest to help extinguish the flames, rather than letting it ruin an important harvest and causing the evacuation of the convent itself. The arson worked to perfection, as the priest - and a cavalier named Thomas - allowed the potato farmers entry to form a bucket brigade. Alas they were not farmers, but bandits who quickly seized the lone cavalier and affected the rescue of the maidens.

Just as they were making their exit, something went terribly wrong. It seemed that Heather had attacked Borges and grabbed one of the bandit's daggers, which was actually the confiscated dagger of the cavalier. Heather managed to stab the priest but then the priest pulled out the blade and slit her throat. It was not the deepest of wounds, but fatal enough. The chauvre de sois escaped to the forest with the two remaining maidens. You arrived back to the convent and know the rest of that tragic end. Yet there is something worse at play.

According to the bandit who was guarding the priest and cavalier, Heather's attack on Borges was so primal, that he believed it could have been personal. I have taken it upon myself to develop a contact in the convent, and it has been confirmed that the priest Borges has raped some of the women, including Heather. The reason you have not heard this is because Herndon swore everyone to secrecy as to not needlessly pain our fellow Janeau any further.

Four other maidens were rescued from Roucy. But without Herndon present the bandits used violent force and two of the cavaliers were killed. Maurice, I must tell you that it was deemed that it was Christopher who started the bloodshed. Nobody has been named in either of the convent raids, but Herndon Calais is wanted as the leader of the chauvre de sois in your region of France and anyone daring to wear a feather in their cap does so at their own peril.

The six freed maidens have been under Herndon's care since their liberation. He had each one housed with various catholic families who he trusted as sympathisers. I hope that you will see the maidens of Laon in the flesh before this letter arrives as I do bear good news. Pastor Rhon has successfully appealed to Abbe de. St. Clair who has appealed to King Francis. The enforcement of the edict of reeducation has been suspended indefinitely. Again I do hope that you hear of this from your own heralds (or better yet a news periodical) before receiving my own modest report.

Now that I think we both have a full understanding of what has happened, let us look to the future. Your last letter troubles me. You should release yourself from any guilt over what happened to Heather, Jan, and even Torry. Learn to believe in yourself again as I always have. I was glad to give you the good news about the repeal of the edict, but I beg you not mistake this for any true progress between the reformed and the Catholics. The Guise faction of Lorraine are radicals and, for the time being, they hold all the power. Catherine de Medici is beholden to them or she risks being as isolated as Montmorency has become. I agree that you have made errors about how this regency would materialize, and about the edict, the banker, and the reeve. However, I still believe in your superior judgement. Act now, join with Charles Avon and Admiral de Coligny. You can make a difference.

I wish I could tell you now more about who I am, and why I was sent to Germany and with what. I sense that you are important, and we are linked. I know we fool about my boasting but there is something more about my background that I fain to reveal. Let it suffice for now that I see only the good or evil. I know you are good and more importantly that it is not Protestantism that makes you good or Catholicism that makes one evil. Look beyond the cloaks and you shall do well at court. Everything that is to happen next has little to do with Catholics, protestants, radicals, or moderates. This has to do with power. Great houses dating from the Capetian line all vying to fill the void that was created the day King Henry took a jousting lance to the eye. The Guise, Medici, Valois, Bourbon, Habsburg, Tudor and Coligny hold no principle higher than their own noble houses. This is what makes them evil. I ask you to work with the devil, for the admiral de Coligny is one of them. Build your own house, one for the oppressed, and lay safeguards against the seeds being corrupted. I see white and black, in you there is a shimmer of white, but approaching you is the blackest of black. Time whispers this to me.

Danilo,

p.s. with a clear view

Seigneur Phillipe visited the Millet household but would not allow a fuss. The lord came only to look upon baby Mary and speak directly with Jean. Phillipe had done much for the Millets since the tragedy at the convent. Merline, Jean's elder brother, took notice that Seigneur Phillipe only sought out Jean directly, leaving the rest of the Millet men to pay their respects before receiving any.

The Millets of Laon had come together to rejoice and bless their newest member, Mary. The babe was baptized by Pastor Etienne on the morn of the Lord's day - the first child of Laon in 1560. Maurice's heart was gladdened. A welcome bright spot in such dark times.

Uncle Merline commented on the distinction. "Our Mary is both the first of the year, but also the first of the decade. With such an honor, I wonder why there was so little Catholic presence?"

Christopher retorted, "Was the half dozen papists screaming for Mary to be baptized a Roman not enough offence for you Uncle Merline?"

Maurice heard and witnessed all whimsically. *As if it were a play.* Jean stared down young Christopher, not satisfied that the lad's hostility showed any signs of waning. "Tis what our Lord ensured me dear brother, that the papists would restrain themselves outside our own house of worship, plain as it may be." Maurice could tell that Uncle Merline was irritating his father, then Uncle Bichtel tried to help. *Which would be in vain.*

Uncle Bichtel, their brother-in-law made suppositions of his own. "Seigneur Phillipe has done much for us in this crisis—"

"Not any more than expected of a noble lord, uncle."

You see Uncle Bichtel, it is quite in vain to bring an olive branch when Christopher has a stick to wag. Maurice wondered this and if his family would ever come to recognize the trouble Christopher was becoming?

Bichtel, perhaps understanding the futility in his present line with Christopher, shifted his attention to Maurice. "Well then Maurice, you are the celebrated father of the day. I should fain to know why you could not expect less."

"Do not get him started Uncle Bichtel," Christopher said. "Or he should bore us all with his slavish devotion to moderation."

Maurice wished he could watch the play forever and forget his lines. "Yes little brother, condemn the very politique which has harbored you from the gallows."

"You will not speak of the gallows again Maurice. That is your brother!" Jean's eyes ablaze. Merline and Bichtel heated as well, only pouring more fuel.

"Why exactly would Christopher have any fear of the gallows?" Merline pretended not to hear what was all the gossip in Laon.

"Come now brother, the reeve claims that Christopher was working with the chauvre de sois who attacked the convent in Roucy."

Pay him no mind father, thought Maurice. Uncle Merline only feigns ignorance of the scandal.

Jean stood up. *Maurice wondered if father was as drunk as he.* The leading patriarch of the Millet family in Laon, though not the eldest, his house produced a successful book shop from the family library, which both he and Merline had equal shares. "You want to know the truth, Merline? I shall give it to you. That vile priest and I came to a treaty, guaranteed by our Seigneur. The Millet family supports the findings of Reeve Gascon, which concludes there was no false imprisonment, and that the true kidnappers are the chauvre de sois, led by Herndon Calais. Christopher Millet and other accused farmers of the southern fields have been exonerated from any association with the bandits."

Father and Uncle Merline drifted out of earshot, but Maurice could imagine their conversation.

Merline, not satisfied, said, "That still is not the whole truth is it Jean? What is the whole extent by which you have attached our good name?"

"What of your truth Merline, do you care to elaborate on how you represent the Millets?"

"You first little brother, you first."

Jean stamped away towards the women folk and requested to hold baby Mary. Tonya of course obliged. Tonya's sister, Violette, asked, "Sister do the men of the Millet house always quarrel so?"

Maurice crept closer to eavesdrop on the women. *Tonya, how diminished is my trust in you?* He took another sip of wine. It should have been watered down further, we can't afford such extravagance; he mumbled to himself.

Marie took the indignation to answer herself. "I assure you the Millet men are gentle and thoughtful. It's only these times with the wicked cloud around Christopher and the loss of our dear friend Heather."

"If that were the only cloud it could not come to rain upon my special day." Tonya remarked with just a tad of venom.

Marie was recalling how different Tonya could be when surrounded by her own family again. Returned to her natural state of jealousy. "Sister, don't you mean Mary's special day?"

Tonya with an air of obviousness: "A child's joy is a mother's joy, you would not understand that sister."

Violette became confused. She never heard the in-laws address each other so. "How long have you been calling each other sister?"

Marie ignored the distraction. "Never mind that, tell me Tonya, what should you mean 'if that were the only cloud'?"

Tonya replied with a bored yawn. "Let us not fumble about like the men, about that which all of Laon gossips. The feud is not just between Christopher and the priest, but that we feud with la Paussion family as well."

Marie could not believe that Tonya would mention that name under any circumstance. She thought she saw a knowing twinkle in Violette as well. She let the matter drop with the same air of boredom, mimicking Tonya's countenance. Uncle Merline found Maurice and insisted a private toast. Maurice could not quite make out what the women spoke of, but it clearly vexed his sister.

Maurice was congratulated so many times that day, yet Merline offered a truly genuine show of concern.

"You shall be a fine father Maurice. Just remember you must put your family first. That is what your father has always done. Christopher could be a folk hero right now—"

"A *dead* folk hero."

"Precisely Maurice. Would it be better for Calvinists of Laon to know that her maidens were indeed kidnapped by the Catholic shit eating priest? It would serve the Millet name if we claimed Christopher and Herndon as heroes, rather than go along with this farce. Yet for Christopher's life, this bargain was made."

"Uncle, you speak as if my brother had been brought before our *cour d' assises*. Perhaps all I mean when I speak of moderation is to keep our spirited accusations…moderated. We cannot prove Priest Borges kidnapped the women any more than they can prove Christopher raided a convent. Each side, in cool moderation, came to agree to drop the matter entirely."

"Since you still cling to a peace we can never have, let me tell you what other deals your father has struck on our behalf."

"I would rather know of your own dealings Uncle Merline."

Merline ignored the redirection. "To settle matters with Claude la Paussion they have agreed to end the boycotts and support the resignation of Reeve Gascon. Their demand, however, is that your bookshop never again be opened. Yes

Maurice, the Catholics would be the only book sellers in Laon. They have finally figured out the power of books."

Maurice found himself dizzy. He knew his father had to make certain concessions, but he never expected he would make such a decree without his eldest son's consideration. He grabbed for another dip of wine. Without a toast.

"You can get the library back from this Charles Avon couldn't ya?"

How does Uncle Merline know about Charles?

"You sold your half years ago uncle, what concern is it of yours?"

"My concern would be as the principal investor in helping you buy it back. Don't answer Maurice, a good father would think about Tonya and Mary a night or two."

Maurice proceeded to get quite drunk. He found one last cause for toast. "To the hero of the maidens, Christopher Millet!" There was truth in the boast. Underneath it all, Maurice respected his younger brother. He was a man of action. He rescued maidens. *Heather was killed after I retreated.*

Uncle Bichtel joined in, "To our hero Christopher of the chauvre de sois! Maurice tell us would you fight alongside your brother now, or run off with your daddy and sister?"

Christopher pushed Bichtel into a wall. Maurice struggled to understand what he heard. *How could they know all this?* The two feuding were calmed down by the women folk. Maurice sat himself down and drank by giant swigs. Tonya's mother looked distressed by Uncle Bichtel's words. Tonya hid her face and cried. The mother was then having a perfect fit. Through groggy haze Maurice could almost make out Tonya crying, then laughing, then crying. Until a satisfied smile. Grandfather Jean had held fast baby Mary nearly the whole evening when upon him stalked the other grandfather. Mary was out of his father's clutches then a frenzy of panic. It was all haze and commotion. Maurice could not quite comprehend what he saw. *Had the play ended as a tragedy?* Spiteful words and grizzled heart. Love and hate comingled before picking sides.

The birth of Mary. The first babe of the 1560's in Laon, France. A celebration resplendent in guile and mistrust.

Chapter Eleven

February & March, 1560

Loire River Valley, France

The whole affair which led to the book broker's demise happened in a whirlwind. Charles Avon arrived in Nantes later than expected. He should have arrived the day before the meeting. The Admiral Gaspard de Coligny had requested that Charles act as his chief agent at a small meeting of conspirators.

"A conspiracy to what aim?" he asked, but received no proper answer.

"That will be for the conspirators to decide, no?"

Admiral de Coligny further hinted that the mission would be fraught with danger, and of utmost importance. What convinced Charles most of the magnitude of this quest, was the fact that the admiral was willing to depart with his only literati. They had hoped Maurice Millet could be elevated to such a role at court, but he had refused the call. Pity, but the ignorant Maurice still did not understand the nature of the threat posed by the Guise faction. Still did not accept that his people needed him, not just his family. Perhaps I should send him another letter. Something else that I know which you do not: King Philip adores his new wife, Elizabeth of the Valois. The Emperor cringes at the thought of the proliferation of heresy in his beloved's home country and his dear neighbor. Never have relations between France and Spain been on more

solid footing. Another ally for them, and by what degree do our ranks rise?

Charles was convinced that this mysterious conspiracy was to be bold and daring, which follows, likely to fail. The admiral could not risk himself. I would be disassociated and left to hang, he concluded.

On the day of his scheduled departure, he cowered and remained at his inn near Anger. By the next day, he stewed in his cowardice and chomped to board the next vessel down the Loire River near Nantes. When he reached Port Hugues, he disembarked and frantically asked around for guidance to the laundry district.

Charles encountered a group of men trying hard not to appear wealthy and decided they must be his new friends.

"The sky falls from below," Charles uttered the password.

"Yes yes enough of that. Where have you been?" said La Renaudie.

"Undecided is all. But I am committed now."

"Are you certain?"

"I would take a blood oath. Who's man are you?"

"No, we decided without you that does not matter. None shall reveal who he represents. We are the conspiracy. I am La Renaudie of House Perigord, and have been assigned to lead."

"Ah so the sky falls from below, but a nobleman must lead." The group chuckled at Avon's wit. "What is the conspiracy then?"

"Let us proceed to the tavern called the 'Prancing Pony', from here on that shall be our rendezvous point.

The Prancing Pony was a mean establishment. There the underemployed teamsters played a card game of *poque*, which mostly involved them staring down at their hands and then themselves for long spells. The conspirators eyed each other with similar suspicions, but with no money on the table.

"First let us discuss means that the four of us can muster. Can anyone present, trust an agent to hire foreign mercenaries?"

"I can. My name is Arthur Pontillon and gather I have been selected for this very purpose."

"How many?" La Renaudie asked.

"Perhaps a dozen."

"Can they be trusted?"

"Three I would stake my life on."

"Those three should be present at our next meeting. In fact all three of you should bring three others for the next meeting. Secrecy is needed, but then again so will be redundancy. Arthur, in which region do your men operate?"

"Gascony, the mercenaries there have been clamoring for pay since the Cateau-Cambresis peace."

"Would it be possible for them to accept a contract with an anonymous chief?"

"Given their desperation I assume so, it would cost more."

"I pray hope this is where you come in Charles?"

"Indeed, I would rely on circa twenty men and women to collect funds from their patrons up and down the Loire valley. These are sympathizers who owe me many favors and never once have I asked for money. That in itself should make quite an impression. Which currency is preferred, Arthur?"

"I shall find that out for you, for now take whatever our patrons give. We will deal with an exchequer if needed."

Charles Avon considered a moment. "As far as I know, ecus are still strongest, I shall collect those as often as I can."

La Renaudie now turned to the final member. "And you my friend, what do you bring to the table?"

"Barry Benique, gentlemen, I have several inroads with the Chauvre de Sois, they could make up a saboteur wing of our own protestant army."

"Our own army," Avon scoffed.

"Yes Charles," La Renaudie retorted. "Perhaps it is a bit of an exaggeration, but I am pleased with the three of you this evening. I represent dozens of noble houses with dozens more retainers which can bring to bear a considerable force. I can estimate 2,000 gendarme. Now with chauvre de sois, mercenaries, and funding—"

"Gentlemen I must press upon you, precious few ecu crowns will flow into our hands without more specifics on what exactly they are funding."

All eyes were on Monseigneur La Renaudie for the reveal. He reached into his pocket and produced a letter. "This was an oath signed not two months ago at a secret assembly of confederates in Nantes, headed by the prince of Conde. His only stipulations for us:" Charles considered with exhilaration how a conspiracy could reach so high. The conspiracy must be led by Prince Conde and the Constable of France Anne Montmorency-maybe even Catherine herself.

"Providing nothing be done or attempted against God, the king, my brothers, or the state; I accept my election to chief of this most noble confederacy."

La Renaudie passed the letter to Barry. "Look upon it with your own eyes before I burn it." They passed it around with solemn reverence, and when the Lord of Perigord lit it aflame and held it outwards, he spoke with sheer gravitas. "Gentlemen, I propose that we should storm the royal train and liberate our King Francis II from the Duke de Guise. We lay down our arms, plead our allegiance, argue our case for the reformed and most importantly request that Francois de Guise be tried for corruption and plotting against the crown."

Charles, Barry, and Arthur were inspired with the manner of the delivery and content of the speech. Not a single utterance of apprehension was voiced. Rather, glasses were raised, oaths were sworn and boasts were boasted. They continued onwards with the details of their plot. Piece by piece the impossible seemed possible. The quest being wholly necessary was worth the noose. *I understand the lateness of the hour Maurice and I beg you to take my place at court for I will not return.*

The relatively minor port along the Loire River was bustling. Groups of men hurried to-and-fro, devoid of any signs of engaging in commerce. No products were being exchanged, boats were carrying more men than goods, and few of the conferences concluded with any letters being drawn. Hardly a crown passed hands along the busy docks.

On their second meeting at the port of Hugues, each of the three provocateurs brought along their three most trusted agents. From that point forward those ten would constitute the high level conspirators, and the only ones privy to the logistics of the plan, such as the date of the plot's commencement. March 10th had been decided. On that day forces would surround Blois from all directions. Blois, being the place where the Guise currently held young King Francis and Queen Mary of Scots.

A newcomer made a chilling remark almost immediately. "Strange we should establish a base at these taverns of Port Hugues given that our enemy has taken to calling us Huguenots as of late."

"Say that again, Huguenots?"

"Yes I almost punched the romish pig who called me that—"

"No brother, wear it with pride. Huguenots, sounds mighty,"

"I heard that they are calling us that because of the rebel protestants that gather at Port Hugues—"

"What!" La Renaudie exclaimed.

"No lord Renaudie," Charles assured the leader. "That cannot be, we have been called that for at least a year now, perhaps more. It translates loosely to home worshippers—"

"Ah so they burn our churches then mock us when we have nowhere to pray!"

Charles spoke louder, "Lord Renaudie please also understand that perhaps this isn't the best base of operations—"

"Nonsense, let Port Hugues be known as the birthplace of the Huguenot revolution. A political revolution where men of integrity meet. Where a man of popery will be thrown right into the river. A place where men declare Death Before Mass!"

The tavern roared. Perhaps the place truly was filled with Huguenots. Charles pulled Renaudie down to speak some sense to him. "Listen please, we should not be drawing so much attention to ourselves."

"I understand monsieur Avon, and you are quite right to be concerned. The secrecy of this conspiracy is paramount. However, that introduces a dilemma. The conspiracy is in service of the protestant cause. But why have the conspiracy if there is no cause." Charles did not know how to respond to such circular logic. "Hmm Charles, I propose, no specifics will be spoken outside us ten."

Charles now thought back on the third and fourth meetings at the port tavern, trying to recall clues. He had starkly concluded that the plot had been discovered. With nearly two weeks left before the launching of the attack upon the chateau grounds, things inexplicably changed. Foremost, the royal train had moved to Amboise. From a chateau to a fortress with a central donjon. Charles' source advised that the move was quite unexpected and hurried. As if that signal was not grave enough, Catherine de Medici was ordering the release of some religious prisoners and offering a general amnesty to still others. The queen mother was extending the olive branch. To which offense? Ours of course. They know. They probably know everything. How? He recalled Renaudie had begun so carefully but had become boastful and reckless of late. Their meetings tended to end in drunken celebrations at the tavern. They always met at the 'Prancing Pony'. Why the same place? It seemed port Hugues was becoming infamous for being a protestant hot bed. During their meetings "The Ten", disallowed eager protestants to join in the committee, but by evening all comingled together. At one point Avon overheard Renaudie boasting to a haunt that he received support from Queen Elizabeth herself. All at the tavern were staunchly protestant but what did that matter? Were the freed prisoners reprieved based on information given by rascals? Yes, I will hang for this. *I will finally write to Maurice, pleading again for him to take up my cause*.

Maurice, I can promise this will be my final appeal only because I am not long for this world. If it were not so I would only pester you without end. I write you now knowing I will be executed for conspiring against the crown. I hope I left an impression upon you of not being foolhardy, yet I sit here a fool all the same. Once you hear the news about our pathetic plan, you shall agree. I do not regret my participation nor general design. I only regret that I did not take charge myself. If I had,plots would have executed quite differently. Enough of my regrets, let us talk about yours. Do you still believe in Catherine and the moderates? Something I know, even their motto is un roi, une loi, une foi. One king, one law, one faith.

Ignore my pokes, we both know you are the greater academic. I am only the greater cynic. Made so by court life. In no other situation would I fain you nearer these jackals. In no other situation would I fain you as jaded as I. Have you ever asked a friend something you would not wish on an enemy? I ask that of you now. May it be my argument and not some personal tragedy that changes your mind.

A friend in waiting, Charles

The final meeting at port Hugues went as Charles expected. All agreed that the plot had been discovered. There remained a general confusion about if their names had been revealed. The conspirators eyed each other suspiciously. The strongest piece of information which all confirmed in their own ways was that Renaudie had been identified to the Cardinal of Lorraine. The informant was a sympathetic lawyer who Renaudie lodged with in Paris. The Ten cursed their bad luck as Renaudie flushed with embarrassment. Defensively he mumbled that could not have been the only informant, as it must have been corroborated to elicit such a reaction. Charles sprung into action as he should have done much sooner. He argued that he should be made the new leader, but the group balked at such a change. The final decision belonged to Renaudie alone. He desired to proceed with the attack. Rather than March 10 upon Blois, it would be the 16th upon the fortress de Amboise.

"Our forces far exceeded what we initially expected thanks to all at this council. We shall breach the donjon, rescue King Francis, and arrest the foreign usurpers. Much blood shall be spilled, but we have the force necessary to take the fort. This is the direct advice from the captains of the mercenaries, the chauvre de sois, and most importantly our Huguenot gendarme knights."

"Why should the Guise move the king to such a fort anyway?" said Arthur.

"I can advise you on that score," Charles answered accusingly. "The Lorraine faction has everyone convinced that this is an English plot. They now have the justification to take the most extreme measures and leave us no quarter. Just another of your boasts which has doomed us."

Renaudie blustered and rushed the literati but was held back by the others. It was a rebuke to his honor to be blamed for their discovery, and he demanded a duel.

"No!" Charles Avon proclaimed, "Our heads belong to the Guise and I shall not begrudge the foreign princes their right."

The knock came at the hour of vespers. Charles took that as a sign. I thank you Jesus for the day and shan't ask for another. He turned the knob fearing he would face some arresting dragoons. Avon opened the door to a single chauvre de sois boldly wearing a feather in his cap.

"Ready sir?"

"No, but coming anyway. I have no experience as a fighter."

"I assure you battle comes naturally to any red-blooded Frenchman."

"I have no weapon."

"We have stores."

Off they went to the rally point in the woods of Amboise. For some time it was just the two of them, but then he saw a line of impressive figures outlined by moonlight upon a ridge. They followed the brilliant glimmer of armor and upon reaching the ridge, a few campfires raged, surrounded by dozens of warriors. Charles knew his prayer had been granted. The Guise shall have my head, but they will collect it from the field of battle rather than the butcher's basket.

Horns billeted to the rally. Charles Avon was supplied with a simple sword and he followed the queue to a single gendarme who was the most valiant knight he had set eyes upon. The gendarme knight held high a banner of the Huguenot cross: four sedan triangles meeting tip side at the center. The knight bellowed and they rushed, for there was nothing else to do. The attack proved feeble and not nearly as deadly as the literati imagined. They stormed out of the tree line with no apparent enemy in sight into a sudden peppering of muzzle flash. Whenever Avon caught sight of a Huguenot bannerman he was zagging, but the Catholic banners held their lines. They had rushed into an ambush and the shrinking intellectual part of the book broker pondered at which point he abandoned reason for fervor.

Charles did not care for reason anymore, only the Huguenot cause mattered. Then he saw his own banner knight unhorsed and facing a single catholic gendarme. Words were exchanged, which Charles could decipher. They had faced each other before and vowed it to be their final match. From behind a tree Charles bore witness. Swords sparked in parry, the movement of their feet vigorous in finding and launching from purchase. His Huguenot hero finding the opening for a death blow, the enemy smote at his feet before enduring a flurry of quivers. The intellectual part of him now completely murdered, Charles rushed out with his simple sword and sparked a block of his own before being gashed into a dank stream.

He was taken prisoner and brought to a hellscape upon the banks of the Loire River. There was all brutality. Prisoners were being interrogated on the spot as the king's men were grouping the captured by class. Any known nobility or suspected leaders were set aside and being led up to the castle. Mercenaries were also being prepared for release, as was the custom, but this process too was frustrated. The royal dragoons complained that the mercenary companies were not flying under the proper banners of the lords who had paid them. Though the mercenary captains identified the purchasing agents they also explained that they accepted the contract from anonymous masters, hence they did not fly customary banners, but rather these Huguenot flags, nought before seen. They took the risk and should now pay the consequences, some argued. The mercenaries eventually got their reprieve and some clever chevaliers at least secured future terms for services they surely believed would be needed. A war of religion loomed.

The protestant rebels were being disposed of in the most horrendous fashion. Charles screamed as he watched men crammed into sacks alive, then thrown into the river. Some had limbs hacked off instead of being sacked, but they too were thrown in the waters. There were a few who earned the indignity of being hung from the branches.

Charles would not have to wonder long about his own fate as he was next approached by a dragoon officer and a...where do I know that man from?

"Who are you?" asked the familiar man.

"A faithful son of Christ." Charles Avon was impressed with himself. The true test of faith comes down to a single moment. "We are the martyrs of this age ordained to sacrifice ourselves so that Christianity may be reclaimed from your Babylonian grip."

"You are a pretend reformer and we shall baptize you mercifully and pray that you don't end up in limbo for your heresy. You are not a fighting man as that is as clear as day. Were you recruited by the chauvre de sois? Just give us one name and you save yourself a limb."

"Another son of Christ recruited me."

The officer stepped in, "may you pretend to swim without an arm then." The soldier pulled his arm and readied the hack.

"Wait, I know this man. Do we know each other?"

Charles turned away. Did his evensong prayer go unanswered? He shuddered. Am I to be tested further?

"Oh this is the literary broker sometimes at court Chatillon. He supplies humanist trash to some of the ladies, it is something of a trend."

"Is he nobility?" the officer asked.

"No, I doubt that."

"I have orders to only save the nobles."

"Certainly you must understand the larger scope, he most likely was leadership. Perhaps one of The Ten. Tell me of the port of Hugues?" Just like that Charles Avon had his left arm severed. "No, let me take him in for interrogation."

"No." The dragoon kicked the broker into the rushing waters. Avon still felt his left arm attached and swam as hard as he could. Finally, he gave in and found the peace to pray in his time of drowning. He floated out of the water and into the sky. Below him, sparks of the burning trees nipped after him. Charles rose above embers' reach. Burnt out now, tiny ash balls were marooned to gravity. The pull caught one in the arc of a swinging blade. From ember to ash to dust.

The possessed soldier's inner light was now too a dying ember. No figment of reason would be relayed by his tormentor so he hacked yet another arm. All those faint and wispy embers below were casting out the full lights from their presence. Trumpets sounded a beacon and there all the lights were collected.

Charles Avon was no longer a singularity. All became one. One now sat with Jesus and that tiny itch, only bothered One for a moment, was gone. Once again One knew only bliss. Charles was handed to his mother and they smiled to one another.

Chapter Twelve

March 16, 1560

Laon, France

Jean had parcels of mail to distribute. Father, Maurice, and Marie convened in the den for such domestic matters. They crowded around Jean like beggars seeking sustenance. Mail day was usually cheery and optimistic, but the Millet home had been one of souring undertones. Silence reigned between the inhabitants since the tragedy at the convent. Since the stork's delivery there had been no quarry worth a chase, only regrets about hunts long past. Since holding tiny Mary in his hands, Maurice had begun to grow doubtful. It was in this very room that Maurice read to his father the contents of Danilo's last letter postdated two fortnights earlier. Jean was increasingly furious with his two sons as he learned the measure of their complicity.

Leaving Laon had since become a dangerous expedition and so Jean's plans for escape to the Netherlands had stalled. Marie took pains not to appear too giddy given the somber mood. Truly Jean was coming to his senses about leaving his sons behind. Disdain from his brothers he could handle, but Tonya's father's admonishment of him, could not be brooked so easily. Jean had been reminded that Tonya, and now of course Mary, was not only married to Maurice, but they gave her hand to the patriarch of the Millets to care for them until days end. Marriage to Maurice meant marriage into the Millet family. Ultimately Jean was responsible for each of them. It

was maddening to see an upcoming storm and not being able to convince your loved ones of its imminence.

"Here a letter from monsieur Avon." Jean crammed the paper into Maurice's open hands. "I assume the birth of your daughter has had no affect." Maurice harkened back to the question Quentin had last asked. Is it to be a girl Maurice?

Christopher strolled into the tense scene to which Jean promptly yanked the feather from his belt and threw it onto the ground. The feather's meandering descent maddened father even more. "As long as we are Frenchmen we shall be loyal subjects to the crown. Millets do not raise arms against countrymen."

Christopher sulked. "So what do we do father?"

"You raise the sword in defiance of me, this one disappoints by not wielding the pen." Jean gestured to Christopher then Maurice respectively. "What is a father to do?"

With so much fury aimed at her brothers, Marie could not resist the chance to finally reveal her heart.

"I fain to remain French for the rest of my life and so father I tell you what we should do, we abjure." The room stifled at the unspoken brought to voice. "The Chevrols have converted quite willingly, as have the Hapier family from the briar patch village." Stunned silence allowed her continuance. "Last year a quarter of Laon's bachelors were reformed yet today it is more likely that I am courted by a Catholic—"

Jean asked his daughter pointedly. "Have you a suitor Marie?"

"No," she lied. "No you don't see."

"Oh I see quite clearly. We are a family of four seeking four different paths—"

Red cheeked Christopher shot back. "Father that is what you suggested—"

"Did I son? Or did I simply give in to what you and your brother desire? Now that the haste of that choice is worn away and my departure retarded, it all feels so unnatural. Perhaps they are right about humanism, it destroys families. You are all dismissed. Let a father think."

Maurice reined in his younger siblings. "I insist we go to the stables and decide this once and for all."

At the stables, the siblings convened. Their secret meeting place, since their youth, inducing them to reveal their secrets.

"It is time we lay everything out." Maurice was determined to clear the air. "Here I have a letter from Charles Avon. The man has connections with Gaspard de Coligny." Maurice paused momentarily for effect.

Marie bit. "The admiral Coligny?"

"The very one. He, rather I should say they, have been giving me an extraordinary invitation. I have been asked to join the admirals court as a library curator and a broker—"

"And you have refused this?" said Marie.

"Repeatedly, because there is an ulterior motive. I am to gain trust and sympathy of the Catholic nobility through teachings of humanism, and to a lesser extent, the reformed religion."

Christopher reeled at the opportunity. "I know Maurice, you expected things to go better concerning the regency. If you initially refused based on your misplaced expectations, why have you not yet changed your mind?"

Marie wisely interjected. "Brothers, this sounds treasonous."

"With all that has happened?" Christopher clamored.

"Even with all that has happened I still believe Catherine de Medici works towards moderation. The admiral and Charles Avon think I may even be able to meet the queen mother personally, by gifting her our family's Machiavelli letter."

"Would it be possible for our family to make such connections?" Marie said quietly aloud with a whimsical flutter. "It would be much too dangerous Maurice."

"I could judge it myself and simply leave. Here is what I propose for the sake of our father whose authority we too long have trampled. I would consider taking on this task if you Christopher would quit the chauvre de sois and concentrate your efforts on finding father an escape route. For all of us, I shall stay behind only as long as it takes to get that meeting with the Queen Mother, then I shall join you in the low countries."

Gallantry and honor came naturally to the young man once error was so introduced to him. "Yes, I promise."

"Et vu Marie?" Time to clear the air.

"We know about your romance with Robert la Paussion."

"Those are but nasty rumors."

"I do truly hope the nasty bits are only rumors but there certainly is a romance. House la Paussion hates our family Marie, this is not one of your romantic tragedies. Furthermore, you drag my wife into it as an aid to your rendezvous."

"She told you."

"No sister, but you have just now confirmed it. Now all three of us are going to do right by father. Our disobedience ends here. You will travel with father contently and hope that these rumors do not precede you." She ran off sobbing. "Now Christopher, let us read this letter together."

After reading the letter the Millet brothers stood in silence. Charles Avon dead. Father is going to be devastated. Maurice scratched his head incessantly. Christopher knew that meant his brother was trying to puzzle it all out.

"I am sorry about your friend Maurice."

"Oh we only met the one time, but he was fascinating. We have exchanged a few letters. I think we would have become friends." Maurice looked beyond his brother, into the distance.

"I am sorry about our sister."

"Me too Christopher, she has not been herself in sometime, it had to be a man—"

"But Robert!"

At that, something within Maurice faltered. Christopher saw a gloss in his brother's eyes. A crack in his voice.

Maurice looked up, beyond the roof of the stable. "In Charles a friend that could have been and in Robert a former friend turned rival. Loss comes in many forms."

"I am sorry about your wife, too."

The levee broke. Maurice broke down crying. He sobbed into the embrace of his brother.

"An arranged marriage," his sobbing turned to a pathetic laugh, "why brother did I ever agree to this marriage?"

"I remember why," Maurice straightened up and wiped his face. "You did it for the family. The union between our families has allowed us to resist la Paussion thus far."

Maurice nodded with a deeper appreciation than Christopher understood. With a pat on each other's shoulders and Maurice looking down at the letter, scratching his head, the brothers had entered into a new relationship.

"What plot does he speak of?" Maurice asked himself.

"I may know a little about that," Christopher hesitated.

"Go on."

"I promise brother I have no direct involvement and I will not associate with Herndon and the others any longer. If there is truth to the contents of this letter then the hour is much later than either of us imagined."

"Indeed, now out with it."

"There has been a lot of activity at port Hugues on the Loire. Rebel protestants called Huguenots. The stories mostly tell of chauvre de sois captains, not Herndon, but others. Bandits meeting with mercenary captains with designs on an attack in Blois where supposedly the royal train currently presides."

"A direct attack on the king, a rebel army! No, Avon would never." The words hung in the air.

"Brother, he says it himself, he has been fooled."

"He a fool? Me a fool? You are definitely a fool." The brothers laughed. "I must tell father about his friend. I do hope I can trust you Christopher, father needs us more than ever."

"I do believe I am ready to be my own man, but you are right, the way I have disobeyed him is shameful. I am sorry about Tonya."

"Yes, I will have to deal with that too."

Marie came to warn Tonya about the development, and to beg her for further assistance. "Sister, sister please they want me to discard my Robert."

"What, they know?"

"Christopher and Maurice are going to obey father's wishes and demand I do the same. Christopher will quit the chauvre de sois and Maurice is off to the admiral's court."

"You speak nonsense."

"Did you not know of the admiral and Charles Avon?"

"No, I don't know anything of this."

"Oh Tonya my heart breaks for you. If your heart breaks for me you must help me at once."

"What sister, how?"

"Maurice is going to be angry with you—"

"Well it sounds like I may be angry with him right back."

"Please promise me that you will work with me just like last time."

"Obviously last time did not work if Maurice found out."

"He only suspected, I gave it away. Surely he has noticed what close friends we have become and with the rumors about Robert and I."

"Sister, those rumors, are they just rumors?"

"Of course they are, don't be lewd."

There was some shouting from back in father's den.

"Go Marie now, act the part. I shall do what I can."

Tonya thought about the previous rendezvous. The girls thought they concocted a clever enough plan. Tonya and Marie would go to market together, nothing odd about that, as long as they shopped for something truly needed and came home with it. Last time it was for paper stock - The Millets being part of the literati always needed ample supply of paper and other scribe materials. Off they went together but it had to be a Wednesday around one o'clock. That would be the time each week that Robert would wait for her at the old butcher shop. He was there, so Tonya did the shopping herself, but made sure not to delay in her errands. The couple would have only the time it took for Tonya to return outside the shop. She knocked when nobody was around and that signaled Marie to exit. Tonya often fantasized about their rendezvous. A young man and woman alone in a closed up shop for over half an hour. What could be more inappropriate? When she had knocked there was no answer for many moments, so she panicked and let herself in. They were kissing passionately. She didn't know two people could be so attracted to each other. Afterwards, Marie told her that they heard her knock, but Robert was too inflamed to release her. Tonya wondered now if he had wanted her to come in and witness their embrace. Another mouth to utter the gossip.

Would Robert even be still waiting for her each week? The idea of that level of hold on a man excited her. Should she even help them again? Did they really have love or was this just lust? Did she even care anymore if it were love or lust? She would take either with Maurice. Now with their baby girl and surely more on the way, her fate was to be stricken to the mundane. What was this talk of an admiral and his court? She would know soon enough she thought, as she heard Maurice's familiar gait advancing the hallway.

"Dear wife, how is the baby?"

"Sound asleep dear husband."

"Good, we have much to talk about and we should remain calm for our sakes and the baby's."

"What is happening? I have been hearing your father booming from the den."

"Yes, well much has happened. Is happening really."

"Tell me Maurice."

Once Tonya heard it all, she bowed her head obediently, but privately vowed to continue to help Marie. She and the baby were to now join Jean, Marie, and even Christopher on the exodus from France. Only Maurice would remain. He would leave his wife and child behind while he adventured off to some noble admiral's court. Not so easy Maurice. No, she would help Robert get Marie, and let it be seen how the man could in turn help her.

"Tonya dear, father grieves now for his friend. Yet he has proclaimed his friend a martyr, burned for the sake of baby Mary."

Town life marched on under the singular vision of the lord of Laon. There were hardly any bogs remaining. Seigneur Phillipe, with that protestant modernity, would have all lands be fertile, tamed, and curated. The first potato harvest in the region had been a success. Town folk chatted with the farmers who could not convince them easily that the potato was not a fruit. Raw potatoes were bit into anyway. Spittles and giggles, one even claimed to like it like that. They were tossed back and forth naturally and upon a thousand other sniffs were finally accepted into kitchens.

Women gazed at the dirty little weirdly shaped masses. Tonya in her role as an authoritative figure set various women to attempt different methods for cooking this strange new food. Dinner parties convened and people cared not a fig for the others' faith. Recipes were shared and the women with the favored results were showered with glee. Skinned, unskinned, boiled, baked, and fried. Mashed, whole, or something in between. All agreed it was a dense food leaving behind full stomachs in the craze. The men even took to eating contests. Maurice placed near to last only eating a potato and a half. He was glad for the return to normalcy, but hesitated to grant the potato great unifier status.

Maurice was still unsure of his decision, but felt obligated to follow his father's lead. Time to rely on his earthly father's judgement as well. If Maurice were being completely honest, he still thought that things were improving in Laon. There had been some positive outcomes after the convent incident that involved the abbe and perhaps even the king paying more attention to Laon. Discussions had begun to end the boycotts and even a joint committee to appeal to the artists' train to consider coming back with a guaranteed sum in patronage. However, that aspect deteriorated into a question of reparations to be paid accordingly by those groups most responsible for losing the festival in the first place.

The lord truly does show the way, Maurice acknowledged. For the next day Maurice received another letter from Danilo. The final report on the lost maidens. The wily traveler used a different encryption method which took Maurice some hours to crack. The de Guise faction? Maidens to be released? It could be no coincidence that both Danilo and Avon had postscripted their letters to me with haste, to take up the cause and recognize the dire straits we find ourselves in. Then came the final insult.

Could Heather truly have been raped? Were the papish as depraved as some protestants believed? Wolves in sheep's wool. Maurice never believed in that. He knew they had corrupt practices and arrogant traditions, but ultimately his differences with the Catholics were dogmatic, and he tended to revere the ecclesial men of God. He hurried to Christopher's room but the young man was not home.

Maurice fretted all day over the matter. He and Tonya looked over Mary together by taking turns. She would be cooking while he read to a cooing Mary. While she breast fed the babe, he would go outside to chop wood. This is how they passed the day and thankfully Christopher returned home before the dinner hour. He pulled him into the stable.

"Where have you been?"

"I wanted to tell Herndon myself, like a man."

"How did it go?"

"It is not easy asking a man to help you and your family escape while at the same time quitting his company." Maurice waited for more. "Of course he will help. He is an honorable man and I am damned if I don't want to be just like him. However he may have used one shameful device upon me. He—"

"Wait, let me ask you something first." Maurice interrupted Christopher, yet balked at such a question. "Do you think it was possible, that Heather… was raped?"

Christopher looked away shamefully. "That I do not know brother, but two of the maidens of Roucy could not contain their cries, saying that the priest Borges had raped them."

Maurice plopped onto a bale haphazardly. "Oh Heather, bless you. Oh Janeau my friend, bless your soul."

Christopher noted. "His pain will increase now with the maidens coming home."

"What is that…you know?"

"Yes, Herndon told me the edict has been repealed. Well, go on, you were right then. The edict is repealed, the boycotts may end soon, Father may even begin to believe you."

"No Christopher it was you who was right. They rape our women, shutdown our shops, and the killing comes next. No, I have been so dreadfully wrong."

"You may not want to hear what else Herndon told me."

"Go ahead."

"I am not sure if I even believe him, it is too far-fetched."

"Go on."

"I mean who would we be to House de Guise?"

"What, de Guise? Danilo warns me of them too. Brother what is it?"

"Herndon claims that one of the reasons he took me in so quickly was because the Millet family is being targeted by de Guise, well by la Paussion via house de Guise. He speaks of la Paussion house being licensured as a new noble house in return for them ridding Laon of the reformed."

"Herndon speaks the truth, I see it now." Maurice explained at length. "King Henri dies and, given the young age and poor health of King Francis, a regency arises as the true leader of France." Maurice talked out loud, half to himself, half to his brother. "Who has King Francis' ear but his own wife, Mary

Queen of Scots, and who has her ear?" Christopher opened his mouth slightly but Maurice answered himself. "Her uncles, the Duke and Cardinal de Guise. They are controlling our king through the young queen!"

Christopher was skeptical. "The Queen of Scots, House Lorraine, blood does not get any bluer. What are the Millet family to them?"

"Nothing. They don't even know we exist, but they support Robert la Paussion and he certainly knows we exist. Robert is behind the boycotts and he may even be connected with the Reeve and the Priest Borges on this."

"How does our sister play into this?"

"Perhaps Christopher, they are in love and he wants us to convert so they can marry. No doubt he has bragged about pending nobility to her. Oh Tonya, it just occurred to me, Tonya mentioned that she and Marie would be shopping on Wednesday for nut oil for the baby."

"So what of it?"

"I think we should follow them, it could be a rendezvous with monsieur Paussion."

"If it is, then what?"

"I don't know yet, but let us be ready for anything. Christopher I should like your advice about something, should I tell Jan?

"Big brother yes, I never agreed with Herndon's decision for us to keep it a secret. I would want to know, I would want you to tell me."

"I understand little brother. I shall think more on this and quickly, in fact I should pay him a visit now, as he often takes a rest at this hour. Think on Wednesday and how it should go, and Christopher ask yourself how would Herndon handle the situation."

Christopher beamed at his older brother. Suddenly the horseshit induced Maurice to gag. It was Christopher's chore to clean out the stable, but these were unusual times. He grabbed the tin pail and began scooping then dumping into a wheel barrow. His eyes watered and even threw up a bit. Maurice was not a man unaccustomed to animal dung, but the nagging thought of Priest Borges raping Heather had poisoned him to the pit. He had to go then to his friend, to deepen the wound.

"Jan I am glad to have caught you. How do you fare my friend."

"I walk the earth sure enough. I scratch away in the fields. That is good enough for me, the lord is great."

"I have some things to speak to you about, and I am afraid none of it is good, and perhaps will hurt you even more."

"Impossible my friend."

"The Millets will leave Laon."

"Your whole family, you Maurice?"

"Yes. My family is planning to start a new life in the Netherlands and I shall accept the admiral's invitation."

"You will? What changed your mind?"

"Many things friend, but at this moment I would do anything in my power to bring justice to you."

"I am at peace Maurice—"

"My dear friend there is more. According to the rebel that witnessed it all, Heather had no reason to attack the priest while her escape was nigh. Furthermore he thinks the attack seemed personal and that she was crazed." Maurice looked pleadingly into Jan's eyes to interpret this wicked train of thought. "Also, Christopher states that two of the Roucy girls were raped and Danilo has learned from someone at the convent that they believe rapes occurred, but can't know if it was Heather exactly."

"You are telling me that the priest raped my Heather."

"I am saying it looks that way, and that would explain her actions. Now the other girls will be returned to Laon as soon as the Edict of re-education has been officially repealed. You could find out more from them. I am sorry Jan, perhaps I should not have told you."

Janeau said nothing for many moments. He rose up to prepare to return to the fields. The fawn skin gloves from his back pocket were set once again over his hands. The long reaper hoisted against his front shoulder looked menacing.

"No Maurice, we are the sophists of the brook, we deal in truths."

"You are wise my friend. So let us speak more truth and put names to our enemies. The priest Borges, Thomas, the reeve, and Robert la Paussion." Jan looked surprised. "Yes he is behind the boycotts and apparently he works directly for the Guise faction who have promised him a title. The rascal even has seduced my dear sister. Yes the rumors are true, and worst my own wife aids in the trysts."

"Maurice, I am sorry."

"I shall follow your stoic example Jan. Christopher and I plan to follow them on Wednesday to discover more truths."

***

Maurice insisted that his brother finish his work as a rebel until the departure date which had been a fortnight away. The family split would be clean and as short in duration as possible. Marie and Christopher both were renewing their interests in the family business and showed eagerness about starting a new life in the Netherlands. For Maurice's part he hoped to work his way up to a meeting with Catherine de Medici, in order to plead the case for peace and tolerance. God willing both elements would work in their favor so they could have the wonderful dilemma of then choosing where to live. They prayed on these matters with open heart and gratitude for whatever the Lord's plan was. Jesus need not show us the door, for he is the door.

Jan and Maurice awaited with the other men. Both relations of the returning maidens and Heather's kin were present. Waiting upon Christopher the posse was seething. All had been told the same as what Jan heard. Heather's father and brother faced each other and made their solemn oaths in a strange calm. Various implements were being stacked near the anvil. Hammers cracked on machetes, testing their suitability. A stinging vibration sent a surge of pain through the arm nerves of a farmer, as he yelped. Forgers of war weapons these men were not. Christopher would arrive with instructions from the chauvre de sois and would also no doubt be questioned further about the Roucy incident. Maurice fought back multiple urges to calm the men down and suggested disbanding for a while, but he held his tongue. Who am I to judge, and what can I suggest anyhow. I need to find myself at court. It feels right, why am I finally seeing it now? At court is where I can make a difference, here I am useless. Christopher is not, and I have been quite proud of the young man of late. Maurice pondered upon the cross road lying just ahead. Christopher arrived with instructions of where to pick up the girls.

"I also have this message from Herndon Calais. We bandits of the shire do what we can with full heart and empty pockets. Give what you can in coin or provisions and know that the most valuable form of support is that of safe houses. We ask that you work to construct such buildings. Houses under your control, secret doors and plenty stocked."

The men all promised in their own way some general form of thanks and acceptance of the task, as well as handing him a pouch of coins that they could collect.

"What of the girls of Roucy?" A man asked.

"Returned safely," Christopher replied.

Another then asked. "Where have all our girls been since the convent?"

"Safe houses. Many catholic families have aided your children and have uttered no words of conversion."

Yes, Maurice was quite proud of the change in this young man. The posse would not be so easily swayed, however.

"Christopher, will you tell us about these rapes?" inquired Heather's own father.

"I have witnessed no rapes my good man. Two of the girls from Roucy were crying out in the first eve of our escape about being raped by the Priest, Borges that is. The girls embraced each other, and generally wailed before God in the night sky. They would talk of it no more after that."

"What about Heather?"

"I was not there so Herndon would know better than me on certain points. Was it true that you found her just outside the convent with her throat slit?"

"Yes," replied Janeau. "She spoke final words to me."

Christopher continued to confirm details with Janeau before positing the assumption that hanged in the air like a stifled bee. "Did you see a wound upon the priest?"

"Yes, he seemed to have been stabbed just below the front shoulder."

"That lines up perfectly with what the rebel who was there told me, a man I trust. He said that when the attack began the lone cavalier was knocked out and that Herndon ordered him to stand guard over the cavalier and the priest. The rebel kicked the cavalier's sword away and took his knife and tucked it into his belt quite haphazardly. When the guard witnessed the escapees coming towards the anteroom, he gestured to the girl in the lead to run past through the entrance. The priest hurled an insult, something about winning in the end, when she suddenly attacked him with nails and tiny fists. My friend was surprised by the ferocity and intervened, to get her to continue onwards, with the others who were then passing by. When he had her turned around she lifted the dagger from his belt and drove it into the priest's shoulder. All wide eyed was the priest when he pulled it out of his own body and swiped it across her neck. Herndon knocked out the priest and determined that Heather's odds were better waiting for you all, than being taken directly to the forest."

Heather's father spoke solemnly. "You tell him from me that I am eternally grateful and he made the right choice. At least she was able to pass on surrounded by her own people."

The Millet brothers made their way home.

"Brother they smell blood."

"I fear so, you did commendable, no riling them up, just the truth."

"On that score, I decided that what Herndon would do about tomorrow is restrain ourselves if we do discover la Paussion. He has taught me much about the value of information."

"Sounds like Danilo."

"I should like them to meet someday."

"Christopher, something tells me they already have."

They laughed at their new world of connections, gossip, intelligence, and spying.

Lisbeth la Paussion rode upon her horse past the outer gates of her estate. Father would not approve but she had a score to settle. In her sights was her despicable brother Robert. He had been a fink in her eyes since she understood what a fink was. She rode hard upon him causing the rascal to dive into some spiny plants. He of course whined in pain, but she paid that no regard.

"You who would surpass father act the princess."

"Mind your business sister or you too will feel my wrath."

"Your wrath prickles me not brother. For you shall withdraw your name from selection now or see us in ruins under your lead."

"It is my destiny Lisbeth, do you not see it so?"

"I see only a weakling who could not dream to thwart Christopher Millet. Maurice perhaps, but eventually Christopher you need face, and would fall."

"I shall handle Marie and Maurice, and your Christopher, what quarrel do we have sister?"

"Only that which excludes father you ingrate."

Robert trodded off then, quite defeated, determined to execute his plans. Priest Borges he had impressed. The chevalier his dog would follow suit. Lisbeth was late to the game and as such would pick at the leftovers. She desired Christopher, so be it, he too could be turned.

Chapter Thirteen

March 19, 1560

Laon, France

The Millet house was nearly empty. Candlesticks were piled separately from silverware. Furniture outlines appeared on the walls, marks of discoloration diverging from the grain, harkening back to its original hue. The game began on that Tuesday evening. Tonya and Marie both had commented about their intentions to shop on the morrow, and they also inquired about the brothers' affairs. Maurice replied that he and Christopher would be tending to the animals as they made final preparations to sell off their modest livestock of horses and mules.

At the appointed hour Tonya and Marie left and the brothers followed. The Millet brothers kept far back behind the women, deciding to let them disappear from sight and to only close the gap as they approached the village markets. Unbeknownst to them, they too were being followed in a similar fashion. The posse of the men of the maidens sought revenge and had then looked to take it out on Robert la Paussion, once they learned from Januea about his involvement. The boycotts, faire, and the convent rapes were all on Robert's hands. Jan then felt ashamed that he let his anger lead him to betraying Maurice. He ought not have told them about the suspected rendezvous. He ought to have found a different way that did not involve Maurice. It now was

too late, for the boiling blood spilled over and took control of all intent and action.

The brothers watched as Marie and Tonya walked by the closed butcher shop, when Marie stopped for just a moment at the door. The girls then walked on.

"Did she just knock on the door?" whispered Christopher.

The girls stopped again and looked around. Satisfied, Marie walked alone back towards the butcher's entrance and the door opened from the inside allowing her to scuffle in quickly. Tonya turned and continued to walk further along, presumably to do the shopping, as not to come home empty handed.

"Who was that inside there?"

"Robert."

"How do you know?" Christopher asked.

"He knocked down that domino and I could not even put up another in its place—"

"What?"

Angrily, Maurice proceeded. "He knocks them down, I fail at erecting them, now he even corrupts my sister. Look brother, if you desire, we can go in there and confront the rascal now."

"Yes Maurice, we could do that—"

The brothers were startled as Jan and his posse were upon them from out of nowhere.

"I am sorry Maurice, I hope you can forgive me someday. All present has sworn to secrecy about Marie, but we must do something about monsieur Robert."

Maurice looked upon Jan knowing that there was nothing to forgive. Now another began to speak, a man Maurice knew to be kin to the old butcher.

"That was a protestant business he shut down and now claims for himself. A thriving business whose family now struggles to pay alms."

Christopher, the ironic lone voice of reason, suggested, "You are here for blood Januea is that it? Perhaps you deserve it, but if we all walk away now, with surprise on our side, we may gain a better opportunity later. We should pass this information on to Herndon and—"

"No, he does enough. Today we must do something," said Heather's father.

At that, the men rushed forward, and Jan, like a raging bull, kicked the door of the butcher shop in. However as the posse rushed in a Catholic family strolled down the road and a pair of protestant kids also soon turned the corner. There would be no secrets today, Maurice realized as the events blurred around him.

Jan had kicked down the door. Primal beasts set upon prey so quickly that Robert and Marie were caught in the most inappropriate way. Marie laid on a table with her breasts out and her legs open, and Robert stood in between her thighs with his own pantaloon down around his ankles. Unmarried or not, what was presented to the posse was hedonistic sin. The sight drove Janeau mad with rage. Some of the men held back Maurice and Christopher as they were at the rear of the charge and did not possess a good vantage point.

"You catholic devils are dirty sinners." Jan raged with immense strength, pulled Robert by the throat and reeled him back into the wall. "Pull up your pants, I shan't pummel a naked barbarian." Robert complied with the snickering mob.

"You call us heretics."

"Rape, Rapists."

"Dirty papist."

"Babylonian whore."

Marie was dressed enough and standing by the time Christoper and Maurice emerged but they had the proper sense of the scene that was revealed.

"We have some questions for you monsieur la Paussion." Maurice reached out his arm to Robert with accusing demand.

"I love your sister Maurice. Yes, I love her and intend to marry her either as a protestant or a catholic."

"I love you Robert," cried out Marie.

"Whore," a woman yelled from the rear.

The gossip had spread to the market goers now crowding outside. Jan unleashed a square punch to Robert's stomach which caused him to double over.

"No time for lies now Robert."

He spat out, "Fine, she is a whore so I used her as such."

Christopher spotted Tonya who began to run away. He was about to give chase but when he saw his sister nearly faint to the floor, he went to gather her and help her outside.

Maurice looked down at Robert and offered a hand up. "These are the least of your concerns. Admit to us that you are behind the boycotts running good protestants out of business and snatching up their storefronts."

Robert rose himself ignoring Maurice's hand. "Yes, so what Maurice, what can you do about it."

"And the reeve?" asked Maurice. "Is he with you, do you both work for de Guise?"

"Maurice I would tell you that I am proud of you for finally figuring it out, but no you are the fool who took too long. My nobility is at hand and anyone who does not leave my shop immediately will suffer the consequences."

At the promise of wrath from a new lord many onlookers began to flee, but the men of the posse all remained.

"So be it. Tell us of the rapes of the maidens."

"You mean Heather don't you. She was raped no more than Marie, and no less a protestant whore."

Jan wondered how long the ringing had lasted. It was excruciating in the ear and was descending in volume as his blurred vision began to recover as well. Robert's mushed face was turning side to side. He drove his fist into one side of the jaw and then the other. Again and again until Jan no longer needed to keep punching.

Chapter Fourteen

March 19, 1560

Laon, France

The reeve suspected that the mob would not respect his authority alone. He stopped two witnesses he trusted, one of each religion; and they told the same tale. Marie Millet and Robert la Paussion were caught in the act of sexual rendezvous when a mob led by Janeau, the Millet brothers, and other protestant men of the maidens had barged into the old butcher shop. Also Jan had beaten la Paussion to death. No, the reeve thought, I will need to assemble a force. He would gather Catholics and the boycotters and have them spread the tale. They should gather a posse of their own and surround the Millet household. The reeve himself would head to the Paussion estate and inform them of their young lord's death. The men of that household could help him hunt down the chauvre de sois who were most likely involved.

Christopher pushed Marie into a chaise and advised his father of the terrible news.

"I must go to Herndon immediately to affect an emergency escape—"

"Damned all of our plans again," Jean yelled lividly.

"Gather what you can, Maurice is on his way." Christopher pulled his father closer and whispered to him the closest catholic safehouse. "Maurice knows of this place as well, if need be, you and Marie can go without him. Maurice is thinking of something that could work for Jan, in case the safehouse owner won't accept a murderer."

Marie began to stand up but Jean threw her to the ground and begun kicking her in the stomach. "There can be no bastard you whore, what have you done to us."

"Father no please stop."

Jean then struck his youngest son. "I have been far too soft for too long and this is what becomes of us."

"Strike me father all you want," he cried, "but if you strike her again I vow—"

Jean kicked again, whipping her head back into unconsciousness.

"You bastard, you're the bastard!" The son pulled the father away with surprising strength. With realization of how he could dominate the old literati, he released Jean by hand and Marie by heart. She had damned her worth for saving and he to be saved.

Jean stared at his still daughter and knelt down in a sob. "My Marie, no, my baby Marie what have I done? Jesus help her, Jesus please." She opened her eyes slowly, Christopher turned and ran.

"Thank you Jesus lord. I am sorry."

"I am sorry father, so sorry. Jesus left me."

"No daughter, never. He is always with us. Even as I kicked, he was with me. I ignored him but he does not ignore us."

"Father, what are we going to do?"

"Let us get you up."

"Father, he said he loved me."

Tonya was hiding in the house with baby Mary and shuddered when she heard Maurice's name being called. His inexorable stomp placed him standing above her as if an apparition bent down to take form and yank her up by the hair.

"Son no. Are we not all children of Christ. Are we not all sinners."

He released his wife but not their gaze. "Yes father, we are all sinners."

Laon was lost to chaos in those hours until Seigneur Phillipe mustered a retinue under his five gendarme and restored order. Members of the retinue argued with the boycotters outside the Millet home. The protestant lord arrived from the temple district, which he just secured and at his presence the boycotters obeyed his orders to return home.

Phillipe emerged out of the house sometime later looking around and wondering where the Millets were. One of the most respected protestant families fleeing in shame. One of the most respected Catholic families losing a son. Civil war looms, and soon he too must make a decisive move. Not on this eve though, for tonight he must remain a loyal subject to the crown and work in concert with the reeve to track down these protestant fugitives. How long will we reformed be persecuted, the seigneur pondered.

Maurice, Marie, Tonya, Jean, and the baby were led down to the sub cellar of the barn which housed the farm's large hay bales. These bales were arranged with a false center affording the owner a secret shelter to which he concocted as a favor to Herndon Calais.

"God Bless you Jean, I can't assure you our grounds won't be searched given the importance of the young man killed, but I doubt we are under any suspicion."

"Only the lord knows that. But we are armed with a shield of truth."

"Us Catholics would say the same thing, a pity that it has come to this. We are so much more alike than we are different."

Maurice was half listening to the farmer while calculating a mental juxtaposition of how precious little they got away with, versus, how much was left behind. He now wondered in anticipation if he made the right choice. The son urged the father that they leave everything behind except their contracts and letters of credit, that they somehow could still collect on in the future. The ecus they had between them all would only be enough to pay the chauvre de sois and a winter's rent in foreign land.

"I don't see how we can start over with this. We should be peasants in our new country. Ghosts."

"We still have one hope, son. I did not want to influence your decision, but if it is true that Avon has perished, then with a signature from Admiral de Coligny, a better portion of our library will be returned to us."

"Ever the shrewd businessman father."

"No Maurice, it was charity from Avon. A symbol of how much they believe in you."

"We all do husband," stated Tonya with surprising adoration. "You can save us, not just this family but our people."

Marie felt disgusted with her sister, for she had seen Tonya derive pleasure vicariously through this wicked affair. Locked in a box however she plays the fawn. Entombed by hay bales they wrestled to find comfort against prickly walls, and to adjust to a poorer reality.

Jean now gave unto his son a renewed northerly star to remain fixed upon, speaking with great volume despite their state of hiding:

"Go to the courts and teach them of humanism. Christ works through you and with your men of the Mausien Brook. You were born to do this. You are a man of clear discernment. Judge those that are wicked and beware. Judge those with an open heart and speak to them in their language. Sit across the Queen Mother and gift her family with our own family heirloom. Leave such an impression and army of allies behind that we may have a tolerant France to return to. Now my children let us all pray in silence."

Maurice prayed from a place of overwhelming shame and guilt. A fatal choice he repeated over and over, each with its own consequences. I am responsible for all of this lord. You sent me angels, Beatrices and I turned away from them. Father, Danilo, Avon, each of your instruments to light a path for me to which I rejected for pride and the comforts of inertia and safety. Heather's blood is on my hands and I do not pray for your forgiveness for you are a merciful god, rather I pray that one day I can forgive myself. I pray that I can make it right. I pray that Heather transport down one more Beatrice, to whom I shall follow blindly into the abyss.

The family's prayers beamed into the heavens until they each fell asleep one by one. Jean was awoken first by a loud thud. Your will shall be done my lord.

"Wake children, our fate awaits us."

Phillipe's retinue circled the bales and commanded the owner explain the best way to gain entrance. This was explained and the men began their breach.

"We are retinue with authority from the seigneur and therefore King Francis, to place you under arrest. Can we expect a peaceful surrender?"

"You can son, we are at peace."

The final bales were separated, and the Millet family came out with the lord's light shining upon them.

Baby Mary cried and a soldier demanded the child be brought more blankets and baby food if the catholic family had any to spare. "These are the orders of your lord and liege Seigneur Phillipe. The seigneur has decided that there is not sufficient evidence to hold the Millet family and decrees that you may not be detained."

Maurice looked at his wife in disbelief and joy. "Praise Jesus."

"However Janeau must be brought in to face justice. So before God you must tell me his whereabouts." Each vowed their ignorance before God. "Maurice, are you certain?"

"He would not allow me to aid him in any way. I assume he went off into the forest to seek the chauvre de sois."

"Indeed. Well enough, Maurice your family has a choice, but you do not. You are to come with us back to Phillipe's manor. Your family is invited as well but he is not certain how long he can keep them safe."

"Why would I be safe with Lord Phillipe but not they?"

The soldier ignored his question to continue. "Our lord doubts he can keep your family in reprieve for long. Their other choice is to seek out the chauvre de sois, as both Herndon and the seigneur believe it their best option of escape."

"There is nothing to decide, clearly the lord works here the only true plan," Jean stated with purity of submission.

"There is one more thing. Maurice, the reason Phillipe need not be concerned of your safety, is because you are already dead. Jean, Tonya, Marie; you say goodbye to Maurice Millett forever here and now." The family was befuddled. "Maurice Millet is to be declared dead. Henceforth, you will know him only as Nicolas de Piefuin."

Tonya shook frantically, "No Maurice, no come with us, let us come with you."

For now it was not a temporary separation for which a reunion lay just beyond. For now it was to be a death such that the symbolic bear no distinction with the real.

"Wife, sister, father…my child," he kissed gently on her head. "I know this name."

"What."

"Jesus is great, I know this name. Danilo uses this name for French characters when we write stories together."

"Jesus is great," exclaimed Jean, "but that wily Roman is pretty good, too."

Without understanding of any technical details of god's plans it was evident that the likes of a mystical traveler, a conflicted seigneur, the Huguenot Admiral, and a most merry captain of the woods were each used to deconstruct Maurice Millet into Nicolas de Piefuin. Chefs each, with their own ingredients, concocted a backstory which Maur…Nicolas would need to memorize.

Jean asked, "Will Nicolas be off to Chatillon then?"

"Certainly not," answered the guard. "Lord Phillipe shall get word to you on Nicolas' destination."

Maurice Millet was rushed away promptly, but he took opportunity to embrace his father and sister with a full heart. He obliged a kiss with Tonya, but the taste of hatred had invaded his contented marriage. For baby Mary all he could give her was a blessed kiss on the little head. A little kiss, which transmitted his very soul to remain with hers.

The family's good spirits dwindled as the sun began its rise, and they had yet to find the forest rebels. With Mary crying and the light of day, they surely would be discovered soon enough and they were warned not to expect similar treatment from other of the retinue. Certainly, "Not to expect mercy from the reeve and run for their lives at any intersection with a Paussion band." However, by the western edge of the forest a few feathered caps popped up and hurried them into the fold.

"Jean," Herndon called low. "Good, the seigneur kept his word. I was only a coin toss sure that he would." It was no wonder his men were kept so merry, Jean thought, however, Christopher was not. He approached his father directly and clenched his fists.

Marie interceded, "Christopher, all is forgiven...I don't blame him."

"I don't forgive you sister. Or you." He threw a stare at Tonya. "So you decided to leave Maurice behind?"

"Eh heh," chimed in Herndon. "Maurice is dead. He died somewhere out here on this very morning. Yes?" He looked around at the entire band to make sure that would be the story they would stick to if captured. "As it stands right now Nicolas de Piefuin is more important than even I."

"So what now?" Jean asked the captain.

"Well for us it is yet another coin toss. Either a baggage train will arrive from the west. Or some blood thirsty Catholics from the east. Nothing to do now but to eat, drink, and be merry. If I may Christopher." Herndon pulled his young apprentice aside. "You may want to make good with your family now. Truth be told this is no coin toss. It is far more likely the Reeve gets here first."

Jan approached Jean and extended his hand. "I am sorry for the trouble I caused your family."

Shaking the young man's hand. "No Jan, we all did what is now done. No more apologies."

"Allow me one more then. Marie, I violated your sanctuary of the heart for my own personal vengeance. I will forever be ashamed as my Heather truly frowns from above."

Marie, too embarrassed to speak, just stared at the ground.

"I will take my leave."

"No Jan, please stay. You are brother to my brother."

Marie and Jan sat together on a mossy cushioned stone. "I too was in love, and we fancied ourselves a secret. I never properly announced my intentions to her father, as I could not bear my being denied. I understand where the beating of the heart can lead one."

Tears ran silently upon Marie's cheek. Here in the forest nature offered canopy to the brokenhearted. "With you and Heather the loved flowed both ways at least. I was, I was used…" she broke down bawling.

"Perhaps, but perhaps not. You must understand men. When overpowered as he was in the moment, Robert would've said anything to hurt us. He lashed out insults to hurt both myself and Maurice. He never considered we would press our advantage to his doom, not with his family standing."

Her eyes pleaded with his. Please don't let that be just a kindness. Please allow there be some truth.

"Bad news Millets. I just received a scout report. The Reeve and about twenty Paussion men at arms approach. My honor won't allow me to leave you undefended so you must run with us—"

"No," Jan stood up. "Herndon, you are a man of action and command. In this moment I ask you to follow my lead. Jean, take your family west in search of the baggage train. Herndon, you and yours escape south. They will make quick work of me, but I shall tell them you all ran north."

"This is not the best plan; but I have none better so I shall yield to your request gallant Janeau."

Christopher trudged to Janeau's side. "Well I won't yield, I remain with you Jan."

"Son."

"Go father, perhaps it be best we never see each other again."

Utterly dejected Jean gestured to the women, and they sprinted away towards the west.

Herndon neared Christopher. "Christopher, it doesn't make sense. Jan is willing to sacrifice himself for the off chance that he can throw them off. Sacrificing a second is pointless. I still have so much to teach you."

"Thank you Herndon, but I am done learning. From you, from Maurice. Even from my father. I will die today my own man."

Janeau and Christopher shared in a terrified look as they tracked actual gendarme bearing down upon them. The scouts reported men-at-arms only, as if that wasn't damned enough, somehow they missed the knights. Claude la Paussion issued two clear directives: "Cease him. Kill him." Fates for Christopher and Jan respectively. Some of the gendarme wondered why their soon-to-be-lord offered no personal venture in the death of his son's killer. They remained horsed, a simple farmer and a book boy playing bandit would be the men-at-arms' dirty work.

Christopher had little time to process the mystery of his special fate, yet remained resolved to die with honor. The men surrounded him but kept their swords sheathed. His own arced with the small competence Herndon was able to teach him in such a short time. Jan's own blade work was yet more clumsy, but he fought with the same ferocity as would any man facing his death. Jan, being stronger than most men, did manage to shove one aggressor away just in time to parry another. Christopher was snatched upon by the shoulder from his rear, yet a smart swipe ripped through heavy pant and drew the ire of the soldier. Though only scratched, it was enough for the trio to widen their circle leaving Christopher precious room to continue his guard. La Paussion declared to him, "Young Millet you would be wise to yield before I order swords out."

The gravity of his words magnified as Jan took a stab directly into his shoulder blade. He elbowed the assailant causing a gushed nose, but was nonetheless worse for wear. Christopher then pleaded, "I shall yield if you let him live!" Janeau's thigh was next impaled and he roared with a madness of prey that defies all rules of death. "They went south!"

A gendarme shot a look towards Claude, "Scout the north, go." Before riding off they hesitated at the wonder which played out. The hearty farmer refused to fall after yet another devastating blow, and instead swung with herculean might and lopped an infantryman's head nearly clean off. In earning their respect Janeau earned their death blows, dying at last with three more gendarme spear points driving down into him. It was the honorable death Christopher dreamed of, but the young man could only drop his sword, satisfied that at least he drew them northwards.

Christopher only spent a day in a dungeon. The dungeon was in fact a wine cellar closet. By evening vespers Claude had furnished a room for his guest. On the second day Christopher was given access to an entire wing of the Paussion Villa. Claude had not explained much, only that his family had not been found. Christopher was asked to be patient and that arriving guests would reveal the truth. Indeed, on the fourth day, the guests had arrived and Christopher was summoned for a meeting.

He was surprised to see his uncles, but then it dawned on him that they were probably being forced to pay some sort of ransom. In short order even that realization would disappear as the truth was finally conveyed.

Claude made introductions for his young guest. "This is Priest Borges," to which Christopher scowled, "and Chevalier du Lay."

The chevalier warned, "You shall remove that countenance or I shall be forced to change it for you." Christopher did not relent. "Perhaps permanently."

Christopher knew he was no match for the chevalier, but wished to earn a measure of respect. With softened features he spoke up. "The Guise Princes of Lorraine had indeed made an alliance with la Paussion?"

"With your uncles here, too."

Christopher was rocked to the core by that, yet replied icily. "I should hear that from you Uncle Merline."

"Christopher, yes this is true."

The young firebrand spit at his uncles, but could not help hitting a priestly bystander as well. Chevalier du Lay rose up and leaped upon the table facing down the young Millet. Christopher got up and backed away but the chevalier calmly dropped down from the table where Christopher once was and stalked him. One sharp back hand followed by another.

"I have pledged my fealty to Duke Francois de Guise. I defend his honor and that of his clients. Do you yield."

"I do." Christopher said stunned. He had never seen chivalry like this except for in his books. Fealty was supposed to be dead. Christopher sat quietly and listened to Claude explain the intriguing situation.

The general nature of the exchange was a noble title to the seigneury of Laon, if la Paussion could oust Phillipe and convert a majority of the protestant subjects. However Claude doubted that he could accomplish the task without aid from an influential protestant family such as the Millets. Robert was to court Marie properly and apply a general positive pressure for at least her conversion. Claude and his uncles had maintained friendly relations for many years, and were convinced of this opportunity to become a second family in Laon. They had been preparing to convert themselves, and apply pressure on Jean.

Robert's inexplicable hatred for Maurice was not truly understood. The young man had also been working to usurp Claude, such that the claim to Laon began with the son and not the father. The boycotts and general escalation of matters were all Robert's doing.

Uncle Merline leaned in and spoke directly to Christopher now as if they were alone. "The Millet family now has an opportunity." He tapped his finger firmly onto the table. "Not to become the second family, but the noble house of Laon. House de Guise has agreed to change the name on the scrolls from la Paussion, to Millet."

"Conversion of the entire remaining house is of course required." The priest added. He waited for Christopher to face him without hatred. Borges got what he waited for and continued. "If you can convince Jean and Marie to return then they too would convert, if not you are to disown them and demand they change their name."

Claude stated bluntly yet with a tinge of horror. "You will also marry my daughter and betroth your first daughter to my distant nephew who is now of age two."

Of course, Claude la Paussion needed something out of this accord.

"I decline your offer Monseigneur Paussion."

"In that case you shall remain a guest for a short while, but surely you will soon be freed to go."

Priest Borges inquired further. "A man with no prospects and no family. He would most likely fall in with the next chauvre de sois band he happened upon—"

"Which is why we also must consider your lawful execution," the chevalier stated frankly.

"Tell me sir du Lay, if I were to become a client to lord Guise, would you defend me with such vigor?"

"To my dying breath lad."

Uncle Merline proposed that a decision need not be made that very day, and it was agreed that Christopher should ponder awhile.

Christopher and the Millet uncles retired to their wing to speak privately. His uncles explained that only his father was so adamant about remaining a protestant. They valued the status of the Millet house and rationalized that un foi, one faith, would save France from being plunged into bloody civil war. Christopher also argued along national lines reminding them that de Guise were foreign princes. Uncle Merline posited that a hundred years earlier it would have made no difference.

Christopher Millet fell to his knees and clutched upon his necklaced cross. He thought solely about only one question as he fell into slumber. He awoke with the words to pose his lord. Christopher asked Jesus if perhaps this new world that was emerging, was not folly and fraught with error. Aloud too, "Jesus tell me, should the chapel be returned to holy mass, the nation back to a kingdom, causes back to fealty?"

He heard noises of chatter and looked outside his window. There she was, Lisbeth la Paussion and two maid hands attending her stroll. His uncles, also imparted some familial praise upon him. He was told he had grown much, seen much, and done much since they last laid eyes upon him. They told him that he was a man now and men make choices. How long he wondered had it been since Lisbeth laid eyes upon him, surely when he was still a boy. Something stirred within. Christopher and Lisbeth Millet, Lords of Laon. She was around seven years older but he calculated that she would now see him as a strong man. A man of action and honor and duty. Time to find out.

"Ladies, lady Lisbeth. I am not sure if you remember me, I am Christopher Millet."

"I know you Christopher. There was a time when my brother and yours used to pal around."

"Now they are both gone, I am sorry for your loss."

"Yes condolences to you also Christopher." Lisbeth wished to begin the courtship on pragmatic terms. "The games our families play, somebody always loses."

Christopher was surprised by the break in etiquette, yet she had long been a woman. "Somebody wins, too."

Lisbeth ushered her hand maids to allow them some private talk. The pair walked to the other side of the court but remained close enough to witness as was only proper. "How do we win then Christopher?"

"My lady?" He was off to a poor start. Men make choices.

"How would we, as husband and wife, emerge as victors?"

"We should be Baron and Baroness." Christopher almost believed his own boldness, but it sounded absurd.

"Laon is a seigneury."

Christopher looked around casually. "It looks like a barony to me."

"That is a start. If you were to propose to me, and if I was to accept, how would we achieve this?"

Christopher was taken aback by her liberalism. What to do? "First off Lisbeth, if I were to propose, you would accept. On the second, I would accomplish my quest by any means that arose. I am not much for planning."

Now it was Lisbeth's turn to be awed. She had not let on, but she had noticed him many times since he'd grown into manhood. Strong and dark, unlike his brother. She was excited at the prospect of this man living up to her expectations; had been so ever since father had confided in her that a match between them could transpire. If her silly brother continued with his schemes, father would initiate the alternative plan of offering the title to Christopher Millet, and herself the prize. Attached would be a marriage arrangement. If Robert did not heed, he would be shut out completely. She thought of the time she pleasured herself dreaming of the youngest chauvre de sois ever. Christopher Millet racing to save the poor maidens from their evil captors.

"May I expect such a proposal?"

"I feel inclined to be honest with you Lisbeth. I find you to be exceedingly beautiful. I would very much like to court you further. I warn you not to fall in love with me, for if I decline this offer it could very well cost me my head."

"You would choose death over being my husband?"

"I may very well choose death over dishonor."

"Christopher, will you take me horseback riding tomorrow?"

"Yes, a thousand times yes. But I doubt your father would allow it."

"Leave my father to me. That chevalier may be at our stalk, but it will be allowed."

Indeed the next day they rode. Christopher and Lisbeth were glad to feel the wind at their backs and not think about all the seriousness of life. For Christopher, the ride was a chance to show off his riding skills that had much improved under Herndon. He was disappointed when he realized how easily the two pages stalked their pace. He was in a new world. These were men who dedicated their lives to the field. Christopher would first have to match off with the chevalier's pages before he could compete with the gendarme.

For Lisbeth, the ride was an opportunity to chase danger yet again. Another test perhaps.

The pair, and the chaperones, reached a gully and an apple tree. The horses had their rests and Lizbeth had her games. She picked an apple and approached her prey.

"I am curious about your reformed faith, is that one of the dishonors you fear."

"Remaining protestant is the least of my concerns."

"Do you protestants believe in Adam and Eve?" She toyed with the apple playfully.

"We do. Why have you been talking to snakes?"

She giggled but gave no immediate response, only a slithering sound as she flicked her tongue around the apple in mimicry of the serpent. Christopher was aroused, she could tell. "I shall hand you this apple and make you an offer. If you accept the offer then take a bite, if you reject me, then cast it away." She handed him the apple.

"I am all ears."

"I offer you a way to keep your honor and have me. Take me now, or whatever moment you deem fit and let us escape. Together we could outrun these runts or you should have to defeat them. Once away, you could take me there in body and soul. Once your conquest complete, you could discard me or marry me after all. We could be protestants or lords or peasants or whatever you wish."

He made a motion to speak, but she pressed three fingers to his lips. "Don't speak. Just bite; or throw."

Christopher was excited beyond all imagination. He never knew such a woman could exist. They were matched and equal in so many regards. He was going to marry her, he decided. He was going to accept the offer. A whole new world was opening to him and he was ready to navigate with high adventure. His family was dead. Father dead, he winced. Sister, gone forever. Maurice now a ghost.

He handed her back the apple. "I choose another option—"

"You must—"

Now it was his fingers' turn to feel the sweetness of her lips. "Does your Catholic bible read the same as mine? Genesis. Your desire shall be contrary to your husband, but he shall rule over you."

He had done it again. Twice in as many days he had won her heart. "Christopher, whatever you choose, know that a man of your immense honor is what I have dreamed of my entire life. Had you betrayed your honor, yesterday or today, my affections for you should surely have withered. I swear to you I will never question you again. I only have one final question to ask. Is the betrayal of a misplaced or expired honor; not honorable?"

Chapter Fifteen

March 25, 1560

Mons, Belgium

For Marie this part came easy, obedience to her father was important. God, father, and husband; only the order could get muddy. There was little conflict within her with regard to her father. The pain in her jaw and stomach still stung with a loathing of Robert. She had forsaken her father for a man. A grave sin she would need to repent for. Despite it all, she found herself mourning Robert. Jan's blows and words were a two-fold blessing for her. Janeau gifted her a seed of redemption and the finality of Robert's life. She was almost convinced that Robert's cruel words at the end were lies. Robert, now muted eternally, gave Marie permission to believe his final insults a façade.

Robert lay dead now. Marie need not kill him metaphorically as he simply was dead. If her devotion to the Paussion prince was misguided, it no longer mattered. Pit for pat, the present truth filled Marie's head with purpose. All that mattered now was father. As it should have been all along. As it had been her whole life before the affair. Her dear father writhed in pain. Jean's left leg and right arm were broken.

Miraculously they made it to Mons, Belgium - to a reformed church now working as a hospital. Wounded refugees from France and their own rebels nearly filled the structure. War was not official in France nor the low countries. Tell that to these people. Maries' father and her niece were all

she had left in the world. She found herself concerned with nothing else but their safety.

Baby Mary had been fretting all through the evening, and Marie suspected the change of blankets was the culprit. Some of the volunteer ladies were less sympathetic to the foreigners than the others. Mary knew that a particular hag had doled them out uncleaned linen. She was frantically inspecting the blankets inch by inch, seeking out the source and figuring what the fabrics were lousy with.

The nurses had been complaining about this woman for several days straight. She had been desperately attempting to block entry into the church hold. Rats of course, could find their way in, and this crazed French lady was deathly afraid that their mere presence in small numbers posed imminent threat to her baby girl and her father. She was lately stalking the perimeter by stacking rocks upon any crevice she deemed a vulnerability. Now that she had taken to accusing some nurses of not washing the blankets, a task they worked tirelessly at, the gals were running out of patience.

Marie caught a glimpse of a scurrying rat. They are carrying disease. It took my mother and now they will get my father. She grimaced and thought about what more she could do to eradicate the danger. Something else glimpsed. It was a glimmer from a surgeon's saw. The wielder was heading straight for her father.

Can't leave him alone for a minute Marie exclaimed inwardly. She rushed over and physically blocked the 'surgeon' from removing father's arm. "Stop," she said in a rudimentary Dutch. She called over back to the French nurse who could translate. The translator shot an annoyed glance back at Marie. They are all against us here.

"What is there to translate? It is as we explained to you before if the arm does not come off he could die."

Marie shot back, "As I explained to you I am still praying on it. The lord's will shall be done."

In addition to her neuroticism, the others were growing tired of her preachiness. "Fine, we have plenty of patients to care for."

Marie pondered on the confusing messages from the lord. What if he lost his arm? For some inexplicable reason she sensed the losing of a limb was more dreadful. She felt the hand of Jesus upon her, she felt she knew the arm must be saved.

Just that moment her own arm was touched by a man. It was the newcomer who arrived alone just that day. A Frenchman, he was singing a miracle into the ears of a believer.

"I am a doctor, I overheard, may I?"

Baby Mary was now crying at full pitch and Marie was terrified to see a nurse holding her. She wanted to rush back over and save the babe from these frightful harpies, but the doctor's touch turned to a slight grip on her arm.

"Let me go at once!"

While releasing her arm, "May I suggest you let them care for your child while we look after your father?" The doctor had a calming presence on Marie, and she saw that she was being pulled apart. "I have observed you today, I think you may be in a state my dear. Can you tell me what happened to your father?"

"We were running through a thick forest, escaping from men-at-arms, and he…" Marie broke down in an uncontrollable cry. "A pit, he fell into a pit."

"Marie is it?"

"Yes."

"Will you please go to my cot and get some sleep. Your child and father are being taken care of."

Marie laid out on the gentleman's cot worrying about the different ways more harm could fall upon her father. She tried to rise, but found the will of the body unmoved. She heard no cries from Mary and could muster no more of her own. With the hand of Jesus still upon her, she slept. The sun shined when she slumbered and it shined again when she awoke on the next day. Marie sensed that a terrible nightmare was behind her, knowing she was still in a strange land surrounded by strangers. The nightmare had ended all the same.

The doctor had been working for over thirty hours. It had become apparent to all that he was the most skilled healer and had been unceremoniously thrust into the chief position. He was notified that Marie had awaken and promptly returned to his own cot.

"What is your father's name?"

"Jean Millet."

"Jean Millet shall keep his arm."

Marie beamed inside, but only nodded in gratitude to the doctor. She needed to control her emotions, she could see that clearly now. Like a lioness she would look after her father and niece. A lioness who need not roar so much.

"The broken bones were not set properly. The arm was reset but the broken leg will not heal properly, he shall have a limp."

"The witches," a roar began to form.

"Now Marie, you must understand that everyone here has been doing their best. These are mostly volunteers you see."

"I see, of course I see it now."

"Your father is nearly out of his delirium and you shall be able to talk soon."

"I shall see to Mary now, then I should report back."

"Report?"

"To be trained. By her," Marie pointed at the nurse who was the object of such deranged ire. She knew that she would seek redemption with these ladies. They not only had hearts of the lioness, but skills to heal. If they would have her, she too would like to gain healing hands.

Chapter Sixteen

April 5, 1560

Chatillon Coligny

The weathercock, perched high atop the western spire, portended a northerly wind mustering a season's end encore. Through loop holes, sturdy rope drew taut between the two central round towers. Fastened to the rope, banners of great houses gusted to and fro. Nothing could detract the bookman from gaped awe. Such thick banners, could only be shaken by storm. Nicolas spotted the grounds worker's sheds splayed off to the side, daring any onlooker to be distracted from the magnificent palace long enough to consider the mammoth task of maintaining such a building. He could not even imagine the chateau as once being a dreary old castle or even constructed of any of its remaining bastion, which of course it was. This was northern gothic wrestling with southern renaissance. He beheld a wonder of light, openness, and detailed decorations without nullifying the inherent mystery of figures, such as perched gargoyles.

Nicolas was met by his host, Lord Admiral Coligny himself near the center of the esplanade. A few servants hurried past to gather his cases from the carriage. The bookman considered himself a man of words, but he bumbled out such an awkward introduction to which the admiral replied, "Please don't mind me, take it all in."

The steps of the entrance were made for Plato's giants. As he ascended to the raised platform and passed through a

portal he dared never dream, he looked up at massive chandeliers of such gloss that even the candles seemed to burn a cleaner white than ordinary. The flames too were more illuminating somehow. "But how do the servants clean them?"

Coligny was keen to explain, "Ah, see those chains, follow the links through the loop holes and down to that lever. It comes down about chest high, they can really get in there."

He was given the quick tour, but what made the most lasting impression was the great hall of windows from which the expanse of the estate radiated. One was not sheltered from nature, but was rather within its epicenter.

"What is your judgement of Chatillon Coligny?"

He, still not fully with his wits, relied on his ability to quote. "Alberti would say that if a single thing, no matter how minute, were added or removed…the whole would become lesser for it."

"Avon had judged rightly, you are well read, exceedingly so."

"To the Catholics we are all buried in books, yet I do promise to posit one original thought before I take my leave. In fact, I may have one such thought just now."

"Do go on," the admiral prodded.

"I wonder if this great hall could be the central point for your entire estate? Though not a free-standing structure itself, through these great windows one could estimate we are nearly equidistant from the woods in any direction."

"Perhaps that is so."

"I stand in awe at the openness, somewhat akin to standing at an abyss."

"I don't mind telling you Nicolas that I shall be stealing away with your descripts and dazzling many a future guests." The name Nicolas was used for the first time without irony. A symbolic death of Maurice Millet. "Do give me one more," the admiral pleaded.

Nicolas de Piefuin pondered and allowed the thoughts to come freely. He had recently learned to cease holding his tongue and let his words flow. The admiral, he had insinuated, could be a macabre man. He focused in on the ends of one of the chateau wings and marveled at the distinctness of form. "Those articulated corners are brilliant, almost impossible for man to contrive, if not for seeing them with my own eyes at present. Those edges I could imagine are sharp enough to split skull. One of a catholic priest perhaps."

Coligny feigned dismay, but perhaps secreted new plans for his newest provocateur. Uses for his subjects dripped in and out the pool of his grand plan, and there was no shortage of ways he could manipulate this low born. "Now now, we are on a quest for moderation. Perhaps I shall allow it to be the head of a Spanish priest."

"Earlier you said that Avon had been right about me. Is he truly passed on?"

"Yes, I am afraid so."

Nicolas expressed sorrow and regret at his hesitancy but the Admiral only advised to concentrate on the particulars of the dilemma at hand:

"Though Charles Avon certainly was executed that night for treason, he was not identified precisely nor confirmed to be one of The Ten, or one of the Huguenots. However, there are still whispers about my missing broker being involved. Though my head is still attached there are no doubts about my involvement. Lord Conde may even be arrested as the ringmaster of the Amboise conspiracy."

"Lord Admiral, I know not of any of these persons or matters you speak of."

"You are now essentially replacing Avon here, that comes attached with suspicion. One thing I can think of to do is distance you from me. We shall be using your steward as a go between. Lehman may appear to be a just another servant, but I count him among my many agents. He will brief you. Pressure is on you to make deals right away showing that it is your merit alone which allows you to curate my library. The Dowager's ball will be your first opportunity."

Admiral de Coligny led Nicolas to the apartment which was to be his. Footsteps clicked smartly on perfect glass stone. The admiral's murmurs echoed and Nicolas could not help feel somehow greater walking upon a perfect floor. Coligny would point out a fresco here and a coffered ceiling there, as if any pointing was necessary. The Chateau, if empty of living souls would teem with life anyway. Feminine figures posed succulently in their shells of soft marble. There were also molesting little demons poking about. Stone maidens were depicted with plump sensuality. Nicolas extended his hand to touch merely the mantle where the marble toes grounded. The admiral gestured that Nicolas could free his groping hands, by himself embracing a full thigh of one of the maidens. The bookman followed suit and reached in between her cheeks, mimicking a horned devil-man.

A new method of study was presenting itself. Here the nobles could frolic with the subjects. Commit the sin of adultery vicariously through the wicked as Coligny was demonstrating to Nicolas wordlessly, how to commit the artificial sin to an almost cathartic release. The admiral could see in the bookman's expressions and sounds that he was feeling the art. Christianity was a living theology. The next fresco objectified the female figures in a different light. Here the women wrestled with various mythical beasts while contending not with horny men, but suckling babes who grasped for their love. In either fresco, the females were clawed at, pulled, and dragged. Nicolas took the lead and pretended to nurse from his mother. Coligny made himself the jealous brother who yanked at mother for his turn.

By the time he was finally left to his apartment, his new home, he dropped onto the finest bed he ever imagined and knew at once he was going to be cured of his lamentation over his long-lost sack of straw.

Lehman was to be the bookman's attendee. The trim middle-aged valet would not be a personal servant, but would check in on

Nicolas frequently. Under that guise Lehman would serve as a go-between for the Admiral. With impeccable style he opened and closed cupboards indicating to Nicolas where he would unpack his belongings.

"Really I should do it myself."

"You are not the first commoner I have attended to. I know you mean well, but in this place, we are all here for a purpose."

Returning to his own purpose, Nicolas inquired, "Tell me first of Catherine de Medici. For she is my quarry and I should like to concoct a plan accordingly." Lehman was sorting clothes into three piles. One pile for formal wear, another for daily court life, and a third which was deemed inappropriate for any situation. He watched most of his clothes end up in the last pile and none in the first.

"The primary thing you must understand about her is that she never puts herself first, yet always puts herself second."

Nicolas noted, "Quite precise."

"Her husband, the late king, was the center of the universe to her. Now it is her first son Francis. And next it would be Charles if Francis is as sickly as I hear. From her heliocentric view as a Queen, all are expendable if it benefits the current king. This is true for her loved ones and enemies alike."

"Perhaps my stratagem should be based on her devotion to King Francis, and put things in light that benefit her son if not her."

"Partially right. Remember I said she always comes second. She views herself as complementary to the king and as such, sometimes mother knows best."

"I see now I must tread quite carefully. I can never offend the king to her obviously, but I may also need to dangle fruits for her eyes that benefit the king nonetheless."

Lehman was neatly folding clothes, asking, "What do you know of her upbringing?"

"Nothing."

"Just like her husband she spent much of her youth as something of a hostage. Both of her parents were dead within mere months after her birth. She was raised by a great aunt and her Strozzi cousins were essentially her siblings. She holds the Strozzi clan dear to this day. When her uncle, the pope, died; the Medici lost their new duchy of Urbino. Nobility stripped from them before the inked name in the scrolls could truly dry."

"Ah I see now, this is why she was hated here in France and that many were appalled that King Francis I married his son so low." A commoner in lord's clothing was still a commoner. An irony doubled as Lehman held up a doublet, jerkin, and cloak. "Am I supposed to wear each of those at once?"

"Yes, and yes about the tradesman's daughter. Barren for a decade did not help. And then ten children out of nowhere, a sure sign of a witch." Lehman looked at the new library curator for a thought.

"An Italian friend once told me that us French have so many names for lady Catherine and that they are all in error."

Lehman was pleased that Nicolas had at least someone in his previous life that understood matters beyond common thought. "Yes, I am afraid her reputations are each flawed in their own manner. You see at least twice in her life she was in grave danger back in Italy. First when Pope Leo died. Second when her other uncle Pope Clement watched the sack of Rome under his watch. When the Medici were at their most vulnerable, the other great families of Florence had Catherine under their 'care.' She faced execution and even being sold to soldiers who would forever rob Pope Clement of his most valuable bachelorette. There were other times when she was placed in a convent controlled by more sympathetic Florentines, and there she met other important women of elder age. These women were also confined to the convent, being hostages as well to whichever their current political plight was. It was from these women who she truly learned to endure such a precarious upbringing. Now here in France, her chief rival had been Diane de Poitiers, King Henry's lover."

"What should you mean King Henry's lover?"

"Nicolas, please don't tell me that such a quest has been entrusted to a gullible bumpkin."

"Perhaps that is precisely what the admiral has contrived. I sir am under the impression that our Kings and Queens are pure and noble, truly anointed by God to caesarian thrones. If I were to wonder privately that the King would have a secret lover, then I would also assume it were a secret."

"No, quite wrong. Lady Catherine has always had to endure life at court with her husband's favorite consort openly known as his true love."

"How did she endure all of this. Grown up as a hostage in Florence, and held responsible for the *mesalliance* here in France."

Lehman continued with the history lesson. "Yes, the mesalliance years were especially dangerous for Queen Catherine. Her Uncle, Pope Clement died without ever delivering any Italian holdings to King Francis I. Not Urbino, not Milan, not any of the Italian ambitions, obtained. Furthermore, most of the dowry was never paid. Many Frenchmen those years declared that the marriage should be nullified and the alliance with the late pope declared a mesalliance. Truly, all King Francis received for the marriage was four new French cardinals, one of which actually reformed. Ha. Yes, the black witch could have easily lost her head in those days."

"I think all these years I have imagined Queen Catherine in my mind, I may have even conflated her to be like my own mother who I lost to the plague."

"I am not that much different than you. I am a mere servant, but I have been employed by the Admiral for near thirty years now and I think I could no longer relate with common folk ever again. Don't get me wrong, for the servant's quarters is a place where we remain humble, but truly the noble men and high ladies we attend do rub off a little. I don't know your mother and truly I don't know Catherine. But I highly doubt they are similar, which you should be grateful for."

"What do you know of Catherine personally?"

"I know some people well enough that know her well enough, and the descripts have been quite consistent. King Francis I never gave the people her head on a spike because he adored her. More importantly, he respected her and saw a valuable matron for the House Valois for times such as these with young King Francis II lacking the energy to truly rule alone. Catherine is known to be spirited, quick witted, and physically tough. She has grace and is well mannered and never betrays her high status. Her husband, King Henry, may have loved another, but he never would have placed Diane de Poitiers above Catherine politically. Catherine de Medici is a scion of her great Florentine house, truly some of her instincts may be in that hot Italian blood. The Medici bide their time. Methodically she has risen to now be the Guise faction's biggest threat. She even got the last laugh with Diane as she was ordered to return royal jewelry, which had been gifted to her from our late king."

"Quite petty."

"Perhaps. But Nicolas you must understand this above all else. She needs money most of all at this junction. Not only are you to gift her your Machiavelli letter, but any deals that indirectly fund her shall grant you an audience."

The ball for the Dowager was magnificent in splendor. Lehman told him that her name was Lady Emily Smolliet. She was a dowager countess of some county which Nicolas was unfamiliar with. The dowager was a handsome woman with a plain sturdiness much like Catherine de Medici. She was the highest-ranking bachelorette that had visited Chatillon Coligny in some time, and the Admiral would not miss the opportunity to throw for her a grand ball. Grand it was, as was it gluttonous, in Maurice's eyes. The exquisite architecture of Chatillon enchanted him. Still he felt remorse for the starving folk of Laon, who could be restored to blush skin by only a portion of the evening's viands.

There was a stir of men surrounding and following the dowager nearly always. Some were young, some old, some were handsome, and some were objectively ugly. Yet they were all nobility. Your blood had to be the right hue of blue to even be a part of her train.

That is what Lehman called it, and to which Nicolas snickered at the absurdity of the astuteness of such a moniker. For where she went they followed. The randy bachelors did not form in a proper queue, but there was a rhythm in play. The more you made her laugh or blush, the closer to her person you could remain. Offering a statement met with Lady Smolliet's disdain, allowed those from the outer ring to rectify her good spirits by ousting the latest offender. Of course, she could dismiss or call upon certain gentlemen to enter the vicinity. And she did. Not by explicit command, but by the magic of her implications. For she was Aphrodite and men's ears suckled on the vibrations of her notes.

Nicolas was able to gather as much because he dared a reconnaissance of the train. He tarried about ever so nudgingly and was given some latitude due to the peculiarity of the situation. I am a nobody, that was plain to see. A nobody should not even be in the ante room, yet there he was, also plain to see. The bluebloods had themselves a paradox to solve. Were they to act on their prejudice and oust the ruffian on the strength of his general anonymity? Or would they risk being excoriated if he turned out a distant Duke? I could even be an imperial prince travelling incognito. Nicolas understood what bewildered the men of the outer ring and credited that for the most likely explanation that a plain outsider got so close to the dowager.

In that time and place, it felt like something he could get away with and he instinctually made his move before the men of the train could converse enough for a belligerent to conclude that he were indeed a nobody and deserving a thrashing, perhaps that would even entertain her ladyship.

When a debate about humanism erupted among some ranks of the train, he took to interceding immediately. Both giving him the initiative for his own grand entrance to court and a chance to regale his ladyship and indeed all present with his own thoughts on the matter at hand which was specifically the blasphemous writings of Rabelais, 'The Unbeliever'. But how could he strike a balance and make not an enemy so quickly? This thought was of the fleeting kind as Nicolas acted quite without forethought.

Lehman watched in frozen terror. Nicolas mingled not, yet somehow made it to the nearness of the dowager. He had not even talked to another soul and was introducing himself to Lady Emily.

"Lady Emily Smolliet, I am Nicolas de Piefuin, the curator of the library of Coligny."

Emily blushed at the secondhand embarrassment she felt for the poor fellow. "Is there nobody here to announce you monsieur?" snickered an outer ring gent. Her admirers shuffled harder, nearly shoving a way to the interloper.

"Only our host Admiral de Coligny, but he seems quite busy so I decided to correct the notion that Rabelais is any kind of unbeliever." The wrestling then ceased as the original speaker would have to defend himself.

The Lady Dowager introduced the gentlemen claimant, "Monsieur Nicolas, this is Gaultien and he quite disagrees with your conclusion."

Gaultien wore more articles of clothing than Nicolas had ever seen piled upon a single person. The entire ballroom presently contained more decadence than he had seen in a lifetime, and he hoped should suffice for the rest of his days. Such waste, he thought.

"That, Monsieur Gaultien is precisely why I am here. If you should like we could visit the library tomorrow and I could—"

Gaultien now commented directly with Nicolas. "I need not be instructed on how to read from a humanist sophist."

"I am a humanist. In fact, my students and I were speaking recently at the brook how we do indeed envy the Greek scholars, but only to the point of where their paganism saddens us. We shall make them envy us. Best of both worlds. We admit to being anti-clerical and would seek to revitalize the church and renew its Christian teachings without the popish hierarchy and rituals."

"Just say it man, to REFORM."

"I must concede, yes, we wish for all our Christian churches to be reformed. But non-believers, nay. Belief in God and Christ always comes first. The humanists only wander at the mystery perhaps more than the scholars of two hundred years ago, but after allowing our rational thought to meander, it always concludes with reaffirming our faith. In short, we would not know how to unbelieve. We are all lost without God."

Chatillon's new library curator received a general applause for the oration as Emily ventured, "Could I meet with you at the library tomorrow?"

Before he could respond Gaultien turned a purplish red, "You dare to intercede on church authority and to condescend us!"

He wisely extended an olive branch and wanted this first discussion to be as neutral as possible. "I do apologize for my enthusiasm. Please make admittances as I have never been in such august company. Reformed I may be, refined I am not. The lessons in the library shall go both ways, clearly I have much to learn from you." The ultra-catholic was trapped, he had to publicly agree. Despite his best intentions, Nicolas had made his first enemy.

"But now tell us of your world, the common world," a man said.

"Oh yes you must, your appointment being quite fresh," now from a woman.

"We are a happy folk. The women dance to the rhythm of the day. A babe suckling with another crawling about bringing oohs and ahhs to all the passerbys. And the scene is laid to bare because she must open the shutters to allow the sun to beam its happy shine upon her home. We do not have such windows as these. I have never seen so many. You can plainly mistake it for the lord's heavenly sky itself."

"But do the women work?"

"Of course they work you twit!"

"Ah yes my lady they do all that I described above, while taking turns at the spindle."

"I hear they work in groups."

"Quite so, it is a marvelous dance indeed. One may bask while the other bleats and yet another turns the wheel laying out ever more fine French cloth."

"How dreadful."

"Not at all, you see they do not toil. Their love and labor are so intertwined that for us poor villeins, they be two primary ingredients for life itself. Surely I have described our women caught in a dance, but it is their husbands singing in the fields. Men woo them at five and ten o'clock, with notes from a musette and into the peak of their godly marriages, the melody continues, echoing from field through brook and village."

The dowager was pleased to hear of country life. "A truly happy lot and if I may say, due to no small spark from your reformed spirit."

The curator led with a favorite psalm of his people before insisting to hear the favorites of the Catholics.

O come. Let us sing to the lord, let us make a joyful noise to the rock of saluation.

At Nicolas' apartment he met Lehman for a synopsis on the evening. "What is the matter? I think I did quite well," he said to a stone-faced Lehman.

"You did Nicolas," replied the attendant. "Perhaps a bit hasty and somewhat condescending with Gaultien, but you did quite well for your debut."

"I am to meet with lady Emily tomorrow—"

"I have sad news for you sir. I hate to be the one to tell you as we have only known each other for a few days—"

"Tell me, what is it?" Nicolas knew it had to be about his family, for what else could it have regarded.

"Your family has not reported to the expected destination in the Netherlands, and by all accounts were not picked up as arranged." He struggled to understand. An air of dumbness confounded him. "All we know for certain is that they are not where they were expected to be, and have thus far not placed letters here at Chatillon, which makes sense because they would only have learned of your destination upon arriving at their own."

"Makes sense? Lehman, none of this makes sense. My entire family is missing, is that what you are telling me...and why should my father have been told Chatillon be not where I was intended?"

"That I do not know. But I can only gather that it was so your family could not tell if they were captured. Otherwise don't you see with our present knowledge we would have to have you removed immediately. Nicolas you are in the midst of a most dangerous affair."

The curator was panged deeply, that Lehman could tell, but the Admiral was his lord, and he was tasked with turning this commoner into a seasoned courtier but before a season. "Your wife, child (Lehman grimaced a mumble), father, and sister are unaccounted for, but your brother is not."

"Good. Where is Christopher?" said an older brother with great hope.

"We have just received confirmation that Christopher, along with the entire remaining Millet line, have converted to Catholicism at the Laon mass. And your brother is also engaged to marry Lisbeth la Paussion."

Nicolas felt freedom in the end. He took in the news of his missing family, and his brother's betrayal. Maurice was dead now. He only lived in a world of pleasure and deceit. For the first time he had nothing to live up to.

The first person at the library on the following day was a senior member of the moderate politique. He wanted to talk Rabelais, but Coligny did not own 'Pantagruel'. He told him if he donated it to the library, they could study it together and he would give a good word to Emily for the suitor. In this manner, the schemes of the curator had begun.

Then he ate all that was offered to him for brunch. He would meet the courtiers on their terms, that of gluttony. He worried that his brother knew of this identity and had already turned him in. Looking around, the library curator realized he had never seen so many fat people gathered in one place. Surely they were not always obese. Surely they must be unrecognizable to their former selves. Nicolas took a giant bite of roasted duck breast and let his mouth slowly chew the succulent sauces and juices. A new name shall not be sufficient, he should need a new appearance, too. Glasses of wine were gulped down greedily and the others took notice. This new curator, this country sophist, was no longer partaking meekly of the chateaux fruits. Perhaps he was coming down from his pedestal of austerity.

Chapter Seventeen

April 15, 1560

Laon, France

Herndon reflected on that day when Jan and Christopher sacrificed themselves. His scouts had only spotted the men at arms. The archers reported back later that indeed there were gendarme in pursuit.

Imagine that, gendarme knights hunting the likes of me, the wily captain thought. With such a cavalry involved, he now would have to expand his tactical capabilities. Herndon wanted to add the new horsemen he had been hearing about. Reiters would be an excellent addition to his band. Herndon sat and stared at blank parchment dejectedly. He listened for any approach to his tent. He then began the painstaking process of writing Danilo, explaining that he had been unable to solve the latest encrypted letter, and as such, had yet to read the contents of said letter. He had asked that it be re-sent in the method that he was comfortable with. Then he explained his desire to learn more about these German Reiters.

Danilo, instead of writing back, simply sent back three German Reiters and a scribe. Herndon was continually in awe over the quality of friends Danilo could make. In his relatively short time in Germany, the old courier now had minor influence with several German princes. Most of the noble houses of Deutschland supported the cause of the French protestants, even though in Germany, the reformation was styled as Lutheran, and in France, it was Calvinist. Aside from

coreligionists sticking together, primarily the Germanic nobility needed to attempt to contain the dominance of the Spanish Empire. The Habsburgs and their unstoppable monolithic machine indeed were the driving force behind wiping the reformation off the face of the earth. Herndon was learning from learned men like Danilo, and the captain's new scribe, that economics played perhaps even a larger role than dogma. What the empire truly feared was the acumen and industrious spirit that the protestant followers exhibited. The papal ecclesial body could find no religious directive from the reformed churches that explicitly instilled this core value, but it pervaded nonetheless. The Spanish Empire, like all empires, wobbled under the weight of her administration. The protestant avarice and good faith dealings, looked to produce nation-states that would thrive economically. The bourgeois had been knocking at the door of royalists for centuries now, and the protestant culture seemingly held the key to breaking it down.

The men, all protestants, made valuable additions to the chauvre de sois. Reiters trained some, but his band desperately needed war worthy horses. The scribe was an asset, too. His first job was to translate the old letter from Danilo.

Herndon was overjoyed to learn that Christopher yet lived, but devastated in knowing of his betrayal. Their friendship was one thing, but to join the oppressive Catholics was another. The scribe was no stranger to the blistering hatred of men enraged by their hearing urgent letters translated. For Herndon, however, rage was a rare emotion. A pot of half cold soup was swiped, dropping its fish gruelled contents onto the wooden planked floor. Herndon burned with fury. It had been a long time since he had been hurt by treachery. He then slammed both fists down onto the now empty table sending a rush of pain up his wrists.

"I can finish the translation later, Herndon," said the scribe.

"No!" He raged on, then kicked the legs of the table which only produced another wave of pain to his shins. He looked at the mess on the floor, that he would need to clean up, and felt his various new injuries. *Well, I am certainly the loser of this fight.* Herndon chuckled to himself and the scribe came to know that the jolly fellow may anger occasionally, but his happy spirit was never far behind. "No please, I want to know everything that Danilo has learned about what happened in the forest that day."

The scribe continued with the events in the forest, as Danilo in his ways came to know and transmit faithfully. "You have come to know not only were there men-at-arms in your pursuit, but also gendarme. The pair obviously did not stand a chance. Explicit orders were given for Christopher to be taken alive, and so he was. Janeau, however, was cut down mercilessly, though it was said that he fought like a lion. Tales of this simple protestant farmer, his ravaged love, and his fierce vengeance, reach even the Germans." The scribe looked at the captain pointedly. "Danilo also points out the likelihood that the tale has been told tall."

"Nearly all my men are simple farmers. It is time to change that."

These Reiters or 'Black Riders', donned in their blackened armor, operated as a cavalry unit which relied less on melee and more on a short-ranged attack. The primary tactic which Herndon's band was working on tirelessly was thus:

The 'Black Rider' should have two pistols and a sword. The Reiters should then fire a synchronized volley into the enemy line before drawing sword and charging. The Reiters then hack away at infantry in standard melee fashion, but they also look to deploy their most dangerous tactic. The Reiter should use his last pistol shot at any opportunity for a point blank face shot.

The scribe also advanced their communications network. They were now even in contact with the lone survivor of the Ten original Huguenots of the infamous port. The scribe corrected Herndon, explaining that the name derived from an early Swiss Calvinist, Besacon Hugues.

With expansion came risk. And such that a spy of Christopher's had infiltrated and was reporting back on the development of the newly arrived Reiters. The spy was given orders to gauge a chance for an ambush.

Christopher was certain that seigneur Phillipe was aiding Herndon Calais. The chauvre de sois were never trespassing in the forbidden forest, but rather granted exclusive entrance. The young Millet could see that now. He could not yet challenge Phillipe, but he could harry the bandits under the reeve's authority. Christoher realized that he did not need to prove that Lord Phillipe was illegally aiding the bandits, because the lord had to deny it. Therefore, the bandits were either trespassing or they were being harbored. Either way, the new Reeve had the lawful authority to seek public aid in capturing them. The Millets and la Paussion were merely helping, not engaging Seigneur Phillipe directly.

Thinking about the latest error made by his lord, Christopher grew confident that he could overthrow him. Phillipe had relieved Gascon of his duties, *but the fool only promoted another who was loyal to de Guise*, and by extension Christopher and his new wife. With the knowledge of Herndon's tactics, Christopher prepared to ambush his old band.

Strange did not even begin to describe how Christopher felt sitting at the head of the giant conference table. He still was not used to being back at home, if it could be called that. This was the home of his father. The home where he was a child. It was empty without his family. I am an impostor. An impostor for sleeping with his wife in his parent's room. An impostor sitting at this table that his uncles gave for a wedding present. "At this table we shall divide up France between us." But their jests were empty, and now that he sat there, Christopher found he had nothing to offer.

Present at the giant table were the chevalier, Uncle Merline, Uncle Bichtel, Cousin Jacques, Claude la Paussion, and Andre la Paussion. They all sat together, Catholics one and all, and the Millets had even taken their eucharists. Between the back slapping and burps they tore from a roasted pig with their hands until bellies were full. They eventually quieted to sips from jade encrusted cups.

Christopher, feeling ever the figurehead, opened. "I have information that Herndon is expanding his operation and now has three German Reiters. They are conducting drills using those tactics."

Claude said, "When will strike an ambush then, surely you are finished gauging their position?"

"My spy was only just admitted to the chauvre de sois shortly before the Germans arrived, he should be given more time to become embedded."

The chevalier put in, "Christopher, the addition of Reiters is significant. With proper training, horses, and firearms; Herndon would become twice as formidable."

"I only mean that my spy should be given more time, but, I have an ambush plan ready to execute," Christopher lost his courage and began to stutter, "I should not want to be there personally though…"

Chevalier du Lay was surprisingly calm. "Christopher, you have made a pact."

"Killing my friends myself was never part of the pact. The pact is that I give up the information so that it could be used, and that I was to be elevated to nobility, surely that means to delegate."

Now du Lay was red with anger, "Are you learning nothing from our lessons? Honor demands that you lead this first foray to prove to yourself and everyone else here that you are not ashamed!"

Establishing himself as a leader would have to wait, Christopher decided. "I won't do it. I am not ready for that yet." *Soon I must be.*

The men of the giant table, of this new Millet house, looked invariably to the chevalier for judgement, to which du Lay responded. "Very well. Then I shall lead the ambush myself, like a true gendarme. I tell you this Christopher, if the ambush turns out to be a falsity of yours, I shall march directly back here and kill you myself. I would ask for the Duke's forgiveness after."

"I shall be ready soon, just not now. And the ambush really should happen on the morrow. I have become certain that Herndon does not actually trespass the seigneury woods as he would have his band believe. Seigneur Phillipe is allowing him passage, so his route plans are much clearer to me now."

Claude, raising a hand slightly, as if asking permission, "If I may?"

The strangeness of this new reality took shape as Christopher watched Claude la Paussion defer to *him* for permission to speak. "Of course."

"The chevalier will be our true captain in the forest but officially we should be led by the reeve, to bring legality to the confrontation. The action is not against our lord seigneury, rather on behalf of his ancestral hunting grounds."

"Quite right," Christopher concluded. "Officially this will be an action of the new Reeve to clear the forest of bandits. Lord Phillipe must only congratulate us if a capture is made. Capturing Herndon himself would be the happiest of outcomes."

Like natural creatures of the Laon woods, one could barely fathom the band of rebels passing through her lushness. The chevalier fathomed them with ease. Christopher's information was superb, there may be hope for the young lad yet. If the chauvre de sois escaped the trap, Christopher would die.

Du Lay signaled with his fist to the Reeve of Laon that their quarry was snared. The reeve and the chevalier were to call out the chauvre de sois, denouncing them for royal violators. Escape would only be had back across the creek which had presently been flanked by three gendarme and young Jacques Millet stalking as a page in training. The boom of the reeve's call froze the bandits, too long had they run of the woods. "Halt there in the name of the seigneur for you trespass upon his woods!"

Prepared well by Herndon, they scattered each to their own. Only a single bandit was needed to escape the trap, to advise the others that all routes known to Christopher Millet, were known by the enemy. One bandit attempted a glorious pass through the reeve and chevalier. Two other bandits diverged along the creek bank and the other two attempted a retreat across. Quite predictably the charger was thwarted by du Lay with ease. The chevalier simply dismounted and launched himself, a tackler, as in the no-rules ball of his youth. The reeve placed this one under arrest, leaving any other captives quite superfluous. A gendarme across the bank speared his man from twenty sticks and then gave chase to a river runner. The other gendarme bound his quarry, leaving him with Jacques before bounding off.

The ambush was a success. Two captured and three killed in the forbidden woods, in clear violation of ancient laws of the second estate. The pair of bandits were captured and placed under arrest by the reeve.

The capture put the Seigneur of Laon in a difficult position. Phillipe had to come to terms that a second reeve had now betrayed him. Officially however, the reeve acted lawfully. What could be more natural than a reeve policing the noble woods.

Christopher Millet was also on precarious footing. Chevalier du Lay had talked loosely about Jacques' performance, and how maybe he should send notice to Joinville to once again reconsider their candidate for Laon.

Christopher had no choice but to lead the next ambush. The chevalier would accompany them for oversight only and the reeve too would remain behind. No arrests were to be made, only execution. The chauvre de sois needed to comprehend that Laon was lost to them. Without a rebel force in the forest, protestants would lose to the ultra-Catholics if war came.

Once again it was only a small group of bandits and again Herndon eluded the new Millet house. Three slain rebels were left in Phillipe's woods for Herndon to bury. The captain bid adieu to the seigneur and wished him luck. Christopher Millet had removed any outside interference to the question: who had legal claim to the seigneury of Laon? A protestant nobleman? Or a Catholic pretender?

Christopher Millet had rid the town of the chauvre de sois and was quickly becoming a hero to the local Catholics. Soon he would have a legal claim to usurp the seigneury from Phillipe. Phillipe would have to decide whether he would give up his ancestral home freely or put up a fight.

Seigneur Phillipe was livid. The herald seemed to be a bearer of only bad news for over a year now. Or has it been since always? The lord of Laon was beginning to feel his ancestral title slipping away from him. Not since the days of his grandfather had another noble pressed a claim for Laon. Now Phillipe may have to deal with such a claim from Christopher Millet of all people, who everyone knew was not of noble blood. Yet here the herald reported that the brothers Francois and Charles de Guise had already successfully installed several new noble titles in their time as regents and treasurers of France.

Phillipe was beginning to realize just how isolated he had become. He had a faction of supporters he could call upon if he took more of an active role in the Huguenot cause, but he did not want to be a protestant leader. There were also clergymen willing to help suppress the licensure of House Millet, if he only convert to Catholicism, but he did not wish to do that either. A third option in possibility would be that he abjure, and appeal to Francois de Guise to ally with him. There was too much bad blood between the two since the 'Italian Wars' to even consider that, though they were once friends.

The final insult was that he yet again entrusted a friend to the position of Reeve, only to find that he had no friends. The latest reeve had sanctioned an ambush on the chauvre de sois without consent. Rather he led, the yet to be established, House Millet through his woods. Had the reeve suspected that Phillipe was harboring the chauvre de sois, which indeed he had, there were official channels for the reeve to have taken.

Phillipe was going to have to give in on some front because he could no longer defend his land by himself. He owed it to his religion to take up the Huguenot mantle for at least some time until he could retreat back into the isolationism of his tiny kingdom.

The herald attempted to argue with Phillipe as he took down the dictum. Phillipe valued his opinion, but on this matter, he would not be moved. The letter to Admiral de Coligny would declare the following:

Dear Gaspard,

I would ask not for support on the matter of the licensure for an impostor family such as the Millets. I should like to believe that the first estate would not condone such a travesty against our second estate. These ancient traditions of France may prove to be immutable. If, however, the name of Millets shall enter the scrolls, I guarantee that they will be designated as 'unlanded'. I have utter confidence that I could withstand a military assault on my seigneury. However, I would then at that time also be committed to the Huguenot cause.

Let us then begin making accords for such future scenarios. If your forces can come to the aid of Laon on one occasion, then I shall pledge my retinue under my own personal banner at no more than two engagements of your choosing under the Huguenot flag.

Sig. Phillipe

"What do you think Nicolas?" Gaspard wished to know Nicolas' interpretation.

"I don't know what to think Admiral. This is your world. I am not here to tell you what I think, I am here to tell you what I feel."

"You are upset about your family I understand, I am working on it. I will find out where they are."

"I am lost admiral! What am I doing here? This is my first private meeting with you since I arrived and will probably be my last. I have no advice for you on how to respond to Seigneur Phillipe, I am hear to beg my leave. I just want to leave and find my daughter. My daughter is out there all alone somewhere. It is up to me to find her, to guide her."

"I have a young daughter too Maurice. I want to reunite you with all my heart. I would grant your leave here and now, yet my mind tells me that I have a better chance of finding her than you would. My mind also tells me I am worse off without you. The lady dowager is highly impressed with you, and all who seek her favor now understand to seek your favor. I should like to speak with Maurice again. The man of intelligence and rationale. What would Maurice wish?"

"I wish to remain. Yet the longer I go without news on my family, I fear the more you shall lose my intellect and only have my lament."

"How would you judge Seigneur Phillipe?"

"Phillipe wants three things equally. To remain protestant. To keep Laon. To minimize any negative effect on keeping Laon. Therefore he cannot be trusted in our Huguenot cause."

"There you see, you are invaluable to me Nicolas. Do not doubt the efforts I would make to satisfy you. And what of Christopher?"

Maurice was visibly racked to think upon his traitorous brother. "No man in France could speak more truly about his unpredictability. Christopher is daring, and when high adventure calls him he answers. I believe he will take Laon. Besides, Laon, the deep north is a lost cause is it not. Why waste any resources on a lost cause?"

Chapter Eighteen

On December 5, 1560 King Francis II died from an ear infection. The Dauphine Charles IX, being only eleven years old at the time, required yet another regency.

March 15, 1561

Fontainebleu, France

A broad smile escaped the serious Queen's mouth as she purred over the elegant design. Catherine was admiring her royal seal stamped upon the official documentation for her final review. The scepter she held and the phrasing, represented a historical first for France. Being Mother to the king, not merely the Queen Mother, confirmed her status as both *de jure* and *de facto*, Governess of France.

The document she then considered was an appeal. This appeal for withdrawing of request from de Bourbon, pleased her. In her efforts to consolidate this new position, of which France had never seen, she would be no mere regent. Four years until King Charles IX would reach age of majority, perhaps more if he lacked energy as her poor Francis had. Perhaps five years of being a sovereign, lay ahead. In her efforts to consolidate, she made Antoine de Bourbon, Lieutenant-General of France. She also expedited the release of his brother of the blood, Lord Conde. Antoine could not, however, resist the urge to reach further, and so made a

formal request to be inferred sole ruler, in the event of her Governess falling to ill health.

Who did he think she was. Does he not know of the Medici curse of gout? She, as her ancestors, were often of ill health, but always endured to perform their duties. She thought to herself that she could have denied the request. Henceforth disallowing the Bourbon house opportunity to orchestrate a *Florentine malady*, to induce such ill health upon her body. *These men flirt with Florentine ways against a woman with Florentine blood.* No sooner than she would sign the document, some wicked ailment would mysteriously arise. So she counter-schemed. Catherine would not merely deny the request. Rather, she stated that there was simply no need for such measures, as she would *always* be able to perform her duties. Bourbon had no recourse but to formerly withdraw the impertinent request. It was Michel d'Lhopital who she made Chancellor for exactly such issues as that. Her raw Medici political acumen needed to be tempered and concentrated into legal forms for her to properly run the state. The legality of the request was codified such that had she indeed fallen to illness, she could not be discarded. Privately though she surely would allow her Chancellor to make decisions if her condition were dire, as she would never place the realm at risk. *All I do is for my late husband King, and my son Kings, and Dauphines.*

The governess turned her thoughts to the upcoming estates-general. House de Guise of Lorraine would be forced to recognize the authority of this new royal seal as long as her allies remained steadfast. The Constable of France, Lord Montmorency, troubled her only a bit, but could see no other means to pacify the protestant sympathizer.

Lord Montmorency and his nephew, the Admiral de Coligny, were then seen as leaders of the Huguenot movement. In error, the protestants had grown demonstrative under the new regime of Catherine de Medici. Even in the staunchly catholic capital city of Paris, the Huguenots were making their presence known.

The throngs of protestants surrounded a city preacher. Pastor Rohn reveled in the greatness of God and their deliverer, the Governess-Queen Catherine. "The tolerance of the new government has defeated the violent faction of the Guise." The home worshippers as they were called, cheered. A people destined to the sobriquet 'Huguenots'. The reformed embraced the identity and had for so long worshipped in non-traditional places. Atop prairie hills, snuggled in an elder's small home, or stranded in some hillside cavern during heavy rain. The Huguenots committed themselves to continue worshipping in plain places, yet would now do so in the open and no longer in hiding.

Pastor Rohn shouted to his people. "God would not have us worship the grounds. The ground becomes sacred whence true followers pray together with full heart and in un-denying faith." There upon the steps of a most unsuspecting Parisian law office, did Pastor Rohn ascend. The pastor had been summoned to Paris by Abbe de St. Clair to join a catholic-protestant small council, which had successfully suspended the Edict of Re-Education. The small council was then disbanded and Pastor Rohn wandered the streets of Paris.

He had gained a significant following over the year which had passed. Protestant enclaves of Paris still lamented the rape of Roucy. Stories went: "Dozens of cavaliers seized maidens from their homes and carried them out into the fields for an orgy of rape. The men were mercilessly cut down during the mayhem." Such was the way of mythos, and its tendency to exaggerate. The followers of Pastor Rohn had grown even more fanatical now that his sermons were commenced in such places crowded with violent Catholics.

The pastor spoke of Sunday being the Lord's Day - the day of Christ's resurrection. Many followers chirped how the plight of the Huguenots could be compared to the centuries of persecution by the apostolic creed of the Roman Empire. Such were the thoughts of the Parisian learned folk. Christianity was rising from the barbed crown of the papists. Rohn went on preaching, "When a Christian accepts the lord's light, he is then redeemed for eternity." Knees bent to the cobbled road and hands rose high into the air. Eternal damnation be damned by grace.

At that, some of the followers railed against the church for the heaviness of the cross placed upon their flock. There was a catholic in the midst of this rowdy sermon. From his knees he cried out. He begged release from the chains. "Let Jesus into your heart and you shall be released." They cheered him. He wailed that he could not pay for his indulgences. "Jesus loves not your money, yet only loves you." The man, unladened, rose to his feet and belted out gloriously a praise 'Jeeessuus!' He was embraced with amens and hugs into his new fraternity.

Other sections of the street gospel were not so joyous. Pastor Rohn insinuated the grace in turning of the cheek. This section booed at that, and lamented the dozens raped at Roucy. "Not a dozen," one yelled, "but scores of dozens of maidens were ravaged that day." At that exaggeration, a mob broke off into riotous harassment. Curious catholic onlookers, who were not so beckoned to conversion as the other, were harangued with every manner of insult. Once the rest of the Catholics ran off, the emptiness of the square revealed a statue of some bygone saint.

"Why should he be set in stone?" Said an inciter.

"A mortal like us."

"We should free the poor sinner from his limbo."

The heaviest of rocks that could be gathered and pitched could only mar the statue. The missiles they had thrown broke up into fragmented spears. Tapping into their ape brains, two men fashioned a couple of sturdy pieces into miniature axe hammers. With these primitive implements, they scoured the profile of the bewildered saint. The pair found their respective weak spots and hacked away. Pastor Rohn attempted to end the iconoclasm, but was denied. "You, our hero of Roucy and we your hero of Paris."

First the nose finally gave way, and then the left hand severed nearly from the wrist. They marveled at their creation.

"Quite humanist that piece."

"His ugliness and deformity exposed."

"Which Florentine master are you?"

The vandals laughed raucously while being surrounded and cut off by the city guard. They laughed no more as the poor saint would not be the only one deformed on that day of the lord.

Chapter Nineteen

March 20, 1561

Fontainebleu, France

The show of unity, no matter the ratio of pure show to real unity, was impressive to all those who sat across from them. Here seated together on one side were the most powerful people in France representing the Crown, via the Governess who held the sceptre. Deputies representing the estates-general concluded to themselves the many ways each of these men were appeased by Catherine de Medici.

Antoine de Bourbon, who was the nominal King of Navarre, also known as the *First Prince of Blood*, was made the Lieutenant-General and given the illusory role as co-regent with Catherine. His appeasement to the politique, distanced himself from the ultra-catholics, which allowed him space to explore converting to Protestantism as a threat to the Spanish emperor, who could grant him his kingdom back. Navarre had been annexed by Spain during the Italian wars, and de Bourbon was more than willing to convert and re-convert any number of times to gain back his domain.

Louis de Conde, the Second Prince of Blood, was also a member of the council. Catherine granted de Conde his freedom and declared him innocent of being involved with the Amboise conspiracy. The Moderate queen had gained two brothers in one swoop: one from the ultra-catholic side and the younger from the ultra-protestant side to join her politique.

Anne de Montmorency had little to lose by uniting with the Governess. Under de Guise regency of Francis II, he was able to keep his post as the Constable of France, but was excluded from any influence, so for the old general any change could only be favorable for him.

Francois de Guise, who essentially passed the scepter to Catherine and allowed himself to be excluded politically, still was the commanding general of the army.

Lastly, there was Michel l'Hopital who she made Chancellor and would be the official mouthpiece for the preliminary meeting of the upcoming estates-general. L'Hopital who coined the politique party line of: One King, One Law, One Faith, was somewhat representative of the new humanist thinker. He was advancing the language of law faster than the magistrates could comprehend.

Surely most of the deputies of the three estates struggled to understand the fanciful language of the skilled orator. Most of the deputies had little reason to try. The third estate, representatives of the commoners, had nothing to offer. The second estate nobility were nearly as broke as the crown. Through all the venturesome platitudes of L'Hopital, essentially, he was begging for money and only the first estate clergy had any to give.

The chancellor was asking the church to buy back revenue generating rents and offices, so that the crown could begin to fill its empty coffers. To show an initial sign of good faith, he demonstrated how Catherine de Medici had saved two million livres in court spending by cutting servant staff, lowering pensions and salaries, and disbanding offices that earned no revenue. Members of all three estates laughed at this.

The young legal minded firebrand and the still novice queen had made their first blunder. The chancellor's admonishment of the wasteful court was received as naiveté. De Bourbon and De Guise cringed at the notion and understood what had transpired. The other members of the council could not talk Catherine out of her insistence on making those cuts. Household budgets fell well into the world of leading matriarchs of noble houses, but Catherine did not make the discernment between the treasury of house Valois and the treasury of the crown. None of those line items were wasteful, they all gained the crown something.

There were dozens of lower members of the court who could either become nuisances to the king or obedient sycophants. The difference between the two, was having, or not having, a meaningless office that brought home a salary. The difference between a happy lord and a not so happy one, is how many of his own servants he brought when called upon by the king. When attended to by the crown's own servants, one is more amiable to the wants of the king's calling.

As Bourbon and Guise had previously warned, not only did the clergymen not accept the savings as good faith, but announced they could not consider buying back properties until the governess completed her policy of savings. Since she was able to cut the two million livres so easily, one could only wonder how much she could save if she really got her hands dirty.

The sham of the entire new political reality was lost on nobody present at the conference. The traditions of the three estates were established long ago in French culture as a system where parties were obligated to one another. The chivalric knights of the nobility were to protect the peasants from the abuses of the clergy, or the clergy were to protect the nobility from an overbearing king by threat of ecclesial damnation. By the times of the high renaissance, belief in these traditions were still steeped in the common philosophy, but deputies of the three estates had long realized the value system to be dead.

Truly the French monarch had near complete control over the national church. The appointments of bishoprics were made by the king and any possibility of gaining a cardinalship in the papacy came from the king. The church's coffers were the king's coffers. The time of boy kings was now on its second year, and the estates could just not equate the council body, no matter how impressive, as a singular entity with the lasting authority of a mannish king. With another boy king, the political scene remained less stable, yet everyone understood that come the Estates-General at Pontoise in the fall, the church would indeed finance

Catherine de Medici as if she were the embodiment of a twenty-year old Charles IX. She would get her money as if she were a man, but they would play with her first because she wasn't a man. The council concluded with angry men throwing rhetoric to and fro. They ripped up scrolls and feigned shock at the other's ideas. Servants cleaned up spilled wine and tattered papers, the debris of political theater.

Chancellor l'Hopital did gain major legal victories that day that would strengthen the estate system in a modern way. To prevent abuses by the courts on mainly the commoners, magistrates would now be appointed by election. The bourgeoisie were still considered third estate commoners simply because they were neither noble nor clergy. Unification of weights and measures and abolished transportation levies, would solidify the merchant class. Finally, it was decreed that a formal Estates-General should meet every five years. Attitudes were changing fast in this new age and the rulers of France needed to keep up.

Chancellor L'Hopital was in no rush to report back to the Queen. He was not sure what was going to be more upsetting: the decline for funds or the validation of the warnings that she received from the council in regards to the budget cuts.

Catherine was preparing for a ride and insisted that Michel join her. The Governess was a rather plump woman and Michel still could not account for her hearty activities. She rode and hunted with the gusto of a typical noble male her age or even younger. When she finally eased up on the magnificent horse and allowed them a trot, is when she asked him about the preliminary meeting of the estates-general. Bad news first he thought.

Michel dove in, "They shall not consider funding the treasury until we have proven that we can cut no more court expenses." It was not a denial, but Catherine did visibly shudder at the reasoning. As she was warned, they would throw it back in her face that the cuts were made with ease. "They are curious how much more you can save once you really take a go at it." Michel decided not to give the next piece of bad news yet. "All else went as expected. Everything my lady, the magistrate elections, meetings every five years. However, there is another complication."

Catherine stopped for a moment and suddenly prodded her horse to a full sprint over a meadowy hill. L'Hopital decided not to chase after her, but rather quicken the pace and catch up when she calmed down. Instead, what transpired was that she came rambling back towards him on foot and was not calmer at all. The governess yelled at her chancellor with the general sentiment expressed that she grew tired of the disloyalty to the crown. Boy king or not, a king was king.

When he finally was commanded, he blurt out the complication. "There has been a rash of vandalism by the protestants, most notably in Paris. The acts of iconoclasm have been blamed on you. Our policy of reprieve for the protestants until the conclusion of our national religious council, has been said to give the reformed a sense of support."

Catherine told Michel not to blame the policy. "We always knew the clergy was going to find a way to object. The Pope surely does not want our own national religious council to undermine his never-ending council of Trent. The Huguenots are to blame. The moment the boot is removed from their throat they become audacious."

"In the end, we shall have our one faith," Michel stated with certainty.

Catherine put her hand on his shoulder solemnly, "One Faith."

Governess and Chancellor still understood politically the need to remain with the politique, and that civil war would be disastrous. They decided that measures would need to be taken to rein in the Huguenots, especially concerning the destruction of Catholic idols. Lord Conde and the Admiral would have to tighten up discipline within the reformation movement.

Chapter Twenty

April 11, 1561

Chatillon Coligny

Gaultien received his guests with open annoyance. Since the arrival of Nicolas de Piefuin, the dynamic at court was shifting and none he employed, including those presently hosted, could brook the tide.

Feebly, such a guest argued, "Of course this is our Admiral's court is it not? And he is an open protestant—"

"Unacceptable," Gaultien countered. "Gaspard de Coligny has long nurtured a balanced court and all of his courtiers loyal to the end. No, something has changed. First with that Charles Avon and now this new mysterious Nicolas. The Admiral now openly promotes Protestantism." At that notion Gaultien was stung. Had he simply missed the clock hand? Had his opportunity to join them passed?

"Not a protestant court here at Chatillon, non, perhaps moderate."

Another of Gaultien's guests uttered so. That one has betrayed us already. He pretends to still be with us ultra-catholics, but I wonder how the curator has lured him into the politique.

"Please take your leave now, I have much to consider."

There were some utterances of further apologies as they shuffled out of Gaultien's apartment. Left alone, he peered around his home. So empty was this place. He longed to return home to Tours. Gaultien's family was one of the oldest in

France. They were not of nobility, yet for many generations managed to linger in the courtier and clergy classes of society. The last two generations had been hard on them and now only a marriage pact could bring his family back into good standing.

Gaultien still remembered the news of the great Admiral's conversion to Protestantism. There had been a rash of important figures joining the reformation at that time, from which a proposal arose. Gaultien would be granted an apartment at Chateau Chatillon, and in the successful conclusion of holding back the reformation there, would be given a most soft and respected hand.

Nicolas had acquired eight books for the Admiral's library in his year at Chateau Chatillon. He still had received no news about his missing family. He resolved to maintain his pact to gain protestant rights through edict, and make France safe for their return.

Seventeen additional books he purchased for a handful of moderate and sympathetic courtiers. There was even a devout Catholic who sheepishly sought lessons, as long as he was discreet about it. As he remembered from Charles Avon, the trades were rarely for ecus. The new book broker's standard method was providing a discourse with the individual. He always worked one on one, and instilled a humanist or reformed value that could be drawn from the text. He asked his students to not just learn these values, but to exemplify them. Most of his students were members of the politique or very closely associated.

The text that he lectured on that day was, John Ponet's 'Treaty on Politcal Power'. That morning his student was Marcel Ruben. A linen magnate with an unusual family background. His family line could trace nobility back to the age of Charlemagne. In the time of his father, the family became financially destitute. Now the son, sitting before Nicolas with an air of smug amiability, had built a treasure pile. He was both old nobility and new bourgeoisie and as such was keen on renaissance knowledge. After the lesson came the ask.

The curator explained Ponet's view on a major contemporary debate of the time. The treatise had been printed not five years earlier and he had acquired a brilliant piece which had been modified with an elaborately adorned hard covering. The front cover illustrated with embossed figures of angels, men, and beasts. Writers were beginning to collaborate with artists to bring visual highlights to their works.

Nicolas lectured, "John Ponet establishes that men have a moral duty to usurp the autocrat who no longer rules with human reason, who no longer ministers justice on god's behalf."

The student was confused by the contents of the text and the symbolism of the cover which he had opened the lesson with, so Marcel asked, "Is it not true then that a central value of humanism is to preserve the order of things, to preserve man's place between angels and beasts?"

"Yes, quite an excellent understanding of the cover art, except for one key component. Humanism does not have a central value. Rather it contains a set of values that sometimes conflict with each other."

"Then what good is such a philosophy?"

"It is everything, the ultimate gift to men. Guidelines linked with autonomy and free will. Men like you and I will think deep and rationally about our choices." Nicolas peered at the wealthy noble and felt a sudden pang to teach Robiere again, or Torry. Or Janeau.

"I see, on the one hand we must have a strong government to maintain order through degrees of authority. Yet on the other hand, if the nature of that authority becomes wicked, we must usurp the scepter and hand it to a newly appointed godly ruler."

"I could not have said it better myself. With that I present to you the most sought after copy, to adorn your already brilliant library." With grace the curator presented the piece, yet on the inside he was all gloom. The sophists of the Mausien brook, were only a memory.

"Now Nicolas, I must insist on knowing the price—"

"Come man, you know what I am about. I seek only empathetic patrons to support my Calvinists however they can politically."

"Quite trusting you are. I could simply do nothing for the protestants and keep the book."

"Indeed, yet we teach a way of life not only meant to be learned but exemplified. We are both children of Christ, should we not treat each other like brothers."

"Of course, I shall do what I can to help you. I only point out that you ought to be more exacting in your methods. What is it exactly that you need?"

Nicolas was piqued, a genuine intention to help perhaps, "Originally all agreed it was the ultra-catholics acting with aggression. Now it is the Huguenots who have gained the ire of the common man."

"Rightly so I would say, considering the wanton destruction of our idols. They may not mean anything to your lot, but we revere them greatly."

"Absolutely. But you must also understand that the Huguenots have no government, no order, yet. We shall always be loyal to the crown, still an internal hierarchy needs time to grow."

"So, it is patience you seek? With the promise that Huguenot leadership shall control the hooligans?"

"Nothing more. I would also remind anyone you can that protestants lost their lives, along with our holy houses."

"I must ask you, was this lesson in any way to insinuate that we have a moral duty to rebel against the crown?"

"Impossible. God's law dictates that Kings rule with manly reason. We have not had a man king since that damned joust. Patience indeed, Charles IX shall become a man and all shall be much improved on the strength of that alone."

Admiral Gaspard de Coligny made a rare visit to Nicolas at the library. Coligny still feared being linked to Charles Avon's replacement, given the suspicions about the Amboise Conspiracy. Certainly though, the Admiral would want to check in on the progress of his library. The visit was as brief as it was unsettling. He and most members of the admiral's court had been summoned to Fontainebleu, the current residence of Catherine de Medici, King Charles IX, and the rest of the royal court.

The admiral advised him that they had been invited into the snake pit. The invitation of course was compulsory. As for an explanation, Gaspard only told him that Catherine's new regime was on shaky grounds and she wished to gather as many pieces nearer to her scepter.

On the trek, Nicolas de Piefuin tried to keep his horse aloof, as he wanted to be alone upon Lehman's return to their position. The Admiral's train was riding a post through a vast plain. A desert compared to the flowering fields of their last post stop. Ruins of old Roman walls dotted portions of the high road. Christopher was a master rider compared to the elder brother. Even the Lady Dowager, who intruded on him, was clearly the better rider. The more Nicolas saw the woman in action, the more handsome she became to him. Of all the intruders he wanted to keep at bay, at that moment, she would be on top of the list. The temptation of being cloistered with Emily Smolliet worried him. Thinking of her with affection made him think of Tonya and their baby Mary, which only made him lament further into despair over their deaths. On some days he thought of them being dead, all of them: his father, wife, sister, and baby daughter.

How is it that he still was graced with the lady dowager's companionship all that time in Chatillon and now onto another chateau? The tactic that he used for gaining favors in exchange for his good opinion being transmitted to the dowager had become a worthless commodity. Most of the suitors had bowed out, with the sentiment that Emily Smolliet was only smitten with the curator. He came to consider the possibility as well. Being a man of his word, he indeed did pass on praise as he promised, but no matter the compliment, she would redirect it back towards him. If Nicolas described a young *vicomte* to Emily as sharp…she would declare the bookman sharper. Even then, riding together, she was congratulating Nicolas on the deal he made with the linen magnate. Her flattery continued with her declaration that his reputation of the budding intellect at Chatillon caused the governess to summon him for a similar effect upon her councilors.

Lehman was now making his way toward them. He had learned much of refinement and found the best ruse would be to ask the lady for excuse that he may confer with his man on the status of his grooming kit and other gentlemanly matters of the private kind. Men too now were afforded time with their own sex, not for brutishness, but civility and taste.

With Nicolas and his valet Lehman alone, they discussed the admiral's beliefs on the real reason for the summons.

Lehman said, "We have our first signs of civil war looming. Family rifts so deepened to the point of disownment. Like your brother and you, the Admiral and his Uncle Montmorency have turned far from affection."

"Lehman, can you at least pretend to remind yourself that I am but a mere commoner. We would not whisper around campfires about noble family dramas, back in Laon."

Lehman decided to answer question with question, to help him along. "Tell me Nicolas, was your Seigneur Phillipe truly reformed?"

"Absolutely, it cost him everything."

"That is precisely the point. For a seigneur of an unremarkable town, it is all so simple. For these men, assigned to the highest posts, it is anything but. Anne de Montmorency does not care that his nephew has turned protestant. As far as our lord's uncle is concerned, Gaspard has either found his true religion, or a political convenience. De Montmorency only cares that his nephew remain loyal to him, for he would not be the great admiral he is today, without his uncle first opening the way many years ago."

"Has the admiral betrayed his uncle?"

"Why does the lady dowager believe we are being summoned to Catherine's court?"

"She nearly has me convinced that Catherine wishes to employ me for the same purpose I have provided at Chatillon. To sway the moderates with my ever-persuasive intellect."

"The dowager is not far off. Catherine will expect your help because she needs it now." Lehman shot a serious look at the curator. "Our Admiral did not betray his uncle. But he did not remain loyal either. It was Anne de Montmorency who has betrayed Catherine. His uncle also summoned him. A choice has been demanded. He chose the Governess."

Nicolas' head pulsed. The constant bouncing on horseback. *France shall never be safe again for my family and they are dead anyway.*

Lehman took another cautious look around them, but they had successfully cordoned themselves off from the rest of the traveling post. "De Guise, Bourbon, and the Marshall de St. Andre have formed a Triumvirate and quit Chatillon without royal permission. They have been appointed by King Philip and Pope Pius IV, to stamp out the reformation in France and indeed all of Europe. The true reason we have been summoned to the royal court is that Catherine has been forced to pivot. Conde has taken effective control of the Huguenots who now bend the knee to the Queen. Oh the magnitude of these shifts. As if by magic it is the protestants who have proved loyal to the crown."

"Allow me some grace Lehman, to comprehend all of this. In my studies I have found it best to understand and name all the principal entities. We have a new party, called the Triumvir, who are currently challenging the Royalists?"

"Yes."

"One of the triumvirs is Antoine de Bourbon?"

"Yes."

"Antoine, a Catholic, has a younger brother named Louis who is a protestant?"

"Yes."

"Louis is the effective leader of the Huguenots, and Admiral Gaspard is second in charge?"

"Apparently so."

"Is Montmorency aligned with the Triumvir?"

"I doubt he wished to be, but he is probably reading the report now of our post to Catherine. He will align the ultra-catholic Triumvir by the end of the day."

"Civil war then?"

"I told you that the religious differences between these men did not matter, but it will now. Though their difference in faith did not lead to their rift, once the chasm is formed, they will make it about nothing else. These men are not heartless. Gaspard desires not to maim his uncle in battle. Antoine would rather pierce the chest of a Spaniard alongside his brother Louis."

He puzzled out what Catherine could be thinking. A regency she hoped would last four years barely lasted four months, it is all so pointless. "I think I understand. The Queen now wishes to fill her court with protestant sycophants to pressure the return of her council and the inharmonious breakup of the Triumvirate. Can I share this with the dowager?"

"All of whom you trust should understand what we are heading into."

He rode to Emily Smolliet to bring her the news.

"What is happening Nicolas?"

"You were wrong m'lady. We are not being summoned to expand our moderate cause at Catherine's court. We are being summoned because she has been forced to abandon the moderate politique—"

"Why should that be?"

"She has been betrayed by most of her council. They have formed a war party under a triumvir leadership, with mandates from Pope and King of Spain to exterminate all my people."

Emily Smolliet struggled with the thought, then concluded, "So she sides with the Huguenots, your people are to be favored by the crown of France?"

"I think not. I think it is a bluff to draw the triumvir back to her council. The only two outcomes I can envision are: a continued effort to peaceful moderation, or a holy war against all of us reformed."

Emily reached out to hold his hand. Without words they understood one another. *Let us continue the moderate cause.*

Nicolas was personally met by a man named Blauve Mirshelle who was the curator for the governess. His specialty was art and wood cuttings, but he was also competent enough in literature as demonstrated by the fine library of House Valois. There was someone in the library, a slight figure sitting on a chaise in the corner of the reading room.

"I shall leave you to it," the curator said, leaving him another new stranger. Nicolas was taken aback. "Please monsieur Nicolas de Piefuin, you must know your reputation precedes you." Said the stranger.

"I certainly am not aware of that and can neither fathom what account that should be."

"Let me just say that I know who you are, and I am here to assure you that the governess has recognized your role. She thanks you, for your aid in getting the Edict of Romartin passed. We hope that your good works can continue here for further acts of tolerance." He was still dumbfounded. "Anyhow, I just wanted to introduce myself and hope to converse with you further once you get settled in. My name is Effrain Ghant and I work for the Chancellor in much the same way you work for the Admiral."

The mysterious slim man excused himself leaving the bookman agape. The curator returned some moments later and directed him to his apartment.

His new apartment was even more luxurious than his first, which he would have thought impossible. He wondered about the man he met. Could it be true? Were all of his dealings gaining more influence and support for the moderate cause? Could he truly have been integral to the passing of that edict of January, calling for religious tolerance?

All glory to Jesus for the edict which decreed a halt to persecution, release of religious prisoners, and pardons for the suspected ring leaders of the Amboise conspiracy. All praise to the lord for making me an instrument for change.

But had anything really changed? Was this the blunders of Maurice all over again? He did not consider if Jesus had left him because the savior never abandons his followers. He may have lost the vision for god's true will. Perhaps he never had it. For all the progress he apparently made, their position had not changed.

Animosity for the Huguenots was at an all-time high, and now the ultra-catholics were solidified behind the triumvirate. Catherine's son in law, King Philip of Spain, soured by the moderate policies the Governess had implemented. The Mother to the King argued that the harsh policies of the past century had not destroyed the protestants, and even strengthened their resolve. Catherine's reasoning was perfectly natural. Try something, anything new, rather than the same banal approach which had yet to yield the desired result. King Philip would not be moved, and thus shifted his support squarely behind the triumvirs. Once again, Francois de Guise was still the thorn in the protestant side and Catherine de Medici the supposed heroine.

The remaining council were ripe for the teachings of Nicolas. He would advance the modern point of view which recognized that they lived in a new season. A world where ruling elites would have to learn to tolerate less than ideal situations. A world now fully settled into a political age of compromise. He would also help push an agenda to convey new messages to Spain. As it became apparent that Sebastien de l'aubespine, the Spanish ambassador, misrepresented the governess.

Chapter Twenty-One

May 3, 1561

Fontainebleu, France

Back in Laon, Maurice, along with everyone else, had lived off a staple diet of soup and bread. Where he once might have eaten meat a few times a year, he now ate it twice a day. Complete with rich sauces and heavily buttered breads, Nicolas had become nearly as fat as the lifelong gluttons. He convinced himself that the change in appearance would only help his disguise and that by adapting to the courtly norms, it made his progressive rhetoric more palatable. He was taking in a meal at his apartment as he sometimes did. A servant arrived with a tray of food, bending down to place it gently upon the apartment table. He was coughing which led to a fit, and so led to him failing to properly thank the lad. He called out to the retreating servant and yelped his gratitude. His neighbor was exiting her apartment and took the opportunity to gawk at his rudeness.

There may also have been an unintended effect from his metamorphism, which was that it made himself and Emily an even more compatible match. The younger and leaner suitors would say that he won her affections by eating further courses with her; thus, enjoying longer durations of her company. The truth was that he and the dowager were finding they were compatible in every way. Intellectually, philosophically, and with a hint of overlap in faith. He sensed that he could convert her.

It panged him that he was tasked with disseminating renaissance philosophy from a secular angle. Disciple making was one of the highest directives from Jesus, so he thought about broaching the subject with her as a matter of fulfilling a holy obligation. There was more to it, he had to admit that to himself. If Lady Smolliet were a protestant, he could marry her. The hope of his wife and child being yet alive, and their reunion a possibility, was down to a flicker. Nicolas prayed on his sins, for in his darkest thoughts he wished baby Mary alive, but Tonya not. His sin already was adultery. He fantasized about his new wife, a better wife.

The book curator walked a brisk pace from his apartment to the library. The promenade may have been twice as robust over Chatillon. On this day, he decided to take a turn about the garden palisade. Giant trees of heather green lined the walkway overlooking a sparkling clear fountain pool. The pathway was topped with fine pebbles ground to nearly sand, so that each step produced an earthy crackle. The various pack ponies that sometimes accompanied the gardeners, broke down the pebbles even further in an altogether pleasant sight. The pristine state of the garden was achieved by a large workforce of groundskeepers as they trimmed bushes to perfect angles and lopped wayward branches from trees. He had even seen a gardener once stand upon the shoulders of another, so that he could cut down a non-conforming spruce back to size. He thought of the poor folk back in Laon. Four in ten adults had no consistent employment or a house of their own. What could an estate like this do for Laon? How many could it employ? Would Christopher be a good Seigneur? Lord Phillipe helped the poor beyond that of even his father's rule. The protestant ruler sought to excite activity, drawing from family treasury to drain marshlands. This served the idle men seasonal jobs, for no others would work the odious swamps. Upon drainage, a rising family could become landed and buy the improved land from the seigneur, with coffers refilled and poised to survey the next swamp. Surely men of the original project would be fixed to a more permanent wage, as who knew better the irrigation features of the newly shaped land. His brother now being a paper Catholic may not have the same acumen spirit and would for certain not have the treasury to launch such an effort.

He turned the corner and paced the northside on the chalky walkway that gave way to a little garden patch with flowers so exotic he was sure some must have been imported from China. If there was good that could come from all this grandeur, perhaps it was worth it. Maurice would not have entertained the thought, but Nicolas now did. As he approached the northern entry staircase, he was stopped by a guard who had sheathed in his black leather belt one of those wheel lock pistols.

"Halt monsieur."

"I am Nicolas de Piefuin, visiting library curator."

The guard looked doubtful but a second called from across the staircase to let him pass.

"Is that an arquebus you have there?"

"No, it is smaller and I need no match to fire it."

"I should love to see it fired sometime."

The guard gazed at him with a stone face, "Sometime soon you shall." He grunted for him to move forward and Nicolas hurriedly did. It had been sometime since he faced the venomous hate of an ultra-catholic, as he had too long only gazed upon its mask.

Blauve Mirshelle had arranged for his own workstation and the two were getting along quite well. Blauve would often pop in and ask him for literary advice or what book to read next. He would also seek the art curator out for guidance on understanding the importance of the woodcuts and engravings. The catholic and protestant would also have theological debates to pass the library hours away, which they usually concluded with a match of arm wrestling.

Others invited from Chatillon to Fontainebleu were three of Nicolas' most reliable supporters. The dowager, Marcel Rubin, and Daniel Laurent. Each had enriched their own libraries with books the book curator brokered for them along with their own personal lessons about how to comprehend the texts. The charming Lady Emily drawing suitors in. Marcel, advising on the nobility's growing interest in business. Lastly, Daniel Laurent was a banker to the growing administrative class of the Loire valley.

"Forgive my tardiness. The lipid pond beckoned me to walk under the day's rising sun."

The others were clearly holding back something with their poorly restrained grins and shuddering cheek bones. Eyeing one another as if in a game of high stakes cards, Emily blurted out. "Did you not hear about what happened here last night?"

"Should I have?"

The others could not contain the outburst any longer and went about peppering him with gossip.

Daniel shot first. "Do you remember the story about the latest outbreak of iconoclasm in Paris?"

He recalled, "Yes I believe a statue was marred—"

"Well apparently our ten-year old Dauphine Alexandre-Edoaurd was quite smitten with the story, as last night he snuck into the artist's workshop and bit the nose off a soft clay replica!" Marcel said.

"Which saint?" begged Nicolas, causing the group to laugh even more.

"Who knows," continued Daniel, "but Gaultien was here earlier to talk to Blauve about it."

The tone got noticeably somber at that.

"Has it occurred to anybody else that we have crossed some barrier into another world?"

"How so Nicolas?" said Emily.

"I was expecting Fontainebleu to be a snake pit, but here we are being praised for the January Edict, the court is dominated by moderates, and the royal brats are running around playing Huguenots. Someone even suggested that the Queen Mother hire me as tutor for them."

The mood darkened further. Emily gave him a baleful look, but the men's eyes reflected pity. That same pity for the naive Maurice.

Marcel sought to clarify the dire straits they found themselves in. "We are here as bait. Catherine threatens the Triumvir to disband and return to court or she will hand the regency over to the Huguenots. Only a war could result from that. If, however, they do return, anyone here may be forfeited for the exchange."

"I can't quite agree Marcel." The dowager sheepishly made an admission. "The Queen Mother finally sent me an invitation and we supped together, quite possibly while the dauphine was making mischief. Nicolas' name did come up. She was quite interested in all I had to say about you."

Daniel snapped her forearm playfully with a fine cloth napkin. This had been a development they waited for.

"Shall I be tutoring the brat then?" Nicolas marveled.

"Actually, she did make a light suggestion."

The lady dowager certainly had a way of keeping men stunned. Marcel looked down, "So it will be war then."

Nicolas surmised, "No, you both are a little wrong and a little right. Indeed her children are playing at protestants, and yes she, along with her entire court, are flirting. She is not serious. She would never allow any of her children to turn away from Catholicism, and she understands not the dangers she invokes."

He now moved the group away from wonderment and towards purpose. He knew Daniel to be a man of directness. "How do you think we should proceed Daniel?"

"We have achieved much from Chatillon for Catherine's regency so we should not forget that we also have earned a place here at royal court. Effrain Ghant making such an acknowledgment on behalf of d'Lhopital is significant. The lawyer and administrative class have risen to second class citizens, believe me, I manage their growing wealth. I would advise you Nicolas to seek out from Effrain on how exactly we can assist the Chancellor."

"Yes, I agree. There is also a quest we should look to explore with the new Spanish ambassador. As lady Emily points out there is no real danger of a Valois conversion, Sebastien de l'aubespine has misrepresented Catherine to King Phillip.

In the following weeks Catholics fled the royal court as protestants continued to pour in. Nicolas' main rival Gaultien remained, and he managed to keep the politique away from the new Spanish ambassador by the name of Chantonnay.

There was a piece of good news for the book curator which did produce a much jarring conversation. A lieutenant of John Calvin himself also arrived at court. Theodor de Beze quickly associated himself with the book broker and without much haste, but while quite alone said,

"I know you to be Maurice Millet."

A credit to his new sense of subterfuge, Nicolas lied quite easily. "You have been mis-informed, I am but myself—"

"Ah so many apologies. Our Admiral de Coligny told me such a thing, not to betray Maurice Millet, only in well wished hopes that I could help find his family."

"Monsieur it is so and I would give anything to the man that could locate my family."

De Beze promised to dispatch orders to Dutch agents to inquire the whereabouts of his family. He found himself rather conflicted at this, since it raised his hopes for finding them while simultaneously increasing the shame he felt for falling in love with the lady Emily. Alas it was quite a liberation to have another besides Lehman with whom he could speak freely.

One day the courtiers at Fontainebleu were shaken at the news: Chantonnay drafted an official report for Cardinal Charles de Guise as well as King Phillip of Spain: 'The royal court of Catherine de Medici is infested with heretics. The black witch should be denounced as Governess and placed under house arrest.'

Chapter Twenty-Two

May 10, 1561

Reims, France

A dreary group puzzled about the scene, ashen faces to match their plain gray cloaks. None seemed to be familiar with the dead strewn about the hawthorn bush, but the general score was they were Huguenots. Furthermore, a few had feathers in their caps, designating them as members of the gay band chauvre de sois. A pair of Jesuits arrived shortly after to disband the onlookers and issue dire warnings.

"See now what happens to the unrepentant souls, all ye who still hold the heresy of the reformed in your bosom shall know such an end."

"There is not a relapsed convert among us," shouted back a pauper.

"Isn't there?"

As if by cue a single bat flew overhead and flitted a circle twice over before menacing further into the night. The omen was heeded and the lateness of the hour marked, and so the group scurried off each in their own separate directions.

The Jesuit continued, "The reeve will be informed, and I should fain to learn that one of them is the deviled Herndon Calais himself!" Now to his silent partner, "And you should get notice to de Guise's man as well."

They ruffled through the pockets and retrieved a pouch of silver crowns. "Ill gotten gains returned to the true lord, ye better snatch the cock feathers as well. Evidence for the reeve." The bodies were left strewn to carry the message,

pierced organs to tell the tale of the last bandits of the chauvre de sois. The two Jesuits marched away together.

Herndon was eventually hunted down and captured with Christopher's help. He was not of those dead but held prisoner.

Those dead were more victims, and past friends, of Christopher Millet. Before word could fully get out about his betrayal, he used his knowledge of safe houses and forest hideouts to launch several ambushes. Under the tutelage of Chevalier du Lay, he traded one father for another. Whereas Herndon's honor was dedicated to a cause, liberal and malleable to the morality of the moment; the chevalier's honor was fixed to that of his lord. The latter, Christopher decided, suited him better.

Christopher was not at the ambush that eventually captured the captain, but a final confrontation could not be avoided. Duke de Guise wished to interrogate Herndon personally, as well as attend the coronation for Charles IX. Christopher and the chevalier du Lay were summoned to Reims, where the prisoner was also being transferred to. Duke Francois insisted that Christopher participate in his old mentor's torture.

Near the Cathedral de Reims was a minor estate of the Duke Francois de Guise. Second and third cousin families of house Lorraine were granted residence. It was there down the dank spirals, two dragoons and their lone prisoner descended. "It is he, the duke's most wanted of men." One of the dragoon's hand-pistols clanked against stony by-wall as the staircase narrowed. "Andre, we need to get you a holster for that thing, and some proper bearings for thee dungeons, as we shall soon be frequent haunts down here." Andre was too enticed by the beratement of prisoners to listen. "Hey reformed, it's the racks for you. And your whole circle will soon be once more at your company."

The Royal Train of the Valois Dynasty was a travelling court which spent nearly as much time on post than it did fortified at various chateaus. Fontainebleu was a common base for the royal train, but at this time the Valois were in Reims. Francois, Duke de

Guise, arrived for the coronation as well. First, he had a nuisance to squash.

Francois interrogated Herndon personally. He told Herndon of the coronation of King Charles IX. "Another new boy king to puppeteer." Heavy coats of the dragoon guards rustled as they attached the silent captive to the rack. Their boots, which were styled wide and loose at the calf, proved clumsy in the tight dungeon space and one even tripped and fell on his butt. Herndon let out a great laugh, merry till the end. An ominous creak let out once the wooden wheel began its turn. Herndon, now inverted, struggled to keep his senses as blood rushed to his brain.

Someone else was present, behind de Guise, watching from the shadows. Levers, chains, and gears continued their work, separating into semi-circles and increasing the diameter of the wheel to which Herndon's wrists and ankles were bolted. It was pure agony to experience. His muscles and ligaments stretched beyond the natural. Herndon readied his trap. Contorting himself to a single goal, he must utter the correct words. In the intense magma of his brain, pops were then perceived, tissue torn and his world turned hot orange.

Words were being screamed from the captain, so Francois ordered a halt. The wheel of pain was closed back up and Herndon was returned to an upright position. His dizziness would not subside though and he heaved vomit down onto the floor.

"Well done Herndon, that was a mighty display. Now repeat it and you shall have your reprieve."

Herndon struggled to concentrate as lies and truth were intermingled then. "My band is at Compiegne," gurgling blood escaped through his lips, "and shall not remain longer than forty days in my absence." Footsteps padded forward into the light. His trap worked.

Christoper loomed behind the shoulder of Francois de Guise. "That is a lie my lord, and most likely a trap."

Herndon grimaced through the pain and delirium. "I thought that was you back there Christopher you dog!" The once-merry captain wheezed heavily in effort to complete his indictment. "As if it was not dishonor enough to join de Guise…" Christopher watched with pity. "You help in hunting us down rather than fighting us in the open." Christopher looked upon his old captain with a sullen stare. "Well boy, speak for yourself, for your salvation." With great inner strength, Herndon finished his sentence without breaking down.

Even at the end I am impressed by the man. "There ought be words that can advocate for my actions, but I cannot summon them. Perhaps Maurice would have been able to." Herndon allowed some hope in the possibility he did not betray Nicolas also. "My only dishonor was not being on the right side to begin with. My kin were nobles, the Millets were Catholic nobles—"

"Yes boy, keep saying that and one day you may even believe it."

Christopher looked at the wooden rack which was stained with blood, sweat, and guts. His loincloth stained with piss. "I am a man. A real man who took a wife, and a child on the way. I have a family to take care of. This is what real men do, but not you my old friend. You never had the time for a wife. Instead you turned rogue and convinced yourself that handing out trifles to the paupers of Laon constituted a cause."

"You have convinced yourself of much, Christopher."

Francois ushered the dragoons to pull the lever, "Enough of this, we shall try again."

"My lord, if I may," The duke and his young subject huddled away. "He will never tell a truth, I am ashamed not to have been able to live up to his honor, but I wish to rise up to the even higher honor of yourself."

"I suspect you are right, this may just be a waste of time." Francois pondered. "I cannot keep him here much longer and the governess works to put an end to my licensures. You have proven yourself Christopher. Let us be away to the ecclesial and get your name in the scrolls." Christopher smarted with excitement over the nearness to nobility. "You shall be the one to kill him of course."

"Of course my lord."

"I thank you for the mercy Christopher." Herndon looked knowingly at Christopher. There was too much information in that brain of his. Being turned and torn again could have yielded more chauvre de sois blood for the duke. "Come embrace me Christopher…there may be hope for you yet, and Nicolas?" Christopher nodded and plunged his dagger into the heart of the merry captain. Herndon had three mighty gasps in him before his body fell limp.

Christopher was honored to meet the lower cousins of Francois de Guise. Like a ghost, he attempted to mingle among the elites. He was not truly present. He was still down in the dungeon. How long will this haunt me?

"Christopher." The chevalier tried for his attention. "Come, follow."

He followed of course. What else could he do? For all the talk of manhood with Herndon, he knew that he was not just a boy, but even lower, a dog. Christopher then found himself alone with the duke in a study. He was prompted to sit.

"You have done everything we have asked Christopher. Now let me present this." He unfolded a letter that clearly looked like the licensure he had waited for. "This is not the licensure itself, but this is a letter of verification and support from the Cardinal de Guise."

"Your brother? Surely it will take more than authorization from your brother—"

"I assure you all the proper requirements needed attention before Charles could sign this. This, and the pouch that du Lay carries will be all that the bishop needs."

Christopher pondered a moment, still not truly ascended from the dungeon. The poor, the poor of Laon. "Thank you, my lord. But there is a small matter I wish to discuss with you." With a look of genuine surprise and not a little annoyance he gestured to continue. "I shall not say I am happy to have killed a friend only that it was my duty—"

"Well said Christopher, it shall not be the last time. I consider Seigneur Phillipe a friend of mine as well."

"Herndon could not have become the thorn in your side he had become, without the love of the people. Laon has many poor and most of the paupers are Catholics—"

"What is it that you ask of me?"

"Let us make Laon a Barony; I could make Laon a strong, prosperous barony as your liege, we could even incorporate your ancestral lands of De Guise, to help with this strange idea that you are a foreigner—"

"How dare you!" At once Christopher knew he asked too much. Far too much. "You insolent ungrateful worm, I should tear this up and hang you next to Herndon."

"Forgive me lord, I don't understand any of this really, I know not what I speak."

"A barony is no small matter you whelp! And if you ever hear anyone call me a foreigner, you should bring me his tongue without any promise of reward."

Christopher knelt and bowed as he knew the chevalier would have done.

"Now leave at once. Your presence here this close to the coronation is highly inappropriate."

Chevalier hissed as soon as they were upon the rue, stomping to the cathedral. "You stupid stupid boy—"

Christopher turned and faced him. "I shall not be called, boy, again."

To the chevalier that felt almost like a challenge and that made him somewhat proud. "You are right, before the end of this hour you shall outrank me."

"I do not wish to outrank you. I only want to be your equal."

"Would you look at this?"

It was the royal train at the cathedral. The Governess and young King Charles himself were making an early inspection on the preparations for the coronation.

"Perhaps you won't be my lord this hour eh?" Christopher was petrified. "Do not worry, I shall buy ya a pint, and as long as it takes you to drink, or until thee Black Witch be gone."

The young Millet knew that this was destined to happen. On the day he killed his old mentor. On the day he would be conferred nobility. On this day, he would face his brother. Christopher unremarkably perked up whenever hearing about the infestation of Fontainebleu. Nicolas de Piefuin had become a person of some interest to the Guise faction. A literati book broker was earning a reputation for his wise teachings and fostering an alliance between the moderate party and the governess. It dawned on Christopher that his guilt was getting the better of him. That monsieur Nicolas de Piefuin had no more business here at the coronation than did a soon to be Seigneur. Such an idea of the brothers being elevated so was impossible a year ago. Now it was only unplausible. What would another year bring?

It went as the chevalier declared. Christopher was still not a strong drinker and by the time they finished their cheer, the cathedral was open again. The bishop issued a blessing of sorts, though not in any language Christopher knew. And with minimal ritual entered the name Christopher Millet into the books. Even as the son of a bookman, Christopher had never held a finer book. A leather shell with a bony spine which contained a Millet family treasure summoned into existence. Listed were a few generations of his family, but most of the scroll was empty, waiting to be inked in by his future sons upon the strength of their own conquests. The bishop advised him that the ecclesial body would notify Phillipe of the claim, but that he would not turn the manor over so easily. Christopher was also warned that a new class of lawyers were working mysterious magic of their own.

The chevalier told the young man not to worry. That the Triumvir shall have their war and that Christopher would claim Laon by force. No one would call him a boy ever again.

Chapter Twenty-Three

Feb 6, 1562

Fontainebleu, France

Firstly, went the under wear which were of the same familiar type that Nicolas had worn his entire life. All familiarity ended at that step. Next came a frilly top, which he had to entice to remain knee bound, while he attempted to raise fine satin pants upwards and around his now rotund belly. The last thing he wanted to do was to stand around while the tailors updated his measurements. With one final pull around and stretch, the tight pants were fastened into place, barely. While gasping for breath he took a much needed break and allowed his mind to wander. Is this still all for disguise and acceptance? Can I afford to lose some of the weight?

It had been nearly two years at court-- one at Chatillon and another at Fontainebleu. Two years, he lamented. Nicolas de Piefuin had still not been discovered. There could be no doubt that because of this lavish and gluttonous figure he had been both camouflaged and accepted as a seasoned courtier. Surely I could lose some of it, focusing in on the idea. The Triumvir had called Catherine's bluff and won back the regency. These days Catherine occupied herself with domestic affairs, and most importantly, finding a royal husband for young Margot. An oddity at court life, in regards to Catherine's taciturn toward domesticity, held Nicolas' thoughts. The Medici family had long been cursed with the gout and Catherine got it into her mind to do something about it.

Florentine cooks were brought in to introduce Italian cuisine. Lighter and more balanced meals, complete with vegetables and exotic fruits to provide an alternative to the thick sauced, over-seasoned, meaty masses which comprised a typical meal for the privileged. I shall eat vegetables again, and not so much meat. I shall eat more like Maurice again even though I cannot dress simply like him again.

Resumed with clothing himself, deep blue surcoat with almost a velvet sheen over a doublet of course. Why so many layers? He wondered. Finally the periwig, a bit of rouge, and a perfectly placed dot of black face paint dabbed perfectly upon his cheek. I would not recognize me.

Daniel Laurent and Effrain Ghant were waiting for him just outside the cordoned portion of the Oval Court, another construction project that was put into a frenzy once Catherine surrendered the scepter. A thought that triggered commentary from Daniel when the bookman arrived.

"We failed her Nicolas. She will do nothing for us moderates now. She is too busy with this now." Daniel gestured to what would become the new entrance to the royal apartments.

"Oh the oval court, no, that is only a side project for her." He led them away on a leisurely pace to the library, where he still conducted most of his business. "No, her primary concern is the marriage between Margot and Henry of Navarre. What could be a more symbolic marriage?"

It was Effrain who pondered this with great skepticism. "A Catholic Queen and a Protestant King…"

He continued, "No but one can dream. Besides, what I shall show you today is going to give you cause to join me in a fantastical hope."

At the library Nicolas ushered Daniel and Effrain to sit, as he ruffled through his materials.

Effrain now to Daniel, "Yes, we failed. Chatonnay would not heed my advice on offering the King of Spain a different perspective. Do you remember that perspective? It was one of our lessons."

Daniel took his time thinking while the bookman produced a box and joined his patrons at the desk. A curious container brimming with mystery. Daniel then, "Yes it had to do with advising French diplomats that Spanish diplomats needed to begin preparing King Phillip on the idea that Christendom as we know it is coming to an end, and the birth of 'Europa' was emerging. Furthermore, that he should acknowledge that Catherine always remained a devout Catholic, but did understand that the world be changing and that royalists must allow for some concessions, especially along religious lines."

"Precisely!" Nicolas pointed out to his students emphatically. He still loved to watch his teachings recited back to him. "And I was right," tapping on the box. Upon its opening a few maps were produced.

"Maps?" said Daniel.

"Yes, and where is Europe situated?"

Daniel's eyes glittered. "By God in the center!"

"And Europa?"

Daniel submitted, "She is different. Glorious, and that scepter. This could have been Catherine."

"Now look at this one, at the details," he presented a particular map.

Effrain noted, "I have never seen its equal, there are hills, mountains, and rivers yes, but now also notations for distances, heights, and even current flow and strength. Where did you get these?"

Nicolas only gazed, he wasn't going to give him an answer. He wasn't going to tell them that de Beze's men who were looking for his family were on a primary mission of surveying the low countries. He was not going to tell them that the attitudes of Maurice Millet had quite changed. That he now looked upon migration not with depravity, but with holy anticipation.

Daniel added, "I am impressed but what are they worth?"

He only shrugged. "I don't know but I can tell you this as a bookman. Great atlases of the most expensive prints ever run are underway for the Kings and Queens of Europe. I suspect any baron or count would be interested in lesser scale maps of their own and surrounding domains."

"By God you are right. Maps such as these could give commanders untold advantages in strategy—"

"Not just that, but in commerce and trade."

Just at that moment they heard someone approaching the den which caused Nicolas to insert the maps back into the box. Who else but Gaultien turned and gave an obligatory knock while simultaneously opening the door. The air of interruption permeated the little nook and he knew at once that Gaultien would be quite interested in knowing the contents of the plain wooden box.

"Ah Nicolas, monsieurs Laurent, Ghant…" Nicolas was dumbfounded. This was as amiable as Gaultien had ever treated him. Yes, he must now be quite curious about this box. "I have been looking for a particular text to add to my own collection and so I seek out your assistance."

"Ah well you have come to the right man," Daniel put in. "We were just leaving."

The men nodded cheerfully at one another. "How may I be of service?"

"I should like to purchase 'The Prince', by that Florentine, Machiavelli I think was his name."

He tried to master his emotions as he now suspected that his enemy had finally come to him for a confrontation. "I should be able to get you a copy easy enough. In fact I am pleased to advise that you should not need a broker, but only directions to the nearest book shop."

"Ah yes, I have thought of that. But did you know that there exist copies that come with personal letters from the author himself? Copies intended for the Medici house which he desperately wanted to regain their good graces."

"If I could acquire such a piece, the cost to you would be tremendous."

"What no trade for political favor, would you even throw in a personal discourse on the reading. Yes, I know how you operate." The courtiers faced each other squarely as the battle of wits had begun. "No matter, I shall not object to your price and as the copy that you already possess is useless to you seeing as you shall never attain a personal audience with the Queen Mother."

It was only a matter of time, Nicolas thought. He had given his true intent to a few of his patrons who did have access to Catherine and who could put forth his proposal for a meeting. Someone had betrayed him or one of Gaultien's spies discovered it upon their own means. He had his own methods though and had in time, come to realize that Gaultien was a man who just may entertain an alternate proposal.

"Oh but you Gaultien, my friend after all could be the very one to gain me such an audience."

"Name any price and you shall have it you blasphemer. Any price for the book and that ridiculous box you grip too firmly."

"Very well, Gaultien. We could discuss a price, but first you must humor me my ordinary custom. A lesson and then an ask."

Gaultien only chuckled pitifully, "By all means, teach me something then divine my will." Gaultien made taunting motions with his fingers as if the book curator wanted to ensnare him with a magical spell.

"Divide and conquer is one of the basic lessons that Machiavelli would have for a prince. It follows that the prince should not allow himself to be divided either. A homogenous state is a strong state. You are a good Catholic and a loyal Frenchman, you should have France under one faith, un foi."

"I should have every last one of you burned alive."

"Yes, precisely Gaultien, as I should have every last one of us get the hell out of France."

Nicolas had been right about his rival. He was a man who cared more about the cleansing of the reformists than paper conversions. He saw the value of a more direct and simpler solution. Nicolas admitted to his enemy a plan that he had not uttered to anyone. He was ready to quit the cause of moderation. His father was right all along. Escape was the only answer. Maurice's gifts used in duty would show the way, staying always close to Jesus Christ.

As part of their pact, Gaultien demanded to see the contents of the box. He explained that he valued the maps not for military planning or trade, but for planning a route for a great Huguenot exodus to Sedan. The bookman waved the map of Sedan excitedly and Gaultien had to admit the genius of his adversary. Sedan was a principal possession of Catherine's French side of her heritage. Catherine could possibly be swayed to open up the principality to Protestant refugees. A France rid of all protestants could be achieved.

Nicolas convened later with Lehman to update the admiral of his latest agreements. They had conceived a way to hide the secrets under the guise of a notebook which simply read as bad poetry. He kept peering into the notebook as he told Lehman that he made no deals that day, the words sticking in his throat. Court life had corrupted him fully. There were neither friends nor foes in the intrigue of court politics.

A grotesque lordly looking face reflected off the pond's surface. He had not eaten any meat that day yet he looked no thinner, no less hideous. The lady dowager happened upon him at the appointed hour, but instead of delving directly into the latest intrigue they quietly enjoyed the fountain waters together.

"It is quite something that the chattering of the birds can still overcome the washing of the fountains."

"Birds, I hear no birds." Emily shot him a look of mocking disbelief. He closed his eyes for a few moments, "Oh yes, how is it that I could not hear them?" They laughed together at his aloofness and she then found herself fondling his arm before breaking off from affection.

Asking him a question to ease the transition from flesh back to heart. "What do you think of it then, the bird's triumph over this magnificent fountain pool?"

"I suppose God has tasked us to care for each of his creatures and to preserve their order. Man sits above the animals, but not necessarily the machinations of men."

Emily Smolliet was fascinated with every explanation Nicolas had ever made. "If I tell you something that I have been harboring would you tell me something that you have?"

"That implies I have been harboring anything."

"Call it a woman's intuition."

He looked nervously around and accepted that they had total privacy. He remembered that night de Beze had called him by his own name, its delicious sound.

"You are right my lady, I have been harboring something and since you have mustered the courage I could not, I demand to now go first."

"I am not the man you think I am. I am not from the town I told you about. My name is not Nicolas de Piefuin, and most importantly, I am married."

Emily was aghast as she stepped back away from the admission. "That is not at all what I was expecting."

"Please I beg you to allow me to tell it all before you run off as you rightly should." She nodded and sobbed in affirmation. "My name is Maurice, Maurice Millet. I am a bookman. I did indeed operate my family bookstore and I did have a band of sophist farmers who are my dearest friends and most treasured students. My home is Laon, but my family was driven out by Catholics. I have a wife…" She shuddered, "and a baby daughter—" Emily was now crying uncontrollably. He looked around again but still they seemed very much alone and he was now very much determined to bare it all. "I have a father, sister, and brother. Maurice Millet could have been implicated for false crimes. So well placed friends of mine invented the identity of Nicolas de Piefuin to come to Chatillon and use my knowledge of literature to help…well you know all the rest of that." He waited a dramatic beat. "My family was supposed to have been transported to the Netherlands, but they never arrived to their destination, and so now I am but a few fortnights away from enduring a two-year anniversary of losing my entire family."

Bitterness was giving way to sorrow. Empathy becoming sympathy. Emily stepped closer to him, thinking him a figure of tragedy and not pure deceit.

"I suppose I should not say I lost my entire family as my young brother Christopher has joined the enemy on the promise of a title to the seigneury of Laon."

"Oh I have heard of that affair, that is your brother?"

"I shan't make him a villain Emily for I am the one who is befouled. I fell in love with you. There is no evidence that my wife is dead but I have wished it. I don't know what I have become but I fear the once good man named Maurice is long dead."

The dowager heard others coming around the bend. "Come, take me to your apartment, I fear we are more scandalous about than inside our own rooms."

Neither spoke another word until they reached the apartment.

"Maurice this is the last time I shall address you truly, for once I leave, we must keep Nicolas protected." He agreed. "Who was the man who introduced himself with no humility at my ball?"

"That was Maurice."

"Then you are the man I fell in love with." Maurice looked at her in bewilderment. "Yes I am in love with you, too. However, that is not what I intended to tell you at the fountain, under those bird songs." She had trailed off but recuperated. "What I wanted to say is that, through you I have found Christ. From your teachings I have decided to reform."

A few days had passed allowing the couple to come to their senses. Emily agreed to refrain from any more talk of conversion, and they both agreed that Nicolas must find out the whereabouts of his family above all else. He told her about de Beze and his search party that was dispatched nine months prior. She praised God at that name because she had recently learned from Catherine herself that de Beze was nearing Fontainebleu. He told her, "The only people who knew of Maurice-Nicolas were: Danilo, Seigneur Phillipe, Herndon Calais, Christopher, Admiral de Coligny, de Beze, herself and Lehman."

They spoke of the irony of how he once believed in the moderate queen mother, although presently proven correct, he was still wrong. He wished to tell her all the regrets of Maurice, but she would have no more lamentation. She spoke of her brief encounters with Catherine. They mostly shared their similarities as dowagers and voracious eaters. She, like Lehman, also believed her temperate policies were emergent from her vast savoir-faire. "She seems to always know what to say, and how to say it. The day you two come face to face; I should fain to be ever there."

Emily was growing increasingly confident that Catherine would grant him a personal audience soon. Catherine was quite aware that he had the Machiavelli letter, and also his name had been posited as a possible tutor for Margot. Nicolas piled another item of guilt, as he did not divulge to Emily that once he finally met with Catherine, he would have no intention of furthering the moderate cause, but to take up his own instead. She was right after all, "for now they both must think of Tonya as his wife." The best thing for his family now was to return as Maurice.

He and his patron politiques still met and still spoke of the last January Edict. Protectionist policies that go mostly ignored with the Triumvir in power. They continued to speak of Catherine's various wedding schemes for both Mary the Queen of Scots and Margot. Rumors of Catherine's youngest children still abound. Whispers insinuating the royal children having inclinations towards Protestantism. And that Margot, a gifted child warranting a prestigious teacher such as Nicolas, could be assigned under his tutelage. Emily was shuffling through an assortment of material samples. She thumbed through squares of linen, cloth, and silk. Occasionally one would flit to the floor and he would retrieve it for her with a bow. The old debate within the group continued arguing over the validity of the young Valois' supposedly ambiguous religious tendencies.

He shuddered to imagine. "It would be a death sentence for me to be allowed anywhere near those children. Catherine is utterly ignorant. She may have allowed some childish playfulness to a reckless degree, but this only proves how she still thinks of the split as something that can be mended."

Daniel added, "Catherine was not at mass last week."

The dowager met that information with her own indigestion. She herself had not been able to attend mass for some weeks since her eyes had been opened. *And you talk of a death sentence Maurice.* Wanting to change the subject, Emily interjected,

"Oh yet I am electrified by the news that Calvin's man will be visiting court soon after what he said at Poissy." Nicolas mimicked De Beze:

"His body is as far removed from the bread and wine as heaven is from earth!"

The group heckled on.

"Scandalous and so inspiring."

"I, like lady Catherine, have both been duped."

"A tear which cannot be mended back you say."

"I do mon fille."

"Hmm," Marcel nearly choking on his wine. "There is another party arriving soon, ultra-catholic ambassadors from

Joinville, along with a Priest Borges. Does that name mean anything?"

The bookman felt a pit deep in his stomach. He had only eaten meat once in the last few days, but he still looked no different. His disguise now for once seemed useful. The priest and him had only met that once, and the latter events of the day surely blotted the inconsequential bookman from Borges' thoughts. He then thought, perhaps Maurice need not be afraid of Borges, but Borges be afraid of Nicolas. The man who raped and killed Heather in his midst. If I called in all of my favors, could I orchestrate an assassination?

Nicolas not only quickly exorcised those murderous thoughts, but he decided to stay in his own apartment until Borges' departure. However, leaving his room became unavoidable as he was called to a small meeting to be recognized as the man of the hour. De Coligny, his brother Odet, Louis de Conde and de Beze announced that another of their edicts had passed, and that the final wave of support came from his dealings.

"Our literati teacher raised the crucial question to his moderate patron-students. If a Frenchman need not be Catholic to be a citizen, then why should he be disallowed from Protestantism?"

"Our edict shall remove the religious aspect of statehood and citizenry. As a measure to restore France to unity based on secular citizenship and loyalty to the king."

"This is the final chance to stave off civil war. Huguenots are already attacking churches in the southwest as such that a line of demarcation is manifesting."

"Where would you reckon this line?" said Conde.

"From Lyon to Bordeaux."

Nicolas watched as each of the men studied and marked off their own personal maps. They looked like schoolboys looking over shoulders to see how the other had done. He thought little of that though. All through the meeting he prayed to the lord for de Beze to bring him the good news.

As the meeting concluded de Beze pulled him aside.

"I have news for you my friend." Nicolas was shaking. "Your father, sister, and daughter are in Mons."

"They live. They are in Mons?"

"Yes."

"Where is Tonya, where did you find my wife?"

"No I am afraid we have not found her."

"Tell me everything Theodor."

"My man Thomas Sunstone has found them in a church in Mons. It is acting as a makeshift hospital for protestant refugees from both France and their own uprisings which the Spanish king is squashing out without mercy."

"Why are they at hospital?"

"No, they are fine. They have been there this entire time! During the escape your father was injured badly, but your sister nursed him back to health. Sunstone reports that she has become an accomplished nurse and does God's work there."

"Marie, Marie does this. She always was protective—"

"Listen, Marie told Thomas that during their trek through the Ardennes they each went a bit mad, but more so for Tonya. In the end she cracked and in essence had abandoned your daughter to her. It is doubtful she ever got out alive. Now listen, they have been advised on your status and told not to write any letters to you. Nor could I risk it, I am sorry I waited to tell in you person."

"Brother, you have given me the greatest gift, thank you. I might have another problem. An ambassador from Joinville has arrived." De Beze chuckled at that and ushered over the admiral, "Yes the Guise refuse to set foot in court, clamoring on about how there are still too many Huguenots afoot all the while keeping us quite penned in."

"Yes, well he is with Priest Borges." The admiral clearly needed reminding. "He is the priest who kidnapped our women during the re-education. I met with him once, to formally demand their release. Surely he will remember me."

"Just the one meeting you say?" said de Beze.

"Yes."

"You look so different from the old monsieur."

"He really has quite taken to eating like a lord."

"I doubt we need worry but why tempt fate. You deserve a break, so remain in your apartment and I shall design an escape, a cause for you take holiday."

"Will the edict truly gain protestant official rights?"

"We must praise Jesus for any victory we can, but in truth, the parlement of Paris will never ratify it. However, your job was to change the composition of attitudes of those who wish to remain at court. In that you have exceeded."

In fact, Nicolas had done too well of a job in both Chatillon and Fontainebleu. Too many incidents of politique sway involved this mysterious bookman. The origins of Nicolas de Piefuin were investigated and found lacking. The priest and the ambassador were hurrying to the small council which they learned of too late. Still, they could catch him leaving, and they did, all alone to boot.

"There is one of the heretics that has been befouling our court. He has been described to me thusly as Nicolas de Piefuin." He stopped to allow their confrontation. They had no men-at-arms. He at least would not be arrested in the hallway. The ambassador continued explaining to the priest. "A literati curator of Admiral de Coligny. Furthermore, he replaced Charles Avon, a man we suspect was part of the Ten of the Amboise conspiracy."

Borges took the fat man in carefully. "Monsieur Nicolas de Piefuin, I should most like to make your acquaintance. I am Priest Borges, and I declare before God that you are a heretic. France is ruined as long as you and yours pollute such holy houses as these. For royal houses of Catholic creed are as sacred as any cathedral. You dare defile God's house with your protestant preachings!"

"Not so. I am not a preacher, only a humanist teacher working towards legal policies to help find common ground." Nicolas was struggling to incline his face to contort somehow differently than that of Maurice. He avoided eye contact which only brought further scrutiny.

"Ah well protestants and Catholics do have ample common ground. Would you not agree?"

"Surely."

"Yes, a bookman, such as yourself actually; once remarked that to me and it has stuck. Ample common ground, he said. Very well, Nicolas is it?"

"Yes father." Nicolas used the title with only vitriol.

"I have warned you honorably, you are binding yourself to the depths of hell, but you too can seek me out one day for salvation, for there may be a lifetime of sacraments yet made to atone."

Nicolas rushed to the arms of the dowager and poured his heart. He told all. His family was alive. Tonya abandoned their daughter and is believed dead. He had been identified by the Priest Borges. Finally, he told her about his new plans, about the maps, about the pact with Gaultien, about an exodus. They wanted to make love. All of the emotions culminated into a mixture of glorious news tinged with tragedy. A new hope paired with a fresh danger. They made their own pact. They would escape France together and she would become a protestant. If in that duration, no news of Tonya would arise, they would bury her and consecrate their own union without guilt.

Without surprise he opened the door for a pair of men-at-arms to take him into custody. Surprise only began to creep in when he realized he was being taken to the Royal wing. Could this be it, will I finally be able to look Catherine in the eye?

First impression was off-course from expectation. The Governess looked frantic and had scrolls strewn about. Candles burned low and mis-shaped, waxy coagulate drifting. She began addressing him with such steel determination so as Nicolas reckoned reality to be back on course.

"I have heard much about you monsieur Nicolas de Piefuin."

"Greetings my lady Governess."

"I have heard the most dreadful news, then it dawned on me that it is you that I should put off receiving no longer. My understanding is that you have a gift for me, a family heirloom."

"If it pleases you I can fetch it, your family heirloom..." She then produced the package herself.

"Your apartment and study has been searched." She handed it to him. "Then you offer it back to me," which he did. "There I accept your gift."

"That is an original and personal copy of Niccolo Machiavelli's "Prince", it has handwritten inscriptions directly to both your uncle and father. There is also a letter addressed to Francesco Vettori, but very much meant for your family, suggesting that Machiavelli wrote this book to showcase his experience and insight in vain hopes to gain employment. There is also a draft of the provenance, explaining how this set was won from Niccolo by my own grandfather; in a game of cards." The bookman paused for the impression to sink in, and trudged on when it was not.

"Do you know if any of the other copies made it to the Medici library in Florence?"

"I do not."

"I should fain to know if this book is destined to be reunited with all the others, ah the provenance of such a set."

"If provenance is so important to you, then how dare you make counterfeit this one." At once it dawned on him, his critical oversight, if Priest Borges had recognized him and turned him in, then Catherine now has me trapped in advertising the piece as a family heirloom. "You are Maurice Millet are you not? Come now, that priest reported you straight away. He said you were a lean bookworm from Laon, and now you are a fat bookworm from Chateau de Chatillon. A wanted man to boot."

"This is true."

"Very well, then modify the provenance letter and I shall happily accept your gift."

Maurice did as commanded. "Am I to be excused Queen Mother, onto my judgement?"

"Am I to be deprived of what all the other ladies at court received. Do they not receive an intellectual lesson to go along with their acquired edition?"

"Yes this is true, but for those meaner ladies they purchased favor."

"Treat me the very same, this is how you garnered support for yet another January Edict of Tolerance."

"On your behalf Queen Mother, oh kill me now if that were not so."

"It pleases me. Both means and ends. Now what would you ask of me?"

"Let me go, leave court safely. My quest now complete, I desperately want to go home, wherever that may be."

"Done."

Maurice racked into a more erect posture as if his ears could better make any repeat of her unthinkable words. It dawned on him that she was probably playing him false. "There was a time that I fancied a lesson or two, on 'The Prince', for you my queen mother, but being at your court has taught me that the virtue Niccolo only wrote about, you exemplify in your everyday industry. I fain to believe you could teach old Niccolo a thing or two about how to rule."

"I am flattered, but amuse me."

"The most cogent chapter for you is the one on the mistakes made by King Louis, which has had a direct affect on you and I sitting across each other this very moment."

"Go on."

"The mistake King Louis made weakened France and Italy, and strengthened the Church and Spain. If not operating from this present handicap, I wonder if you would not be Empress by now."

Maurice hurried to correct his faux pas. "Empress to the Emperor in waiting of course."

"What mistakes did he make?"

"Giving up on his weak allies prematurely."

He was not surprised that she was an astute student of history. "Yes, King Louis became Master of Italy and immediately went to the aid of Pope Alexander."

"Indeed. Remarkable grasp of royal history. As I have predicted, other than being an artifact, The Prince's contents offer no new knowledge to impart."

"Surely Maurice you can cite one useful example."

This being the critical moment, he thought to himself, that he had nothing to lose by pressing back. "What of your dreadful news? No news of urgency obviously, as you would not have beckoned for the bookworm for a hasty introduction."

"Great import. What I learned today has caused me to now see that war is inevitable. Not just any war, but a civil war. Civil-War, quite the contradiction eh Maurice?"

Two years now Maurice had heard the guarantee of civil war. Now on the day he finally meets the moderate savior, she utters its vile oath upon him. "What makes a war, a civil one?"

Catherine recognized the tactic of a wise teacher, striking with precise questions, "Civil wars are personal." She answered.

"Exactament." Catherine, not satisfied with the teacher's praise prattled further support. "The Bourbon, that waffling fool, has attended mass and made a full commitment to Catholicism, shunning even his own wife. Is that not personal? Montmorency has disowned his nephew, your admiral. Through all their differences in all years past Lord Conde and Duke Guise remained close friends, and now they are mortal enemies. Is that not personal Maurice?" She struck at his non-response. "You and your own brother may very well cross swords over this Maurice, is that not personal?"

Nicolas broke down in shuddering tears. He was lost again. Is this not the path Jesus? Whose plan is this? He had one secret plan left. A secret he shared with no one, not even Maurice. "Of those who come to power through wicked actions. Of those who come to power through wicked actions!" he cried out. "That is the chapter for you. Gather up all your enemies in one place."

Now Catherine was as stunned and emotional as he. "For what purpose?"

"At the heart of Machiavelli lies the ability to separate what can be done and what cannot be. What is possible and what is impossible. Is it possible for you to round up all of your enemies and kill them?"

"Yes it is possible. Yes by god that is possible."

"Consider all things that are possible, then and only then do you consider moral implications. Machiavelli knew, that you Catherine, can either be a strong yet wicked prince, or a weak and yet good one. You may not be both. For those who commit the blackest of acts, will forever be known as black actors."

"Why would you tell me of this, lay this at my table. What do you want of me?"

"Make sure parlement ratifies this January edict."

She burst into laughter. "It's done, poor Maurice. They have softened and will register its legality. Another worthless edict for the hall of records."

But he knew that already. "I don't betray my people for two reasons. Firstly, I don't suggest who your enemies are, only you know that. Will you gather up the Huguenots or the ultra-catholics? That is for you to decide. I am inclined to believe you will gather the former which brings me to my final request. Sedan."

Catherine realized then it was wise to fear even meeting with this upstart literati who came from nowhere. He had surprised her at every turn. "Sedan, what of it?"

"It is a principality of your family's holding, on your mother's side that is."

"Correct, a protestant principality at that."

"Precisely. Final lesson for the Machiavellian Prince. Do not put off war when conditions are favorable. I offer you favorable conditions. Let me, help me, orchestrate a mass Huguenot exodus from France, using Sedan as a base of operations. A sanctuary for refugees and a way point for their dispersal. At best there may very well be nobody left to fight. At worst, your odds will be better than otherwise."

The royal chamber, one of the most prestigious rooms in Europa was perfectly still. The rich mahogany desk offered not a creak. "I should think King Phillip would have something to say."

"Unify France under one religion and he should be pacified. Besides, I do not plan to migrate to the low countries exclusively."

"So I am to help the reformers proliferate through Europe?"

Maurice took in a deep breath before his next utterance. This was the final piece. He had gathered so much information on Catherine de Medici for so long and he kept coming back to the same thought. She fears the supernatural above all else. Her love and devotion to her children is her weakness. A seer predicted the demise of her husband and that demise brought ruin to everything.

"Why not? After all you are no Catholic. I know of the seers you employ; they rule your heart. They foresaw what the young

Lion of Montgomery would bring about. All this debate whether you would abandon the church for the reformists and nobody but me dared to question if you had already left the pope for another."

"Insolent, how dare you!"

"Kill me now if I am wrong. The superstitions of the Catholics comfort you, as do superstitions of the occult. I employ seers, too. I am no Christian and you are not Catholic. You said you only just learned of de Bourbons' conversion and of his disgraced Queen of Navarre. Should you not at least have called upon your seer before my humble self? Or was I, the next seer you needed?"

Catherine writhed in humiliation, covering her face.

"Today I am your seer. I will to you, the true omen of this devastating news. How long for this world do you think the King of Navarre is? What of the dauphine Henry? Would the shunned wife not raise a Huguenot? A Huguenot King of Navarre destined to marry not one, but two Medicis." She raged. "Today, I am your seer. I see our way out. Help me induce exodus from these wretched lands so that you can set about repairing them."

Maurice and Emily were spirited away under Catherine's personal guard. Effrain Ghant was called in to draft a land deal between Catherine and Emily. Emily would give up her French holdings and gain lands in Sedan. Emily was poorer for the transaction yet risked losing all if persecuted as a treasonous heretic. They each felt pangs of guilt for betraying their politique friends, but gathered that through correspondence, reasoning could win back some level of trust and future cooperation.

Emily asked him how he had managed to win her over. He reminded her that he had been reading books his whole life and that he could spin a yarn when needed.

Chapter Twenty-Four

March 15, 1562

Germany

In front of Danilo were news pamphlets from five of his most trusted printers. He had always known their work to be most diligent. They employed well-informed people, sometimes even himself. "Sell a lie once and you won't be able to sell another." Further, these printing houses had agents of their own to double check certain facts; they also coordinated with local administrators when prudent.

Danilo puzzled on how he found himself looking at five different headlines about a massacre at Vassy:

Duke de Guise the Butcher of Vassy
Sunday Mass survives Protestant assault
Illegal protestant service, shut down
Protestant Women and Children slain by the hundreds
Princes of Lorraine retaliate against Edict of Toleration

Danilo was recalling the debates he would have with Maurice about these news periodicals. He thought the new phenomenon for people to have access to the news was positive, but Maurice warned it could be invasive, and differing stories would have a destabilizing effect.

The cult masters looked down upon the papers arranged such that they too could consider these contradictions.

The ex-courier decided this would be as good as time as any. "I should like to be tested for the second order. The German princes have their role to play in all of this, that is clear to us all, is it not my masters?"

"You have been warned that any single failure results in your automatic status at the current level being so deemed for life."

"This life anyway," the other master put in. The second, older master continued. "We have much faith in you Danilo and will not risk your eventual advancement."

"I have done some research of my own. I could demand to be tested." The masters were aghast. It had been sometime since a student demanded to be tested. "I have made many partnerships with the German nobility and if I could present myself as a second degree gnostic, the support we could gain would be two-fold."

"You are being drawn in by your emotional attachment to your friend Maurice Millet—"

"No, I swear it. I love my friend, but if I did not see his importance in my own visions, I would not risk my own path. I sense he is important, and he needs us more than ever. Right now, not later."

"Tell me Danilo, have you pondered upon the meaning of dualism and why it is a core tenet of our Cathar Order?"

"Yes master I have. The conclusion I have come to is this. When God made man in his own image, he saw the world as an amalgam, a great grey. Once man ate the forbidden fruit, he was then cursed to see the world in black and white, good and evil. In our arrogance our wisemen state to judge with sophistication and consider the nuances of the behavior of men. But this is folly because we already lost that right, for now we must make stark judgements. There are white acts and black acts, nothing more. Finally, we must not be so vain to place the black acts below, but we of the Cathar Order must strive to keep the balance."

The masters were not sure when the last time a student demanded to be tested, but they knew they had never heard such a profound thesis from one. "Very well, let us commence with the test. If you pass, you shall be a second order gnostic."

The potions, plants, and perfumes were summoned for which gave Danilo time to ready himself. He sat cross-legged, still as a sloth, and focused on the one-armed man. A visionary could not be certain which allegory the test would weave, but he could be certain it would be based on the consistent subject of his dreams. In Danilo's case it was a one-armed man.

The ingredients arrived and the masters prepared the test. Once the potion was ready Danilo was given a final opportunity to forgo, but Maurice needed him now. Leaf was alit and Danilo inhaled deeply, followed by a strong pull of the broth. The effect was immediate and for only the shortest moment of time did Danilo receive his vision. Following was grueling pain, heckling doubt, and the deepest fears. Once the torture ended, which took not the shortest moment of time, the test begun. If Danilo was unmoved, then the vision would return wholly unaltered from the original. The masters, through decades of training, could tell if the student spoke with any doubt. His screaming words came to an abrupt start and the masters had to act quickly.

"What will be?"

"A one-armed man."

"What can be?"

"A second one-armed man."

"What may not be?"

"A third one-armed man."

"What is the greatest calamity at hand?"

"War, protracted, yet in pieces."

"Will there be balance?"

"Only with a blackest of black acts."

"What ends the first piece?"

"Duke de Guise will be shot and killed."

"What ends the second piece?"

Danilo looked around frantically not knowing where he was. "What? I don't, I don't understand."

The masters were out of time. Danilo had passed the test and saw the truth so clearly that the masters got far more answers than they could have imagined. They agreed that if the specific prophecy of the Duke came to pass, that Danilo should be elevated to the third order without another test.

The test was grueling for Danilo and though there was ambiguity between who the one-armed men were, he believed it was Charles Avon, one of the three already manifested.

Danilo was admitted to the meeting of the second order. He was welcomed as the thirteenth member and their five masters convened the council. His test had brought much clarity to their purview, and they established the following mandates. Maurice must lead an exodus and light the way for the coming crisis. He shall plant seeds and take care to remove any spoiled roots. For as all great crisis events, revolution is to follow and these seeds remaining mostly uncorrupted, will be a concern for the Cathars for lifetimes to come. Danilo had dreams of Maurice and seeds before, but he was astonished to know that second order gnostics knew even more about his friend than he did. Lastly, they concluded that Maurice had already begun the exodus, but floundered.

The Cathar masters summoned Danilo. They advised him that Maurice needed help. Yet they also advised him that the help of the secret society superseded help to his friend. While both overlapped, Danilo could serve both. But upon any divergence, Danilo must serve the greater good. Danilo, greatly confused, could only ask, "What do you order of me?"

Chapter Twenty-Five

December 12, 1562

Principality of Sedan

Maurice awoke and found himself restless. He gazed upon his pregnant wife and wondered if she carried a boy. If so, they had decided to name him Luke. Emily was enamored with the idea that salvation was meant for all. Furthermore, the book of Luke contained themes of reversed fortunes. Something that their new family considered their chief experience.

Upon their departure from Fontainebleu, not quite a year ago, Catherine's chancellor Michel l'Hopital, worked his new wave magic lawfare, which not only pardoned Maurice Millet, but also involved land deals between Catherine and the Dowager. Catherine gained more holdings in France and in return the Dowager received holdings in Sedan, where she could convert from Catholicism and not risk seizure. In the end, she had been half as rich as she was, and Maurice was incalculably richer than any book broker could have dreamed.

Sedan was a magical place for these reversed fortunes. There, Maurice was reunited with his family, and in one of life's inexplicable miracles came the man Thomas Sunstone. He was the Calvinist surveyor who found Jean, Marie, and Mary in Mons. The son of a rich shipping businessman from London, he was striking out on his own to found another branch in Belfast. Thomas Sunstone keenly understood the importance of these new Mercator maps to better survey the northern seas, as well as do his part for the reformation. When he heard of the search

for the missing Millets he was drawn to the quest although he had no intentions before to venture inland so much.

He found Marie there and they fell in love. Indeed this knight in shining armor fell in love with baby Mary as well, even after he learned she was not truly Marie's child.

Then in June a spurt of seventeen refugees began to pour in one day. On the next, eleven more, all from Laon. Christopher had done it. Seigneur Phillipe never received assistance from the Huguenots, so when the war began Christopher came and pressed his claim by force. It was a bloody fight, but in the end Christopher emerged victorious. Maurice and Marie would marry rich, but Christopher, the youngest of the lot, gained true power. The Millet family contained not a drop of noble blood, but there he sat, the new Seigneur of Laon. Knowing that the new lord's policy would be conversion or death, many found the escape route to Sedan.

Among the refugees, many people of Laon found Maurice Millet and exalted him as a local hero. Dearest of all though was the reunion of Maurice with Torry and Robiere. The friends resumed their scholarship at the nearest brook and talked of all their tales. They were duty bound to inform him that Christopher demanded he renounce the family name.

Shadows of Laon flickered in by many forms. The magistrate had made a brief visit to inform Maurice that the Troyes family had just arrived, these were the kin of Tonya. Maurice told Emily and sent out invitation without delay. The magistrate was a man of strict adherence and so if their marriage were to be annulled, there could be no avoidance of Luke being born a bastard.

Jean-Baptiste, Victoriete, and Violette sat stone faced and received their acquaintance to their daughter's replacement with as much grace as could be expected. Jean Millet began to talk but Jean-Baptiste said, "No, Maurice is the man of your household."

The elder Millet accepted the insult realizing it was altogether true. Everyone knew of Maurice's great works in constructing escape routes from France into Sedan.

"Monsieur Troyes dear sir, my grief is only surpassed by your own. Though I wish it ever not so, all the information could only be concluded at the passing of dearest Tonya. I fain to now know if you have any material to suggest otherwise?"

"No Maurice, we for ourselves have no solace in comfort. I accept that dearest Tonya is dead, and I place full blame on you and your father. Your father will be burned for his abandonment and you Maurice shall burn for sacrificing your own wife on your virgin quest. You perfected the craft of escape to usher in a new wife, a woman of great means, yes Jesus sees you." Maurice had no recourse but to accept the shame, for intentions aside, it all came to pass.

Now Tonya's mother spoke. "We could abolish your union, for we have no body to bury. None to bury." Her display was only a preview of what would appeal to the magistrate. "We could claim Mary, for you have all been shown to be unfit!"

Jean-Baptiste in tacit, "There is another way, Maurice. You who are so skilled at moving lost souls. Get us to Amsterdam, that city which is much closed to us Huguenots. Deliver these means to me and you shall keep your wife, and poor Mary who was cursed from her very christening." He stood up and spat on the floor, leaving behind nothing unsaid.

Upon the departure of Tonya's family, close personal matters would be resolved. Maurice announced he would atone and grant their poor family all they asked and more.

Maurice made the arrangements for Jean-Baptiste, but also included a position into a fledgling trading company which possessed much speculative value. The magistrate agreed that Tonya should be declared legally dead; and that Maurice and Emily's marriage remain intact.

Another decision required Maurice and Thomas Sunstone to also come to terms. Mary was nearly three years old and knew only Marie to be her mother and Thomas her father. Thomas formally made known his intention to marry Marie and wished very much to be acknowledged as Mary's father. Marie, though she would not fight it, was horrified to lose her baby girl. Emily even stated that she preferred Maurice and her to get a fresh start of their own.

Maurice pondered about that further and decided to invent a new family name. Thomas told him how the Anglican way often used the family occupation as a surname. His family was a long line of seafarers who claimed Viking descent and used the 'Sunstone' to navigate west. Thomas asked if the whole family could return with him to London, and eventually Belfast, so Maurice took the name Bookman.

On June 21, 1562, the dual wedding between Maurice and Emily Bookman, and Thomas and Marie Sunstone took place. The former: a symbolic renewal of vows under the new surname. The latter: a fresh marriage covenant that recognized Mary Sunstone of being born out of wedlock.

After the weddings, Maurice had doubled his efforts on the logistics of refugee routes to Sedan. The guest housing they had been assigned to left him little room, but that he did have was crammed with diagrams, time-tables, and contacts. Any paper with immediacy found a spot on the floor or any surface that could be found. The rest of the papers rolled into tight scrolls and piled, nearly a man high, in the corner. He thought about the refugee network he built and how Danilo saved him when he was stuck. His old wandering friend came to him when needed most. Like a ghost from the past, Danilo re-entered Maurice's life. The travelling Greek reminded Maurice of the importance of priorities. "Categorize groups of refugees." He said.

His chief patrons worked together with Gaultien as agreed, to first categorize the protestants of France. The initial category they dubbed the unwanted. A swath of society which the ultra-catholics couldn't care less about. A second group would have been the exact opposite: nobles and even clergymen and some from the wealthy merchant and administrative class. Gaultien advised that this group, the ultra-catholics, would be determined to hold as hostages in their own homes. Supervised and surrounded and pressured to abjure at each turn. Only as a last resort would these families be under threat of death. This group is where Maurice needed to use Marcel Ruben, his renewed friend; his task, to find trade routes that he could arrange smuggling these people using the old method of Herndon Calais' influential Catholics as above suspicion safe houses. The final group was the majority of bourgeoisie who could buy their way out. Daniel Laurent would help these individuals sell their holdings and possessions to Catholics in exchange for papers to travel. For all three groups the terminus was to be Sedan.

In theory, the plan was sound, but Maurice lacked the manpower and security forces and so the refugees only trickled in. Then arrived Danilo from out of the blue, and Sedan once again proved to be the place of reversed fortunes. Danilo, who was always well informed, was also now well armed. He was evasive and secretive about his advancement, but he could now be found ahead of three bands of German Reiters. Once Maurice had the strength of these horsemen, more fully stocked trains of protestants would be escorted out en masse. Cover as traders was always used. But when in a pinch, the reiters could fight off patrols and flee.

The old iron midwife also escaped unscathed from Laon, and in a final irony, she visited upon Maurice just that day advising that Emily needed fattening up. The couple had vowed to repent for their sin of gluttony and had done well to reserve meats for special occasions. They spread the Florentine cuisine of Fontainebleu even further north where vegetables were no longer to be designated as the food of the poor.

Maurice continued staring at Emily's stomach when he thought he perceived a ripple. Was their child awake? Now instead of the people trickling in, they came by torrents. That day, aside from being reprimanded by the midwife, he found himself harangued by provincial administrators as well as Danilo. The administrators had been warning that Sedan was bursting with newcomers, and they could not all remain. Maurice put all of his efforts on the escape and had henceforth washed himself of any duty for his people beyond that. His father and the Sunstones were preparing for London, and he and Emily were to be not far behind after the birth and the midwife giving her approval for sea travel. All Protestants must draw upon their own industriousness now, he would declare.

Danilo was concerned about the latest threat from Christopher. Apparently, Maurice's successful exodus had gained the attention of de Guise and now dangled a Barony, if he could indeed sever the escape routes and secure the ancestral Guise lands as he once boasted he could. Danilo urged Maurice Bookman to return with him to Germany to find a new destination with their own new routes.

His father's words before bidding him goodnight comforted him now, as did the little kicks of his baby. "You have done extraordinary things already son, and have endured many costs." Jean took Mary from Maurice to return her to mother. Maurice gave a tight squeeze before letting go. "Its not the same as losing a child, but it is close. Don't risk losing another. You had a duty and you eventually reached it, now you can afford yourself that simple life you wanted from the beginning."

Chapter Twenty-Six

February 3, 1563

Paris, France

One of Pastor Rohn's converts in Paris was the cavalier named Thomas. His self-appraised honor became so diminished in the years following the convent rapes, that he had grown upset with the church. Thomas recalled the times he was dismissed by that wicked priest, so he had been left alone with the maidens. It sickened the cavalier that he had been an unwitting piece to those great sins. Thomas thought about the days when his own wife beamed with pride to be married to a cavalier, a protector of maidens. Borges stripped him of that dignity. Thomas was made to endure many more months of guarding the black priest before finally receiving a patrolling assignment in Paris.

The new mission proved only scantily more honorable. Parisians were extremely intolerant to the protestants, and since the reign of the Governess and her edicts of tolerance, they came to worship more freely. Despite the edicts coming from up high, his own captains gave quite starker instructions. "Search out and torment any Huguenot gathering."

It would be said that the city arms came to ignore their edicts only after the few crimes of iconoclasm. To Thomas' memory the edicts were ignored before any Church property was destroyed.

Thomas happened upon the street preaching Pastor Rohn on more than one occasion. He always did what he could for the pastor, advising him of the quarters that would be least

patrolled for the fortnight. The pastor sensed in him a man ready to convert, and he was ever right. The cavalier complained to Rohn when they were quite alone about his dissatisfaction on how the church handled the affair of the edict of re-education. Thomas felt an urge to confess to Rohn and to be forgiven for his own ignorance.

He sought redemption and yearned deeply for a church leader he could trust. In time, Thomas found himself ready to convert, but Rohn also preached patience to the man. He advised that there were other men at arms, city guards, and captains who were also ready to convert. Rohn had warned them to not convert individually, but to wait for such time that they could form a unit together, and thusly, be unshakeable in their solidarity.

Thomas heeded his pastor's advice, but had announced to his wife and family of their upcoming conversion. Thomas' wife began showing that hint of pride in her husband again, and she prayed that the other wives would see the light of the protestants. Its warmth was comforting and its light guiding.

On an evening of a new moon, a harlot that Thomas knew ran to him begging for assistance.

"He is tearing her up, he goes too far this time!"

Thomas knew of the brothel she worked, and so set off without any further incitement. The cavalier arrived at such a scene that would prove too much for him. It was the damned priest! He held a bloody knife and the woman lay to the side bloodied and stripped.

Priest Borges shown that look. That look of relief. The look which washed away guilt and replaced it with the usual arrogance. Borges saw Thomas and at once believed he was saved yet again.

"I shall do what your bishops would not, I shall cast you to hell."

Sir Thomas drew his cutlass. The sound of steel reverberated and it pleased the cavalier to see the priest quake. *That sound of steel tolls for thee.* Thomas lunged with a practiced death strike, driving the tip of the blade through heart. To his surprise he found himself twisting following his thrust. He had killed many men, but never in hatred. Borges' eyes widened to their limits and as such remained as his lifeless body slumped down. Thomas cleaned and sheathed his cutlass with a deliberate motion when the other harlot had returned. To her he only said, "Whether I was here, or were it another of your drunken guests, I shall leave up to you."

Chapter Twenty-Seven

February 24, 1563

Orleans, France

Defeat was at hand, the Admiral decided. Gaspard was pondering the events of the war and how things could have gone differently.

Antoine de Bourbon was the first of the Triumvir to perish during the fighting. He was mortally wounded in his successful charge to capture Rouen. This was an important victory for the Royalists, as the Huguenots had handed the port city of La Havre to the English in exchange for their help. Rouen being near La Havre, could block English advancements into the fray. The strategy worked and forced the Huguenots out, in order to join with their new allies at La Havre. The Catholics moved to block them, which resulted at the battle of Dreux. There the commander of royalist forces, Anne de Montmorency, was captured, but so too was Lord Conde setting up a possible prisoner exchange.

That was a mistake, Gaspard de Coligny concluded. At the beginning stages of the Civil War, it was all mobilization and blustering, but neither side had truly desired to spill the blood of their kin and countrymen. By the Battle of Dreux, the boiling blood had infected all. Surely we could have been civil enough to exchange our prisoners? He had only balked at the offer of trading Montmorency for Conde because Gaspard thought it an uneven trade. When St. Andre was captured though, he was more amiable for that swap instead. Before he could draft the letter for immediate dispatch, it was reported that the

Marshall St. Andre had been slain. Gaspard had eschewed his impetuous brother for the transgression, but of course Odet claimed no responsibility. The Admiral had Montmorency spirited away before another accident occurred, but the rules of warfare had escalated beyond all control.

Gaspard continued to look haughtily at his brother through his recollections. "I still blame you brother but worry not, for I may have a surprise for Francois de Guise."

The battle of Dreux concluded with another Catholic-Royalist victory, but the over nine thousand corpses drenching the battlefield told an uneven story. The Huguenot cavalry remained largely intact while the Catholics had hardly any left. Francois, the Duke of Guise, now the sole commander of the royalist army, called in reinforcements until he had a 2:1 advantage in his final push for Orleans. Demands, promises, and victory drunk promotions were issued, such as the raising of Christopher to Baron de Millet.

The protestants now only held Le Havre, though physically held by their English allies. Orleans, defended by the brothers Coligny and their Huguenots. Orleans, the last bastion.

Francois de Guise watched his informal prisoner chew on a flank of fried pork. "Brothers against brothers, out there and in here. Time was we were fast friends."

"Still are," Louis Conde circled his head in an arc gesturing to the plush conditions for an enemy prisoner.

"You against your own brother, who died in this unnatural war."

"Now you don't have to share in the victory." Pointed out Conde.

"The admiral versus his uncle who is now a prisoner such as you."

"Oh I am quite certain his arrangements are better. Get to the point man."

Francois lamented on. "The point my friend is that this war is pointless. We are not fighting over faith."

"Aren't we?"

"Is it because I am a foreigner? A Kraut?"

Lorde Conde grew bored. "No, Francois let us not pretend."

"You are right. I want to be King of France. You want to be King of France. Your brother wanted to be king of France. Catherine wants to be King of France."

"There we have it. So all this is not pointless," Conde posited for a conclusion.

The Duke of Guise begged an alternative. "But it is, because we could simply sit down and all agree on the following, un", as he pointed to himself, "deux," as he pointed at Conde, "Catherine trois."

Conde was up for the fantasy. "Neh, King Charles trois,"

"Neh, Montmorency trois."

"OK, un Lorde," Conde at himself, "du" at Francois…and the men guffawed away at the joke. What a joke, all that death over a childish game of king of the hill.

They were interrupted by a guard. "We have a Huguenot deserter."

"What of it? You will have plenty more with their doom being now imminent."

"He states he was working for you, over at their camp spying."

Conde shot an accusing look at the Duke.

"What? As if you don't have a few of your own here in my camp." Conde only shrugged innocently. "I have some artillery inspections to conduct, but I shall return so we can finish this. But there is no way you get to be King."

The Huguenot was twenty-two years old, yet short as a boy. He was immediately recognized by the Duke and ordered released. Francois took the spy's report of enemy morale and a short list of important leaders, then the double agent was dismissed. The man was more like a triple agent, and most aptly an opportunist. The short man had noticed the Duke was not wearing any chain mail, and here he was still armed with his arquebusier.

A few minutes later the shot rang out and a guard rushed over to the Duke. "This was to be expected, but I think it will be nothing."

The bullet could not be removed and so it festered and poisoned Francois' blood and soul. On the eighth day he quaked a final confession, and begged mercy for the butchering of Vassy.

Once again Catherine seized regency and had another chance to rule with the moderate politiques. Conde and Montmorency were released and thus the Edict of Amboise marked an end to the war in March of 1563.

Protestant nobles earned religious freedom, but not the commoners. All church property was to be returned in exchange for the crown paying off the Huguenots debts to the mercenaries. Paris and Lyon remained hotbeds of conflict, but in time they calmed. The war was over.

Chapter Twenty-Eight

Peace did not last. Catherine de Medici mustered a united French force of both religions to oust the English from La Havre, leaving the islanders disbarred from the continent for good. A unification under national lines was short lived and at age thirteen Charles IX was declared an adult and the official sovereign King of France. The era of boy kings was over.

The Council of Trent concluded in December of 1563 with Cardinal Charles, Pope Paul III, and King Philip II of Spain united against further protestant expansion. Cardinal Charles de Lorraine gave up the Gallican cause and influenced his nephew the new Duke of Lorraine, Henri, to religious lines.

June 1, 1570

France and Ireland

The royal train departed Fontainebleu on a national tour that would span several years. The young King and his ever-present mother heard grievances across the domain. Yet rather than pull into centrism, in their wake were only new Catholic leagues determined to do what King Charles could not. The Catholic leagues represented the primary source of fear for the Huguenots, resulting in a delicate peace. Leagues conspired directly with Spain, just as the Triumvir had, but now there were not well-established heads to cut off. The

protestants were saved at Orleans when Duke Francois de Guise fell.

Spain had a new king as well. The 1567 Dutch revolts caused King Phillip II to order the Duke of Alba to put it down. This was all that was needed to end the uneasy peace in France. With Spanish forces mobilized along French borders, the worries of a Catholic conspiracy with King Phillip II, sparked the 2nd war of Religion which ended in 1568 and then a 3rd in the very same year.

It was not like his first noble appointment. Christopher now had a contingent of supporters. He also had accomplishments which won him a higher level of legitimacy. Henri, the new Duke de Guise, spoke with enthusiasm and grace. This time Christopher learned of the Latin phrases for such ceremonies. The bishop's strange tongue was now meaningful and young Christopher puffed his chest out, "Blessed be the noble families appointed by God to rule over the Earth," phrased in Latin.

Upon the ending of the ritual, Duke Henri spoke to Christopher. "I have a surprise for you Baron Millet. We have another formality to attend before we can quit the business of lords and attend to our enemies."

"Surely every possible praise and title has been conferred upon me, let us quit now and seek Huguenot blood."

Both noble men, being in their twenties, fed on the other's thirst for glory. Henri embraced his friend with bellicose zeal. "You have captured and executed Captain Herndon. You have won Laon, then you expanded your territory by disrupting your brother's plans and exposing the treacherous lords of my own family homelands of Guise. Now your Barony extends from Laon to Guise, which makes us practically brothers. I must make you a gendarme today as well, I could not hold such relations without it being so."

"My duke, I have not yet truly led a charge. The others hold back as to let me appear so, I also cannot properly joust—"

"I understand Christopher, but still it must be done. Besides, your horsemanship improves by the day, and I think we should begin training together as well."

Henri de Guise, the 3rd Duke of Lorraine, performed the simple ceremony. The knights and pages were lounged around a fire and were enjoying their feast upon a hare du Lay had trapped. Many of the gendarme were not too pleased during the ceremony. The young Baron was a brave fighter and a decent commander, but his rise through licensure could not replace a lifetime of training that true gendarme undertook. With no outlet for such talk, they instead spoke of the enemy.

"Take the fight to the Dutch heretics!"

At that, a protestant pikeman punched the antagonist and they wrestled about a bit before they both tired and came back to the meal. Christopher was still trying to understand the realm of France. Here they were a band of catholic forces that enlisted several protestant men. He came to accept this dynamic, but then became upset that he was not allowed to remain protestant since it now appeared not to matter much. War induced craziness and strange alliances.

It had been explained to him that he was now too important to consider reforming again, and he came to accept that in time. Christopher was getting a lay of the land. Mercenaries were far more important than he could have imagined. Men of various creed, nationality, languages, and faith could fight as one when it counted. Men who have fought in scores of battles, sometimes with each other, sometimes against each other. The mercenaries were loyal to whoever kept them paid and fed. A master failing in that for too long would find himself deserted before long. Henri, the new Duke of Guise never failed in that. Christopher was also learning about chivalry and lack thereof. The mercenaries were less likely to pillage a townfolk such as he once believed. Bigots however, like the man who got himself punched, were the real threat to the innocent. For the zealots, the conflict was religious. Any opportunity to terrorize a commoner of the protestant faith, was seized with glee.

The new head of house Millet continued to adapt as he learned about the real world and all of its nuance. It was up to chivalrous gendarme to protect the innocent, even in war. He once hoped that the chevalier was proof such chivalry was indeed not dead. However, he had come to find that when an evil doer who stopped to rape a farm girl was rarely challenged, it was not so simple. Even du Lay, who was gallant, knew when to choose his battle lines. The morality of Christopher during these formative years came to a resting place less like du Lay or Herndon, even more like Uncle Merline. "Do what you can to protect your own family through status and power." He would say. Lisbeth, and yes still Maurice, is who he wanted to protect. He wondered how Maurice must be a changed man, too. He wondered if he could convince him to convert. Had Maurice too learned that the religious divide was a farce?

Maurice Bookman had become an important figure in the wars, and Christopher had heard much about his brother over the years. He had become the chief architect of protestant exodus out of France. It was said that he and Admiral de Coligny had a falling out over the soldiers Maurice was costing him, but his brother would not yield from the vision of their father: escape at all costs. Now that the Dutch were at war for their independence from Spain, Maurice had transitioned his land routes to sea routes, with many refugees bound for England and Denmark.

Looking upon the desolate landscape, Christopher, for the first time, began to feel genuine hatred for his brother. He rode along passing by a pile of bodies, a sight he had grown much accustomed to. This pile, being prepared for mass burial, were not victims of battle. This was a pile of victims of the war. Starvation ushered in by the black horse who rode too about these lands. The crown was broke. The people overtaxed. Battle ravaged crops and salvageable harvests were taken by the soldiers. Whoever won the battle of the day did not matter to the people, for the aftermath remained the same. Trade stifled to a trickle as many attempted to leech upon any lifeline emanating from the rare cities hosting no armies.

Joining up with whichever army won the day became an increasingly tempting option. Better to steal from another than have it stolen from you. Christopher was inspecting a group of men who were asking for such admission into his band. This always led to a point of contention between Christopher and his war party. Millet believed deeply in lightning-fast movement. Strategy be damned, just get there first. First to survey wins the proverbial high ground he would argue. Christopher was forced to accept the ragged and malnourished farmers as his force was nearly depleted of bodies, and at present had more food than mouths. At the very least he could feed his countrymen, if for no other reason. "Check them for disease," he barked, indicating his approval of their joining up.

Damn Maurice and all the Huguenots. The war is pointless. Christopher asked questions mentally that he directed telepathically to his older brother. If this was a war of religion then why do both sides fight with mixed forces? If this was about faith, then why do the commoners care not about who wins? If Maurice, in your infinite wisdom, accepts this is not about faith, then what dear brother is it about? For what Christian reason should you not abjure so that our country can unite and raise ourselves back into glory. Christopher never in his darkest nightmares believed the French could fall to such piteous depths. The eucharist. A pope in a pointed hat. A mass. These all flicker against the blackness of despair and suffering that could be ended with a simple sign of the holy trinity.

Not only were the Baron Millet's forces not first to the next major battle, they were hopelessly chasing the Huguenots who were racing from Toulouse to Paris. Christopher continued his alterations with formations. He ordered change from a one to five format, into a one to three, concerning the number of Reiter to number of pikemen. The Catholics finally caught up and they were defeated at Arnay le-Duc.

Four security towns were established, by decree of the treaty of St. Germain, signed in August 1570. La Rochelle, La Charite, Montabaun, and Cognac were granted protestant control as the third war came to an end. Armed peace was no peace at all. Most rights were won for Huguenot lords and not the commoners. The ascension of both Maurice and Christopher was remarkable, yet both brothers felt deeply connected to their more common roots. The Robieres and Torrys of France. If only Maurice would have abjured. The Millet brothers could have been powerful agents for a true and lasting peace.

Christopher took to looking upon his letters. Counting all the children born up to that point. In one letter, his father also asked him to live simply and stop trying to soar and polish his grubby crown.

Maurice and Emily built their new life together as simple Christians. They lived in London for a year before settling down in Belfast. They were diligent about learning English and dropping their native tongue. They were elders of their church due to the important role Maurice Bookman had in the Civil Wars, but the couple did not abide much reverence. As far as they were concerned, they were guest peoples in Ireland and only wished to help a community of Huguenots contribute to their new countrymen. Their children, of which they had four, were being raised by the values of the gospel. Emily praised the lord to be able to raise her own family outside of the stifling catholic monolith and thanked god every day for bringing Maurice into her life.

Of their four children, comprised of three boys and a girl, the fourth, they christened John, had just been born. Since that birth Maurice had begun growing restless. France was embroiled in the 3rd war and now the low countries were in open rebellion against Spain. He had attempted to pass on his network contacts for other protestant leaders to take up the cause, but they were not nearly as successful. Personal oversight was required, but Maurice would not make that sacrifice again. Watching baby John coo, he remembered when Mary was only a babe. No. He would not make that sacrifice again.

Thunderous cannon blasts rained down on the already defeated town. Acrid smoke choked a group of fleeing protestants, but the haze also provided cover. Only yards away swiss pike pierced heart and brain. What lay beyond the fog of war was a terror muted in their minds until they heard the screams. The runners rushed on. "To the watermill at Edou crossing," is what they heard the day before. The seven survivors took stock only after they outran artillery. The water mill at Edou was perceived, and once in sight, their cries and tears then flowed. In a torrent of release, they told of Baron Millet's men at arms who had broken and scattered the defensive lines. The terrible cannons retrained upon their escape, while pikemen drove down man, woman, and child. A woman had slipped on the blooded ground and was trampled into fleshy mud.

Potato soup and milk was given. They rested, and were given time, for the shock to pass. Eventually they were told that the only passage was destined for Denmark. None in that group knew anyone that had fled to the country of the Danes. Ten others were relayed to port the night before, and two were said to have relations already there. The seven of that iteration were rowed downstream and taken to a port warehouse. They met the other ten and learned that they were to be secreted away within the stores of chateaux wine crates, bound for Sjelborg. Among the group were two sisters, a father and son, and three cousins. Of course they all knew each other well enough as fellow town folk, but they were now destined to become linked tightly as strangers in a strange land often do.

They spoke of Maurice and how he continued to prepare the way for the Huguenots. Exodus was made possible, comfortable, and safe due to his works. Pamphlets and tickets of sorts were issued, and it was explained that they would be directed to a church upon arrival and that many Huguenots were obtaining jobs salting and pickling fish on the western coast of Denmark. New world opportunities were discussed as collectively the group seemed to have the greatest number of relations with those who fled to Halifax in Nova Scotia. The smugglers warned them though, as Maurice warned the missionaries, to not make a settlement in Brazil. The fools tried and were expelled. In the New World, the Catholics plague the protestants as well. North Ireland, England, Netherlands, Germany, and Scandinavia were the only safe domains.

They prayed together and praised their liberators and asked them to pass on their eternal gratitude to Maurice. The Huguenots boarded the ship and left France behind them.

Belfast was much like Laon in that it was primarily an agricultural town with some trading and shops. For the scholars of the Mausien Brook, it was the harbor along the coast of the Irish sea that presented the landlocked farmers a fresh world to live in. The rough fishermen, in their rickety boats, belied the range they could venture. Huguenots would watch them disappear to the eastern horizon and wait for their return. Torry and Robiere came to give a report to Maurice.

"Sveyn Gnordsson sends confirmation that he can fill fifty more positions at his fishery." "I shall send my thanks, then I shall cease further contact. From here on it is between Sveyn and Daniel Laurent."

Robiere pleaded, "Too many immigrants too quickly for your replacements to handle, even with the addition of Monsieur Laurent."

Maurice snapped, "Don't you think I know that. My brother-in-law fears the customs agents are no longer happy with the size of their pouches, fears his ship will get boarded sooner or later. My instincts tell me he is not far off. Should I risk his family or mine...again?" He looked at his old friends and cooled down. "I fear we are nearing the end my friends."

"Fifty-four thousand Maurice." Torry had become a great lover of arithmetic.

"Stop giving me updates on the—"

Torry did not relent. "Thirty thousand souls you have saved Maurice. I have worked out the calculations with the others, we estimate fifty-four thousand more Huguenots seeking freedom."

"Do you really believe you can put a number on when you have finished the lord's work?"

"No I do not—"

Robiere interrupted. "That is just it Maurice, do you even speak with Jesus anymore?"

"Clearly you both have something to say."

Robiere went on, "It's only, you seem to be drawn further away from the gospels and leave our academic teachings nearly entirely on us."

"And you Torry?"

"Ever since we came to Belfast, you got closer into Thomas' world, the world of commerce."

Robiere felt the tension in the air, something the men of the brook rarely shared. Torry looked ready for another blow, but Robiere gave him that look. That look that said, come now friend, let him alone. The same look Jan used to give Torry to give Robiere a reprieve. They hoped he would pray with Jesus. He did not pray, but rather turned the gears of his own powerful mind. Slowly yet surely, he had backslid to his old ways.

Indeed, Maurice had fallen into the pride of his great works and the even greater works to come. His master plan was building each day in his own thoughts. Deep down he knew his replacements would fail. Though Daniel Laurent and the other patrons had many capabilities, only he it seemed, could see all the pieces fit together. How many letters have I sent to them? Maurice had tried to convey his plans to them all, but it had become apparent that only he could accomplish the monumental feat. That notion comes with vanity and its pitfalls.

The master plan began to form in his mind as they departed Sedan. From that terminus the plight of the Huguenots continued. It was an error to consider the task complete at that juncture. I was still responsible for them.

The path that Maurice constructed was not only a physical route but also a secular guide. Communities and occupations needed to be planned. Initially, the communities would be enclaves so the refugees could feel a sense of familiarity. Maurice though learned how crucial it was that they assimilate into the host country and to their languages and customs. Each refugee should be told to: "Adopt their way of life as long as it does not violate your faith." In the matter of uncompromised faith is precisely why Maurice chose to not transport Huguenots to the New World in the efforts of colonization. That path would invariably lead his people to become slavers. Slavery was becoming the moral high ground that Christians held over the Catholics.

The final phase in his master plan did involve a colonization of sorts. What Maurice envisioned was developing a commercial center for both the Huguenots and Irish to thrive. He retrieved his beloved domino blocks and began setting up the layout of this commercial center with blocks representing different buildings and zones. Maurice had done this a dozen times, with each iteration involving a schematic change or improvement of some kind.

"Playing with those dominoes again?" Emily had snuck in. The glint in Maurice's eye shuttered as he embraced his wife lovingly. "You never did finish the story on how you acquired those toys."

"Ah yes, well remember back when I had to treat with Grace o' Malley?"

"Yes that terrible pirate woman."

Maurice shot her a discreet look. "That pirate woman happens to control the Irish sea. No trade is allowed if not by her consent. Which is still no guarantee her pirates won't board you but still, I had to treat with her when I was more involved with the exodus." Emily gave a baleful look, she knew he missed running that enterprise. "Apparently, they captured a Spanish galleon sometime before and among her captured was a China-man. A catholic China-man the Jesuits converted. He was on his way to mother Spain to receive further education, one of their favorites, a wise man indeed. I spoke to him about dominoes of course. This sparked an idea and he began crafting sets and introducing the game to the Irish. They apparently love it. When I was last at O'Malley castle he gifted me this set."

She was gazing at the plaza model being constructed. "I tease about playing with them, but this looks quite serious."

"What I have planned here is an investment to our very own business district. Funded by wealthy Huguenots, I am making inroads with Irish and English officials for a three-square mile plot with extensive roads to act as a distribution hub. Do you remember when Danilo came with the news of King Henri II's death?"

They sat and thought on it, they had shared so many memories of their individual pasts. "I do. The boycotts."

"Yes, but even without the boycotts his press master was going to stop making deliveries. Danilo also said that other presses were abandoning transportation as well."

Emily caught on to the genius of her husband. Her affection for his mind as strong as ever. "If you can move people efficiently, why not move goods."

Maurice kissed her for that. "Yes, I want to build a waystation here in Belfast. From this center we would pick up directly from the manufacturers and centralize all the goods here. The cost savings and contracted quantities would net a wholesale price, and the merchants would buy directly from these offices and warehouses. All run by a thriving protestant manager class."

Emily detected a down note at that last part. "Husband, what troubles you?"

He knocked the dominoes down and began putting them away. "You were right dear, they are just playthings."

Chapter Twenty-Nine

September 10, 1570

Belfast, Ireland

Marie awoke and heard the gurgling of her second son. Though this was only her second baby, and indeed the process she was quite used to, the delirium of her sleep post-partem had never been this deranged.

Her dreams were terror-filled, and her waking hours were replete with reminiscent nightmares. Her son was brought to her during breaks of the madness, for as much suckle that could be had before the craze resumed. Baby would be ushered away screaming with the nanny proclaiming that her mistress still needed more time.

Within the mind of Marie swirled memories both true and false. A love affair was it? An evil sister-in-law. Lost in a jungle, then a pit. That woeful endless pit. Her father fell, then fell further, then fell again. He was crippled, but still struck her with thunderous force. "Whore," a boot. Blackness.

Marie awoke to her husband eating soup while looking over her like a frozen squirrel not knowing whether to approach or retreat. "Thomas, tell me of me. I fear I don't remember anymore."

"Hmm, let's see. It was so long ago wasn't it. At least a fortnight," he chuckled to himself. "The doctor said I must test you, to help with your memory. Dear, do you remember what brought me to that church hospital?" She winced in pain and beckoned for medicine. "This isn't helping either," denying the request.

"A brother was it?" Marie thought.

"Yes, your brother."

"My brother, not your brother?"

263

"No, your brother. Maurice."

"Nicolas."

"No, Maurice."

It was all muddy. "He came for me, to save us."

"No dear, he couldn't, so he sent me."

"You saved us?"

"I suppose if our life was a fairy tale then that is what the author would say. Ok, good job Marie. Yes, I was sent to look for you and your father. When I met you I was smitten. Sure I fancied myself a knight on a quest, but that did not include a beautiful princess in that fantasy. Yet, there you stood. Stunning." Marie smiled. "Oh but that was nothing. Your father was the center of your universe, and your niece too. He was so sick all the time, and crippled. You nursed him day and night. A fiercer mother hen I never knew. I would have thought you a nurse your whole life. To earn your keep there, you volunteered to nurse all the other refugees. You would later tell me though that you knew not a single thing of healing, but learned from every doctor and nurse you could." She looked about the bedroom and was indeed remembering more things. The armoire which she had selected herself. It had a cream finish and was not nearly as ornate as those most popular. She would have no carvings of mythological scenes containing their linens and night wear, even the wrought iron handles were a little too intricate for her taste.

"My father is dead?"

"No, no, I am sorry, forgive me I was only speaking in past tense."

"He is crippled."

"He is."

"How?"

"Your turn dear."

"Please tell me how."

"I can't. You would never speak of it." She reached her hand for the bottle. "Dear please."

Marie gestured with her hand again. He removed the cap and handed it to her sullenly.

She turned the bottle slowly emptying the contents into a nearby pot. "I have children to take care of, and a father."

"And a ridiculous husband."

"And a good husband."

Thomas headed back to work, quite happy with his wife's progress. His brows furled as he remembered that he must first regain her true memories before reminding her of their secret about Mary. At the port of Belfast, Thomas was to supervise disembarkation of their arrivals from France.

He made a final personal inspection of the port's gangways. Satisfied, he authorized the orderly transfer of passengers and crew from ship to wharf. Quite shortly into the hour there was a loud noise followed by a growing commotion. Thomas drifted to the small window afforded to the office to find a quite common scene. They had done it again, he noted to himself. Protestant rabble who hide among the wharf's many stacks and emerge only when their target party appears onto the planks. Visiting catholic dignitaries from the continent were the usual objects of such harassment. He issued some preliminary order of readiness, but watched on. The protest began peaceful enough, which set him a little towards ease. Thomas could not help but be moved by their production of music. Stringed instruments poured out chords of worship and they singed in hums of soulful lament. Thomas flinched as one of the catholic retinue grabbed an instrument and smashed it to the ground. The wooden guitar split as did the peace. Thomas ordered his own sailors into the fray. Politics aside, he had a duty to protect his passengers. His sailors and port workers rushed into the crowd. Fists were being thrown and even a French Baron himself, presumably their quarry, wrestled with a large ruffian. A human shield formed around the impressive baron, allowing Thomas' men to push the Protestants away from the port.

Baron Christopher Millet and his entourage completed their exit from the Port of Belfast. There was to be an official celebration for a noble betrothal in Ireland. As was agreed upon so many years ago, his first born daughter was promised to the la Paussion. Christopher's rise had been sharp, and thus, soon he became powerful enough to renegotiate the terms with Claude la Paussion. Aurelie, then of age eight, was to be promised to a higher rank in Ireland, belonging to a boy called William Lynch. The melee at the port between catholics and Protestants troubled Christopher to a degree, but he was quite happy with the port authority's handling of the mob.

At the party, Christopher was celebrated for his victories and he regaled his own tales, including Herndon and the chauvre de sois.

His new Gaelic cousins were bawdy. They danced and sung without inhibition. Certainly owing some degree to their immoderation in drinking. Lawrence, the gallowglass, was dancing with Lisbeth. She seemed quite at home here. Or at least in her element. Hers was a wild spirit, so she would not allow Lawrence to teach her any of the steps. The gallowglass' feet may have well been unhinged, for they moved without care of possibility. And Lawrence wasn't even the best of the Irish dancers there. All around, Christopher could zoom in on any pair of feet and be dazzled. They thumped in rhythmic patterns. Lisbeth too was performing quite well, and he loved her very much at that moment. The dance came to an end and Lawrence returned the Baroness to her husband. Another gallowglass drew closer, followed by another. Christopher knew they were hungry for another tale. As much as he would have loved to regale them with addtional adventure of the chauvre de sois, he knew it was time to speak of more heady matters.

"You men wish to know of our war, our War of Religion in France?"

266

"We do lord Baron," Lawrence turned severe. The gallowglass were the sentinels of Ireland and as festive of people known to the emerald isles. Talk of war straightened any man's back though.

"We have found peace, the Treaty of St. Germain held fast when I left."

"Excuse me lord but hasn't peace been struck before?"

"Yes, this is our third peace."

"And do you reckon a fourth shall be needed?" Lawrence was speaking for the other gallowglass. "We hear, that it may be time for the gallowglass to cross the sea, to fight for the Pope, and our own homelands."

"I am uncertain about a fourth war," Baron Christopher looked the men in their eyes. "But I can assure you, if you come to France you will fight for nothing but coin."

Lawrence shot back, "No, the gallowglass are not mere mercenaries."

"In France you would be, trust me cousin, the very soul of my country is in disarray. Come, let us dance now and be festive. For the Huguenots have territory now and you shouldn't expect anymore come to Ireland."

Lawrence motioned for the music to begin again. Once again the Lynch clan reveled in their changing fortunes. Their ancestral titles stripped by the English nearly a decade previously, now obtained a marriage pact with French nobility. Baron de Millet clumsily led his wife, but Lisbeth understood the Celtic steps at a primitive level, so she took the lead and Christopher accepted. The papacy, now done with the French protestants, would surely move on. This, the Irish sung and danced to. Aurelie and William also found a pattern to match. Perhaps in their time, Ireland, with support from France and the Pope, would rid themselves of the English invaders.

Marie got back to her old self and then could join with Jean and his tutoring of Mary. At age ten, grandfather Jean suspected she had inherited the brilliance of Maurice. Mary excused herself and kissed her mother hoping that her illness would continue to desist. Marie could tell that Mary was pleased to see her mother carrying baby sister herself.

"Father, I want to finally tell Thomas about the pit. Can we see if together we can remember the right of it?"

"Oh Marie, its best to let things go."

"Please father. We were running west, looking for the coach which was supposed to pick us up for Brussels."

"Dear it had been two nights in those woods, I'd be damned if we weren't heading in circles. On the third day I fell into an old hunter's pit, thanks being to Jesus that it had been long defanged. My body and mind were broken. We were beginning to starve and each of us were quite mad. We had endured nearly a week of being bedeviled at every turn. My spirit held, and yours too. Tonya though, when she volunteered to search for help, I knew she wasn't coming back. She had given up."

"Yes, I remember. I argued with her that I should go, a mother should remain with her baby. She insisted. You finally convinced me not to wait for her and go save myself. I left you too, I left you to die for beating me."

"No." Jean cried. "No, you left to live and with forgiveness in your heart, Jesus led you to his nearest church. We had not been making circles, we were in Mons, we made it out. You brought help and came back for me. When I saw you again I could have died then and there of contentment. I still had a son whose forgiveness I sought; I seek."

"Father, he should beg for an eternity for your forgiveness."

"Daughter, let me tell you of how Jesus works. My father gave me the good news and you shall give it to her." He stroked baby Heather's cheek. "Before you and those men returned to the pit, it had rained. Rained hard. A deluge Noah would be proud of. All of our papers destroyed for good. Had that not been the case. Had I still had those important letters," he stressed the comedy of their once held importance. "From Mons we would have made our way to Brussels and never looked back. Jesus showed us didn't he. Stay, stay put my children."

Marie was following along, her memory seemingly returned with clarity. "We grieved so that we could not write to Maurice, and that silly moniker, Nicolas de Piefuin. What of your terrible cold Dad, had we got there before you were drenched in a freezing pond—"

"Yes, today I would not get the chills from a gentle summer breeze, but I have grandchildren who will be free to worship." Marie swam in the profoundness of that truth. "Jesus knew he was coming for us. Thomas was coming for you. This is the way of Jesus."

On that evening, Marie told her husband about their escape and being lost in the woods. "Father fell in a pit. Tonya was to look for help but never came back. She ran away from motherhood, but I am learning to forgive her."

"You have now told me all this dear. We need never speak of it again. Yours is a guarded heart, but once won, beats fiercely."

Marie shuddered visibly. *If he knew the whole truth I should be beaten again.* He thought her cold, Marie could tell, so rubbed her for warmth, but she shivered on with guilt. She remembered all the guilt she waded in back in Sedan. When her town folk from Laon met Thomas she dreaded that somebody would spread the gossip about her affair. That never came to pass, too many things of more importance had happened. Too many lives lost. Nobody remembered or cared.

"You said something of a fairy tale. When I was young I read them and believed in them with no proof that such love existed. Now, you are all the proof I need and I should never read another fairy tale again."

"What if our young Mary writes one? Your father certainly thinks she could."

"Then I would read another."

Thomas knew then his wife was returned. She remembered both the truth and the lie in regards to dearest Mary. Now that she was wholly herself again, he was able to give into his yearning for her, but Marie was tormented by the guilt of her and Robert la Paussion. She buried the memories away and made love to her husband. She owed him that much. If she could not reveal her secret, then she must not reveal its weight.

The next morning at the Belfast port, Thomas was approached by an underling who had the initiative to advise him on a small matter that would change their lives. The worker wondered if they should prepare special security for that visiting noble that caused such a ruckus last time, as he was scheduled to depart in two days. Thomas agreed and asked for the principal name on the manifest, to which his ears took in, "Baron Christopher Millet et al."

Thomas rushed home to tell his wife, and they shared the news with Jean and Maurice. It was decided they would go meet with him, and bring all the children. Thomas could arrange a meeting room in the yards office for a private meeting. There were contradicting sentiments between Jean, Maurice, and Marie, but they concluded that it was peace time after all, and if France could heal, then maybe so could their splintered family.

The house would be a pit of nervous energy until the reunion, but for Marie she was living a nightmare. Her past was hard on her heels. The next evening when Thomas returned home for dinner, she was rocked again.

"I have more news of your brother."

"Oh."

"You see since the extra security was approved, I have been able to gather more information about why Baron Millet's arrival caused such an uproar with the Protestants in the first place."

Marie struggled to calculate how much surprise she was to convey. She drew in her lips before venturing, "He is considered somewhat of a traitor among my people."

"Yes but I wish to ascertain more specifics. Tell me, do you know of the Lynch family from Antrim?"

"No, they are unfamiliar."

"How about La Paussion, in Antrim."

Marie froze, she tried to think quickly. "Antrim no, but of course La Paussion were the head family that chased us out of France. It was them that Christopher betrayed us for."

"Yes of course I am sorry dear, I just don't remember you actually telling me the name of that family. Anyway now it is making more sense."

"How so?"

"The Protestants that attacked him the other day were not of your Huguenots but more of my Anglicans. The visit had to do with an arranged marriage which would help solidify Gaelic-Franco relations against the Tudors. Do you know of Christopher's children?"

"I do not, dear husband we are quite estranged."

"Perhaps you would have learned by other means, but he has a daughter named Aurelie, aged eight, who was betrothed at birth to a La Paussion noble boy in Antrim. However, since your brother has gained a barony, Aurelie's status has been upgraded. They finalize and celebrate a new marriage pact between Aurelie and William Lynch, of a similar age. Young William Lynch by all rights would be a Gaelic chief if the Tudor dynasty did not have anything to do with it. You see Marie you may have ample time to repair things with your brother as it seems he will have powerful connections here in Northern Ireland."

Marie could hear no more of the farce. "He is not powerful Thomas. The Millet name means nothing and never has except for what my ancestors had humbly built. A noble wedding? That is a comedy. He is an impostor and nothing more and you should know better than to grant him any honor. Now I should like to be excused to visit with my real brother."

Marie went to visit Maurice and confided in him to sorts. "Sister, you know I have always supported your choice to not tell Thomas the whole truth. Once known he would be left with no other choice but to be shamed. There is no cause for him or you being shamed. I will simply pull the rascal aside tomorrow and demand he bite his tongue. I daresay I am the master of my younger brother."

"And what of this marriage nonsense?"

"Your husband is wrong. Whether separated by the channel or not, we will forever be separated by faith."

On the day of the embarkation, the Millet party was greeted personally by Thomas.

"I am told you are to thank for the security, I thank you," said Christopher.

"I assure you that is our policy to ensure safe passage for all of our passengers, regardless of creed. You may not believe that once I tell you who I am."

Christopher was quite puzzled, "Who exactly are you?"

"Thomas Sunstone, I have the pleasure of being the husband to your sister Marie." Thomas hurried in as much information as he could to fill the gap of dismay. "She is here now. Just that way. And our children. And your father Jean. And Maurice and his family. This was pure coincidence, not an ambush. I only learned your name on the manifest yesterday. Your family decided for me to come out. You can proceed with boarding, or join us with a little reunion. It is your choice Baron Millet."

Christopher talked with his wife and with their children, too. They followed to the meeting room while the rest of the party boarded along with their baggage.

The family reunion was altogether an honest affair. Being a total surprise for Christopher, and mostly a surprise for his old family, a type of utter honesty was induced by the spontaneity of it all. Secondly, there was little time for awkwardness, as Thomas would not delay the departure by much. Lastly, there were children. The family had many beautiful and innocent children.

Christopher saw his father crippled and ran into his arms. "I am sorry father, I am so sorry."

"Who do you pray to son?"

"Jesus Christ."

"Then you have nothing to be sorry for."

Maurice then pulled away his brother and somewhat whispered to him closely. "Two secrets brother I should have you keep, one Mary is the daughter of Marie and Thomas, and secondly Thomas knows nothing of that bastard Robert."

"Maurice, I have no wish to hurt your family." The dock attendants meeting room was a strange place for a reunion. If it were any indication, then Thomas certainly did keep his affairs ship shape. The sterility lent to the softness of Christopher's words.

Thomas then figured he was somewhat the host. "Let us attempt introductions." Each of the three families gathered together like newly purchased cattle being shoved with the herd. Jean remained with Maurice. "I am Thomas Sunstone, Christopher if I may?"

"Of course."

"Let me present our children: Mary, Richard, and our newest Heather."

"My heart is warmed by this meeting Thomas and may I present my wife Lisbeth and our children: Pierre, Aurelie, Antony, and Henri. I should love to meet yours Maurice."

"Yes Christopher this our 'Bookman' family: Wife Emily, Luke, Antoinette, Seamus, Lawrence, and a boy we expect to be christened John."

They exchanged other pleasantries and mingled, but were on a limited time table.

Christopher told his father about the battle of St. Denis where he fought most honorably. Jean was unimpressed and it darkened Christopher that he still sought validation from his father. He thought to himself that his ascension continued in the same way, opportunities arose and he seized them. "Father, brother, sister, let us have some words in private."

They gathered and sat around father like the old days. "We have little time so let me get straight to it. Sister, Maurice told me of the secrets and I am happy to keep them. I also name Robert a bastard, and I too still spit on his grave. You think me a traitor and there is nothing I can say here to change your thinking, but consider this. First, there is much that father kept from us regarding our uncles and the other Millets. Secondly, did I join La Paussion or have I buried them? Even now I deny them the hand of my daughter and make for her a better husband. We ran from our home, for our lives from them. You could return home now as Millets, come back to Laon and look down on la Paussion and they would have to kneel."

With nothing left to boast they each gave an answer of their own.

"Brother it pangs me to see you walk this false path. I did that as well, and I too thought it was for my family, but I eventually turned back. You say you have done this for your family and I accept that. So now turn back around. You renounce your title and proclaim your true faith."

"Son, you did none of this for your family. You did it for glory and a corrupted sense of honor."

Christopher stood, embarrassed to the core. "Bookmans and Sunstones then, quite the Anglican clan. Invaders here to the Irish and you dare condemn me. I must ask father, nay demand. Drop the Millet name, it does not belong to you anymore."

Jean beckoned Thomas with a wave. "Thomas, please come here. I humbly ask if I can adopt your own surname. To be henceforth known and buried as Jean Sunstone." Thomas bowed with trouble. The reunion soured.

"So now son let me say one last time as a father. Christopher, keep praying to Jesus Christ and know you made your father very proud. Now as Jean Sunstone, a Protestant to a catholic. May you burn in hell you slaughterer. Repent before it is too late and accept no letter of indulgence to make right. See here now in Ireland, where it is the Protestants who rule the catholics, yet see how their humanity is preserved. See how this good protestant ensured a papist to pass." Christopher gathered his family. "See to him how one should rule with tolerance and not a blood stained cross."

"We shall take our leave, but it would be an ill uncle of me to leave my niece and brother-in-law under false pretenses." Now at full shout and only partially directed, "Mary…Maurice is your true father and you should seek to him about your mother. Thomas, we were forced to leave Laon because Marie made a whore of herself and you should seek her about his name."

Maurice tackled him to the ground and punched angrily upon face and guts. Christopher had only grown since they last met, only trained, only warred. Christopher threw him aside and rolled into a fighting crouch. He leapt toward Maurice with an uppercut that lifted him off the ground and into the dazed world. Christopher's knife had carved into his cheek before Thomas could pull him away. With a shove, Baron Millet led his family away, onto the ship bound for triumphant return to France.

Chapter Thirty

August 18, 1572

Paris, France

A singular vision was conveyed to Catherine as she looked upon the clerestory windows. The blood red tint of glass projected images of Christ and his apostles. With the Catholics attending mass, the Huguenots were left alone to mill about Paris unabashedly like foreign sailors with a day's leave. The capital city was brimming with the multi-day festivities to celebrate the marriage between Margot Valois and Henri de Navarre. A royal marriage between her catholic daughter and a protestant king had finally brought the Huguenots out of hiding. The two-year peace was as fragile as ever. Despite the co-mingling between the two factions during wedding celebrations, there was a single issue that could ignite the city. Paris was the ultra-catholic capital of France, and the Huguenots were quickly wearing out their welcome. What they conversed about in their protestant enclaves mattered not as much to Catherine as it did for the common Parisian.

What concerned Catherine was what they discussed openly, within earshot of members of the radical Guise faction. Goadingly so they would announce their intent of quitting the city the moment the wedding celebrations concluded. "To war in the Netherlands." Gaspard schemed in obvious abrogation of king and council's orders. The bellicose Huguenots bragged to each other on how well armed they came to this city of iniquity. At times they donned themselves in battle regalia, to bring proof to their boasts. Groups of Parisian maidens would

draw closer to this clamor and feign innocence once amidst the mania. Then the Catholic male suitors would swoop in to save their beloved from the fray. The dustups were tame, yet altogether disorienting. The most inflaming of declaration came from the Admiral himself, that he had already begun mobilization so that he could rendezvous with his forces just outside Paris. Catherine's scouts had not been able to substantiate the claim though.

A plan crystallized as she thought upon another troubling trend. She knew for certain that her son, King Charles IX, was growing more envious of Admiral Gaspard de Coligny. This envy now seemed to run parallel along other feudal ranks. The hampered King was no longer a boy, and became envious of the absolute authority the Admiral held in his mini-state of Rochelle. A young page of the Guise faction, in youthful exuberance, clamored for battle. The boy would witness the other Huguenot boys preparing at once to war in the north. The Catholic lord who withered beneath the gaiety and gaudiness of weddings and balls while these Huguenot men called for a unified France capable of taking down an empire.

Paying little attention to the mass, the single conclusion was forming in Catherine's mind. He must die. He must die now. His assassination must be cordoned off as an act of Guise-Coligny blood feud, and nothing else. Catherine knew just the way it would be done. What the black queen did not know at that time was there already was a plan in motion by Henri de Guise to kill the admiral, however, that assassination attempt would fail.

Gaspard then saw clearly the errors he had made. They were now as a clear as the missing fingers he stared upon. He played the fool. The Admiral de Coligny was often warned to not enter the romanist metropolis, for any reason. His most trusted friends never questioned him though. They reasoned that since Gaspard was an abundantly cautious man, his sense of security surpassed their sense of security. They had been lulled in. Daily, weekly, and monthly invitations, since the Pacification of 1570. Fetes and privileges heaped upon Huguenots and King Charles, with the ever-dangling promise of war with Spain. The admiral had been blinded by that dream. Huguenots banned from Paris, now suddenly invited enthusiastically and without end? That was the puzzle Maurice Bookman begged him to consider. Coligny could not take Maurice too seriously, as the letter also revealed the bookman's paranoid delusion that he put it in Catherine's head years ago to gather up all her enemies and kill them. The one sign that Gaspard regretted most was the fate of Jeanne.

Jeanne d'Albret was the matriarch of House de Bourbon and father to Henri Navarre. Jeanne, Henri, and himself were the leaders of the Huguenot cause. Like him, she was vigilant to a fault. Like him, she was drawn in by a passion project. The promise of war with Spain meant an opportunity for Henri to regain Navarre, who he was then only a king du jour. However, she seemed to know she was being strung along yet unable to cut the strings. Catherine had eventually convinced her to agree to the consanguine union and visited Catherine personally at court. Soon after, Jeanne would die under mysterious circumstances. Of course they killed her. There is no doubt now that the rumors were true. It must have been true that a Florentine perfumer had poisoned her gloves. Gaspard didn't believe it then. He truly did now as he lay there shot, only for a miracle not lying dead. Was it God that induced him to bend down at that moment. Who was his God truly? It had been so long since he wrestled with religion. For too long he had been seduced by the mistress of glory. King Charles had deceived him, but he'd told lies of his own. He quipped to the king, "an army of Huguenots nay, an army of romanists nay, an army of Frenchmen." While de Coligny welcomed and may have even needed a united force, the endgame he envisioned was a completely reformed Europe with England, France, and Germany leading a future where any stubborn Catholics would be left behind in medieval backwardness. It was humanists like Maurice that convinced him of which side to stake his life. The culture of the protestants was industrious, practical, and morally sound. How could they lose? Now facing the miracle that saved his life, yet also the probability that they were hostages in Paris, he asked himself if he ever truly left the church. Should I not abjure before I die? Should I not confess and go to mass? These were Gaspard de Coligny's ponderances as he winced in pain. The admiral rang the bell for his valet to attend him, for his pains had returned tenfold and he wished for root tea. Benoit, his valet, made not an appearance, so he rang again, this time more loudly for any of the servants to beckon.

Chapter Thirty-One

September 11, 1572

Belfast, Ireland

Maurice had been writing consecutive letters since he read about the terrible news from Paris. He scratched at his head, but his fingers were cramping. Nearly out of ink and paper at his desk, tremoring fingers dabbled away furiously. Next in turn was meant for Danilo:

Dearest Danilo,

I write to you to keep you informed on the wedding in Paris. Catherine de Medici has committed a blackest of black acts. On Monday August 18, Prince Henry and Margot de Valois were married. Cardinal de Bourbon received the vows, yet they stood outside of Notre Dame and without sacrament. Grounds for divorce can later be presented on two items. Margot never voiced assent to the marriage. The King simply nodded his sister's head with his own hand. Secondly, it is believed that Pope Gregory had not sent the final accord and that the Cardinal was presented with a forgery. Moods between the enemies were reportedly amiable, while the bride and groom then splintered respectively into Huguenot chapel or mass. By the evening the festival was dismal at best. The feasts and spectacles of those four days became increasingly hostile. My trusted sources of the metropolis cite the Huguenots as the principal antagonists. In open defiance of the King, they looked upon their captured Huguenot banners and vowed to replace them with Spanish ones. Tuesday evening the 19th a pantomime tournoi was performed in which the nymphs of the elysian fields witness King Charles prevent King Henri into paradise. Quite the delineation of Heaven and Hell that meets so well into your own inclinations. May you regret forever your absence from this spectacle. Broken lances were even incorporated to symbolize the death of the King's father all those years ago. May your scorn be doubled as you desired to be at that tournament in 1559. Coincidentally, Sir Montgomery, that accidental jouster, still lives, and was present. Weds. The 20th a thousand royal arqubusiers were posted about the city to keep the peace between House de Guise and House de Coligny By Thursday the 21st it seemed the arqbusiers prime directive was to disallow the Huguenots from abruptly quitting the celebrations. Coligny had grown most impatient with the king remaining undecisive on the campaign to the low countries. Friday morning of the 22nd the celebrations were officially closed and business resumed with a council. The King and Duke de Guise were absent and playing a match of tennis. The council ruled against the admiral. Gaspard was shot somewhere along his path back to the Huguenot quarters. His hand and arm wounded in what was an obvious trap. Much fuss was made by King Charles and Lady Catherine and apparently a genuine investigation was issued post haste. What would happen next will be so contentious that I wish now I could simply conclude this faithful report to my dear friend.

On the butchery at hand, I can no longer dwell. My hands will never be clean of it, as it was I that planted this seedling scheme into that wicked woman's mind. On Saturday evening of the 23rd, Catherine and her war council confessed to the King. They had been behind the assassination plot. The investigation would surely prove this and is already spoken of in the Huguenot quarter as matter of fact. Charles was outraged but was made to realize that there was now no alternative. The Huguenots would never believe it was not sanctioned and their army was approaching the city. A council member presented a list of the Huguenot leaders all gathered together. Such an opportunity would never again be presented. King Charles IX uttered only, "kill them all."

Guise led swiss pikes, as the bell ring of St.Germain rang out at dawn, which was their signal for the attack. The admiral was beaten to death by Henri de Guise and thrown out of the window. The leaders on the list were subsequently murdered but once the Huguenot soldiers were neutralized, civilians were then killed in a door-to-door extermination. By the 25th the King's orders to cease were ignored and other provinces followed suit with massacres of their own. Apparently the killings in Paris have ceased and order restored but fresh reports come to me of mass murders throughout my beloved France. The news pamphlets not containing these details cannot be blamed, for my source is an English spy who was there in Paris for the entirety and barely survived himself. His latest letter came to me while enroute to England. God save us. He states the number of those slain should be counted by the tens of thousands. I fear there shan't be enough water in the oceans to clean *the blood from my hands. I beg of you to do what you can to get refugees into Germany. I believe every last protestant should make exodus at once, but surely the Huguenots will make war again. A fourth civil war ensnares my homeland as I write, I have yet to receive the report but know it in my soul to be true.*

Faithfully, Maurice Bookman

Upon sending out the letter Maurice fell into an even greater sorrow. He fasted for days and barely spoke. He imagined Danilo reading the letter. He knew what he would say. "Stop torturing yourself my friend. Only God is righteous."

Maurice prayed to the lord and asked for forgiveness. The bookman felt Jesus' love and the greatest comfort surrounded him. Once his mind was clear he went back to the letter he received from the English spymaster who survived the massacre and was his primary informant of the events of the St. Bartholomew's Day Massacre. That man took in fellow protestants and shuttered in. By grace his door did not give way to the blood thirsty murderers on those wicked nights. He would not open the door again until well past the last drop of water was consumed. It was from this spymaster that he learned the details which he had transmitted to Danilo. The survivor was returning to England with cause to rid Elizabeth of Bloody Mary and her Ridolfi plot.

A dismantled church of England could be a death knell to the entire reformation. Elizabeth and Mary. Mary and Elizabeth. Maurice wondered why those two names were associated to him at a deeper level. His daughter Mary, who had only recently begun talking to him again, meant the world to him. Yet there was something else. What are these names to do with each other? Those biblical names. Of course!

Jesus was answering his prayers and lighting the way. Guided were his fingers, scrolling the pages of his worn-out bible. The blessed virgin Mary, Jesus' own mother. Now the lord turned the bookman's thoughts to Catherine de Medici, and those barren years of the mesalliance. His thumb stopped at the Gospel of Luke. Here it is, Elizabeth, the barren old woman who would birth John the Baptist. John who would clear the way. John's father, Zachariah, who doubted the angel Gabriel, and retorted that the old man and woman would never bear a child. With Old Testament severity, the man was muted for nine months until indeed the son was born. Maurice then and there declared that he would not speak again for nine months.

For the next nine months he would finish what he had begun, this time with no doubt. England will not be the only bastion for Huguenots, nor would Sedan be the only terminus. The network he once concocted would be resurrected and mightily expanded. Routes would be multiplied and destinations nurtured not to only receive refugees, but sustain them. Maurice the mute would begin his Belfast project as well. He would erect his dominoes for God alone.

Thomas Sunstone proved to be a man of resounding faith as he found it in his heart to forgive Marie for that affair which now was finally buried in the past. It happened on an evening upon their porch wickers. Thomas and Marie were looking upon their children playing in the grassy knoll of their yard. Without a single word, Thomas offered out his hand. Marie interlaced her fingers with his and never a word of it needed ever be spoken.

The sea beggars and privateers of La Rochelle's navy would also be employed. Old contacts would renew financial support after Catherine's transgressions against the moderates and the sympathizers. To each of them, her blackest of black acts, required atonement of their own. The St. Bartholomew's Day Massacre, which lasted nearly a month and ended only after tens of thousands of protestants were murdered. The rift, made no longer bridgeable, ushered in an era of anguish and guilt. Permanence washed over certain members of either side, leading to a resolve, for redemption or revenge, or some measure of both.

The children did not know what to make of Maurice Bookman. To his five children, Father had a strange illness that took away his voice. To his nieces and nephews, Uncle was playing a funny game communicating only by his ever-present writing slate, and often refusing to use that as well. Two of the boys were wrestling in the courtyard after a perceived offensive look. The bigger found himself pinned with his arm quite locked, dirt riled up and a fresh strawberry welted an elbow. Twelve-year-old Mary was becoming the matriarch of the children and so she chided her uncle as many of the children took to playing silent games as well. Maurice explained through scribe, that he had made a covenant and would not relent until he had fulfilled his mission to aid the Huguenots to flee France where they were being massacred by the thousands. What started in Paris spread like wildfire and the Pope did nothing but wave the fan.

Maurice was feeling the lord's work through him as never before. By remaining silent and even refraining from dictating on his slate, his commands were being interpreted without his own ego blurring the cause.

"He wants us to remain home," Thomas was saying to Marie. "You should not travel with child and he thinks I would be of more use here overlooking the shipping business personally."

Emily looked only at her husband and asked, "What of us Maurice?"

"He wants to keep your family together. The Sunstone estate near London can accommodate you all, dear sister."

Emily continued, "Letters of support and outrage are pouring in. Catherine has betrayed so many back home. Should I request that the notes be sent to the London exchequer husband?"

Maurice scribbled on the board, 'What do you think wife?'

"Yes, I shall send out our replies and prepare for our travels."

"Off with me as well. The new director is going to think himself troubled, for my sudden interest in the day to day business." Thomas made motion to leave.

The slate, tapped on lightly, 'Is he a supporter?'

Thomas answered, "I don't rightly know, but if he isn't I will make him one."

Marie and Maurice were left alone.

Marie read the next statement from the slate. 'Mary hectored me about this foolishness.'

"It is not foolish. The Bible teaches us many lessons few can follow. You my brother are one of those few." She kissed him on the cheek and sobbed as she hurried off. Maurice opened his mouth but only shouted internally. Take care of *her*, sister.

When the Bookmans arrived at the Sunstone estate, not only had financial support begun to pile up, but so were visiting dignitaries awaiting Maurice 'The Mute', also known as 'Our Zachariah'. For Maurice did not represent John the Baptist, but the shower of the way to the shower of the way. Maurice Bookman had regained his confidence in seeing the capabilities of others and showing them how and where to aim their virtues.

The English spymaster was given authority to help move elite Calvinist families to the port of Brittany and on to Scotland. There the spy would work to unravel the Ridolfi plot.

For Robiere and Torry they were lead field scouts. They established safehouses and kept a steady stream of refugees flowing in the right direction. Huguenots primarily were sent upon the route to Sedan then deeper into the Netherlands with

Belfast being their ultimate destination. Maurice also judged that Huguenot commanders would not always welcome losing soldiers who would rather flee than fight. Robiere and Torry were imparted to parlay a bit with them. Lessen the blow by sharing supplies or encouraging young men to fight in one more battle before quitting the country. Ultimately the bottom line, right from the mute's slate: a man who wishes to run has every right to do so and no Christian can deny him this.

Chapter Thirty-Two

The 4th and 5th Religious Wars of France commenced immediately following the St. Bartholomew's Day Massacre. The mini-state of La Rochelle stood after the purge. They stopped paying taxes to the French crown and formed a confederacy with other independent towns.

1572-1576

France

Upon the isle side of the English Channel a mariner could glean the white cliffs of Dover. Sailors heading to the continent side could, similarly, catch glimpse of White Town, La Rochelle, basking in the light of the rocky coast. The fourth war ensued in September of 1572. La Rochelle's fortifications included angled bastions, medieval towers, and ports that were difficult to blockade. The city folk were a staunchly protestant people led by missionaries returning from Brazil. The bankrupt king took months to mobilize a siege upon the defiant White Town. Henri III, King Charles' brother, led the attack, but found the inhabitants willing to fight to the end. In May of 1573, Henri quit the assault and left to Poland to become their new king.

A one-armed Huguenot named La Noue came to the protestant sentinels with offerings from King Charles IX. The king was ill with consumption and offered La Rochelle favorable terms if they abandoned the confederacy. In the tradition of the protracted civil war strange alliances continued to confound the populace, and the wavy line between friend and foe gave endless materials to the poets and satirists alike. La Noue

'Bras de Fer', so named for the artificial arm he bore, not only did not strike the peace King Charles sought, but he remained there to become the latest commander of the citadel. He governed the city with vigor, yet remained loyal to King Charles by frequently encouraging the people to consider French overtures.

La Rochelle stood as vigilant sentinels for their brothers in Christ, and so ultimately won their independence for themselves and their confederates allies of Montabaun and Nimes. Three Huguenot cities were now erected at the conclusion of the fourth war in June of 1573.

Uprising and rebellions continued after the peace of La Rochelle. The peasantry had been overtaxed to fund these religious wars and began overthrowing lords without any discernment of religion. Huguenot bands outside the control of the confederacy battled with local catholic leagues, and contributed greatly to the famine of the commoners. When the fifth war began in February of 1574, one could not find a peasant who was aware the fourth war ever ended. Truly most people in France thought 1574 was simply the twelfth year of the civil war.

For the younger generation, the war had monopolized their lives and they sought to put an end to the ever ambiguous crisis of conflict. Known as the 'Young Malcontents', the runt of the Valois litter ascended to their lead. Francois-Hercules Duke of Alencon was the youngest of Catherine's sons, and the least favored. When King Charles IX died without an heir on May 30th 1574, Alencon forwarded a claim to the throne on the basis that his elder brother, Henry III was already a King of Poland and Lithuania. That dubious legal basis and the liberal mantle of the malcontents he bore, prompted Catherine to once again gather the reins of France in her vigorous hands. Now an old and quite fat lady by any standard, she had her youngest son imprisoned and beckoned her favorite, Henri, to quit Poland and claim the throne of France without haste.

King Henri III returned to France and was crowned king, though his little brother Francois-Hercules was able to escape the dungeon and raise the malcontents into such a fury that Paris was surrounded and the new king beaten into submission. A new peace would need to be contrived. Perhaps, some wished, the Huguenots were to finally get each of their demands met.

Chapter Thirty-Three

April 1, 1576

Belfast, Ireland

For all his travels, this was the first to Ireland. The tall grass danced in the wind of the emerald island. He came upon a pauper who assured him to be heading in the correct direction, or at least he thought he did, as the lilting Irish-English language was strange to Danilo's ear. The Sunstones and the Bookmans were well-known in Belfast. An ecu flipped to the pauper, then Danilo wondered if the poor man understood the wealth of a French Royal Ecu. To not be shortchanged on an exchange. Then it occurred to him, too many of my friends are now in high places, time to make new friends. The pauper did not fright when the strange rider turned back around. He was flipping the ecu and was calling out sides, beckoning to make a bet.

Oh I like this rascal indeed. Plopping down from the horse the old courier's boots crunched into the sandy path. An ancient stone long since grounded into dust. A sudden whip of wind stung his eyes causing a shift, so as to sit next to the man, facing away from the wind. Danilo did not have a hood like the poor pauper, but at least he was then oriented properly. The flipping ecu rang sharply. The landing was padded by his woolen gloves. He pointed to the side showing the likeness of some long ago king. Danilo determined the pauper mixed his broken English with old Irish Gaelic. He deemed it the most musical language he had ever heard. Once Danilo figured the word for 'heads', he turned the coin over and pointed to the

fleur-de-lys side. A stream of song was invoked, and the pauper was clearly excited that they were understanding each other. And that he wanted to bet for another coin. Upon hearing a softer sound repeated several times they understood 'tails'. The next few minutes were spent wagging fingers at each other, a wordless negotiation about who would call it was underway. Danilo bested the man in a stare down. After blinking first he handed Danilo back the gifted ecu. Danilo repeated the soft Gaelic word for tails and sent the coin ringing out to the skies to decide fate. It was heads and the pauper rose to his feet and begun a most fantastic dance. His feet were moving every which way and he was singing, too. Perhaps he was still just speaking, Danilo truly could not discern melody from speech. Danilo handed him another coin and blurted out in English, "You buy."

The pauper froze and looked at Danilo like a lost hound. Apparently, his English was better when the words were favorable. Perhaps they were just both happy to make a new friend. "I buy," he agreed.

He hopped onto the horse and Danilo turned to beseech him to translate between English and Irish. They would spend their time building a shared vocabulary. Danilo knew English well enough, but was much more interested in this Gaelic tongue of the mythical druids. The hours passed with grunts and lyrics passing to and fro. A carriage rumbled past them going the other direction with folks staring at the pauper. One could believe the man had no luck or friends until just that afternoon, until just meeting Danilo. Could he be a prospect for the order? Danilo would have to observe for any signs of prescience.

Shortly arriving at a pub, the poor Irish man began to realize the scope of his luck. The bar-keep was both willing and able to exchange the crowns for their local coinage. The pauper had won himself a veritable treasure. As agreed, the first round was on the Irish man, and they next introduced themselves. D-a-n-ilo, Dan-ilo, and Danilo was introduced to Muu-togg, mur-tog, and finally, Murtaugh. The new friends were also able to converse more about the Sunstone and Bookman families. As it was, the pauper did understand the traveler's purpose back those many hours ago when he stopped looking for directions.

Danilo came to make the pauper understand that he was heading to see Maurice Bookman, an old friend of his. "You and me are new friends, he and I are old friends." The pauper was invited to come with. It was only natural for friends, but Murtaugh seemed skeptical about being allowed anywhere near the denizens of that zone. *Imagine that, Maurice an elite.*

They got quite drunk and so it was decided to take up a room above the pub. Though Danilo knew Maurice would welcome his old and new friend, the welcome would be much reduced by the late hour and all but evaporated by their potted condition.

Danilo was all the more happy to see Belfast by the light of day. Within the confines of the Huguenot quarter, a livelier economy he had not seen in all of his travels. There was also an order to the operations that was not present in Paris, Berlin, or even London. Wagons and carriages with imports came in one side of the city, while exporting out the other. The logic of the roads continued to even connect with the harbor along the Lagan River. A third entry gate and plaza for the folk people and a market. This was far more than a market center. Maurice had done it. He built a distribution center administered by a management class of Protestants. The Huguenot newcomers had demonstrated to the Gaelic and Old English alike that the Protestants lived for heaven, but with a humanist work ethic, to be as productive as possible here on Earth.

Danilo looked proudly back to Murtaugh, but he looked sullen. Danilo had to consider the negative effect on the Irish. Was he always a pauper or did these newcomers displace him? Surely Maurice's project created jobs, but no enterprise can bring prosperity to all. They came upon the Bookmans' estate, sprawling and high. Several torches blazed around the exterior, suggesting the presence of groundskeepers.

The door knocker produced a flat toll and when he went to give it another go, Danilo detected a hysteria just on the other side of the door. There was Maurice, and his, well, family. Maurice and Danilo embraced, and for a brief moment, they were back in the old bookshop. Here now was Maurice Bookman. Maurice and an entire family that needed introducing:

His wife Emily Bookman, who Danilo knew was the former Dowager de Smolliet. His eldest Luke who was thirteen, though he knew this was not truly his eldest. Antoinette, twelve, aptly named for a girl who could never pretend to be anything but French. Seamus was ten, already stronger than Luke, like Maurice and Christopher perhaps. Lawrence at eight, and finally John of six years. For the Sunstone family Danilo hugged Marie and again felt the presence of the old bookshop. Her husband Thomas, the shipping magnate who was at least half responsible for this half miracle. Their eldest Mary, a sixteen-year-old maiden. She looked like a mirror image of Tonya, who Danilo regrettably could never account for, lost and dead in the middle of the Ardennes was her most likely end. Richard Sunstone, quite a name, aged eight, another John of six, and Heather, being four, promised to be the apple of his eye for the duration.

When it came for his turn to introduce Murtaugh, he had already disappeared. "What an oaf I still am Maurice."

"Worry not, a friend of yours is a friend of ours, I shall send a couple of men to find him."

The women excused themselves to prepare a dinner feast and the children too went along their merry way, leaving the men to their business.

"Maurice, Thomas…I salute you. You have made a shining example of what a refugee town could become. Surely you have advanced Belfast a hundred years into the future."

Maurice, somewhat embarrassed, "We have our problems here too—"

"Tah-, problems there shall always be, but we rarely get to celebrate solutions."

Thomas leaned back and put in, "You know, we did not even have a word for refugees in English."

"Keep it, because the refugees have only started."

Thomas rose and said, "I will grant you two some privacy, but allow me to thank you Danilo, from what I can gather you played a critical role for Marie's family." Danilo stood up and shook his hand wondering just how much they really knew.

"Shall I pour us a drink?"

"Why not."

"A strong tonic will be required for what I am about to tell you." Maurice was wide-eyed and that amused the old courier.

"Now now, I exaggerate, or have you forgotten me already."

"I think I may have, and you surely must have lost certain aspects of my personage as well."

"I am forbidden to tell you of this, but you have trusted me so now it is my turn." A dark pause portended harsh seriousness. "I am, I am a member of a secret sect of Cathars."

Maurice winced at the bite of his drink. "I have forgotten you Danilo, I remember your jokes used to be funny."

"Do you remember the last day we were together in Laon?"

"It's somewhat foggy."

"Your bookshop was being boycotted and it was my last delivery as I was then moving to Germany—"

"Yes and you carried something with you. A secret treasure that was going to change your life. Now that was a good jest."

"I wasn't jesting then nor am I jesting now. Revealing this secret could end me, so if you want me to stop now let us just chalk it up to a bad joke. But if you want the truth then let us be serious now."

Maurice put down his glass. "I'm sorry Danilo, please go on. And of course you have my word that your secret remains a secret with me."

"What I transported back then did change my life, and yours too as it turned out. The young lion will overcome the older one, on the field of combat in a single battle—"

Maurice completed the presage. "He will pierce his eyes through a golden cage, two wounds made one then he dies a cruel death. Nostradamus?"

"Nostradamus indeed. My order investigates visions and predictions such as that very one."

"What I carried that day was the shield used by King Henri during the jousts. The shield was emblazoned with a lion."

"What of the shield of his opponent?"

"I was unable to recover his shield, but by all accounts Sir Montgomery also branded a shield with a lion on it."

"It cannot be, Nostradamus wrote that years if not decades before the joust."

"Maurice, my order believes he not only predicted the jousting accident, but also predicted the ensuing civil war."

Maurice pondered at that, "It has always seemed to me that it all came apart with the death of the king. I thought the Cathars were exterminated."

"We almost were. But then again so were the Bogomils and the Templars, yet the legacy remains. I am a part of that legacy."

"What does your sect believe, what do you believe? I know the papacy has decreed your kind as satanic, but given they have attempted to annihilate us with the same vigor, I am inclined not to believe them on any matter of faith."

"Maurice, I assure you I am a Christian, however, we deal with a mysticism that you would judge not that different from the ritualistic papists."

"How did your journey change your life? How did that shield change mine?"

"I have been a Cathar since I was a child. I was born to a father who raised me to always concentrate on the duality of life. The material world is evil and the spiritual is good. Our human form is material Maurice, but inside we have a divine spark, which can be freed and reunited with the spiritual world."

"Salvation through Christ."

"Amen. Where dualists differ from protestants is in our Gnosticism. We believe that Jesus gave us access to the knowledge we need to be saved. We would say that learning Jesus' knowledge is even more important than faith alone. Eating from the tree of knowledge got us into this mess, and eating more is going to get us out."

"Danilo you are blaspheming in my own house!" Maurice felt as light as a leaf, picked up by a hurricane and dropped at the bottom of Olympus.

"I am my friend, I know this. Forgive me—"

"Just tell me how my life was changed—"

"I saw the future of the Huguenots and led you to a different path—"

Calmness showered over Maurice. Where once confusion and anger would have prompted him into dismay; now only the lord's will mattered. "It was said that Catherine called upon Nostradamus once or twice. A seer was never far from her presence, always stoking fear about the fate of her children. Is that who you are Danilo? Do you count yourself a seer?"

"Yes my old friend, I have become a seer of a third degree sect of the Cathars, I am a reincarnate. The knowledge Jesus passed to us cannot be fully understood in a single lifetime. It takes multiple lives for his teachings to truly become coherent. Through my visions I have been able to guide you."

"I command you to desist from blasphemy. Jesus showed me the way."

"Jesus works through me, too."

"No. I follow Jesus alone. You reveal to follow another force. I too know of duality. There are friends of god or enemies of god. Which are you?"

Danilo stood stunned in silence, Maurice had become much more pious.

Maurice continued. "The anti-christ...heretic...a false prophet?"

"Perhaps you are correct Maurice. Your wisdom has never been in doubt, and I have heard the tales of the mute guide for the Huguenots. I see for myself how righteous you have become. Let me then tell you of my prophecy before you judge it false. This vision has been with me for nearly twenty years. I have been trained and tested by master Katharos, the True Ones. I have seen three men, each missing an arm. A true knight who I now know as La Noue 'Bras de Fer'. A false knight who my sources indicate was Charles Avon."

"Avon, how? What of a false knight?"

"Yes at the end Avon chose to fight in the attack of Amboise, fight gallantly he did not. He was captured, identified, had an arm cut off, and thrown in the river."

Maurice prayed for him, "Jesus is great."

"No horror Maurice? Your faith is now truly unshakeable? Know this, the last man is to be you. A father with two names, in addition to other clues and all this I have surmised. The masters have been so impressed with how I have honed my divinations, they wonder if I may have two or three visions in me before I pass to the next life."

"Danilo listen to yourself, these are not your masters."

"If you lose an arm Maurice the Huguenot cause dies. This is the prophecy. I sensed you could not appeal to Catherine. I saw that exodus was the only option. With great heartache I discovered you needed to become this twice named father. That is how I was able to save Maurice and get Nicolas to court."

"This is the end, Danilo. I have both of my arms, all grace to God. I was able to lead many of my people to a new home, all grace to God. I am grateful for your help, but I will give no grace to your prophecy nor your cult—"

There was a knock and a valet reported something to the ear of Maurice.

"Your friend has been found. You shall be escorted to him but I must ask that you leave."

"Maurice?"

"Danilo my friend, you were right to tell me the truth, but with that I am afraid we must part ways."

Here the heart of Danilo broke but not his will. "If you step foot in France again you shall lose an arm and doom your people."

Maurice's eyes sparkled and Danilo hoped it meant he was finally believing.

"Oh blessed Danilo, Christ does work through you. How else could you have known that I fully intend to return to France. One final work for the lord then I shall be relieved to have my own peace."

"I tell you never to go to France and the lord tells you to go precisely there with haste and purpose. Perhaps I am the anti-christ."

"I don't believe that, repent now Danilo."

"Only time will tell, it seems only one of us can be saved. Bon voyage."

Danilo took a few steps, then froze, "Learn discernment Maurice, not all which is dark is wicked. Beware the corrupted seed."

Maurice would have begged him back, for his teacher to explain, yet his devotion to his savior stayed his hand. The nudge of the staff, making him lay down in green pastures.

The family was shocked to see Danilo being led away without even a farewell. Marie asked her brother what happened. He told her why he had turned his friend away. When she heard of the prophecy she exclaimed, and begged for Danilo to be fetched back immediately. She told quickly the story of how she somehow knew she was to have father's arm saved. Their father who now had a second name after Christopher demanded he renounce being a Millet. Maurice did not rush to retrieve the old courier, instead he soothed his sister with praise for guarding over their baby Mary and their father in those darkest of days. "Be glad, the lord's will has been done."

Chapter Thirty-Four

May 6, 1576

La Rochelle and Bealieu, France

A river birthed a rowboat with two oarsmen taking a break as a steady wind pushed them along. The glassy reflection inverted the chateau's tower into the deep. Half a century ago, Vikings upon their versatile long boats would have struck a less joyful profile. A landscape artist sat upon the bank and framed the scene.

Maurice and Luke watched the artist more than they did his subject. The bow of the vessel served as the line of axis between the reflected images of blue sky, pink castle, and heather green trees. The waters were not as placid as the artist expressed nor the faces of men as rough. Maurice taught his son that in the humanist style, man was shown not in the image of God, but in the ugly and pathetic flesh as outcasts of Eden.

"This is your home father?"

"This is southern France, your grandpa and I both grew up in the north."

"Can we visit there too?"

"No Luke, it is still too dangerous there."

"Look father."

Luke pointed to a man running towards them. Maurice stood up and recognized that it was one of the valets from the chateau.

"I was ordered to bring you this letter with haste. It comes from Lady Catherine de Medici."

"Very well man, thank you."

Understanding the curious look in his son's eye, Maurice explained the reason for such an interruption, "Catherine Medici son, has been the queen mother here for nearly twenty years. Her sons die one by one, King Francis then Charles. She survives though."

"How does she survive?"

The boy asks the right questions, "She really isn't French, she is Italian. She was born for this war, but her sons were not. Her husband was never supposed to die that day of the jousts. France was supposed to have a strong king." Luke searched for a response. "You don't understand and that is good, may it always be so. I suppose I shouldn't be surprised that the Florentine Witch found me here." Even here at La Rochelle, the Catholics and royalists have spies.

Maurice laid on the grass and opened the letter to read. The nearby artist gathered his materials as Luke ventured closer to see the finished painting. The letter was short. Maurice got up and joined his son.

"Does it please you son?"

"Yes, they are the ugly oarsmen from Eden."

The artist proclaimed, "A better title I could not have come up with."

Maurice offered three crowns to the man. "If it were mine, I would call it: 'My Peace'.

"Sold, but I like his name better."

Like the letter from Catherine, their meeting had been brief. She thanked him for accepting the invitation and gave him the details to attend the peace council. All the weight that he had lost she had evidently gained. She spoke as confidently as ever, but now with a noticeable gasp. She stamped her seal upon some letter and gave Maurice a long look. Her eyes darted back and forth, and Maurice noticed a new guard sliding around. He could not help his shaking hands as he was writing down the details for the council. The Black Witch, he imagined, was considering her options. Could she ever forget the way he exposed her when they last met? The Queen Mother he cherished, his only hope. Inside of a dreamer, having a dream, he had met her. Confronted her and stripped her down. The look released and she began peering at the next form for her approval, curling it carelessly.

"Our old covenant continues to serve in its own way. Some would like to hang me for aiding the Huguenot exodus, but most just are glad to be rid of protestants one way or another."

"It goes for me much the same. My people have mixed feelings about my works. On one hand I am depriving their ranks of more men. But on the other, I am helping my people escape before you orchestrate the next massacre."

Catherine, unperturbed, hurriedly revealed her agenda. "Whatever your present standing with the Huguenots, if I were you, I should convince them to give in on church permits, and eight security zones is too many."

Maurice lavished in the irony of it all, yet held his amusement at bay. Since they had last met, he had only grown in importance. For the lady Catherine it was quite the opposite. Yet she beckoned him to attend a sliver of her audience, mere moments, while she burrowed herself in paperwork. Thinking of one of Erasmus' adages, Maurice replied.

"My lady I won't be advising anything, I am here only to receive my condemnation."

"Oh that, nobody cares about that."

"I do."

The peace talks concluded with the Huguenots receiving all their demands. King Henri III, namesake to his father, had no other qualities to suggest that he would not be just another weak king.

A herald passed out pamphlets to a few print-masters for publication, but were ushered then to leave. The herald rose:

"First for the delicate matter of condemnation and condolences."

King Henri III remained seated. "I will state here officially, as my brother always had; the crown bears all responsibility for the St. Bartholemew's Massacre. King Charles found his authority wanting, for all the unlawful executions that continued through Paris and indeed the realm. I swear before God, noble lords and all the people, that my brother had nothing to do with the assassination attempt on the admiral. Gaspard de Coligny was a dear friend and a mentor. However, the Huguenots would not accept this truth, and so they did plot to commit regicide. Only they need to atone for that choice. King Charles authorized the immediate execution of the plotters. All the bloody carnage that was brought to the households of the plotters and the households of the innocent were done so by exceeding royal authority. Though not his intent, the corpses lay at his feet. For my part, I shall punish any party who dares to celebrate the massacre. Furthermore, I shall instruct our cardinals to ensure that St. Bartholomew's Day celebrations are to include honor to martyrdom, regardless of creed. Our flayed saint was danced upon too. So any good Catholic should well know the pain of such injustice."

The herald then spoke. "Turning to reparations."

The new King Henri continued, "I should like to correct a common misunderstanding that the Huguenots were here as wedding guests. This could not be further from the truth. Many of these protestants own property and other holdings in the city. Not so long ago they were Parisians. Charles and our mother had spent the better part of two years beckoning for their return, which slowly re-integrated them back into our fair capital. Thus was the symbolism of the union between my own Catholic sister and the protestant King Henry of Navarre. I authorize the proposal to return ownership and rents as they were recorded before that tragic day." The king sensed the council growing bored with the empty display so nodded to the herald.

"Now onto more pressing matters."

Maurice stood up.

"Sire if I may." The king turned for a reminder on who stood before him.

"You are no longer a French citizen?"

"No sire, English now or perhaps even Irish." The room was flabbergasted as Maurice awkwardly rambled. "I know a man with around a dozen different nationalities—"

"If you must."

"I too wish to stand here before God that I profess my own guilt for the massacre. I, in my own way, accept responsibility." Maurice spun theatrically to be witnessed by all. "If anyone feels the same, I invite you to stand with me and be absolved by the lord." Nobody else stood, and the frustration towards this sideshow was palpable. The bookman would not yield. "I shall then myself acknowledge that King Charles was not alone. Condemn me as well for these transgressions—"

"Granted, and your punishment is to remain quiet for the duration of these proceedings." Maurice obeyed with grace and not a hint of irony to the bedazzled spectators, who could make no sense of what they just saw. Catherine alone knew what he sought atonement for.

The agenda moved on. Free worship was granted everywhere with the only exception being Paris. Proper churches would be licensed for construction. Parliaments, chambers, and courts were to be mixed in representation of both religions. There would be no position that a protestant could not hold based on faith alone. Huguenot leaders would also be permitted to attend the general-estates. Eight towns were assigned to Huguenots for security detail, thus allowing them to maintain their own forces lawfully. The terms agreed to were a dream. The farce of the Edict of Beaulieu council, came to conclusion.

The Huguenot camp exploded into celebration as leaders returning from the council trickled in with the news. Groups hugged and cried out in joy. A lady wept alone as the wars had taken everything from her.

"How come we are not celebrating with the others Dad."

"There is nothing to celebrate."

"The war is over, you helped achieve peace."

"Five wars there have been. This was the fifth peace treaty. In the naiveté of my youth, I celebrated the first one. That peace lasted four years. I give this one to the end of the year."

"Seems like a fantastic waste of time to come all this way."

"I came for forgiveness."

"Hasn't Jesus already forgiven you Dad?"

"You know son, this was a fantastic waste of time."

Maurice let out a forlorn sigh followed by a private chuckle.

"What is funny father?"

"The strangest thing. I can't wait to go back home."

Father and son enjoyed the celebratory faire after all. A band of violinists stung the ears of most attendees. Maurice explained to those offended by the screech, that the pitch would take some getting used to. His son joined in a game of no-rules ball. While listening to those high notes registering now as waves of calm, he watched the boys pass the leathern ball to a catcher who had to run for his life before being unceremoniously tackled. He decided they played a gentler version than when he was a kid. Luke followed suit and tackled a catcher with like restraint. The ball rolled through fumbling little hands until his son secured it himself and safely ran away to the boughs. He raised the ball in victory while his new friends laughed and cheered. Notes of climax were violently strummed and the song came to an end.

Future Books by Danny Aglugub

Scribes and Scripture Series Book Two 'Beyond the Pale'

Blooded Iron Series Book One 'Pilgrimage of Gold'
(working title)

Acknowledgements

To my editor and publisher Keith Hayden at HAC Studios:

Cliché, it's true, but I could not have done it without you.

A special thanks to Conrado Gallardo, my consulting architect. And Dr. Roland Moreno, my consulting physician.

About the Author

Danny is a historical novelist and native Californian with a background in data and history. The Lord called upon him to write historical novels.

Away from writing, he enjoys spending time with family and playing with his GI Joes.
By Rod and Staff is his debut novel.

Read more of Danny's writing on Substack.

Don't forget to RRS (rate, review, and share) this book!

Thanks for reading!